Love OF MY DEATH

D1304345

DALE FOWLER

Love Of My Death

By Dale Fowler

ISBN: 979-8-7097443-6-3

Published in the United States of America by Dale Fowler Books

Cover Design and Layout: by Jutta Medina

First Edition

Printed in the United States of America

There may be aliens in our Milky Way galaxy,
and there are billions of other galaxies. The probability
is almost certain that there is life somewhere in space.

~ *Buzz Aldrin*

DEDICATION

Love of My Death
by Dale Fowler

Life can offer many privileges, and one of my most blessed and cherished is the many friends I have met over the years. In the eighties, God saw fit to let me cross paths with Dr. Edgar Mitchell and we became fast friends. Ed had a distinguished career in the Navy flying jets, and he eventually joined the space program at NASA becoming an astronaut.

To say Dr. Mitchell is an American hero is a giant understatement. Not only did he fly Apollo 14 to the moon, he also had the longest space walk ever on the moon more than nine hours. He helped design the lunar landing module (he had a Ph.D. from MIT in physics) and when the crew of Apollo 13 got trapped in orbit behind the moon, Ed's calculations rescued the crew from certain death.

In his post-NASA days, he spent much of his life challenging governments to release their full knowledge surrounding UFOs and alien visitations to Earth. This coming from a man who had access to the deepest inner workings on space programs, and knowing Earth's relationship with other worlds throughout the vast and unlimited space we all travel through.

Dr. Mitchell was one of the most sought after experts on the UFO phenomenon, appearing in countless programs for National Geographic, the History Channel, and all the major networks. In a DatelineNBC interview, he stated that thousands of UFO recorded sightings since the 1940s belong to visitors from other planets. UFO encounters like the 1947 Roswell incident were covered up by our government and alien beings were found on the crash. UFOs had provided "sonic engineering secrets" helpful to our aircraft design and other military advancements. In another interview with Kerrang Radio, Mitchell stated alien beings have contacted Earth many times, but governments continue to hide those findings from the public.

In a providence of fate, Ed and I lived within minutes of one another in South Florida. He was often a guest of honor at my home to speak about UFOs and their technological impact on us to invited friends over a meal and wine. He shocked thirty of us at one such event when he stated that microchip technology came from the Roswell crash and led to our computer driven world.

So why is Dr. Mitchell mentioned in *Love of My Death*, a work of fiction? As you can note from the book cover, UFOs have a role in the storyline. What, you might ask? You will have to read the book to find out. Dr. Edgar Mitchell unfortunately passed from this Earth in 2016, and we lost one of the most unique human beings ever to live.

This book is for you, my dear friend.

INTRODUCTION

New Orleans is one of the most unique cities not only in the United States but the world. It was my home in the nineties, and I met some of the friendliest and most well-mannered individuals this great country has to offer. The citizens are deep South and take pride in their food, and certainly what kind of alcoholic beverage they drink and offer to you.

"N'awlins" people don't go looking for trouble; it has a way of stalking them. One of my neighbors, in his wonderful Cajun accent, once told me, "The Devil wasn't born here, but he raised a family and comes back to visit on a regular basis."

New Orleans is the backdrop for *Love of My Death*; and yes, it is a love story. One the Devil would approve of. It has murder, mafia hit men, UFO abductions, affairs, and a myriad of other human evils that come to haunt this sexy city. Just your average week, on and around Bourbon Street.

All of this human tragedy falls into the lap of Detective Chris Dale and a reporter for the local newspaper, Jessie James McGaha. Both are charged with figuring out the evil individuals from the saints. Something that is anything but obvious when reading the book. So, many people are good, but bad. Some characters steal your heart, and then beat you to death with it.

Love of My Death has at its foundation a love affair between

Trey Stephens, a wealthy, aristocratic pillar of New Orleans' society, and Gayle Kidd, a mysterious and beautiful city newcomer. The Stephens family wields power over gambling, hotels and other nefarious institutions. But they have met their match in the wickedness that Gayle has performed in the past.

Detective Dale is introduced to the ongoing death while investigating the murder of Bailly, a street musician with connections to the mob. Bailly's grandson Emrik witnessed the death of his grandfather and ran for his own life into the underbelly of the New Orleans night, barely escaping the same fate. When asked by Detective Dale, "Who killed your grandfather and gave chase after you?" Emrik swears it was "the Devil."

Detective Dale has never investigated a case like this, so he solicits the help of Jessie McGaha to paint the true picture of what happened that night. Jessie and Chris fall deep into a rabbit hole of voodoo, cop and mob killings, and the conjuring of a real devil known by the locals as a "Hell Raising."

Take a tumultuous ride into the depths of Hell, way beyond this planet, with Detective Dale and Jessie McGaha, putting the pieces together and walking down a trail from which they can never return.

One

THE REAPER

Devon Childers' lipstick touches her pressed mouth in the small bathroom mirror and, backing away, she likes the result. A generous application of perfume on the neck and wrists make her feel sexy. Devon has spent most of her adult life denying any femininity in the name of family functionality and respect for her mother. Two younger brothers needed Devon's guidance because Mrs. Childers worked long hours and was gone much of the time.

One of those brothers, Dallas Childers, is rousted out of his bedroom to drive her to a rendezvous she really does not want to discuss with anyone in her family. On the way out the door, Devon has to run the gauntlet by her mother and aunt avoiding any details on whom she might be seeing.

Mrs. Childers is watching a speech by President Ronald Reagan when Devon and Dallas walk through the living room.

"Where you two going?" Momma Childers asks.

"Got a date, I bet. Is he good-looking?" The aunt jumps in, wildly guessing.

"Meeting a girlfriend. Not a big deal."

"All that lipstick. You can't fool me." The aunt smiles, thinking she knows the answer.

"Headed to the movies ... sorry to disappoint," Devon responds.

"Maybe I'll go with you. Your mother insists we watch this actor turned president."

"Be quiet, Mr. Reagan is my man. Reduced my taxes," Mrs. Childers insists.

"My goodness! You have to be the only black woman in Louisiana who voted for that man."

Devon kisses her mother and rides away with Dallas to a restaurant. Dallas never inquires why she wants to be let out or whom she is meeting. He drives away.

Devon sits in the far corner of the small diner looking anxiously at the unfamiliar faces in various stages of eating. She tries to make herself smaller in the chair to avoid attention. The waiter has walked by on two occasions but pretends to be busy, not making eye contact. That's okay by Devon; she's not here to eat or drink but waiting on Reed to pick her up. Why he chooses this bigoted corner of New Orleans for their meeting place seems

9

harebrained, at least from her perspective.

New Orleans in 1988 is fun and games to millions of white visitors coming to Bourbon Street for conventions and partying. Still, a black woman like Devon must pick her entrances and exits carefully. She could go outside and wait, but it's Halloween night, and getting showered with eggs or worse doesn't have allure. Each flash of lights shining into the front window pulls her up from the seat to check for Reed's new red Buick; and getting away from the glaring eyes, questioning her seating choice.

Reed is always late. Devon is always early. She smiles slightly at the thought, not too boldly. Nothing in Devon's life can be done boldly. At twenty-six, she feels and acts much older, having had to grow up early to life's realities of raising younger siblings, helping as her single mother worked two jobs. Devon didn't mind. Her heart and soul were used to the giving, while most are used to taking.

She found a first employment two years ago when her two brothers finally graduated from high school. A job at Stephens Publishing in the mail room. The job is rather easy; sorting and delivering to various departments and senior staff. She didn't have to be in until 9:00 a.m., making the bus ride a lot more convenient. Her mother worked at the brewery at 5:00 for job one, and when she got home little energy was left to eat, bathe, and crawl in bed.

Devon had it easy compared to her mother's grueling schedule.

When Reed started flirting eleven months ago, it was scary trying to balance how much to ignore and how to respond. She knew who he was. The Executive Vice President and son of the company founder, Reed W. Stephens. Reed Jr. didn't ease into the flirting but came on like a gorilla in heat.

To the point, she dreaded walking anywhere near his office because he always spotted her. He never touched her, but his boldness made it uncomfortable. Not that she didn't think he was handsome. Lord no. She was instantly attracted to his good looks. But she was aware of his marriage and, even more mitigating, he was white. Devon understood all too well the remote distance between their worlds.

After five months of cat-and-mouse talk, Reed came out and said it.

"Please have dinner with me Thursday night."

It took Devon two days and more moxie than she had ever mustered finally to say, "yes." Not sure why she agreed. Maybe it was his boyish grin and the "please" that flipped the switch. Twice she went to his office to decline the offer afterward but lost the fortitude to carry it out. If saying "yes" suddenly turned into a "no," Devon was certain she would be fired. A position allowing her mother to resign job number two and arrive home long before her usual 8:00 at night.

The first date was awkward. Devon stayed distant, self-preservation kicking in. Reed bubbled over with energy, taking her to Houston's for dinner, an experience Devon had only observed in magazines.

Looks did resonate from the crowded restaurant; a black woman and white man will do that. Devon saw the hate from several sources, but Reed was oblivious, making her feel less intimidated as the evening wore on. She evolved to the point of staring into his blue eyes across the table and for a couple of hours forgot about the color of her skin and his. He ordered champagne. A first taste for her, forging a quick buzz after only two glasses. The evening flew by into the night. Dancing and more champagne followed.

Reed never asked her to go to the hotel room. He assumed it would be fine. It was. Devon fell down a rabbit hole of wonderment and fun never experienced in her life. If it was wrong, so be it. Reed gave compliments for months on how beautiful she was and made her feel all woman inside. Now it was time to be a woman for him. Devon figured once the sex was over she would be sent back to the mail room and forgotten. If that was her fate, she was settled with it. Surely he wouldn't fire her.

Instead of being fired, she received roses at the house—six dozen roses. Mother was beside herself with curiosity. Who's this new beau hidden from her view? Devon lied, not sure whom she was trying to protect; a young black man in shipping asked her out once and sent the roses was the story. She wondered what mother would think now, fourteen months later, if she ever did get to meet Reed. Her mother didn't have a clue Devon did, in fact, fall down a white rabbit hole.

Devon saw the Buick turn into the parking lot and stop. She stood and walked to the door to meet him outside; the righteous could then eat in comfort. On the way out, a casual glance from a young waiter revealed eyes following her body up and down with something on his mind besides disdain. While walking past, his subdued appreciation made her feel like an attractive woman. Those looks came her way on occasion, but most of the time escaping her attention and muted by the ominous stares that never ceased coming.

Reed's broad smile meets the opening door.

"Been here long, beautiful?" he asks, knowing she is uncomfortable roaming the streets by herself.

"No, I have your timing down pat. You tell me 8:00, I show up at 8:30." Devon reveals a slight variation of the truth. "How was your day? Didn't see you at the office."

"Board meeting downtown. We're thinking about building a hotel on the river. Everyone's convinced gambling will be legalized sometime in the future. We need to stay one step ahead to make sure we're part of it."

"Big business. Looks like it's going to get bigger,"

"Where are we going to eat? I'm starving."

The Buick pulls away from the diner.

"Got a surprise. Won't tell you—have to show you," He piques her curiosity.

"We're not getting on another shrimp boat?" Devon asks, not pleased with a previous surprise that ruined her favorite dress and required multiple shampoos to remove the smell from her hair.

"I thought it would be romantic; boy, did I miss the boat, so to speak." Reed's sheepish grin confirms Devon's point of view.

The Buick heads along Canal Street and makes a few turns into a rugged slum area Reed usually avoids. She reaches over and takes his hand.

"You're definitely off the beaten path. How did you find this restaurant?"

Before Reed can find the words to answer, several eggs are thrown from behind a parked car, landing on the windshield and hood. Reed slams on the brakes.

"Dammit!" he shouts.

Four teenagers run in front of the car to the opposite side of the street dressed in Halloween costumes then stop to look back at the latest egging victim, daring a response. Reed opens the door, bent on fulfilling their provocation.

Devon leans over and grabs his arm. "Reed, it's not worth it. Let them go."

"You little bastards!" he yells at the disappearing goblins running toward an alley as he steps out of the car.

A look back to Devon changes his mind, and he gets back in, shutting the door. He grabs the steering wheel and squeezes it, trying to relieve his zero-to-80 temper. "I just waxed my car."

"They're doing what kids do, getting into trouble," Devon

says, thinking back to her brothers' egg-throwing days. "It's Halloween. Everyone becomes a little crazy."

Reed drives off. "Must be cause for celebration. The monsters get to take their people masks off during the day."

He turns the windshield wipers on to rid the mess hindering his vision. It only smears.

The car is silent for a few minutes except for the rubber sliding back and forth on the glass, Reed trying to cool down and Devon letting him. She saw his temper at a bar one night when a drunk made reference to his coziness with a black woman. He pulled a gun, and she jumped in front of the man to keep Reed from shooting him. They left soon afterward at her insistence before the cops showed up. Devon was terrified at the thought of him shooting someone over her, and she didn't want anything to do with the police. Reed didn't seem too worried about the law; in fact wanting the guy arrested and willing to plead his case. Devon ushered him away from the scene, confused about his petulance toward authority.

Reed pulls over in front of a gated cemetery entrance, revealing an endless view of above-ground burial vaults as a backdrop. He moves out of the car and heads for the rear. Devon thinks there must be a flat tire and cracks the door, leaning out. Reed opens the trunk, but Devon can't understand his activity.

"What's wrong?"

"Celebrating like the other monsters." Reed's voice is clear, but the statement doesn't make sense to her. She climbs out and walks to the back.

"Celebrating what?"

Reed rises from the trunk, filling his arms with a bottle of champagne, two glasses and a blanket. He leans over, kissing her.

"Our love, and freedom to love," he announces, moving toward the cemetery gate.

Devon eyes this strange place to celebrate and decides to follow, not wanting to be left behind.

"Can't we celebrate in a hotel room?" She tries to add what she perceives as common sense to the discussion.

Reed opens the gate, waiting for her to catch up. "Where's your sense of adventure? It's Halloween. There are monsters all over the city throwing eggs—not any here, ironically."

He sets the champagne on an angel's outstretched arms, and pulls his jacket back, revealing a pistol holstered against his chest. "The boogie man won't bother us."

The bottle is retrieved; they go deeper into the array of small buildings covered by biblical concrete figures in various stages of the aging process. Devon is uncomfortable as Reed's flashlight dances along the footpath. The light creates shadows that bounce off the buildings, adding to the eerie scene and her thoughts. Reed has always done things off the beaten path when it comes to romance, but this is extreme even by his standards.

"This may come as a surprise to you," Devon reveals, "but something about this place is taking the romance from my body."

Reed stops at a bench and lays the blanket over the cold concrete slab.

"And what a body it is!" he proclaims, opening the bottle and pouring the glasses full. His strong arm embraces her shoulder, giving a temporary sense of security along with a full glass of champagne.

He leans low and kisses her passionately, but soon Devon pulls away.

"The police could see your car and find us together. That would be front-page news in the land of the free."

"Alright, this is pretty kinky even for me. One drink and we'll go back." They clink the glasses and take a sip.

"To our new life in Atlanta." Reed throws the glass back, finishing it off.

Devon lowers the glass, no longer interested in the champagne. Tears start to form in her eyes. "What did you say?"

"I told Helen I want a divorce, and she's willing to give it." A smile grows on Reed's face, proud of the statement.

Devon pulls back even farther. "But the business, the baby. You'll have to give up everything."

Reed pulls her closer. "It means nothing without you."

Devon drops the glass and wraps her arms around Reed's neck then lowers her voice, barely audible. "Maybe you should think this all the way through."

Reed whispers back in her ear. "I have. My mind's made up—if you'll have me."

Before Devon can respond to the question she never thought would be posed, a large, hooded figure walks down the path dressed like the Grim Reaper and carrying a harvesting scythe in hand.

She pulls away. "Somebody is coming." She turns him back toward the advancing figure.

Reed places his hand on the pistol and moves Devon behind him. "No problem. Just some fraternity kid stealing a headstone."

The Reaper glides closer, seemingly with no effort or foot

movement below the grey cloth covering the body. The giant, imposing figure stops a few feet away, a face covered by a draped hood revealing only a small opening for visibility.

Devon sinks lower behind Reed hoping for defiance. She wants to look away but is compelled to watch every move in a bazaar sense of obligation.

Reed, fearless in everything life offers, makes light of the moment. "The neighborhood is a little short on candy tonight. Keep moving."

The Reaper's head turns slightly in the other direction, as if looking for someone to approach from the cemetery. He speaks. "Time."

"What did you say?" Reed tries to affirm what makes little sense to either of them.

The Reaper turns his hooded gaze back to Reed. "Time". The voice raises in octave.

"Oh, what time is it?" Reed moves his left hand away from his body so the watch is exposed and glances down. "8:40," he confirms.

"No," the Reaper voices as Devon closes her eyes, somehow realizing all hell is about to break loose. "Time to die."

With lightning speed, the Reaper swings the scythe across Reed's watch arm, slicing it through at the elbow. Devon screams as Reed pulls the pistol out, fires a point blank shot at the figure before the scythe rifles through the air cutting Reed's head away from his body. Reed crumbles to the ground, his severed head beating it to the path by a split second.

Devon, fear now pumping through her veins, runs the path to the gate, screaming. She looks over her shoulder expecting the scythe to slice the darkness at any moment, but the figure is nowhere to be seen. The gate comes into view, and she barrels through the small opening, bouncing the gate outward. Running around the car, Devon grabs the handle and starts to open the door. The harvesting scythe comes out of nowhere and cuts her arm off above the wrist. Blood pours from the wound on the asphalt, and Devon raises her other arm trying to fend off the thrashing weapon with no hope. Silence returns to the cemetery.

◆

Helen Stephens, Reed's wife, sits up in the large, four-poster bed with a baby crib beside it. Her ten-month-old son, Reed W. Stephens III, is sound asleep, but she is sure someone is in the hallway outside the bedroom door.

"Reed?" she hopefully asks. Only a bad answer is walking the Victorian mansion.

Helen rises out of bed and looks at the sleeping baby. She turns attention to the door. The movement beyond is not trying to be silenced. "Reed, is that you?"

Not waiting for an answer, she moves to the door, locks it, and grabs the phone next to the bed. The receiver gives no hope of a tone as she desperately tries to dial out. She picks up the baby, rushes to the window, and looks through the third story glass that has no escape. The harvesting scythe's blade rips through the door, knocking a large hole. Helen screams, and the baby cries. Again the weapon strikes the door, blowing wood onto the floor and inching closer to entrance.

Helen paces back and forth, cradling the crying child, while tears of her own join the helpless feeling swirling inside. A gloved hand reaches through and unlocks the handle. The door swings open, and light from the hallway outlines the Reaper's giant figure, standing silently in the doorway. Helen huddles in the far corner and watches the figure for a brief second, staring at her fate in disbelief. She places the baby gently on the floor and stands, a concession of sacrifice Helen hopes the monster will not accept.

Two

ANGEL EYES

The hedge clippers move along the outside edge of a bush next to the nine-story Stephens Building in the New Orleans Financial District. The man holding the clipper halts the cutting when a tall and attractive woman comes into view, climbing the steps to the front entrance. Gayle Kidd is used to men stopping what they are doing and paying attention to her. The attention is appreciated, but today is business, and she is dressed professionally to make it happen.

As Gayle signs the book at the reception desk, several floors above, Reed Stephens III—also known as Trey—is on the phone with his stockbroker. The open veranda gives Trey a look at the reception area through the glass office wall.

"Where's Microsoft at?" Reed asks, pulling opera glasses from his desk drawer to obtain a better look at the long-legged beauty signing in.

"Down one-and-a-half," Jeb Wallace relays.

"Looks like you pay for golf."

"Trey, I always pay for golf."

"We're into the second quarter of 2019, and I don't like my return worth a damn this year—fix it." Trey watches Gayle take a seat on the couch and dials the receptionist.

"Gabby, who's the young lady that signed in?"

Gabby glances toward Trey from her desk. "Her name is Gayle Kidd. She's got a two-o'clock with Mrs. Jason for a book review."

"Call Jennifer, tell her I'll handle the appointment then send Ms. Kidd up to my office."

Trey straightens the clutter on his desk and goes into his private bathroom to comb his hair and spray cologne on his neck. Trey is rarely this self-absorbed and interested in a strange woman, but something about Gayle Kidd, even at a distance, is ringing the bell.

Gayle rounds the corner of Trey's office, and he waves her in. He stands, as if working the phone.

Gayle walks in, hand extended, and Trey shakes it. "I'm Gayle Kidd."

"Have a seat," Trey points to the chair. "I'm Reed Stephens, but please call me Trey."

"Thank you, Trey." Gayle sits and opens a briefcase. She retrieves a manuscript.

"Jennifer Jason is tied up with another appointment, but I didn't want to keep you waiting."

Gayle focuses on the briefcase file and doesn't look up.

"It's an honor receiving attention from the top." Her piercing blue eyes redirect to Trey's side of the table. "Are you familiar with my conceptual outline?"

Trey is caught off guard, not only by the question but the eyelash-guarded eyes, painted blue. "No, profile it in ten thousand words or less."

Gayle smiles slightly at the boyish joke, but it is hard covering those perfect teeth even when she tries.

"It has a New Orleans setting, high-class society aristocrats, an interracial love affair and..." She hides the perfect teeth. "Murder for all the right and wrong people."

"Must not be fiction." Trey quips, trying to lighten the moment.

"Perhaps a little stretch of the imagination," Gayle says, as she sets the briefcase by the chair. "There's Cajun voodoo and a Hell Raising."

"Hell Raising? Definitely not fiction." Trey knows the city's history well.

"Are you familiar with the legacy of a Hell Raising?" Gayle asks, cocking her head with an inquisitive stare.

Trey instinctively moves his head to match. "I've spent many Julys in New Orleans, proving Hell is not fiction."

The blue eyes narrow. "I appreciate a man with a sense of humor, but I have invested a tremendous amount of time and energy in this book. I thought Stephens Publishing, being based in New Orleans, would be a natural fit. I write for the Boston Globe, and countless other columns in The New Yorker and the Times. Perhaps it's not your cup of tea."

Gayle rises and offers her hand.

It takes a few seconds for Trey to grasp the sudden turn in attitude from the black-haired angel falling from the sky into his office.

He stands. "Please have a seat. I have a smart-ass sense of humor that doesn't always compute with people. It will grow on you, I promise."

Gayle sits as Trey leans over on the desk. "Like every publishing house in America, we're looking for the next James Patterson. Give me your manuscript. I'll read it personally and give you an honest opinion."

"The first sixteen chapters are here." She places the manuscript on the desk. "I'm doing field research in your city to close it out." She writes on the folder. "I'm staying at the Hilton Riverfront, Room 1223. Give me a call when you finish reading it."

Trey turns the file around on the desk and absorbs the room number, afraid it might disappear. Gayle extends her hand, and Trey shakes it. She heads for the door, and he opens it like a Southern gentleman.

"Ms. Kidd, how do you know about a Hell Raising?"

She turns and softens her expression with a smile. "Call me Gayle. My grandfather grew up in New Orleans. In his youth he worked for the Macuch family in their brewery. He lived the dark side of your fair city."

Trey watches the cut calves walk out into the hallway. Sounds of the tapping cadence from the stiletto heels soon disappear around the corner. He goes back to his desk and taps three digits on the phone.

"Jennifer, have you read the manuscript by Gayle Kidd?"

"She sent me the first few chapters. It was riveting. I've never read better, and I invited her here to work on a contract. She must be good-looking if you stole her away from me."

"She's bright and attractive. Marketing would be easy with that combination. I have more of the manuscript and will forward when I get through the read."

"Must be impressive. When was the last time you read a manuscript?"

"When I hired you," he says, hanging up.

He brings up Google and types in: "Macuch family New Orleans". He is very much aware of the crime family that controlled Louisiana in the 1960s and '70s involving Mafia lore. A dozen stories appear on the screen surrounding murders, loan-sharking, gambling, and narcotics. He immerses in several articles before opening the *Hell Raising* manuscript. He loses himself in the smooth and intriguing writing, and admires the talent it must take to compose such literary genius.

Trey has grown up pampered, anchored by all the trappings associated with family money. Things have a way of falling in his lap through the divine providence of cash, not luck. But he recognizes Gayle is special and, by no recruitment of his own, walked into Stephens Publishing to be discovered. A smile erupts on his face as he heads for the parking garage to go home.

◆

Trey drives the Mercedes into one of four garages attached to a seven-thousand-square-foot mansion hidden by massive gates and two acres of pristine landscaping. He opens the kitchen door and walks behind an older black lady peeling potatoes.

She stops her knife movement and looks at Trey with mistrust.

Trey stares at his shoes, knowing precisely what rule of hers he has breached.

"Hi, Lilly... what's for dinner?" He doesn't make eye contact.

"You understand the routine Reed Stephens the Third. Get those shoes off in my house!"

Reed bends over, takes off his Ferragamo Drivers, and redeposits them in the garage.,

He walks back in, determined to take control. "Under the impression this is my house."

"I wiped your ass when you were a baby," Lilly snorts, slicing another potato with aggression. "That gives me the right to run this house. In the near future, I will be senile, and you can wipe my ass. Then you have earned the right to wear your shoes."

Trey starts out of the kitchen. "God, I love you. Will you marry me?"

"I saw both sides of that white ass of yours. You can assume the answer."

Trey is oblivious to the never-ending Lilly wit. He has been jousting with her since he could form a sentence. A large leather chair welcomes his attempt at being comfortable. It sits in a massive den, graced with a hundred-and-twenty-year-old grandfather clock announcing each second. Trey continues reading "*Hell Raising*" until finishing the last chapter.

A glance at the old clock reads 9:10, and Lilly walks in.

"Supper is ready." Lilly retreats but is stopped by Trey.

"Put it in the fridge. I still have work to do."

Lilly walks out of the den and gets louder with each step. "I cook for two hours and you can't move your ass from that chair to eat? Eat it cold. See if I care."

Trey ignores the rambling and talks into his cell phone. "Call the Hilton Riverside." He moves the pages over to the table. "Yes, room 1223, Gayle Kidd." The distinct sound of a slamming refrigerator door can be heard in the kitchen. Trey shakes his head.

"Gayle, Reed Stephens. Have a few minutes?"

"Sure, did you jump into the manuscript?" Gayle is caught off-guard by such a quick response.

"The manuscript is excellent. Couldn't put it down. Can we meet to discuss?"

"Absolutely, what time tomorrow is convenient for you?" she asks, trying to hide her excitement.

"I was thinking more like tonight. Can you get to Jackson Square in an hour? We'll talk over beignets at Cafe Du Monde."

"That's only a few minutes from the hotel. See you shortly." Gayle shifts her thoughts to what to wear.

"One last thing. What's your cell number?"

"Sorry, I should have given that today. It's 617-231-9056."

"Got it." Trey ends the call and heads to the kitchen, pulling out Lilly's fried chicken and making a biscuit sandwich to go. He won't be late.

Three

TO DIE FOR

Trey finds a parking space two blocks from the cafe and surveils the dark street before getting out. He opens the glove box and takes out a 9mm holstering it inside his pants. Trey has a carry permit and takes the weapon seriously. He shoots an array of weapons in a makeshift gun range in his basement. It provides a comfort zone when out on the streets of New Orleans, which can present problems if at the wrong place at the wrong time.

The Louisiana night has thick air, but Trey makes the short walk with minimum loss of moisture. Cajuns are somewhat immune to the oppressive heat. He searches his pocket for a small bottle of Dior and splashes generously. A habit since high school.

A distant reconnoiter across the open-air seating at Cafe Du Monde does not produce a tabled Gayle. Several groups of people are seated, giving the scene a crowded look in spite of being in the middle of the week after 9:30 p.m. Of course, the cafe is open twenty-four hours, serving its world-renowned square donuts that attract locals and tourists alike.

Trey walks onto the deck, and Gayle is seated in the far corner away from the street. She stands and waves. Her thick black hair is pulled back into a ponytail, and a running suit clings to her perfect body.

Approaching, he notices the orange running shoes are quite the change from the heels earlier in the day. It doesn't matter. She could wear overalls, and any man would take note of her presence.

"Are you a runner?" Trey extends his arm and takes her hand.

"Not so much now, but I did run over from the hotel." Her smile lights up the shadowed corner of the restaurant. "If I'm going to stuff my face with donuts I'd better slide back into the routine."

"Let's jump into the powdered sugar backed by strong Cajun coffee." They walk to the service window.

A sense of ease in the smalltalk crosses Trey's mind walking to the table, donuts in hand. Gayle appeared to have a hair-triggered focus earlier in the day, but for the time being it seems to be placed on the back burner, adding fuel to her attractiveness.

"So, what did you think of the manuscript?" Gayle asks, taking a donut bite and leaning back for the answer.

"Honestly," Trey hesitates with a sip of coffee, "you have an incredible gift."

The smile from Gayle is intense. She has worked hard to hear the compliment, and to receive it from the head of a major publishing company lifts her energy.

"Now, let's talk about the management it takes to place a book on the street." He watches to see if she can take criticism. "Are you open to having our writers hone the edges to get the book finished?"

"Sure, anything to polish the end-product. But the heart of the story can't be changed." She leans across the table for his response.

"I understand your concern. We won't change the base premise, but there's not an author in the world doing their own editing. Eyes beyond your beautiful set have to..." Trey's voice falls off, emphasizing the slip of the tongue.

Gayle tries to ignore the slip, but it sits on the table staring at both of them.

"What about my eyes, Reed Stephens the Third?" Gayle draws a serious mask of anger, quickly falling away to a smile.

"They are beautiful. So at least you don't have a bullshit-speaking publisher on your team."

"I can't thank you. It would upset too many feminists I know—who, by the way, helped my career get off the ground. Let's move back to the book and away from my eyes."

"Fair enough. I like the premise and your style," He looks around as if to keep a secret. "Tell me, is it a hired killer hacking the bodies up or the father that can't stand the thought of his blue-eyed son loving a black woman?"

"You will have to buy the book to gain the answer." Her eyebrows furrow at the thought.

"That's what we intend to do. I'll have the option papers drawn up in the next couple of days, and we'll give you an advance to finish the book." He presses forward, pleased with his decision.

She leans across the table, placing her hand on his. "That's wonderful! This is so exciting. You've made me speechless."

"Still a lot of work to be done on both sides of this transaction to produce a launch date, but I have no doubt our team and your skillset will make it happen. Tell you what. I'll walk you back to the hotel, and we'll seal the deal with a glass of champagne at the bar. Big day tomorrow."

They leave the deck and start the ten-block walk to the Hilton.

Trey points out all of the historical sites steeped in tradition. Gayle is engaged, asking beyond the typical tourist babble. Each step pulls him deeper into the heated abyss, with little fight on his part.

The street is lined with jazz bars and strip clubs, the New Orleans bread and butter. In front of a bar, an old man is playing a clarinet, and his twelve-year-old grandson is tap-dancing next to him. The music and tap are highly synchronized, punctuated with splits that draw photos and tips from the crowd walking the strip. Trey leans over and drops a tenspot in the hat placed at the old man's feet, and the two continue their stroll to the Hilton.

Once they pass, the old man stops playing and watches them stride along the street.

"Time to go, Emrik." The old man packs the instrument away as the boy gathers the coins and bills dropped in the hat.

"It's a good night, Granddad. Why are we leaving now?" The boy stuffs his backpack and pocket.

The old man speaks not another word. He simply walks the strip with the grandson following closely. Each step brings a kiss against the concrete with a metal tap of Emrik's steel-toed shoes. Emrik senses something is wrong with his granddad but does not dare challenge him.

Both have been working the streets for seven years together. The old man has been pandering and doing con-jobs on the same streets for sixty years. His thinking is tilted toward staying one step ahead of the law, the landlord or, in his younger days, a woman trying to get money for one of his seven children.

The young boy and old man come to an intersection and take a left off the beaten tourist path, confusing Emrik even more. He has never been on this street. After several blocks, the old man walks to the door of a three-story house. The two stand for a few seconds on the porch, and Emrik wonders why his granddad doesn't knock on the metal-framed door if this is their destination. A six-inch opening appears in the door, and doubting eyes stare out at them. The door cracks slightly open and a booming voice jumps around the metal, causing Emrik to step back.

"What do you want, Bailly?" the Voice commands.

"Have to see Mr. Fleck, it's real important." The old man answers the command.

"He's has no time for you. There are rules. You know them well." The Voice is not in a good mood, Emrik thinks.

"Ain't about money." The old man seems to be begging, a first for Emrik to witness.

"What else could be so important?" the Voice counters.

The old man moves forward next to the door opening. "Tell Mr. Fleck that she's back."

"Who is back?"

"The Devil." The old man's body seems to lose its balance, and the air barely clears his lungs.

The opening closes, and the Voice retreats.

Emrik's mind is racing wildly. His granddad is the toughest man he has ever known. Two bums tried to rob them one night, and even being sixty-plus in years, Bailly beat them so severely that the next day one still laid in the alley. But his granddad is now the one scared, and Emrik knows he doesn't believe in Heaven or Hell, yet he has seen the Devil? Emrik pushes his recollection about the last hour dancing on the street. No one with horns walked by. It wasn't Mardi Gras where the costumes covered devils and saints.

The door opens, and the man connected to the Voice towers over granddad and Emrik. The old man sets the clarinet case on the porch and steps through the opening. Emrik picks up the case. "Granddad, your instrument."

The old man turns toward him. "Leave it."

Now, Emrik is shaking like his granddad. He would never walk away leaving their ability to make money on a deserted front porch, ever.

The Voice leads them through the hallway and on either side, people are playing blackjack or poker. Slots line the walls, but little play is being made on them. At the back of the converted house, the Voice stops at a large wooden door.

"Wait here." He opens the door and once again disappears.

Emrik's vision is redirected by a clapping noise to his right, and a naked woman is upside down on a pole attached to the ceiling. He has caught many looks at lightly clothed women inside doorways walking the strip, but this is his first totally nude view. He stares.

The vision is interrupted by a granddad tug on his shoulder. A strong smell of bourbon and cigar smoke greets Emrik's nose inside the belly of a mob operation beyond the wooden door.

A man in his seventies holds court behind an ornate desk that escaped from a seventeenth-century English castle. The desk participated, unwillingly, in spilled booze, blood, and sex on both sides of the ocean.

"Bailly, I understand the young man can dance the taps off those shoes." Louis Fleck, the man responsible for much of the booze, blood, and sex on the table greets Emrik's granddad.

28

Bailly pulls Emrik closer to his side. Emrik leans heavy against his leg, fearing something bad is about to happen.

"The boy got the talent from his momma ... Mr. Louis, the Devil is back in town. Seen her walking with a man on the strip."

"What makes you think it's her?"

"Some things, and faces, never leave your thoughts. She has crawled out of the ground. Pretty sure she has come back for us."

The room is dead silent, even the mob king is humbled by the thought Bailly has neatly laid on his ornate desk.

"Okay, I believe you saw the bitch. If she wants a war in my town, we'll be ready."

The three young hoodlums in the room do not have a clue what Bailly and their boss are talking about. To them, someone coming to Louisiana looking for a fight on their turf is mindlessly stupid and soon to be sinking to the bottom of the Mississippi River.

Fleck pulls a hundred-dollar bill from his pocket, hands it to the Voice, and motions toward Bailly. The giant of a man walks over to the old man who has Emrik clinging to his belt.

Bailly holds his hand up, refusing the money. "Thanks, Mr. Louis, but money ain't no good now."

The old man turns around, walks out the wooden door, and the boy follows closely. This night Emrik has seen many firsts, but his granddad refusing money has torn away all his core beliefs. He is confused and frightened, not understanding how this night is going to end. His wildest thoughts are about to fall far short of reality.

The Voice shows them a back door to exit into the night. A set of steps leads to an alleyway and darkness. A few yards down the alley, the old man turns Emrik around and leans low, face-to-face.

"Listen to me, son, you are going to grow up far too soon. Remember all those things we talked about working the crowds? Your Uncle Randy can play the music for the dancing. Tell your momma I love her. Love you, too. You will do well in life, but don't look back. Don't ever back down from anyone." The old man's voice is soft and caring.

He takes Emrik's hand and walks slowly along the alley's descending grade. An Emrik glance at his granddad's face shows a man settled with his life's work and whatever fate demands. For the first time tonight, Emrik feels comfortable and safe.

Time suddenly stands still as it often does in tragedy. Emrik feels a sudden jolt grounded in granddad's grip on his hand. The old man straightens up and takes a heavy gulp of air.

Their eyes meet in a flash, and falling off the old man's lips, Emrik hears him scream. "Run!"

Emrik's vision witnesses the tip of a long blade protruding from granddad's chest. It doesn't immediately register the gravity of a fourteen-inch blade swung with enough force, to go completely through a man's back and stick out the other side.

What did register was the order, "Run!" And, run he does. The old man leans backward with all his dying strength, pushing the blade even further into his body. He is buying precious time by hindering the blade removal and pursuit of his Emrik.

The grandson flies down the alley with the taps hammering the street. Adrenaline, and dancing endless hours, kick him forward faster and faster. Emrik rounds a corner but isn't sure where to go in this strange neighborhood. Several commercial buildings appear in the distance, and his speed turns him in their direction. Two blocks later, he slows to grab a mouthful of air and glances over his shoulder. A giant, hooded figure is gaining ground.

Another hundred-yard sprint places him next to a warehouse with a partially cracked basement window. He kicks the glass out and crawls through, dropping five feet to the floor. A sting to the arch of his right foot gives a frightening reality to his decision-making. The shoes are removed and tossed aside to stop the calling-card tap of each step. The stairs leading to the second floor beckon, and he makes the climb despite the increasing foot pain.

The second floor is a storage facility for Macy's mannequins, haphazardly lying among props used in countless parades the New Orleans aristocrats have created for religious and fundraising causes. Emrik limps several feet into the figurine maze and hides behind a five-foot-tall Donald Duck.

Tears form in his eyes, not for his plight but the knowledge the man he has loved and worked with six days a week is gone. The only real male figure in his life was his granddad. Emrik wonders what he is going to say if he ever sees his mother again.

Footsteps on the stairs bring back the immediate fear of death stalking him. Emrik looks around for an escape route, but the only way out is straight toward those footsteps walking closer. His small hands tighten into fists; he will make his granddad proud. A tall figure comes into view, and Emrik rises to fight.

"Hey, you have any money?" the figure asks.

Emrik digs in his pocket, pulls out a handful of change and the ten-dollar bill that fell from Trey's hand on Bourbon Street. The street bum reaches low and takes the money.

"This is my place," the man asserts. "You can stay the night, but out tomorrow."

"Thank you. Be gone in the morning." Emrik leans on Donald Duck, falls into a deep sleep and dreams about dancing with his granddad.

Four

THE DEVIL DOWN IN GEORGIA

Chris Dale sips from a coffee cup, his third of the morning. An eye on his watch confirms the habit of reading about the Saints online is over. Joanna Dale walks into the kitchen with a tie matching his jacket and places it around his neck.

Chris is colorblind and depends on Joanna to avoid having his wardrobe blasted by his peers in the office for the unwitting choices made over the last twenty-three years. His first eight with the New Orleans PD, he constantly was teased about the mismatched clothing, before his marriage to Joanna. Chris has a highly sharpened wit and misses the exchanges about his misfit clothing combinations. But he would never acknowledge as much to his wife.

"How is Detective Dale feeling this morning?" she asks, pulling the tie tight.

"Tired," Chris deadpans. "Tired of pulling dead bums and hookers out of dumpsters."

Joanna leans her head sideways to show disagreement. "Less than two years left. Then we can head to West Palm Beach. Your brother will love having you so close."

"Not sure about that anymore. Nancy will drive me crazy with her politics." Chris loosens the tie.

"Your sister-in-law means well. It will be fun sleeping in and fishing, and playing golf with your brother."

"I may shoot her. No sane jury would convict me." Chris actually believes this.

A phone rings for attention.

"Started already." Chris answers the call. "Be there shortly."

He turns to Joanna. "Love you." He starts for the door.

"My love to you." She follows him and watches him drive off.

◆

Chris draws a self-appointed smile on his face. There was a time he would run to the car, flip the lights on and drive twice the speed limit to the scene of a murder. That ceased a long time ago. He now understands that time stops having meaning to a dead body.

The crime scene tape is draped between a stop sign and a police car. An ambulance parks nearby, like a vulture waiting its turn. Chris steps out, looks up and down the houses lining the alleyway where the old man lies, covered by a sheet. He is looking for a security camera, but none jumps into view.

A familiar face greets Chris a few steps short of the body.

"Detective Bobby Rabold, what have you found for me on this beautiful Thursday morning?" Chris sees a large pool of blood gathered well beyond the sheet. He shakes Rabold's hand and leans over, lifting the cover.

"Bum?" Chris asks.

"Not really, he's a street guy named Bailly that worked the tourist trade," Rabold waves a police officer over. "Tell Detective Dale what you know."

Chris pushes a handshake to the young officer, who is surprised by the offer. Most detectives keep their distance from the street cops.

"His name is Joe Bailly. Worked the street with his tap-dancing grandson. Played all kinds of instruments for handouts. Been arrested a few times for some minor stuff since I've been working downtown."

"What kind of stuff?"

"Got in a shoving match with a tourist a couple years ago. Nothing came of it. Two homeless guys tried to rob him. Didn't work out very well for them."

"Tough guy, huh?" Always a bigger badass. Please hit all these houses within a couple blocks for witnesses or video. Then get back with Detective Rabold."

"One more thing," the officer says. "That three-story house is a gambling joint. An FBI guy told me Louis Fleck runs it." The officer points to the house eighty yards up the street.

"Really? Haven't heard that name in a while. Good job officer...?"

Chris wants the man's name.

"Officer Dalton." The young cop walks off.

"Big fish in the casino, let's go harass the old bastard." Chris waves at the ambulance driver who comes over.

"Don't touch the body until the coroner releases it, or they will be picking up two bodies when I get back." He and Rabold walk to the three-story house, and Rabold pounds on the metal door.

The door slat retreats. "How may I help you?" The Voice knows who is at the door.

"Open the door," Chris orders while flashing his badge.

"Have a warrant?" The Voice defies.

Chris moves close to the opening. "I don't give a baked shit about your illegal gaming or hookers, but if Fleck isn't out here in thirty seconds, I'm calling SWAT."

"Yessir." The Voice comes to his senses.

Rabold smiles at his directness as Chris shakes his head. The door opens and the diminutive mob boss appears.

"What can I do for you officers?"

Chris flips his ID open. "I'm Detective Dale and this is Detective Rabold. Do you know a Joe Bailly?"

"Yes, he comes by from time to time to play pool," Fleck calmly lies.

"No slots? No blackjack? He plays pool? We know what goes on here. If you don't answer my questions truthfully, I'll turn my investigation over to the FBI, something you don't want to happen," Chris says, barking like a drill sergeant.

"Why is this even necessary?" Fleck inquires.

Rabold jumps in. "Bailly was stabbed to death less than a hundred yards from your back door. Was Bailly here last night?"

"I don't know personally, but I'll confirm with the staff. Report back to you. To answer your other question, Bailly delivered packages to people around town for me on occasion. Never saw him gamble, ever."

Chris pulls out a notebook and pen. "Give me a number you will answer or the FBI can wiretap you."

"That's been going on for a long time," Fleck says, pulling out a business card. "My personal cell. Call me tomorrow. Tell you if he was here last night."

Chris retreats to the car and taps Bailly's home address into the GPS. It directs him to a housing project on the west side of town. He knocks on the door.

A large man opens it.

"I'm Detective Dale. Does Joe Bailly live here?" Chris knows the answer.

"Yes, he's my father. Come in," Randy Bailly answers.

Eva Czapleski comes into the room. "Is something wrong with my father?"

"I'm sorry to inform you that Mr. Bailly was murdered last night." Chris hates this part of his job.

"My God, no!" Randy grabs Eva to keep her from falling to the floor. "Did you find my son, Emrik?"

"No, how old is Emrik?

"He's twelve. Works with my father downtown." Eva cries, scared out of her mind.

"I need a photo of Emrik," Chris says. "We'll push it out to the black-and-whites to bring him home." Eva retrieves a picture of Emrik, Chris shoots it with his phone, and passes a text to police headquarters.

"We'll also put out an Amber Alert. He will be found."

The door opens, and Emrik Czapleski stands barefooted for a few seconds, surveying the crowd. Eva rushes over and envelops her son with kisses.

"Where have you been?" Eva stops the kissing and begs.

"Walking home."

His bloody feet upset Eva, and she walks to the kitchen for a wet cloth and returns.

"Why didn't you ride the bus?" his uncle asks.

"No money," a meek voice responds.

Eva places Emrik on the couch and starts cleaning his shoeless feet. Chris leans low in front of Emrik.

"Were you with your grandfather last night?

"Yes." His young voice seems even more tender.

"Do you know who stabbed your grandfather?" He softens his voice.

"Yes." Emrik is mentally rushed back to the night before.

"Who, son?"

"The Devil." Emrik grabs Eva with a hug.

◆

Chris opens the door to his car and sits for a few minutes, pondering the story just heard from the young man about being chased around New Orleans by the Devil. At this stage of his career, if a victim told that story he would have the city commit them until the truth surfaced. But he is aware Emrik believes every last detail, and it is now his job to disconnect the pieces of the puzzle and then reassemble. He pulls out the mob boss's business card and calls Louis Fleck to start that reassembly.

"Mr. Fleck, this is Detective Dale. I spent this morning talking to the old man's grandson. Want to revise our conversation earlier?"

Fleck looks at his ornate desk, contemplating his answer.

"Okay, Bailly came in last night with the boy, but not to gamble. Out of courtesy, I spoke with him."

"What was the conversation about? Stop the pandering, Mr.

Fleck."

"Bailly said someone was after him. He was looking for a little help.This will sound crazy, but the old guy thought the Devil came to town after him. You can imagine what I said to that. He left."

"Maybe the old man wasn't as crazy as he sounded. We'll talk again shortly." Chris ends the call and drives toward the station.

Fleck looks over at the Voice. "Go buy a burner phone with an hour on it. Need to make an important call." The Voice is gone for thirty minutes and returns with the non-traceable cell phone.

Fleck pulls out from the desk a small book containing telephone numbers—the old fashioned way. He taps the number of Billy Macuch in Chicago.

"Billy, how's business?"

"Couldn't be better. How is Cajun country doing?" He respects Fleck for his forty years of iron-fisted control in Louisiana.

The Macuch family had moved their crime empire to Chicago in the late seventies for bigger money, after the sudden death of a crime family boss a Macuch hitman orchestrated.

"Blew it out with Mardi Gras. Going to retire pretty soon." This is a running joke for the mob crowd every time Fleck brings it up.

"You will die sitting at that fancy desk of yours. What can I do for you?" Macuch knows Fleck's calls are not made to wish someone a happy birthday.

"I need real talent for a couple of weeks. The best you have."

Fleck is taking the threat seriously, especially with Bailly being killed in his back yard.

"That would be Israel out of New York, but he ain't cheap."

Macuch stops short of giving the full name Israel Hamric.

"Money is no object. Need high-level trash taken out."

"Okay, he'll text you an arrival date in the next twenty-four hours."

"What does he like? Dope, women, booze? Want to welcome him properly."

"Women are his thing, but he can be pretty rough on them."

"I'll make him happy. Thanks." Fleck ends the call and hands the phone to the Voice. "Burn it."

The Voice takes the phone and starts to the door but stops.

"Boss, we don't need this Israel guy. Jake ... me ... the guys can handle this."

"You let me handle the decision-making." Fleck grabs the telephone booklet and places it in his pocket.

"What makes this Israel so talented?" The Voice doesn't understand how far he has been pushing the conversation.

Fleck is about to rip his head off, but he pulls back to teach a lesson.

"Just because you go to the gun range and blast holes in a paper man does not give you talent. Israel Hamric once killed a man on a dance floor with a hypodermic needle filled with cyanide. Everyone thought he had a heart attack. A VIP daughter was beat up by a thug she was dating in Pittsburgh. Israel taped him, spread peanut butter all over his body, and threw him into a sewer full of rats. Then he set up a camera to record the rats doing their thing while the man screamed his head off. Don't ask me any more of your stupid questions."

The Voice walks off in silence.

Five

SOMETHING LIKE LOVE

Trey whistles as he walks into the kitchen while Lilly is cooking breakfast. A reach into the cabinet retrieves a glass, which he fills with orange juice from the refrigerator.

He sits and opens his laptop. "Good morning, Lilly."

Lilly flips a pancake but doesn't look at Trey. "How come you're chirping like a bird?"

"Met someone really special."

"Like that stripper you met on Bourbon Street?" Lilly sets two pancakes and bacon on a plate to his left, away from the lap top.

Trey pushes the computer aside and repositions the food.

"She was a different kind of special."

"What that woman could do with tassels, can't imagine all her tricks in bed." Lilly places a fork and knife on the table.

"You liked the stripper, didn't you?" Trey follows with a bite.

"At least there was honesty about who she was and what she did. Not like some of those dizzy babes you brought home before."

Lilly recovers the pan from the stove and starts washing.

"When do I get to meet this gold digger?"

Trey sets the fork on the plate. "Why is every woman I go out with a gold digger?"

Trey answers his own question simultaneously with Lilly.

"Why else would she be interested."

"Why else would she be interested." Lilly smiles at the dual thought process and her training of Trey's reaction.

"Wow, now I'm really scared," Trey relays. "Know you so well, we've become soul mates, Lilly."

"You think so?" She asserts. "What am I thinking now?"

He leans his head to the left. She leans her head to the right and enunciates slowly while speaking loudly. He reads her lips and speaks in unison.

"How about a raise?"

"That's total genius."

Lilly opens the door on the thought.

Trey throws his hand in the air. "You would leave me high and dry."

"Best day for both our lives. Tell me about this new honey."

"Just met her," he explains. "Brought in a perfect manuscript, perfect body ... perfect brain."

"Is she a Southern belle?"

"She's from Boston."

"Good."

Trey shakes his head. "What's wrong with Southern belles? My mother was one."

"Your mother and the rest of those Southern girls spell 'belle' as 'b-i-t-c-h'."

"You have crossed the line, nothing is sacred with you."

Lilly changes her tactic. "Bring her over tonight. I want to meet this woman."

"You'll cook something special?"

"You question my cooking at this stage of your life? Want my retro-raise in twenties by noon."

Trey finishes his breakfast. "Lilly, do you know where my golf shoes are?

"Yep."

"Well, where?" He's is losing patience but knows this is her style when receiving a pushback about her ongoing raise issue, even though he gives her a substantial bonus each Christmas that increases every year.

Lilly wipes her hands free of the washwater and turns around. "Polished and placed in your golf bag, where golf shoes should be."

"Thanks, you're the best," He stands and heads for the garage but turns back in her direction. "Plan on dinner for two tonight."

◆

Trey arrives at the country club and sees Judge Raymond Hastings getting dressed in the locker room. "Good day for golf, Judge Hastings."

Hastings finishes tying his shoes and turns toward him.

"Never had a bad day when it comes to golf. See you on the first tee. I'm going to the putting green."

Bill Wycoff walks in, and the judge offers his hand. Trey makes the introduction. "Judge Hastings, I believe you know my attorney, Bill Wycoff."

"Yes, he used to grace my courtroom years ago, until you put him in the business world."

"Great to see you again, Judge. How's the game playing these days?"

"Got down to single digits last summer, but more like a 12 now. Not playing much in the last few months."

"I seem to hear that from everybody just before the Nassau bets are made." Bill understands how the game is played.

The judge smiles and leaves.

"Thanks for the golf. It's been a miserable week at the office and I needed the break,"Wycoff offers.

Trey looks around the locker room to make sure nobody else can hear. He moves close Wycoff.

"Where are we on the riverboat deal?" His demeanor has changed in an instant.

Wycoff adjusts his glasses and pulls back slightly. "It's tough, Trey. The state commission is controlled by Councilman Reynolds. He hates your grandfather and won't let your money in. Controlling interest is impossible."

Trey grabs him by the shirt. "You listen well. We were shut out of the Hilton Riverfront years ago. It won't happen again. Buy Reynolds off, take pictures with a hooker or concrete him to the bottom of the river. Makes no difference to me. Just get it done or suffer the consequences."

He turns his shirt loose. "We own two casinos in Gulfport and can't get anything on our home turf. It's embarrassing."

"Your grandfather muscled the Reynolds family in South Louisiana out of the vending business. He can't be bought off."

Trey smiles. "There's your answer—alligator meat! Let's go hit some golfballs."

The two walk out of the clubhouse toward the first tee. Trey turns attention to his ringing phone. "Be right there guys, have to take this.

"Gayle, I was just about to call you. I'm tied up with a business deal today, but I'm having your contract drawn together as we speak. Why don't you come by my house at 6:30 tonight for dinner and we'll push the formalities along the way. Get you a check."

Trey listens to her confirmation. "Great, I will text my address over shortly. See you tonight." Trey tees off, happy on several fronts.

◆

When Trey pulls the Mercedes into the garage at home, he notices a car parked in the driveway. His watch reads 6:05. Gayle is early. He starts for the kitchen door but places his golf shoes in the garage before entering. No use giving Lilly any more ammo with Gayle present.

"I apologize, but the golf was slow. See you've met Lilly."

Gayle smiles with a glass of wine in her hand. "She has filled me in on quite a bit."

The two women clink their wine glasses in a toast.

"I'm sure of that!" The scary thought rolls quickly through Trey's head.

Lilly sets the glass on the table.

"Bless my soul." She places a hand over her heart.

Trey looks down, taking inventory on what he could have been doing wrong walking in.

"What?"

"You couldn't possibly be carrying all my retro-pay in your pocket. It must be in the car."

"Lilly, we'll talk about this later, okay? I'm going to jump in the shower. Don't you have to finish dinner?"

"Supper is almost done. You go shower, Gayle and I are just beginning to talk about your diaper." She takes a wine sip to punctuate her newly found power.

"God give me strength." Trey heads out of the room while Gayle laughs at the latest Lilly dig.

◆

When Trey returns to the kitchen, Lilly and Gayle are not present. Motion on the back deck beside the swimming pool reveals the two setting a table for the meal.

Trey walks out and Lilly hands him a glass of wine.

"Don't frick this up," Lilly states with doubt and heads inside.

Gayle pretends she didn't hear the latest Lilly direction and stares beyond the pool to the manicured grounds.

"Beautiful property. How long have you lived here?"

"Eight years,"

"Hope Lilly didn't bend your ear to the point of breaking."

Gayle smiles broadly. "No, no, she's quite the character and very entertaining."

"Jack the Ripper and Mother Theresa rolled into one is my assessment."

"She actually loves you a lot. She seems to be a little opinionated about your family history." Gayle winks.

"I won't deny the Stephens' family has some skeletons in the closet, but most longtime business enterprises always have their share of mistakes. Speaking of business, I had the agreement sent to your phone for review. We're giving you an advance of twenty thousand against sales."

Gayle offers her glass to Trey, and they lightly collide in celebration.

"To *Hell Raising*. May it be the first of many successes for you and Stephens Publishing." Trey backs the sentiment by gulping down his drink.

"Hear, hear!" Gayle responds.

Trey pulls the chair out for Gayle to be seated. The table has been set with candles, wine, and flowers.

"This is a magnificent property." Gayle sees a flower garden in bloom directly behind the pool.

"Thanks, it can be overwhelming at times, but my grandfather truly believes that image is everything. I understand the branding aspect for the company, but it's way too much to maintain at times."

"So, you don't agree?"

"Lilly keeps my ego at a manageable level, whether I want it or not."

"Ever thought about a wife and kids running through this vast-expanse?" "

"In all honesty, close once but got cold feet. How about you? Someone so gorgeous must have unlimited men chasing after her."

"I've been focused on my career. It leaves little time for dating. Who knows? After the book is published, maybe I'll sit still long enough for Mister Right to make an impression."

Lilly rolls a table out with plates loaded in her Southern-style food offerings.

"Jump right in, lovers." She retreats to the kitchen while both do as directed.

Gayle is complimentary about the Southern food in spite of her Northeastern taste. Both talk about their family history in guarded terms. She expresses interest in meeting the company's patriarch and founder. It is hard for Trey to maintain his focus on the many subjects flying back and forth. Gayle has an electric aura, forcing him to lean in for the next jolt of emotion.

◆

The glasses of wine waste away to their empty bottoms. Trey

rises, opens a second bottle, and pours another fullness. While leaning over Gayle, his face moves toward her lips for a kiss.

Just then Lilly opens the door and carries out a tray of dessert, interrupting.

"Hope I'm not getting in the way," she happily remarks.

Trey pulls back from the intended target. "Not surprised."

"Ain't life a bitch," Lilly snarks. "Here's my apple cobbler with zero calories. It will make your breasts larger."

Gayle bursts out with laughter, and Trey turns away, mad at the interruption but helpless not to laugh.

"You should be on HBO—and out of my house!"

Lilly cuts the pie and sets a new plate on the table. Without hesitation she continues. "I'm working on one that will help make…"

"Don't you dare say it!" Trey interrupts.

"Miss Gayle, I will let you use your imagination since Trey is so rude."

Trey puts his napkin over his face as Lilly leaves, trying to hide the laughter even at his own expense.

"I swear she has rabies," he says, placing the napkin back onto his lap.

"She is priceless. HBO may not be a big enough platform for her performance," Gayle adds.

The night does end with a kiss, only making Trey lie awake thinking about the possibilities.

Six

A SHOUT OUT

Gayle moves off the elevator onto the eighth floor of the Stephens Building. A young intern walks by, and Gayle stops her.

"Where is the Executive Board Room?"

The intern points to the left. "Second door on the right, can't miss it."

She follows the direction and opens the boardroom door. Jennifer Jason and Trey stand to greet her.

"At last, I'm able to meet the word master in person," Jason relays.

"It's an honor to meet you," Gayle responds, "Without your faith in my early work, none of this would take place."

"Did you have a chance to review the agreement?" Trey inquires.

"Yes. Actually I have a few questions about the marketing costs and how it affects me." Gayle opens a grip and pulls her copy out with notes.

Jason takes her copy of the contract and turns it around for Gayle's eyes.

"If you look at the marketing costs on a quarterly basis, the first ten thousand spent is our expense, and everything after that is split fifty-fifty."

The boardroom door opens, and Trey's grandfather walks in.

Everyone rises to greet the founder.

Mr. Stephens shakes Gayle's hand. "Please be seated. I just wanted to meet this new prodigy."

Gayle flashes her perfect smile. "Thanks so much. It's a proud moment to work with the staff getting my book off the ground."

"Trey and Jennifer are sold on your abilities, which tells me everything I need to know. Please, finish the paperwork. Welcome to the Stephens Publishing family."

"It's certainly my honor to be part of the organization," Gayle answers formally.

Stephens starts for the door but turns back at the last second. "Trey, when you finish here, please come to my office."

Trey smiles. "Absolutely."

Trey never liked being called in by the old man, it rarely meant anything good.

◆

Reed Stephens is writing on a pad when Trey knocks on the door and then opens it. The old man stays focused on the paperwork and points to a chair. "Please sit, Trey."

Without stopping his writing, he asks. "What's going on with the riverboat deal?"

Trey knows this is a pet project for his grandfather.

"It seems the State Licensing Board is under the control of Councilman Reynolds. Not an old friend of our family. I have Wycoff pressuring Reynolds from several angles to push the vote through."

"That pansy-assed attorney? You might as well have Lilly take care of it." I'll talk to Louis Fleck. He'll address the matter quickly. So, who the hell is the bimbo in my boardroom?"

This comes out of left field for Trey. "She's a fantastic writer."

"Where did she come from?" The old man stares a hole in Trey.

"Boston. We've done a background check. She's clean. Writes freelance for the Globe and other magazines. Have you read any of the *Hell Raising* manuscript?"

"My biggest question—are you banging her?" The old man leans forward.

"To answer the question—no!" Trey fires back. "But what difference does that make?"

"We're at a critical juncture on a number of business fronts, and I don't want you falling all over yourself in love. Women are distractions. The company comes first."

"Grandfather, I have enormous respect for what you have built, but my personal life belongs to me. Look, Louisiana people think Stephens Publishing is, in fact, a publishing company. We can't ignore our roots in book creation because vending or gaming is a much better business. We need to employ talent and keep the brand in place. We haven't had a Top Ten author in three years. Gayle Kidd is that talent."

Old Stephens sits back in his chair. "That may be the smartest thing I've ever heard you utter. But don't take your eye off the ball by chasing skirt. I'm watching. Go back to work."

Trey walks out, not sure if a compliment was buried in the conversation. Didn't matter. The old man is set in his ways. He does understand that mixing business with pleasure usually ends up falling to the ground all bloody. That "pleasure," Gayle, suddenly calls his cell and he answers.

"Trey, just want to thank you again for this opportunity to work with Stephens, publishing my book," Gayle's voice drips through the speaker.

"Listen, I've said it before. You have earned this. My grandfather is excited to have you on board. Believe me, Stephens Publishing doesn't give anything away." Trey's thinks his lie sounds good.

"Received a hot tip on a voodoo ceremony tonight. Thought you might find it interesting."

"Is this a formal date?" Trey teases.

"It qualifies."

"Voodoo, huh? Does it take place at the Four Seasons ballroom?"

Trey expects this to bring a laugh, it does.

"More like a barn out in the boondocks. You in?"

"Sure, what time?"

"Pick me up at seven with jeans on. We have a pretty long drive to get there."

"Should I bring a live chicken or goat?" Trey can't help but make fun of what he thinks is a total waste of time. They should be going to the Four Seasons for drinks and sex.

"Only if you're really hungry." Gayle is never short of answers. She ends the call.

◆

Trey pulls in his driveway, and a grounds crew is spread out cutting and trimming the massive lawn. The cell phone rings. It is his grandfather. Leaving the office before six has gotten him in trouble—at least, that is the initial thought running through his head.

"Hello?" he answers, less than energetically.

"Trey, we have a state audit in eight weeks. Meet with Wilcox in accounting."

Before Trey confirms, the cell connection is lost. He laughs at his mannerless grandfather and walks inside. The house is silent and he wonders where Lilly has gone. Just as well. She has badgered him constantly about Gayle, and he has grown tired of answering the same questions.

Trey surrendered a long time ago trying to figure what made Lilly tick. Gayle is the first woman he has brought home whom

Lilly completely endorsed. Strange. Sudden encouragement was not a Lilly forte. Trey has been looking through a positive prism surrounding Gayle, and he takes Lilly's actions as reinforcement he is headed along the right emotional path.

He retreats to the basement gun range, puts on headphones, and begins firing a .40-caliber Smith & Wesson. A box of bullets later, he showers, reads his emails, and dresses in jeans.

A rummage through the refrigerator finds a leftover plate of lasagna he liberates. The grandfather clock rings out six times.

Trey heads for the garage and then downtown.

◆

The traffic is light, unusual for New Orleans this time of day and appreciated. Rarely does Trey anticipate an event before it happens, but tonight is different. An accelerated sense of adventure, hits his body as he pulls into the Hilton entrance. Fifteen minutes early, he tells the young man wanting to park the car to leave it in place. He will be back in a minute. A sawbuck handshake validates the deal, and a look inside the hotel reveals Gayle at the front desk talking to a clerk.

Trey stands beside the car, focused on the front desk through artist's eyes, admiring the completion of a masterpiece. Gayle leans on the desk facing away from the entrance, one foot moving a wedge shoe up and down, completely free of intent.

A flip of the black hair and she turns around, spotting Trey. A wave of the hand confirms her recognition.

She retrieves a paper sack and moves quickly to the car. A kiss on Trey's cheek seals his fate.

"Early, I like a man early." Gayle acknowledges, sliding into the passenger seat.

"So, what is in the sack?" Trey asks, pulling the Mercedes onto the street.

"Thought you would be hungry. Bought a couple of Po' boys because we have a forty-five-minute drive into the country."

Gayle hands Trey the address, and he taps it into the GPS.

"Can't waste a drive in the countryside without a stop for food and..." She reaches in the sack and pulls out a bottle of wine. "Something to free the spirit."

"I like a woman prepared." Trey won't admit the raid on Lilly's fridge.

The road narrows from four lanes to two some thirty minutes into the trip. A country store appears on the horizon.

"Pull in there," Gayle relays excitedly. "Look at the pick-nit tables."

As soon as the car is parked, Gayle moves out and opens the sack.

She looks at Trey inquisitively. "Do you have a wine bottle opener?"

"No, but I'm sure one is inside the store. Give me the bottle. Be right back."

"Nope, I didn't think it through," Gayle asserts, starting toward the store.

"I'll make amends."

"Are you sure? These Cajun country boys will scarf you up."

Gayle flips her hair and winks. "Maybe that's part of the plan."

Trey sits on the bench, more impressed by the minute with this wildcat he is petting. Gayle returns with the bottle open and two plastic cups.

"Was it a guy behind the counter?" Trey asks.

"Yes."

"Didn't stand a chance, did he?"

"Said something about squealing like a pig. This ring any bells with you Louisiana guys?"

"I think that's a little farther east in Georgia, but we might see some later tonight." Trey wishes he was joking.

They finish the sandwiches, and Trey leans over to kiss Gayle.

She pulls back. "Later. The Hell Raising comes first."

The Mercedes drives twenty more minutes, and the GPS directs a turn on a dirt road that quickly becomes narrow and rutted.

"Are you sure this isn't satanic worshipping tonight?" Trey teases.

"Not devil worship. It's voodoo," Gayle corrects. "You watch too many movies. Actually, voodooism is a religious ceremony practiced in many countries. It's a body-and-mind worship that gives the priest or priestess a direct line to the spiritual world. The only place voodooism has been linked with devil worship was in New Orleans at the turn of the 19th century."

"That's going to kill the love-potion business at the botanic stores in the French Quarter."

An old shotgun-style house comes into view with a single light illuminating the inside. Gayle opens her wallet and gives Trey a hundred-dollar bill.

"What's that for?" Trey asks, confused.

"A man at this house will lead us to a barn before the

ceremony starts. We'll hide in the loft and watch."

Trey pushes her hand away. "I'll handle this. Write it off in my expense report—devil-worshipping."

He moves to the house. Gayle climbs out and waits by the car. A knock on the door receives no response. He knocks again.

Seemingly out of nowhere, a man wearing overalls walks from the dark carrying a rifle. Gayle moves quickly to the house.

"What you need?" The man speaks with a heavy Cajun accent.

Gayle arrives as the man approaches the front steps. He glances first at Gayle and then back to Trey.

"Are you T-bone?" Gayle inquires.

The Cajun spits tobacco on the ground. "Could Be. Who asking?"

"Lincoln Jones sent us to see the voodoo ritual. He said you could place us in the loft."

"That Lincoln Jones, he a liar." The Cajun does not sound happy about the intrusion.

Trey pulls out his wallet, and the Cajun moves the weapon barrel lower in his direction. "What's it going to take to make Lincoln a truthful man again?"

The situation is tense, and Trey knows this cracker wouldn't hesitate blowing a large hole in his chest.

The barefoot man looks hard at the money. "Maybe two hundert?"

Trey pulls several bills and hands them in the direction of the bare feet. "How about one-fifty, and you throw in some moonshine?"

A slight smile appears. "I make da' best."

He points to the corner of the house. "Get da' truck. You can't take no fancy car."

Bare feet pad up to the wooden porch and disappear into the house. Trey shrugs his shoulders and takes Gayle's hand, moving around to the side of the house. An old pickup truck is parked there, and the two jump in the cab.

"How did you know he made moonshine?" Gayle asks, looking relieved.

"Everybody in the swamp makes booze," Trey answers, proud of his lucky guess.

The driver's door opens, and the man looks at the two. "Get in the back."

Gayle opens her door, and both climb into the truck bed. The man hands Trey a quart bottle of moonshine and turns to a Bluetick Coonhound standing behind him.

"Get in, Jeb." The dog jumps into the cab.

Gayle and Trey huddle together as the truck bounces around on the dirt road. Trey forces the quart jar open and proposes a toast.

"Here's to coming in second to an old hound dog." Trey takes a sip and recoils. "That will grow hair on your chest."

He hands the jar to Gayle, and she does the same with a contorted face.

"I think it's more likely to remove hair."

Trey laughs and takes the jar back. He looks deep into her eyes, and suddenly the kissing becomes passionate. The truck hits a hole, knocking moonshine on both.

"What do you think, Trey?"

"About what?"

"Driving through the bayou drinking moonshine with a tobacco-spitting, barefooted man and his dog. Ever picture that sitting on the seventh floor of the Stephens Building?"

"I'm impressed sitting next to the most beautiful woman I have laid my eyes on—and of course, the moonshine." Trey moves his hand up and down her thigh. Gayle doesn't resist. Suddenly the truck stops.

The Cajun opens the door and leans out. "Everything over by eleven. You come down the road, I be there."

The couple dismounts from the truck, and it motors away on the dirt road.

"Are you sure you want to do this?" Trey asks.

Gayle looks at the disappearing truck lights. "That option just drove off with the hound."

Trey take a drink; the booze has become easier to swallow. A large barn is fifty yards in front of them.

"To the penthouse." Trey points to the loft.

The barn door creaks open with Trey's help. Gayle taps him on the shoulder before entering and hands him a small flashlight.

"Kinda' figured we would need it."

He turns the flashlight on, and the two gain entrance to the barn. The light cuts through the darkness, revealing a large expanse of farm tools and bales of hay. A flash of the light frames a ladder leading to the loft deep in the barn's interior. Trey finds her hand and moves carefully, avoiding sharp tools on the way to the ladder.

Gayle starts up the ladder when something moves beyond the beam of light, freezing them both. Trey instinctively shines the light toward the movement and outlines a cow tied to a post.

"I guess we can start breathing again."

"Speak for yourself." Gayle climbs the ladder with Trey in close pursuit.

Bales of hay are stacked randomly at the top of the loft. Trey moves a couple of bales to the edge, overlooking the floor below. Their bodies sit behind them, sharing the moonshine.

"I'm worried."

"Why?" Gayle asks.

"This stuff is starting to taste good." He leans over, kissing a welcoming Gayle.

She grabs the light and flashes it toward her pocket, pulling out a plastic baggie. Gayle rolls a joint sprinkled with a silver substance, lights it, and pulls a drag. She hands it to Trey with an offering gesture.

There is an immediate euphoric impact on Trey's body. Things around him slow, visually. In spite of being high, and having his dream girl pulling down his pants and hers, he enjoys a flatline sense of calm. Kisses and groping escalate, but the joint is not ignored, as if part of a threesome.

Lights come on at the barn floor level. Gayle rises and looks over the edge, watching people gather. Trey's first move is exhausting the last bit of smoke into his lungs and then rearranging his jeans to their previous fit. The sex temporarily halted doesn't bother him; that in itself feels strange. His eyes roll over the side of the hay, watching the gathering below. He is tempted to bleat like a goat, but Gayle puts a hand over his opening mouth a split second before their cover is blown.

A heavy black lady gives directions to a number of men unpacking musical instruments. French Cajun conversations flow in all directions, and the barn becomes a sea of activity. Trey hears each word distinctly but remains far more interested in Gayle's body and what little is left of the moonshine. Gayle resists the advances, intent on the scene developing below. A tall man dressed in black and wearing a mass of beads enters.

Gayle leans closer to Trey. "The high priest."

The group is still swaying and dancing to the music as the tall priest contorts and gyrates. The priest suddenly stands rigid and opens his mouth wide. Everyone falls silent.

Gayle whispers. "He's possessed by an outside spirit."

A woman's voice screams from the priest's mouth without lips moving, his eyes rolling back in his head.

"Why would you let this happen, Reed Stephens?" The woman's voice yells.

Trey's thinking becomes crystal clear. His grandfather's name has emerged concisely. Puked out by this country Cajun like a dog choking on a bone. Neither the blue haze of the dope nor the one-hundred-and-ninety-proof moonshine could trick him into hearing anything but, "Reed Stephens."

The event turns worse. Trey stands, unencumbered by any pretense of spying on a Bohemian ritual. The priest is deep into the trance and issues the next shock to Trey's system.

A man's voice answers the woman's question. "Helen, I'm so sorry. Dear God, I'm sorry."

The priest falls to the floor semiconscious. He is visibly trembling after delivering a question from the grave. The crowd of voodoo players watches the priest writhe around on the wooden planks. One of them notices Trey's presence and points to the figure in the loft. Gayle stands, doubling the problem. Several of the men rush toward the back of the barn to climb to the loft.

Trey turns on the flashlight, searching for the 9mm that fell from his jeans when removed earlier. Two men clear the top of the loft and head to the couple without an escape route. Trey pulls the 9mm to eye-level and aims at the first man rushing to them.

A last second sobering decision made, Trey points the pistol to the roof and fires off two rounds in quick succession. The sound is deafening in the close quarters.

It works. The barn is emptied in thirty seconds, and Trey crawls down to the loft floor having taxed his adrenaline to the limit.

Gayle kisses his face and holds him close, not fully grasping the message relevance or intent. Scared to exit the barn, Trey and Gayle wait twenty minutes before leaving. T-bone and his dog have not returned, and the walk covering the two miles back to the car is tense. Surprisingly, the car tires are intact, and the ride back to New Orleans has little conversation.

◆

Gayle kisses him on the cheek exiting to the Hilton driveway.

She turns back and leans into his window.

"Trey, who is Helen?"

Trey looks into Gayle's eyes. "My mother."

"I don't know what to say," she responds. "Maybe we heard something based on the dope and moonshine high or some type of group hypnosis? It could be the priest was screaming Smith or Jones. We heard what we wanted to hear."

"You didn't know my mother's name. You heard Helen, just

like me."

"Truth be known, I was sky high, but Trey, the night was wonderful up to a certain point. Please know that." She turns to leave.

He drives parallel to her walking to the hotel entrance.

"May I ask a favor?" he says calmly.

She doesn't stop walking. She has opened her heart far more than ever before. "Sure."

"Stop please," he implores. "It's not your fault. I never knew my parents. It's left a huge void in my life."

Gayle returns to the car window. "You don't have to explain your feelings. It's okay to hurt. Let's talk tomorrow, I'm still high.

Things will feel different in the daylight."

"Come home with me." His voice now seems boyish and vulnerable.

She looks back to the hotel as if something is waiting for her inside. He sees the look and is certain the drive home will be alone. He has placed all his chips on the table.

Without another word, Gayle walks around the car and opens the passenger door.

Seven

SATAN'S ICE CREAM

Israel Hamric is a patient man when it comes to death. There is an adrenaline rush when committing the actual act of murder, but he has never killed to solicit the feeling. Hamric reads about the famous serial killers like Bundy, Gacy, and Dahmer. He understands what they did was based on a self-centered compulsion to dominate a victim for control, sex, or just the pure joy of taking a life. Hamric has studied serial killers, not to admire, but to note their carelessness and avoid getting caught himself.

His murdering ways are driven by cash and respect. Respect in the underworld of lawlessness means associates who are paid to murder fear him and his reputation. Their self-preservation and insecurity dominate their psyche, pushing fear to the far reaches of the mind to escape the same fate as their victims.

A scared hitman will never take a contract on Israel Hamric.

No one in the murder business will take the time to set up a hit like him. As a result, his murder-for-hire has grown to a six-figure rate. That type of income has pushed him along the rail of leaving it all behind and building a bungalow in the mountains far away from the United States.

Hamric first honed his killing skills as an Army Ranger, serving two tours in Afghanistan. He did not grow up part of the mob but did run the streets of New York as a kid and knew his way around the alleys he frequented.

Two mob muscle-heads came after his uncle over a gambling debt, and both ended up at the wrong place at the right time. Hamric not only beat the two to death, but he swam the sewer pipeline and killed the guy who sent them. Bad news travels fast in the underworld, and he quickly became a celebrity hired gun of sorts. One thing he did share with the well-chronicled serial killers is zero conscience about killing anyone. Children or women getting in his way shared the same fate as their targeted fathers, husbands, or brothers.

Hamric also would kill without being paid if you disrespected him. His path was a dangerous one to cross if you possessed behavioral problems. He has a hate for bullies, although by any definition he is one himself.

Jacob Henderson is Hamric's next target. He is a real-estate developer who ran from a large deal and cost the wrong New York investor millions. Henderson knew it was a bad decision, and so he became hermit-like behind the protective gates of a guarded community in a suburb of Atlanta. He was trying to buy time and hoping the dust would settle.

Hamric has been watching the gated entrance procedures for three days, and access is airtight. Even if he moves past the security gate, he knows Henderson is suspicious and has installed motion detectors to go along with video cameras. Hamric once used a stolen FedEx truck to gain entrance in a gated community for another hit, but he prefers to pull Henderson out of the house to avoid being videoed.

For the second time in three days, an ice cream truck pulls to the gate entrance and is waved through by security. When the music-playing truck comes out of the community fifty-five minutes later, Hamric follows at a distance. The truck moves through four more neighborhoods, two of which are not gated subdivisions.

He observes the routine by the heavy-set owner and is amazed by the amount of ice cream being sold.

◆

Frank Sims is a retired railroad engineer, needing something to do after his wife of twenty-four years died of breast cancer.

A chance to buy the ice cream truck from a desperate neighbor for next to nothing seemed like a deal too good to be true. After three years he has built his route to eleven subdivisions, and many customers know his schedule to the minute. Being an old railroad man, Sims understands the value of being on time.

He runs the truck starting in April and usually quits in late October, depending on winter's approach. Then he drives to South Florida and stays in a condo for the cold months. Most of the ice cream sells for cash, so the IRS does not receive much of it. Sims spends everything he makes on his two grandsons and setting up a college fund for them later in life.

He parks the truck behind his house to keep the neighbors somewhat happy.

Hamric knocks on Sims's front door and produces a law-enforcement badge, demanding to see the city and county licensing permits. When most people see a badge, they follow instructions, and Sims complies. His murder will never be solved.

Hamric drives his SUV two miles down the road, retrieving a bike and peddling back to move the ice cream truck after dark. At quarter-past-noon the next day, the ice cream truck approaches Jacob Henderson's gated community and is waved through by security.

The music is turned on, and children greet the truck, cash in hand.

The ice cream is sold on several streets before approaching the intended target. Music plays as the truck is now parked in front of the reclusive Mr. Henderson's home. Numerous children from several other homes approach and buy ice cream, but Jacob Henderson's door remains closed. Hamric goes about the ice cream business, filling cups and cones with various flavors, taking money and giving change.

Henderson's front door opens, and his six- and eight-year-old run toward the truck. Henderson stands behind a partially opened door. Hamric knows he cannot keep running around in a murdered man's ice cream truck much longer. The clock is counting on the forty-eight hours allowed for the missing person's report to be filed and a police response. Israel makes a fateful decision.

He sprinkles a prescription sedative on the six-year-old's ice cream cone and pulls out a 40-caliber pistol with a silencer below the window's view. A look through the front windshield reveals the earlier-buying ice cream children are moving to their houses, munching on the treats.

The small boy walks thirty yards from the front porch and falls down. His older sister starts screaming, and Henderson rushes to his fallen son. Hamric pulls a bandana over his face and runs from the truck as if concerned for the child's safety. He arrives shortly behind Henderson, who is leaning over the young boy. His eyes lock on Hamric, and there is an instant when he realizes what is about to happen. Henderson turns to run, ignoring his children.

The first shot hits him between the shoulder blades. A calm walk to the front steps, and two more bullets finish the job. The gun is tucked into his pants, and a retreat to the truck is followed by the ice cream music as he slowly moves it out the security gate. A wipe-down of the truck, and a five-minute timing device connected to five gallons of gas burns any remaining evidence.

◆

Hamric is packing his SUV for the return to New York when he receives the request from Billy Macuch for a job in New Orleans.

He, in turn, sends a text to Louis Fleck about his arrival in two days for a meeting to discuss the job requirements. The SUV heads south out of Atlanta toward Interstate 10 and turns west at the Florida panhandle.

Hamric likes the solitude of driving from job to job. There is an obsession with various weapons employed to finish an assignment, and that rules out flying. This arsenal includes not only pistols but a 30.06 Bergara LRP rifle with Leupold Mark 5HD 5-25 scope and Ultra-9 suppressor. A thousand-yard-to-one-mile killer, it is a micro-honed precision tool.

Prescription drugs, like the sedative put on the six-year-old's ice cream, is also an inventory staple. He could have dropped the child with his signature cyanide, but for some strange reason even Hamric did not understand, he let the boy live. All this inventory placed him in position to kill the target, making Hamric the most creative and dangerous person in the business.

A stop for the night in Mobile is uneventful. A good night's sleep produces no nightmares or regrets. Hamric has never revisited dead faces, other than using their deaths as training to become better.

◆

The SUV merges onto Interstate 10. Hamric will be in New Orleans in a few hours, where he will spend the night and get laid. That is part of the welcoming package Louis Fleck has promised.

Fleck has a wall of video cameras watching the property from several angles that changes view every 10 seconds. The cameras have a large recording capacity, but the data are recycled every twenty-four hours to protect the high-profile people who frequent his establishment.

Reed Stephens comes into view on the front porch, and Fleck tells the Voice to bring him to the office.

The elder Stephens follows the big man through the casino, and his mind wonders about running an operation like this. New Orleans is full of illegal gaming, but with the advent of legalized gambling growing bigger every week, the future for this type of operation has to be bleak. Of course, the accessible drugs and prostitution help prop up an ages-old industry.

Fleck has been dealing with Stephens for decades, but they have rarely met face-to-face. He evaluates the older Stephens' health as he enters the office. The last time in the same room together was a Mardi Gras ball twelve years ago. Fleck thinks he is aging better than Stephens.

"How's your grandson doing?" Fleck stands to shake his hand. "Haven't seen him since he was a kid."

"He's doing fine. Wants to run the place but would be disappointed if he didn't."

"All these young ones think they know it all."

"But it's guys like you and me that get the job done."

Fleck waves his hand to clear the room. The Voice and fellow muscle follow direction.

Fleck lowers his voice. "I understand there's a rat problem at your building. We have a great pest service company." Fleck passes pen and paper to Stephens.

Barely above a whisper, he says, "Write it down."

Stephens takes the pen, writes the councilman's name, and hands it back. Fleck looks at the name and furrows his eyes. He shakes his head confirming. A desk drawer yields a lighter, and Fleck burns the paper in an ashtray. He stands and offers his hand again. Stephens rises and shakes it.

Fleck walks him to the door. "Don't want you to worry, but Joe Bailly was killed. Came to me spouting off that the Hell Raising-bitch was back in town."

Stephens' eyes narrow. "What's this going to cost me?"

"Top talent is coming to address both rat issues," Fleck asserts.

"We'll share the expense on the Hell Raising bitch."

Fleck opens the door, and Stephens leaves the casino, not enjoying the sudden financial headache.

Eight

VIDEO HIGHLIGHTS

Hamric parks the SUV across the street from the Fleck casino and observes for thirty minutes as clients come and go. The daylight disappears, and he dials Fleck's cell.

"This is Israel, parked across the street in a black Explorer. Do you have the workup?"

"Yes," Fleck answers. "I'll have one of my guys deliver it."

"No, you bring it to me. Get in the front seat." Hamric hangs up.

Fleck retrieves a manila folder and heads to a dice table, where the Voice is watching a high roller on a hot streak.

"I'm meeting someone in a black Ford across the street. Just in case, go to my office and watch the SUV on the video screen."

"Let me take it to him, boss," the Voice pleads.

"I'll handle this. You watch my back."

Fleck is definitely stepping out of his comfort zone. The man in the SUV is an elite hired killer, and Fleck has made many enemies over the years. Of course, Hamric is Fleck's hired killer, but that does little to eliminate the dread of walking across the street and sitting in the front seat with his back to the man.

Fleck understands the drill. Hamric wants few eyes able to ID him. And he certainly does not want his image captured on video from an illegal gaming operation that could be the center of attention for numerous law enforcement agencies.

Inside the vehicle, Fleck hands the folder over his shoulder but does not turn around to view Hamric. Deep down, Fleck wants to see what the man looks like but does not dare push his luck. Hamric enjoys legendary status, and knowing his identity would be both a privilege and a danger at the same time.

The only sound Fleck hears is the pages being turned in the folder as Hamric reads the details.

"Is this councilman high-profile?" Hamric asks.

A sense of relief falls over Fleck, and instinctively he almost turns around gawking but stops short. With that discipline, he escapes getting shot in the face and being dumped in a shallow grave twenty miles outside the city.

"He is recognized in local and state politics. I won't lie. It will be front-page news in New Orleans."

"Alright, if I need more data I'll contact you," Hamric advises then suddenly lets out a "Damn! You're in the funeral business?"

"Yes," Fleck answers. "My nephew runs it."

"You have a crematorium?" Hamric becomes giddy with anticipation.

"Absolutely," Fleck says, feeling emboldened. "You text me a date and time. Show up at the mortuary then to make a deposit."

"Perfect. The best way to handle a high-profile target is to completely eradicate the evidence. I'm in room 201 at the Marriott, off Fifth. Send one of your ladies over after ten tonight. Get out."

"One more thing. I have another workup when you finish this job."

Hamric sinks back into the leather seat, as if he has a change in thought, and for a moment Fleck's nervousness returns.

"Be back with you early next week. A few more days in New Orleans isn't so bad."

Fleck leaves the vehicle feeling good. Money will be made from the councilman's death, and if he plays the game well, the Stephens family will foot the bill to get rid of this woman from Hell walking the streets of his town.

The Voice opens the door for Fleck. "Everything, okay?"

"Sure it is. Nothing I haven't seen countless times," Fleck's tough guy image returns. "Get the guys in my office, now."

Fleck walks to the office, sits at his ornate desk, and lights a cigar. Three of his thugs gather for a briefing.

"When the old man came in a couple nights ago with the kid, what time was it?"

Jason, the newest of the muscle hires, speaks. "It was ten thirty-five, maybe ten-forty. The strip show just changed shifts."

"Very good, Jason," Fleck continues. "Awareness of your surroundings is big in this business."

The other two goons sit like spoiled kids, pissed at the favorite child for doing something that pleases daddy.

Fleck gives them a chance at redemption. "Does anyone know where the kid did his dancing?"

The Voice stands, convinced he has something to make his boss happy. "The kid dances a lot next to O'Brian's."

"My, my," Fleck says with conviction. "Things keep getting better and better around here."

The Voice smiles deeply. Daddy has acknowledged a job well done, but that is short-lived.

Fleck stands at an odd angle like many over age seventy. He

cuts off the burning end of the cigar and places the remnant in a wooden box. He motions to Jason. "I'm going to further your education today. Let's go to Bourbon Street. Be back shortly, boys."

◆

Fleck never walks anywhere, but tonight he feels twenty years younger and strides the few blocks to Bourbon Street. He lights a cigarette and uses it as a pointer for Jason's education. Jason follows Fleck's extended hand, aimed at Pat O'Brian's across the street.

"So, if I wanted to see what was going on at O'Brian's last Wednesday night, how would I do that?"

Jason shakes his head. "Not sure, Mr. Fleck."

"Video, Jason. Video."

Fleck turns around and heads into the Booty Trap strip club, which sits directly across the street from O'Brian's. The bouncer recognizes Fleck immediately and leads him to the manager's office. Fleck organizes the influx of strippers from neighboring states, rotating among the New Orleans clubs to keep the acts fresh. He provides for the clubs what a high-flying talent agency in L.A. does for the movie studios.

A knock on the door finds Tom Smith's fingers working joyful magic on his computer. Smith has a love for child porn, but with the interruption he instantly switches off the website charging him one-hundred-and-ninety-nine dollars a month.

"One minute," Smith needs only a few seconds to hide his addiction.

"Come in."

Fleck feeds Smith's obsession by providing teenage boys occasionally, keeping a key ally in his pocket. If he had seen the screen forty seconds before, he would not be surprised.

"Louis!" Smith greets with enthusiasm, happy it is not his real boss checking up on him. "You guys out on the town?" Smith lives under the constant pressure of being caught one day with his hand in the wrong place. Rattled, it is all he can speak when greeting Fleck.

"Need a favor."

"Sure, anything for you." This is the real lesson Fleck wants to teach Jason.

"Last Wednesday night, something happened across the street I need to see. Can you load the video pointing toward O'Brian's between ten-twenty and eleven p.m.? That would help a lot."

Smith rolls his chair over to the video control center and enters the date. A fast forward button moves the footage marker to 10:15. Joe Bailly is playing the clarinet, and Emrik is dancing.

Fleck claps his hands. "Perfect!"

"What are you looking for?" Smith asks but has little real need for an answer.

Fleck points to the screen. "The old man playing and the boy dancing."

"Joe Bailly and his grandson. Been doing that for years up and down the street." Smith leans forward, trying to grasp why this has any significance.

Jason chimes in. "Old Joe was stabbed to death that night."

"No shit!" Smith always likes a connection to the details of a death. "When those two finished late night, my cook would feed them leftovers. What happened?"

Fleck jumps in, afraid of Jason's mouth spitting out too many details. "The old man was stabbed behind my place, but the boy got away. I liked Joe and want to help find out who did it. Stop the video."

The video frame freezes at when Emrik stops dancing and reaches to retrieve the money.

"Okay, back up the video, slowly," Fleck demands, and Smith obeys. "Stop it right there."

Trey Stephens is stopped in mid-motion dropping the ten into the hat. Fleck leans close to the screen and points to Gayle.

"Need a picture of those two. Can you print it off?'

"Give me five minutes. I'll make you a hard copy." Smith starts playing with the video unit.

"One more thing," Fleck says. "Put fifteen seconds of the couple walking along the sidewalk on video and email the file to me."

Smith does as directed.

Fleck walks outside while Smith finishes his assignment. He gets on the phone.

The Voice is excited to see the incoming call is from Fleck, briefly lifting his sagging self-esteem.

"What do you need, boss?" he asks, with a bounce in his obedience.

"The cop that does tracking for us. Need him in the office tomorrow. Have a job for him."

◆

While Fleck is playing with the video screen, Israel Hamric drives to the Blue Bird restaurant for a steak. The SUV is parked clear of any vehicles on the street. He can't stand a blemish on anything he owns. The restaurant was recommended by a fellow New Yorker. Finishing the last steak mouthful, he hates to admit the food was better than anything in his city. Being a New York food snob is a heavy burden to carry.

Hamric pays the bill with cash, leaves a nice tip, and chews a couple more cream brûlée bites. The service was very good, a fact Hamric appreciates, spending as he does so much time in strange cities.

As the waiter is thanking Hamric for his generosity, three nicely dressed men enter the door and are immediately led to a private room in the back reaches of the building. Thirty seconds later two more men enter, cut of the same cloth, and are sent back to where the others have gone.

Hamric knows exactly from what cloth these men are cut. He grew up with the mob and their wannabe followers dressed in suits that cost more than their fathers' first new-car purchases. The walk is all the same, no matter what city he is in. He blames it on "The Sopranos," the long-running TV series. Even though gangster types have kept him in business and piles of cash in three separate safe-deposit boxes, he feels superior to their strip-club managing, badass personae showered down on everyone around them.

It does not matter to him at this point. Might even receive business from these up-and-comers along the line. He exits and walks to the SUV, leaving the mob image in the restaurant. But that image comes flooding back when he approaches the SUV. Three-hundred-thousand-dollars' worth of Lexus and Mercedes is parked front and back of his SUV, not an inch of room left between his bumper and theirs. Hamric fumes, his ass-chapping accelerated at seeing all the room available to park away from his vehicle. It is a game to them. Some middle-aged guy, out with his wife, asking nicely if they could move the car and being pounded for interrupting their meal.

Hamric retrieves a silencer from the SUV and replaces his jacket with a different one. Sunglasses on, he heads back to the restaurant and modifies his voice slightly, asking the receptionist how long the wait is for a party of five soon to be arriving? About twenty minutes is the reply.

"Where's your restroom?" he inquires.

She points to the back and turns her attention to the two couples up next.

Hamric quickly surveils the main dining room looking for video cameras but sees none. His walk to the private room is moderate, non-attention getting. The rage boiling up a couple of minutes before is gone. The two-thousand-dollar suits will not be used for the funerals, he thinks. Blood is a bitch to eliminate on top-end fabric.

His entrance into the private room is timid. Only two of the five hoods even notice Hamric standing four feet from the table.

Booze and self-confident arrogance does that. He moves a couple more steps to his left for the perfect angle of sight.

"Gentlemen, excuse me," he humbly speaks. "Do any of you own a Mercedes parked out front?"

A large, round man drops his forkful of pasta. A napkin is pulled from his lap but never makes the mouth. An unconscious insult to Hamric.

"Who the hell wants to know?" The fat fingers, used to beating women not turning enough tricks on Friday or Saturday night, set the napkin on the table.

Hamric holds his hands up in a submissive gesture. "I'm just blocked in. Maybe you can give the keys to the waiter. Let him move your car a couple of feet? I'll tip him for the help."

A second man stands. Tall enough that he has to duck when walking through most doorways, he delivers a matching basso voice. He is fresh off playing tackle for Tulane and itching to prove his manhood to the brothers in crime.

"Move the hell out or I'll pound you into a ball. Throw you in the trunk for a ride to the river."

The remaining four like what is being said by the new guy.

One smiles, while the other three roll into a full blown laugh.

"That's a great offer," Hamric quips. "But I prefer plan B."

He takes the sunglasses off in his left hand and moves them above his head. It's a distraction for the eyeballs now focusing on his every move. The right hand pulls out the forty-cal, loaded with subsonic bullets, and the big man, destined to not see his 24th birthday in three days, is shot in the sternum and crumbles to the floor. Only one of the four pulls his weapon out of the holster, but he is three seconds too late for a shot.

The fat man's pocket yields the Mercedes keys. Hamric rotates right-to-left around the table, firing a second bullet in every head.

He has always shot right to left. The sunglasses again find the bridge of his nose, and he leaves the restaurant. A set of gloves prevents any evidence in the moved Mercedes.

♦

The drive to the hotel is filled with excitement. Not for removing five sewer rats but for the sex awaiting him. A shower is rewarding, washing away the sins of the day. A knock on the door is answered, and a tall blonde is sized up by Hamric before she enters.

"Come in, darling."

The long-legged young lady enters and heads for the bathroom.

"Give me a moment, big man."

She is one of Fleck's prized women, not only for the looks but her love for giving and receiving pain. She applies a new vail of perfume and lipstick, takes off her earrings, and places them in a handbag. A ten-inch handle braided with two feet of leather is retrieved. She rounds the corner and Hamric is lying on the bed, nude.

"Before we get started," he pauses the action, "What's your name?"

"Mercedes," she responds.

He shakes his head. "You have no idea what that name means to me right now."

"An old girlfriend? Maybe an ex-wife? Is there something she used to do, turning you on? Fess up, whatever she did will be a distant memory after tonight."

Hamric pulls her into the bed. "I'm going to do bad things with you."

Nine

REARVIEW MIRROR

Lilly pulls a vacuum cleaner from the hall closet and opens the door into Trey's bedroom. Gayle lies bundled in a comforter next to Trey, trying to hide from an air conditioner set at 60 degrees, leaving the windows frosted. Lilly turns the vacuum on and goes about cleaning the massive bedroom, ignoring the two trying to sleep off a night of moonshine, marijuana, and sex.

Gayle is first to wake, peering over the blanket at Lilly's obsessive nature. Lowering her head back to the pillow, she is beyond the pretense of modesty, desperately wanting thirty more minutes of peace but fully aware it will not happen. Lilly works the vacuum close to the bed, finally stirring Trey.

"Lilly," Trey whispers, but is completely drowned out by the sucking machine. "Lilly ... get your ass out of my bedroom!"

Lilly shuts off the vacuum and looks at the couple in bed, as if they didn't exist three minutes earlier.

"Hell of a party, huh?" Lilly does not know how much truth is in the question.

Trey forces his head to rise from the bed. "Why don't you do something constructive like cooking breakfast instead of making all this noise?"

"Cleanliness is next to godliness—something you don't know much about." She turns the vacuum back on, ignoring Trey's demands.

"If you don't get out now, God will not be able to save you."

Trey is pushed to the wall.

Lilly is always determined to have the last word. "Come into my house tracking cow manure from one end to the other, then bitch at me for cleaning?"

She drags the vacuum outside and slams the door, causing Gayle to jump. Trey buries his head against Gayle's ribcage.

"Can you feel my head pounding through my skull?"

Gayle places her hand on the back of his head in a symbolic way and then kisses his forehead. "The wrath of moonshine doesn't hold a candle to Lilly."

She moves slowly to the edge of the bed, trying to recover an uncluttered mind but failing with the effort. Trey swings over to grab her naked rear end after she raises enough energy to stand and move to a pile of clothes. The hand misses the target, but he admires the graceful walk and perfect body moving across to the couch.

"Where are you going?" He cannot stand the thought of her leaving quickly.

Gayle's white jeans have various brown spots, proving Lilly's manure assertion. "I have a lot of writing to do."

"It's Saturday. Why don't we hang out together and grab some beignets?" He is selling, trolling to see if she is buying.

She comes over to the bed and kisses him on the lips. "The invitation is beyond nice, but ... Stephens Publishing paid me an advance. I need to finish the book. Believe me, I would love to play all day."

"Your Stephens Publishing partner says it's okay to take the day off."

"Trey, this book is far more about me than Stephens. You know that you and I live in different worlds. I'm just trying to catch up."

"Alright, you work today. We'll have dinner tonight."

"Let me see how much I get done. We'll talk later. That's all I will promise."

She finishes dressing and blows him a kiss. He lies back in the bed and falls asleep.

◆

Trey doesn't stir for several hours, attributing his blank, dreamless sleep to the moonshine. Finally, he gingerly moves to the medicine cabinet and opens a bottle of Tylenol. Three pills roll around his mouth and are flushed down with water.

He looks at the mirror, not happy with the haggard appearance.

A shower washes away some of the physical aches, but the mention of his grandfather and mother in the swamp has him more confused than hurt. Answers buried thirty-plus years ago need new questions raised.

The watch reads 1:10. Trey hasn't slept this much since college.

Moving to the kitchen, he drains a Gatorade bottle halfway on the first swallow. Lilly walks through the door silently carrying groceries. He goes into the garage to help remove the numerous plastic bags from her car and returns. A second trip completes the job.

Lilly puts the various cans, meats, and vegetables away. Trey swallows the remaining Gatorade.

"Lilly," he asks. "Do you know exactly what happened to my parents?"

"Trey," she responds in a surprisingly subdued voice. "I was hired by your grandmother about a year after they died. The story they told me was that someone broke into the home. Your parents came back from dinner, surprising the intruders. Both were murdered.

To my knowledge, no one was ever arrested. Far too young to be dying. A damn shame, if you ask me."

"That seems to be the company line. Thanks."

He moves to the computer and Googles "Helen and Reed Stephens New Orleans." He had done this years ago but thinks himself wiser this time around. The newspaper account confirms the story he has been fed all his life. He cannot shake the thought that something is being left out. A sense of emptiness fills his thoughts. Playing around in the Google world, an ad for Mexico pops up. He makes a mental note.

Then a bright star in a blackened sky is delivered via cell phone. He sees the incoming is from Gayle but drops the phone in excited haste. The call is lost, and a return call directs to her voicemail.

He cusses his hangover-induced clumsiness.

Going to retrieve his keys for a drive to the hotel, a text comes through: "Free for dinner … xoxo."

After a confirmed dinner plan from Gayle, he changes his destination to his grandfather's home. The drive is brief on a Saturday afternoon to the massive three-story structure built in the late 1800s. It has taken years, and a large investment, to complete the reconstruction, but the home is New Orleans architecture at its best.

Trey walks to the front porch but hesitates to ring the doorbell.

A lot of memories have been spawned growing up in this house, especially when much of the reconstruction was going on in his youth. The walls lay open for weeks at a time, and he discovered crawl spaces to transverse from floor to floor. The secret passages became reservations for thought. His first kiss, and touch of a girl, occurred somewhere between the second and third floor, far away from grandparental glare.

Treasure-hunting actually produced treasure. He found a leather pouch containing numerous gold coins, all dated before

1870. His first car was purchased with this gift, offered by some-one living in the house more than a hundred-and-twenty years ago. There also were musical instruments discovered, including a violin eventually refinished and now hanging over the fireplace in the den.

The daydreaming complete, Trey rings the bell, and his diminutive grandmother opens the large wooden door.

"Trey, come in. So good to see you!"

He leans over and hugs the woman who raised him with a firm but loving heart. "Great to see you, Me-maw."

A walk to the kitchen produces iced tea and a croissant loaded with cream cheese and homemade jelly. Trey's head begins to regain consciousness despite the night before. A second croissant clears it up completely.

"Where's Grandfather?" he asks, between bites.

"He's gone to Home Depot. Buying a sledge hammer and some other damn tools. We have a garage full of tools, but there's always something missing."

"Sledgehammer?" Trey is puzzled. "What is he doing with a sledgehammer?"

"Don't have a clue. He's been in the basement banging on something the last couple of nights. Even had the yard guy down there this morning. I'm not going to ask. You know when he gets something in that head, better stand clear. More importantly, how are you doing? Dating any nice young ladies?"

His grandmother has always asked the same thing at some point in every conversation over the last few years.

Trey knows she does not understand he is now in his thirties, though still unmarried. Her world order is completely inside-out until he accomplishes her goals.

"Started dating someone new recently. There's hope, Me-maw."

"Bring her over for supper. Love to meet her."

"Soon. Let me walk her a little farther down the trail. But I know you will like her."

Trey tries to get to the point. "Me-maw, what happened to my parents? I understand they were murdered but what were the circumstances?"

The woman who seemed so alive when Trey arrived now sits down, the wind suddenly out of her sails.

"A young policeman knocked on our door Halloween night. Came in. Said your father had been killed. Of course, we went to pieces. I asked about your mother. Was she alright? He said to his knowledge she was fine. Don't remember much after that to be honest. The whole situation just got worse by the minute. Your grandfather followed the police off into the night. I tried calling Helen, but only got the answering machine. Turns out she was dead, too."

The small lady rises and hugs Trey's neck. "Thank God you came through it. You have been such a bright spot for us all this time.

"Thanks, Me-maw. You both always made me feel special. Under the circumstances, a lot of kids would have been an afterthought. Raising a baby at that point in life is not ideal."

"Nonsense, you made the connection to your mother and father complete. It kept us young. Lilly also made it work. How is she doing?"

"Lilly is Lilly. Keeps me in line and the house tiptop. One moment I want to shoot her, and the next want to hug her."

"She's been a godsend for both of us. Did you ever give her a raise? She called me a few weeks ago complaining about it."

"You, too, Me-maw? I pay her sixty-five thousand a year, plus another five-thousand-dollar bonus at Christmas. I'll give her this. She is relentless. If I don't fork over more money, I'm going to end-up dead. You tell the police that after my funeral. Gotta' go, Me-maw. Thanks for the croissant."

Trey walks to the front door followed closely by his grandmother.

Out on the porch he turns to her. "Me-maw, do you remember the name of the cop that talked to you back on that Halloween?"

"Won't ever forget that. His name is Marc Bone. Nice man, he came to both funerals. Always wondered what became of him. Probably retired by now."

Trey moves to the car and Googles "Marc Bone." It mentions the New Orleans Police Department, but the man's status is not confirmed one way or another. He feels alert and charged.

Ten

OK CORRAL

Chris Dale parks a block from the restaurant crime scene. He can not get closer, blue lights be damned. News media are swarming from a local and national level, trying to shoot video of a cop, civilian, or restaurant employee having any connection to what the media are calling the OK Corral. A soundbite, even pure supposition, could be sold for large dollars. Five people executed near a dining room full of customers make headlines. Throwing in, "Oh, by the way, all five are connected to the mob," makes for solid-gold ratings.

This goes way beyond the pale of being a normal investigation—if, in fact, there was ever a normal investigation. The police radio exploded with dignitaries heading to the scene, including the parish special prosecutor. It is only a matter of time before the FBI finishes eating supper and makes an appearance, Chris thinks.

As usual, Bobby Rabold was the first detective on the scene. Chris places plastic booties on his feet and walks to the private room where the carnage lies. On his approach past all the reporters, he counts one video camera located too far away on the street to serve any kind of identification purpose. As Israel Hamric did the night before, Chris searches for internal cameras but comes up empty.

The bodies and their unfinished meals lie undisturbed. Crime scene photographers are shooting one digital photo after another.

"Going to be a long damn night," Chris says out loud. But with all the activity in the room, no one notices. All know it to be true without hearing his declaration.

Rabold is on the floor marking shell casings with a numbered identifier. Chris leans over, runs the tip of a ballpoint pen into a casing, and examines it.

"Forty caliber—are they all forty-cal?" he asks, placing the casing back next to a number.

Rabold stops and looks at Chris. "So far, all forty-cal. What are the odds that five men all carrying weapons could be killed by a single shooter?"

"No way one guy did this. Even Wyatt Earp had help at the OK Corral."

Chris leans close to the victims, examining their various hand positions. "One guy had a weapon out. Everyone else was shot with nothing more than a fork in their hand. This isn't amateur hour. Preplanned and precision execution. Aren't these guys West-siders?"

"Yep," Rabold answers. "Heavy emphasis on prostitution and drugs. Meth kings. Whoever did it is a damn good shot. Five in the chest, and five in the head to clean up loose ends. You'd think with this many guys at the table, someone would return fire. The big guy did stand, but for some reason didn't attempt to retrieve his weapon."

"Meth. Most of that shit comes from Mexico. Has cartel written all over this," Chris summarizes, as additional CSI talent enters the room. "I'll start talking to the staff. Let the scientists do their thing."

He moves to the front of the restaurant where Detectives Joseph and Lee are interviewing customers and staff. The bartender stands next to the bar, waiting his turn as Chris approaches.

"I'm Detective Dale. You been here all night?" He offers his hand.

"James Wilcox," he says, shaking Chris's hand. "My shift started at six-thirty."

"How about a Diet Coke with a lime?"

"No problem." Wilcox pours the Coke and places two lime slices in the glass.

"Thanks." Chris takes a sip. "This crew sitting dead in the back, have you seen them before?"

"The group varies. Different faces occasionally, but they come in every ten days or so."

"Ever any trouble when they come in? Screaming? Yelling? Fistfights? Tonight or in the past?" Chris rarely takes notes. He has a photographic memory.

"Not among themselves, never. A couple times one or two beat the hell out of a customer on the street, came back in and finished eating. The place has a tendency to clear out when they show up. I hate seeing them come in. It kills my tips."

"What caused the fights?"

"One of the waiters told me the … what did you call them?"

"Crew."

"The crew parks close to random cars so the customer can't

drive away—it's a game."

"Looks like the crew played the game with the wrong people."

Chris moves the glass across the bar, and Wilcox refills the Diet Coke. "One last thing. Anybody stand out to you tonight?"

"Like how?"

"A couple of strangers, maybe non-regulars looking at other customers, sizing up the crowd or even the crew when they came in."

"Not really. We were pretty busy around the time all this went down. Didn't have much time to do anything but keep my head low and serve."

"Thanks for the Coke." Chris moves to Detective Joseph, and Rabold joins them from the back.

"Anything of interest, Tony?"

"This place must be haunted," Joseph deadpans.

"Why's that?"

"Cause a couple of ghosts shot the hoods stacked in the back. No one saw anything or anyone."

"Don't think the crew, face down in the pasta sauce, had a lot of friends here. How about you, Bobby, any magic from CSI?"

"The bullet angles are starting to take shape with the lasers.

Looks like one shooter. Ballistics will confirm in the next couple of days."

Mike Broadaway, the special prosecutor, and two other state attorneys head straight for Chris. He doesn't mind their intrusion. All murders eventually end up on his desk, and it's his job.

But Chris realizes this one will be strictly a political ploy. Everyone in New Orleans knows Broadaway's eye sits squarely on the U.S. Senate in the next election. What better way to kick off the campaign than perform for the national media, spread out on the street like floats in a parade.

"What do we have, Detective Dale?"

"Follow me, gentlemen." He leads the crowd to the private room. "Five of Orleans' finest, gunned down in the prime of their gangster lives."

"One helluva mess," Broadaway says, viewing the crime scene.

"Presents one hell of an opportunity." A Broadaway associate reveals the real reason for being in the building.

Broadaway turns to the attorney with a look of distain.

"Speaking strictly off the record, of course." The associate quickly regroups.

Broadaway turns back to Chris. "What do we know?"

"These pillars of society are part of the Reynolds mob on the West Side. Probably distribute more meth than any crew in South Louisiana, primarily Mexican dope. Strictly a professional hit. Looks like one guy shit-canned all five from the shell casings and angle of bullet penetration."

"Well, at least New Orleans is striving to be number one in something. These five bodies move us a close second with Chicago for murder capital of the country. Detective Dale, what the hell is going on in the streets?"

"Katrina moved out a third of the city's population, most of which were middle-income types that could afford the mobility. A lot of businesses and jobs left with them. The poor got poorer. Meth came in to fill the void. We all know what people will do to chase their next hit. This bunch here..." Chris points to the bodies. "They didn't exist until after Katrina. Desperation kills the rich and poor."

"Do your job, bring me answers I can prosecute with." Broadaway heads out of the restaurant to face the media.

Tony Joseph shrugs his shoulders toward Chris.

"We both know whoever did this is already on a plane to New York or Chicago. This will never be solved."

"If you ask me, someone did the city of New Orleans a favor by interrupting this dinner," Chris adds.

"Hard to argue that." Joseph walks back to the front of the restaurant and continues the interview process.

◆

Chris is tired. He had stayed at the restaurant until seven in the morning.

Hastily he moved out when the FBI made their appearance.

The walk to the car provided numerous microphones shoved in his face, but his patience had run out along with the caffeine consumption.

A text beeps its arrival and Chris views the phone. It reads: "Can we talk?" It was sent by a reporter from the Times-Picayune Chris has known for years, Jessie McGaha. Chris types a simple response: "Later."

Jessie and Chris go back on the local crime scene for the better part of two decades. Jessie is a damned good reporter. A well-known writer not only at the local level, she has published several crime novels. Chris has been a go-to source for many stories in the past. He has become more distant and less fact-giving recently.

It is a personal thing. They had an affair for two years.

It cooled off when Jessie let an old high school flame back in her life after a class reunion hookup.

Chris still has feelings for Jessie, and even though he knows it could never be a permanent thing, it hurt to lose at the game.

Chris, at his core, is a taker and has a controlling personality. Making Jessie continuously reach out and solicit a return to a re-porter-cop relationship gives him a sense of control.

There has been more to the relationship than random sex around the city. Jessie helped Chris look at the evidence from multiple facets, and she literally solved numerous crimes while Chris received credit. In return, Chris gave her information critical to good journalism and a big jump on the competition.

He knows she wants an inside angle on the mob murders, but he simply does not have the mental capacity right now to deal with it. That is how Chris has framed it in his mind. He refuses to accept the role of a jaded lover, taking advantage of her need and his position.

The crime scene is only a ten-minute drive to one of his favorite food places, Mother's. The breakfast at Mother's is the best in the city.

◆

After breakfast, Chris rolls his wrist over, and the watch reads 8:10. The energy has returned to a certain degree, though he is not sure whether to credit Mother's or leaving the five bodies in the rearview mirror, probably both.

The schedule has been hectic the last couple of days, but Chris wants to ask Emrik a few more questions. He believes his grandfather's murder can be solved, unlike the one he just spent the night with. It is Saturday and Emrik does not have school, so it fits his timing.

Chris knocks on the door. Eva opens it. "Do you have something on my father's death?"

"May I come in?" Chris asks.

"Sorry, sure come in," Eva leads Chris to the couch. "Coffee, Detective?"

"No thanks, I'm coffee'ed out. To answer your question, nothing new has come around, but I need a little more information from Emrik."

"Absolutely, let me get him up." Eva leaves.

A few minutes later, Emrik enters the room rubbing the eyes. Eva sits down next to him.

"Emrik, you can go back to sleep shortly," Chris assures. "Do you remember where you were dancing when your grandfather saw the Devil that came after you?"

"I didn't see the Devil up close," Emrik says, looking at Eva, expressing pain talking about the subject.

Eva hugs Emrik. "It's okay, Detective Dale is trying to find the person responsible for hurting your grandfather."

Chris tries a different tack. "Here's what we need to understand. I know your grandfather was attacked behind the casino. You took off when grandfather told you to run. But let's back up. Before going to the casino, you were dancing on the street. Your grandfather suddenly stopped the dancing. Right?"

"Yes, I gathered the money to leave."

"Were you dancing on Bourbon Street? Near a restaurant or bar?"

"Next to Pat O'Brian's."

"That's great, Emrik. I'm confident I can find out who this bad person is." Chris stands up to leave, and Emrik returns to bed.

◆

Evil and good minds sometimes think alike.

What Chris does not know is that Louis Fleck, using video, has already figured out the sequence, focusing on Trey and Gayle. Fleck is about to take it to the next level by hiring a cop named Tony Cranford, a brilliant cop but a man possessing a cocaine problem.

He hires out to anyone needing bird-dog services. A cop's salary could never support his habit.

"Let me get this straight, the only thing you have is a photo of a couple walking Bourbon Street? You want me to track them down?" Cranford asks.

"You're the best, Tony, if anyone can do it, I know it's you," Fleck asserts.

"Are they local?"

"The woman is not. The guy, maybe."

"Need a thousand upfront. The balance is mine regardless of the outcome. That's the only way I'll do it."

Fleck reaches into the ornate desk and retrieves a bag of coke.

"Two-thousand-dollar deposit right here. I need this ASAP."

Cranford takes the bag and leaves the casino. A tablespoon

of coke goes up his nose in the car. The feeling of warmth and contentment returns. He drives to Bourbon Street, determined to figure out the mystery and collect the balance.

That much coke would lay the average addict out for twelve hours, but it has only sharpened Cranford's resolve to find answers. Starting at O'Brian's, he walks east on Bourbon Street for a several blocks and spots a security camera located across the road at a restaurant. The manager is eager to help the NOPD and lets Cranford review the video from last Wednesday night. It confirms the continued walking by Trey and Gayle, moving east.

Coming out of the restaurant, Cranford looks east, and three hotels spring into view side-by-side. A smile curls his face. The couple was probably not heading to a vehicle but a hotel. The first is a Marriott, but the photo fails to obtain any bites when passed around the staff.

As Cranford works his way through the line of hotels; Gayle leaves the Hilton at two o'clock after spending several hours pounding on her MacBook Pro.

As happens with all writers, she hits a mental block and needs to clear the mind to re-engage. The Mississippi River flows toward the Gulf with never ending intent. Gayle walks a loading dock watching the water rush by. She had come to New Orleans with a purpose, but having feelings for Trey was never the intended result. Like everything else in her life, these feelings will serve her well in reaching her goal. They have always worked to her advantage.

◆

Cranford enters the Hilton and goes to the bellhop manager, a longtime "Tony associate," bribed on numerous occasions for delivering information on Hilton guests. Barry is a heavy-set black man who can sing much like his namesake, Barry White.

"Ain't got no coke, Tony," Barry bellows in a deep voice. "Gave that shit up four months ago. Not going back, it's the Devil's dandruff."

"Not here for coke, Barry," Tony lies. "Been clean for eight months myself.

Barry shakes his head in agreement but recognizes the coke eyes staring at him. "What do you need if not the white beast?"

"An official capacity." Cranford's second lie. He pulls the photo of Gayle and Trey from a pocket. "Have you see this couple?"

Barry studies the photo. "The woman is staying here. Seen

the guy around a couple of times but don't have a clue who he is. Rich asshole, shows up in high-cotton cars. They in trouble?"

"Suspects in a murder." Cranford drags out a fifty and hands it to him. "Make a call, give me everything you have on her. While you're at it, get a passkey and her room number."

"You have a warrant to do this shit?" Barry knows the answer but is leveraging a position.

"Absolutely," Cranford confirms, handing over another fifty.

Barry returns fifteen minutes later with a printout of Gayle's driver's license and a passkey. "Follow me." They climb the stairwell to the second floor.

Barry turns to Cranford. "Room 1223. Listen, the video is recording on the floor,. I ain't going out there. You doing something bad to this lady, Tony?"

"Nope, I swear. Just want to take a few photos of her things for my report. If she's in, I'll bullshit her and come back later. You cool with that?"

"Don't shit me, I'm clean. Ain't goin' back to jail for your coke-snorting butt. Five minutes, that's it, or I'll be in there jerking your ass out." He stares straight through Cranford with a no-nonsense look.

"Five minutes, got it." He leaves the stairwell and heads along the hallway, stopping in front of 1223. He knocks on the door. "Security, please open." Ten seconds go by, and he repeats the request, but the room remains quiet. He uses the passkey and enters.

He activates his cell phone camera and looks through several drawers, finding nothing of interest. A notebook is photographed page by page. A purse in the closet produces a passport registered in Salt Lake City. He shoots the contents. He rummages through a suitcase, finding nothing but dirty clothes. Stuffing a pair of panties into his pocket, he returns to the stairwell, making Barry happy.

Cranford cannot wait to take another hit. He heads home and parks in front of the TV in an easy chair, surrounded by the tools of his illicit trade. He pours himself a large Jack Daniels on ice. He chases a shot with a lemon squeeze on the tongue. Four lines of coke lay on the glass coffee table; and his nose draws down two lines, followed by a shot of Jack.

Cranford is an artist when it comes to booze and drugs, which are best served alone, with no one else enjoying the fruits of the investigation.

The drug and drinking pattern has changed. Once upon a time

he wanted to share the haze next to a woman then have sex. Not any more. Chemical self-interest has overruled his desire. After three hours of self-adulation and abuse, he passes out, watching "I Love Lucy."

◆

Gayle returns to the room and instantly sees something is amiss. The bed has not been made, so the maid service was not involved.

An inventory of everything in the room is assessed. Going through the dirty clothes bag proves her initial thought. Someone breached her private space and took the panties in a perverse and threatening way. A deep thought settles the anxiety, and she goes about packing her suitcase.

Eleven

DIE BY THE SWORD

Trey pulls into the entrance of the Hilton, and Gayle walks out to the car, losing the valet a five-dollar tip. He jumps out and opens her door.

"Hey beautiful, get some writing done?" He returns to the seat and starts the car before hearing an answer.

"Productive day." she says, less than energetically.

He eases the car into traffic.

"Something wrong?"

"It wasn't easy to write buckled to a hangover, but a walk along the river did clear my thinking to a certain degree. When did you rise?"

He turns to her, showing a crooked smile reeking of guilt.

"I crawled out of bed about one-fifteen. Went straight to the medicine cabinet, swallowing half a bottle of Tylenol. My go-to hangover solution."

"One-fifteen? Why the hell did Lilly let you sleep that long?"

"Not sure. To be honest, she was non-confrontational most of the afternoon. That's scary in itself. Went to visit my grandmother. Lilly solicited her help to hit me up for more money. Of course she sided with Lilly, so I have little choice in the matter."

"None of my business, certainly, but what do you pay Lilly?"

"She's not on food stamps. Makes sixty-five thousand, plus a Christmas bonus. This is not Boston. Numerous management people at Stephens are not making that. No matter what I give her in a raise, it won't stop the bitching. That's Lilly."

Trey turns the corner and parks at Daily's Restaurant. "Is Daily's alright?"

"I've determined all food in New Orleans is beyond alright," Gayle answers.

As they enter, Gayle turns heads, something she apparently is oblivious to. Trey notices, not in a jealous way but proud to have her by his side.

After they order a bottle of wine, peruse the menu, and make their decisions, Trey slides his hand toward Gayle, and she wraps her fingers tightly around his.

"So, feel a little stress coming from you. Am I wrong?"

"Probably not wrong. Things are coming at me fast—the book deal, us. Nothing wrong with either. Maybe, just maybe, I'm a little overwhelmed. Actually had a mental writing block for the first time in my career today. Been around a lot of really good writers. All of them have a block at one time or another. It's different when it hits you."

"That's part of the learning process. To create a work of art, you will have birthing pains. No matter how long an artist has been performing their skillset, the path is filled with obstacles. Hope you will let me ride along." Trey squeezes her hand.

"I would like that. One thing I've never had much of is patience. Your experience will hopefully instill it in me."

The waiter comes by carrying the wine bottle and pours a sample. Trey rolls it around the glass and gives approval. Wine is poured for both.

"To patience in the creative process."

The two glasses touch.

"Wonderful choice." Gayle endorses the wine.

"Ever been to Napa Valley?"

"No. But it's on the wish list."

"One of my favorite destinations. Fly into San Francisco for a few days then drive to Napa for tastings at world-class wineries."

"Where is the sign-up sheet? Put me down." She smiles for the first time this evening.

"Duly noted." He can see her energy return as the evening evolves.

The food arrives, and the conversation centers on who has the best cuisine, Boston or New Orleans. Gayle gives credence to the seafood here but is steadfast on the North End Italian in Boston. Trey concedes, but with reservations. He demands a trip to Boston and a firsthand taste test.

"I need a recommendation, Trey Stephens." She sips her second glass of wine.

"If it's about a restaurant in N'awlins, I'm your man."

"Not food, but a different place to stay. The Hilton is a nice hotel. But I prefer a little more remote location to finish *Hell Raising*. Too many distractions. Plus, I can't cook my own food there."

He leans back. "Know the perfect place for you. Has everything you're looking for."

"I'm excited. Is it far from here?"

"My house," he says, matter-of-factly.

"Trey, the answer is no, for a lot of reasons. It's a wonderful offer, but the distractions are obvious. Come up with an alternative, please."

He leans across the table. "Hear me out. I'm not talking about my home per se. There's a mother-in-law suite on the grounds. A full kitchen. A hot tub. I don't believe it has ever been used. I will stay away … well … most of the time. You can hammer away on the keyboard day or night in complete isolation."

She takes a drink, thinking through the offer. "What will Lilly say?"

"Lilly is an interesting subject. Bottom line, she likes you more than me. With the move in, she will probably give you credit for the raise."

He believes all of this to be true.

"So, what happens if we grow apart on a personal note?" Her eyes widen, spreading her long lashes.

"I kick your beautiful ass out," he says, raises his eyebrows.

"After you finish writing *Hell Raising*, of course. Personal interest be damned. Business first."

"If that's the case, let's do it." The glasses clink again, solidifying the move.

"Speaking of our relationship,I think we should celebrate your new address with a short trip. Bought tickets to Cabo for the morning. Leaving at seven thirty-five. Returning Tuesday afternoon." Trey holds the wine glass high, expecting her to match his enthusiasm.

"Wait a minute, you didn't know about me wanting to move in, so you bought Cabo tickets to celebrate? In Boston, we call that bullshit."

Trey looks at the empty plate. "To be honest, we call that bullshit in New Orleans, too. Now, what's not bullshit is spending time on a beach, drinking fruity shots with you. It's only a couple days. It'll be fun. Probably recharge you on the writing."

Gayle shakes her head. "A lot of assumptions on your part. My biggest issue surrounding your decision may sink the boat."

"What's that?"

"I don't..." she clears her throat. "Don't have a bathing suit."

"I'm sure we can find one in Cabo." He offers the glass, and she responds by drinking the last bit of wine.

"Pick you up at five-thirty. Check out of the Hilton. We'll fly away."

"Meanwhile, want to go dancing tonight, get a head start on the Margaritas?"

"I have to draw the line. So much to do tonight. Let's start the party tomorrow."

"That's a fair assessment. Can't wait to hit the beach."

Trey waves the waiter over for the check.

◆

Cranford rises from the leather recliner as Trey drops Gayle off at the Hilton and kisses her. On TV, Lucy is still giving hell to Ricky. Cranford smiles. His ex-wife was a lot like Lucy, attractive but crazy.

He carries the Jack Daniels bottle to the kitchen, swinging it with two fingers. He pulls a can of tomato soup from the cabinet and pours it into a pan. He is happy. He will put together an impressive file about this chick from Boston on Monday, utilizing law-enforcement tools. It would get him fired if anyone discovered he was using the system to profile someone on a personal level.

Didn't matter. Cranford has been doing side work like this for years.

Probably get a bonus from Fleck. More coke is always the goal.

He sips more Jack as the gas flame focuses hard, bringing the soup to life. A search of the refrigerator reveals an absence of lemons. The crackers that he loves to crumble in the soup have also disappeared from the pantry. Writing a grocery list does not necessarily mean a full pantry. His thoughts about the list wander off in the aisles of the store, no matter how hard he tries. The coke, having thrown Parkinson's Disease into high gear, is rounding the corner of his mind and painting it black.

The last vestiges of a Fritos bag are thrown into the soup. He gently sets the bowl on a TV tray, bought when "I Love Lucy" last appeared on television as a hit series. One of the few things the ex-wife let him keep when she filed the restraining order along with the divorce proceedings.

The cable channel has dismissed Lucy from her perch, and "Married With Children" jumps off the set into Cranford's living room.

He is delighted. One last ounce of Jack is extracted, the empty bottle stares back, encouraging a sister bottle to be opened. His attention drifts to the bag of coke. He pretends to ignore the fun piled high. It has to last a couple more days.

A compulsive thought reminds him of the panties he took from Gayle Kidd's room. He pulls the red thong from his pocket, and a flash of sex races to create an image in the drug haze. He summons her photo, attempting to put a face and ass with the panties.

Even the poor printout gives Tony a long pause to absorb the beauty. It creates the unthinkable: Maybe he should share the coke for sex?

Something drops to the hallway floor on the second story and shatters. Cranford rips away from the daydream, pulls his .38 from its holster, and walks cautiously toward the stairs. In spite of being a drug-addicted drunk, he is an expert with a pistol.

But even more important, he is fearless in times of stress. He made a great partner to other cops on the streets of New Orleans.

A climb of the steps brings the hallway into view and reveals a picture frame lying on the floor outside his bedroom door. He returns the .38 to the holster and walks to the picture of himself receiving a citation from his captain for saving a four-year-old in a rain-ravaged drainage ditch. The photo has been framed for three years but never placed on the wall until two weeks ago. In another drug-induced decision, he bought the "nailless" picture-mountingbrackets from QVC, believing in the back of his mind they would never last longterm. He pushes the shattered glass against the wall with his foot, and he lifts the frame off the floor. He stares at the photo for a few seconds and feels a sliver of guilt. He was a real cop back then, one of the many truths chased away from life by drugs and alcohol.

The guilt evaporates rapidly before he clears the steps, going back to his recliner and "Married With Children." A lean forward plucks a Frito from the soup remnants, but before it touches his mouth a rope is wrapped around his neck and violently jerked upward.

Despite the tightening pressure cutting off the air to his lungs, Tony pulls out the .38 and fires a wild shot toward the ceiling. The rope digs deeper into his neck. Instinctively, he reaches with the free hand to the knot, trying desperately to escape.

He fires a second shot, but the attacker has dropped low on the floor, leveraging weight against his struggle in the recliner.

Being choked to death is a bad way to die. Cranford has seen many bodies over the years that succumbed to this highly personal touch of murder. It can take two minutes before the victim's struggles are subdued and the brain's lack of oxygen stops the heart.

Cranford is aware of the time left to turn the situation around, refusing to panic. Using both hands, he turns the muzzle of the revolver toward the lower portion of the chair and fires the weapon. A scream delightfully meets his ear, verifying the bullet has made contact. He fires again but hears no verbal reaction.

In his adrenaline-induced excitement, he doesn't notice the pressure around his neck has been released. A fourth shot is pumped into the leather chair, and he reaches to free the rope, showing no signs of restraint on his neck. As he turns to fire a shot into the attacker, a ten-inch knife blade sinks deep into his throat, and he slumps over.

Al Bundy sits on the couch berating Peg. This is the final scene, ending the raunchy sitcom's episode flashing on the TV screen, six feet in front of Tony Cranford's blood-oozing neck wound.

Twelve

HANG 'UM HIGH

Chris pulls the jeans to his waist, trying to force-feed the button. After a conversation about losing ten pounds falls on his closed ear, the button responds in a positive manner.

"Joanna," Chris yells. "Need help."

Joanna rounds the bedroom corner a half-step ahead of the plea for help, and two steps behind the ten-pound pledge. She heads to the closet and picks out a sports jacket that compliments the blue shirt that Chris had randomly grabbed off the rack.

"Here, put this on." He complies.

"We need to be out the door in five minutes or we'll be late for mass," he bemoans.

He moves past Joanna, intent on getting to the church in advance of the service. Even though she has been ready for fifteen minutes, Chris will talk about "we" being late. Joanna grabs her purse in close pursuit to the car.

The drive to St. Thomas is quiet. Joanna expects no conversation.

She understands Chris is roiling over the murder events in his mind. Chris is indeed thinking about the crimes but says little in his private life, not wanting to contaminate Joanna's mind about lasagna and spilled brains.

This conversational void has ruined more marriages than explaining what bullet velocity does to the human body upon entry. The cycle of not having a spouse, even when he stands in front of you, takes a strong and loving relationship to survive. Chris is lucky to have exactly that.

Father Joseph had left his greeting perch at the front door, even though Chris and Joanna slide in the door a full six minutes before it is closed. They find seats fifteen rows from the pulpit in a sparsely seated aisle. It is a familiar crowd. Most of the attendees are dedicated to the Catholic way, and virtually everyone recognizes Chris Dale the cop.

Chris has attended church all his life, even serving as an altar boy for three years in grade school. His younger days on the NOPD convinced him he would someday die in the street after a thug had shot him. That fatalistic outlook has never left his thoughts, and he wants to remain on God's good side when it occurs.

In his mind, it is an insurance policy of sorts, even though his later years on the force have made him feel mankind deserves no salvation, him included.

The service follows the Catholic tradition of rising and kneeling throughout, as if sins could be sweated away. Father Joseph preaches mostly in English; the old-school Latin reserved for a few of the ups and downs.

The sermon point of forgiveness creates a smile of sorts on Chris's face, his world dealing in brute force and a "Go to hell" on the way out the door. The smile quickly leaves. As an altar boy, a smile would earn you five hard kisses of the wooden paddle on your butt, deep within the bowels of the expensive wood and leaded glass.

Jesus would approve, or at least that is what the priest relayed before administering the punishment.

The line to exit always has Father Joseph and a priest-in-training shaking hands. Knowing Chris is a cop, the good father grabs his hand and pulls him close. "Bless your service and be safe, my son."

"Thank you, Father." Chris is sincere in his thankfulness.

Those few words always keep him coming back, Sunday after Sunday.

Walking the church steps, Ron McConnell, a fellow cop, approaches him. "Chris, did you see the text?"

"Left my phone in the car, not going to take my ulcers in with me. What's going on?"

"Tony Cranford has been murdered in his home."

"What the hell happened?"

"Not sure. His daughter found him this morning. Headed that way. Want to ride over?"

"Absolutely. Let me get my weapon and phone."

He walks Joanna to the car and retrieves his cop necessities. She straightens his jacket. "Eat some lunch, Chris. Going without food is terrible for you."

"I promise." He knows it will be late afternoon before he does eat, but it satisfies his wife's concern.

Climbing into McConnell's car, he reads the text alerting the police force that one of their own has been killed. Cranford's house will be crawling with rank-and-file cops shortly, which is a bad reaction in Chris's mind because it contaminates evidence

100

at the scene. But nothing could be done about the show of unity tradition at this point.

"Tony was drunk half the time, but a helluva cop," McConnell relays.

Chris adds to the adulation. "One tough sonofabitch. We went through rookie training together. No one, including the instructor, wanted to climb in the ring with him. His uncle was a professional fighter. Tony grew up in a training gym for fighters. He was bad-ass in the younger days."

McConnell counters with another profile. "In the late nineties, we partnered working on the strip. Man, his stories were wild! Tony's father was old school. Beat him on a regular basis.

"When Tony was six or seven, two older kids took his bike. Tony goes back home, crying about these twelve-year-olds kicking on him and taking the bike. The old man slaps him. Says if you don't go down the block, beat the shit out of them, take your bike back, I'm going to whip your ass every day for the next week.

"Tony had no choice. He went down with a bat, beat them up, got his bike back. Whoever killed Tony Cranford had a fight on their hands."

Chris can tell McConnell really respected Cranford and wasn't going to say anything to destroy the image. Truth is, Chris had known he was under investigation by Internal Affairs for drug use. Other offenses pertained to illegal entry and warrant abuses, primarily relating to his detective work outside the department's business.

Cranford's death did not surprise Chris. The man had tiptoed a tightrope between police guidelines and the more shady side of New Orleans crime families. He was a timebomb waiting to go off in his own face. Then again, death has a way of erasing ethical discrepancies.

◆

Tony Cranford's house is buzzing with far more activity than the typical crime scene when Chris and McConnell make their entrance.

Chris has investigated more than three hundred homicides in his career. But he has never witnessed one like this. The body hangs by a rope from the second-floor banister. His feet are tied to the rope, and he dangles, upside-down, six inches from the floor. The broken photo of him receiving a citation has been placed directly under his head, now covered in blood. The scene instantly resonates in Chris's mind as a deeply personal killing, staged to embarrass Cranford in front of his fellow officers.

"Why would anyone take the time to hang him, bleed him out like cattle in a slaughterhouse?" McConnell asks Chris as they weave their way through several CSI technicians examining the body.

"Never seen anything like this. Someone wanted Tony to suffer long after he was dead."

Chris glances at the second floor, where two Internal Affairs officers and an FBI agent are conversing.

"Have to make a call. See you outside," Chris relays to McConnell.

McConnell grabs Chris's arm. "Are you okay?"

"No, IA is talking upstairs with the FBI. The investigation is not going to end well for Tony's reputation. Don't want to be part of it."

"Makes sense. Be out shortly myself."

Chris goes to the front yard, where the usual crowd has gathered when the yellow tape outlines tragedy. He dials Jessie McGaha, and she answers after one ring.

"How's my favorite cop doing?" Her voice gives a sharp jolt to his system.

"You say the same thing to every cop ear you bend for information, Jessie James McGaha."

"You're the only person in my life other than my father to call me that. But let's not digress. You enjoying a Sunday off?"

"Not exactly. Standing in front of Tony Cranford's house. You remember Tony, right?"

"Been a while. He helped me on my second book, the Haley killings back in 2005. Is Tony hurt?" She can sense the answer.

"Not any more, very dead." He stops the information there.

"Sad. He was always generous with his time for me. What happened?"

She seems genuine in her concern.

"Got time for lunch? I need to get away from the fray for a while."

"Absolutely. McGuire's work for you?"

He looks up and down the street catching his bearings. "There's a billiard lounge at the corner of Congress and Jog ... not sure the name. Meet me in forty-five minutes."

"GPS is a girl's best friend, see you shortly."

The call ends as the crowd grows larger. It is a beautiful afternoon in Orleans, and the five-block walk to the billiard hall will help clear his mind.

He texts Ron McConnell about taking a ride on Uber, and McConnel buys it. Chris has the feeling he would not be able to leave Cranford's until he talked with everyone, from the FBI to the techs mapping the crime scene. But Chris does not want anything else on his plate right now. He is being spread too thin to be effective, and his internal clock is rapidly overheating to the point of explosiveness on a personal and professional level. Maybe a look into his old lover's eyes could help manage the load. Time to test the theory.

The billiard hall is named the Irish Green Table, although Chris guesses an Irishman probably never graced the front door. A follow-up text to Jessie narrows the margin of error with the name and actual address. Several pool games are ongoing, and Chris is willing to bet the tables have been played by the same people hundreds of times. Eyes follow him to the bar—any stranger receives undue focus. Like a lion pride on the plains of Africa, the locals size Chris for any weakness. A Crown and Coke is ordered, a sure sign he is not of their tribe.

A story about the LSU Tigers flashes on the dozen-or-so TVs scattered throughout the bar. All activities from shooting pool to serving drinks stop in mid-motion to gain information on the beloved Tigers.

The LSU football team is worshipped in every corner of Louisiana, and even though football season is months away, the Tigers never leave the lips or ears of their dedicated admirers. Adding fuel to the fire is the talent coming back this fall, perhaps the best in school history. When the Tiger review is over, Cajun voices bounce off the beer-stained walls, endorsing the optimism.

Chris returns his attention to the C and C when a hand is laid on his shoulder. Instinctively his hand reaches for the shoulder holster, taking nothing for granted in this darkened, pool-betting hole. A turn meets the smiling face of Jessie, and Chris slides off the elevated barstool. The hug is shared, and Chris feels a warm touch circle his back. His mind sends a reverberated message to other parts of his body, and any predetermined standoffish attitude slides to the floor.

"You're early," He takes a large sip of his drink and returns it to the bar. "Let's have something to eat."

Jessie climbs onto the stool and looks at the bartender.

"I'll have what he's drinking without a lime." She turns to Chris. "Missed you, big guy."

"Crazy busy," Chris relays. "The city keeps lining up all these dead bodies."

"I was beginning to take it personal." The drink is set on the bar as her hand rests on Chris's thigh. "Can't we share the stories … maybe solve one or two together?"

"Don't see any reason why not. Plenty to go around. Really overpowering at this point." Chris feels the Jessie tug and has barely finished that first drink.

The pressure of the job seems to mediate anytime Jessie was involved; and at this point in his professional life, the sides are closing in. The naked truth is, she's smart and has a gift for digging into the deprived human mind and figuring out why people do what they do.

"How's Robert doing?" he asks, wanting to move the obvious out of the way.

She takes a sip. "Chris, whether he is in my life or not, you are a special person to me. You can't deny the fact we are good for both careers. Tell me if I'm wrong."

He finishes the drink and orders another. Food at this point seems a distant prospect.

"Okay, what you say is valid. Missed you on several fronts."

He rubs her leg with no resistance. "You are good figuring out the cesspool I drown in daily. Let's move forward."

He offers the new drink, and she salutes the reunion.

"So, what were the five mobsters eating the other night?"

He can't help but laugh. "Damn, you put everything into perspective. I do miss that. What do you know at this point? I'll fill in the blanks."

"They were West Side guys, heavy into meth. Someone hired real talent for the hit."

"All true. Only one at the table even pulled a gun before falling over in his lobster bib. Forty customers and staff in the main restaurant. Not one saw or heard a thing in the private dining room. Going to call the FBI early next week. If anything pops, I'll forward." He takes another drink.

The bartender approaches. "Menu?"

Before Chris can turn down the offer, Jessie answers. "Why not?"

The menus are laid on the bar, and she opens one. He stares at her choice, a little surprised.

She looks at him. "Can see something smart-ass coming my way."

"Not really. You adapt to the environment," he says matter-of-factly while grabbing a menu.

"What's that suppose to mean?"

"Most women wouldn't take bar food over McGuire's."

"I'm not most women."

"That we can agree on. Sexy in its own way."

She playfully slaps him with the menu. "Don't forget it, either."

After a minute, the bartender returns for their order.

"Chowder, a Po' boy, and another drink." Jessie directs.

"Couldn't say it better." Chris folds the menu and hands it over.

"Fries?" The bartender asks.

She looks at him then at the bartender. "We're all in." The man retreats.

"Anything I can get my writing teeth into before you grab the FBI?"

"The crew came into the restaurant on a regular basis. They played this stupid-ass game parking a car so close to another vehicle it couldn't be moved. Several customers received poundings trying to move their cars. Probably nothing. No fights the night of the shootings."

"Interesting. Did a story a few years ago about this guy. He was an ex-professional boxer. His next-door neighbor came over bitching about this kid that played for Old Miss. Beat the hell out of his son one night in a bar. Now we're talking about a couple of college guys getting into a fight, but evidently the son was half the size of the football player. So the boxer says he'll give the Old Miss kid a lesson, goes to the bar a few days later and really hammers the football player."

"Was the fighter A.J. Justice?" Chris asks.

"No, I didn't use his name in the piece. Turns out there are laws against what he was doing."

"It's assault if someone trained in the fighting arts starts a fight," he summarizes. "Go on, this is interesting."

"The neighbor brags about the fighter on social media. All of a sudden, offers start pouring in for his services. He's out twice a week beating up so-called bullies. Makes more money than fighting professionally. Follow me on this. What if the crew beat the wrong guy with contacts—a professional cleans it up for him." Her eyes brighten with the thought.

"That's crazy, so crazy it may have legs."

"Makes one helluva story, but no one will be able to put the pieces together—except you and me." She takes his hand in hers.

Chris has little resistance when Jessie turns on the charm. Between the drinks and her touching, he is drifting toward what he figures will never work like it used to.

The sandwiches are set on the bar, and it breaks the magnetic pull Chris is feeling temporarily. He refuses to order another drink. More disappointment is coming, and he wants to be sober in his response.

After a couple of bites, Jessie lowers the Po' boy. "See, you don't have to pay thirty dollars for a good sandwich."

"True 'dat," Chris feels a strong urge to kiss her, but he focuses on the fries sitting between them. "You know, I have another case you might have an interest in."

"Tell me more." Her eyes dance with anticipation.

"This old guy, Joe Bailly. Been working the tourist trade on the streets playing instruments for years. Has a grandson. The old man plays while the kid tap-dances. Gathers tips, you know the drill."

"Feel a human-interest story coming."

"Well, if you want to call the Devil human interest, you might have something."

"Now you really have my attention." She leans closer, moving her plate in the process.

"Last Wednesday night, old Joe sees someone on the street. It scares the shit out of him. He takes the boy over to see Louis Fleck. Tells him the Devil is back in town after them."

"Louis Fleck, the strip club king of talent?"

"That Louis Fleck. Fleck tells him to go away, must be crazy. Old Joe and the kid leave the casino. Joe is stabbed to death less than a hundred yards later."

"What happened to the grandson?" She suddenly is knee deep into the story.

"This is where it gets spooky."He looks around the bar. "The kid runs from what he's convinced is the Devil. Ran more than a mile before losing the satan."

"Who do you think killed Joe and chased the kid?" She pulls out her phone and starts making notes.

"I interviewed the grandson twice. He's convinced the Devil killed his grandfather then tried to kill him. Going to run down the video from last Wednesday night. I'll share it with you."

"This is New Orleans. The Devil wasn't born here but raised a family close by and comes to visit on a regular basis. Okay, promise me you'll let me dig into this with you. It will make one helluva book." She offers her hand to shake, and he obliges.

Then she kisses him on the cheek. "Like old times."

"Be lying if I said didn't miss those old times." He drinks the last bit of Crown.

106

Me, too. Want to come home? Talk about those old times?"

At first, the Crown and emotion blur the content of what she has offered. A few seconds of doubt soon dissolve into a helpless response. "Yes, I'd like that … very much."

The best tip the bartender has received in the last month is neatly stacked next to the bill. Chris follows Jessie to the car, watching her long legs slide side-to-side in a skirt. He had paid little thought to the way she dressed when coming into the dark bar, but in the daylight it is easy to notice how sexily she has pulled herself together for him.

It felt good, a woman paying attention to his attention.

Most men would feel a pang of guilt about going to church in the morning with the wife and then having sex in the afternoon with another woman. Self-interest is always the first human emotion under the circumstances, and Chris is no exception. But, he regarded the physical side of the relationship with Jessie as part of the job. She advances his cop creativity and, above all, gives him a pressure-release valve. This logic did not bubble to the surface; he instinctively understands it. Justified or not, no guilt shrouds Chris as he rides away with Jessie.

◆

Walking through the side door of Jessie's house seems cozy and a familiar thought to Chris. The home is decorated well; she has spent a lot of time and money making every room theme-driven.

Fresh flowers greet them in the kitchen, something reserved for funerals in Chris's life.

"Drink?" she asks, out of habit.

"No, unless you want one."

"Not really." she admits, amid a brief moment of awkwardness.

"Your fireplace," his eyes ask a question along with his lips. "Can we crank it up?"

A big smile moves the awkwardness far away. "Going to will that fireplace to you."

Moving to the den, he lights the gas-fired hearth with a match in a manner familiar to him. The blaze extends to the chimney's blackened sides, reheating sparks and causing them to jump skyward. It is spring in New Orleans, and the temperature is approaching sixty degrees, but the fire still charges Chris. It takes him back to a time spent with his grandfather in a tiny cabin in the Georgia mountains. The person who taught him how to be a man in so many ways.

Chris and Jessie sit content on the couch, reconnecting about previous crimes worked together. He puts his arm around her shoulder, and she cuddles closer.

Then she pulls back in thought. "So the old man goes to Louis Fleck. Do you think he is seeking protection from this devil or warning Fleck about impending doom?"

"I interviewed Fleck. Of course, he's evasive as hell. But you bring up a good point. Joe Bailly knew Fleck wasn't going to protect him, but he felt an obligation to let Fleck know someone came to town after both of them." He is betting she will make logic come to life.

"That has revenge written all over it," she states. "Old Joe and Fleck did something in the past together for the Devil to be after them."

"What crime could Bailly and Fleck have in common to create such panic?"

"Give me the grandson's information. I'll contact the family about a possible story on Joe's street life. Dig way down in his history to mirror anything with Fleck."

"Why not talk to Fleck about old Joe? Perhaps add something to the story—connecting dots?"

"This is why we're good together." She kisses him passionately, and the talking ceases.

◆

Chris pays the Uber driver and walks into his home. Joanna has something on her mind, and he reads the expression immediately.

A slight ping of guilt finally hits Chris, but nothing changes his demeanor and tone.

"Sorry I'm so late. We found Tony hanging upside down from the second floor with his throat cut. Several took off for drinks after processing the crime scene." he says, unflinchingly.

"Father Joseph called me this afternoon."

"Somebody die?" he asks, relieved it is not about his lateness.

"When he grabbed your hand this morning, he said it was cold to the touch," she says, taking his hand in hers

"What does my hand have to do with anything?" Now he is starting to become agitated but can see Joanna is genuinely upset about something wrong with his hand.

"He is worried you have poor circulation. Some kind of blockage in your heart may be causing it." Tears rush low on her cheeks.

He sits down on the couch continuing to hold hands with her. "I'm fit as a fiddle. Had a physical eight months ago. Why would he bring up this kind of bullshit?"

"Father Joseph is only looking out for your health. Remember when Dean Sutherland had a heart attack?"

"The ex-high school football coach? He was sixty pounds overweight and smoked. That's not me."

"Father Joseph said he felt the same kind of coldness in his hand six days before he died. He said it was one of his biggest regrets not telling Dean what he suspected." Chris can see she is becoming deathly afraid for him because of where the information is coming from, and he finally understands.

"Look, I'll call the doctor for an EKG this coming week. Everything will be alright." He hugs her.

"Please, promise me!" Joanna begs.

"I will—promise."

Thirteen

JUMPING TO CONFUSION

A Mexican flight attendant serves a drink to Trey and Gayle shortly after take off. She has a beautiful smile and matching personality as the flight makes its way to Cabo. The crew has several members of brown color, and the aircraft cabin is festive and fun.

This flight is a contrast to the one Trey had made with his grandfather several years ago to Mexico City. That trip was to evaluate an advertising firm for the option of outsourcing the company's printing, but nothing came of it. The old man stayed glued to his briefcase and vodka tonics. The pricing would have saved Stephens Publishing seventeen percent annually, a sizable amount of money considering their large printing needs, but the opportunity was nixed. Trey knew it was preordained for failure. The elder Stephens started bitching about depending on Mexicans before the plane had left the tarmac in New Orleans.

Trey did admire what his grandfather built and sustained over the decades. But his open-book prejudice toward anyone of color annoyed him to no end.

Trey had been an average receiver on his high school football team and named All District his senior year, largely because the team's black quarterback had received a dozen Power Five scholarship offers. Denzel Jeffreye not only had a great arm but the legs to buy time in the pocket and complete long passes on the fly. Trey caught forty-seven of those passes, and his grandfather thought an NFL future was in sight.

A trained football eye knew. Trey was too slow to receive a scholarship at the next level, so he earned his BS at LSU watching football instead of playing it. Of course, his grandfather blamed it on racial bias. Not the real bias, but the one that made recruiters think white boys were not fast enough to play receiver in college.

These thoughts had been buried over time, but they came flooding back sitting next to Gayle on this flight, and his anger grew toward his grandfather. An excited smile by Gayle neutralized and temporarily negated his grandfather's shortcomings as a human being, but it was only relegated to the back of Trey's mind for the moment.

Gayle places the drink on the tray extending from the seat in front. "Are you alright?"

"Just some passing issues at work." Trey rubs his hands together, mocking a magician. "Poof, all gone!"

He orders another set of drinks.

"Something you want to talk about?" Gayle inquires, hoping to get the mood back Trey had when picking her up a couple of hours earlier.

"The last you will see of that. Nothing but Margarita fun for Gayle and Trey." He commits with the perfect, formally brace-induced smile.

A limousine is rented for the ride from the airport to the Ritz-Carlton. His grandfather had previously warned him that hiring a private limo could end in a kidnapping in Mexico City. It reeked of wealth.

The city has many beautiful tourist destination points, but not paying attention could get you in trouble with its more-than-twenty-million residents. Cabo is not Mexico City, and he wasn't riding with his grandfather.

Gayle is in a different mental element from the business front she presented when first meeting Trey. Her voice and movement convey a freedom that makes him feel wanted. He soon neatly places his grandfather's shortcomings deep into the mental Pandora's Box.

The check-in leads them to an expansive suite on the top floor of the Ritz. Gayle dances around the suite and onto a terrace balcony. The wind is blowing at a brisk pace, looking off the seventeenth floor to the ocean rolling on the beach below. Trey joins Gayle on the railing and wraps an arm around her waist.

"Spectacular view," Gayle relays, watching the distant people playing on the beach.

Trey stares at her face concentrating on the sand below.

"Spectacular does not do justice."

She turns facing him and catches the fact he is talking about her. "Too kind, Trey Stephens. You were raised a Southern gentleman."

She kisses him.

"You can thank my grandmother for making the compliment. However, you are the one that earned it. You're beautiful."

"That kind of talk will get you in trouble," she says.

"What kind of trouble?"

"Not the good kind of trouble. More like, 'I take advantage' kind of trouble."

"Please don't throw me in that briar patch."

"The only thing needed to be thrown around is a new bathing suit." Gayle walks over to the coffee table and picks up a fashion magazine printed by the hotel. "Saks. Macy's. All these stores offering bathing-suit options attached to the Ritz. Let's go shopping."

Trey is leaning far more toward sex than Saks. Yet he has promised a bathing suit, so the two head to the Gallery of Shops. A tunnel from the hotel to the stores is filled with tourists going and coming, many carrying armfuls of merchandise. Two hours into the process, Gayle has modeled a half-dozen different suits but seems still far from a decision.

"I can see your enthusiasm is waning, Mr. Stephens,"she says, walking away from Saks.

"Cannot tell a lie, not a big shopper. Now, you could put on a knapsack bathing suit and knock all eyes out on the beach. So, maybe I'm biased and naive on what look you want to wear." He is making an attempt at being honest and failing miserably in his own mind.

"That actually makes a lot of sense." She is trying her own patience at this point and sees a Starbucks thirty yards away.

"You get a cup of coffee. I'll finish this swimsuit quest and meet you at Starbucks."

"Deal," he says without hesitation and starts toward the coffee shop.

She smiles and shakes her head, accepting that he has hit the shopping wall.

He finds an empty table and settles in, coffee in hand. The Starbucks has a constant stream of customers. He pays little attention in his focus. He checks his phone for emails and replies to a couple of business inquiries. A text from his grandfather requesting a call annoys him. His response is curt.

"I'm in Mexico. Be back in the office on Wednesday." The return text is likewise curt: "What the hell?"

Trey knows a confrontation is coming sooner rather than later with his grandfather. It is time for him to run the company. The board is in his corner, and he has the votes to pull it off. It will come to a head early next month at the board meeting, or he will leave for the competition that has already made him a substantial offer, plus stock options, to leave Stephens Publishing. He has grown tired of being treated like a college student working summers to get his feet wet in the business. Respect beyond business decision-making has driven this newfound independence.

That, he knows, will totally torch his grandfather from a blind side, but he is beyond worrying about the man's feelings at this point.

Gayle moves next to Trey before he notices her presence.

She lifts a box from Saks. "Shopping miracles do happen, the proof is right here."

"Let's create envious people walking the beach."

◆

He is quick to change into his bathing suit and is rummaging through the liquor cabinet when she walks out of the bathroom.

He returns the small bottle of Grey Goose Vodka to its resting place in the cabinet when he turns and eyes the suit clinging to her body.

"Looks like you fell off the cover of a Sports Illustrated Swimsuit Edition."

"Thanks." She seems genuinely surprised by the reaction. "It's a simple design. Not much to it."

"If that's the case, I don't think the world is ready for a complicated bathing suit on you." He forgets the vodka.

◆

The beach is crowded. Trey and Gayle walk through the human maze focusing only on the sand and sun. Gulls fly above, squawking over the ignorant tourist leaving chips and sandwiches unguarded and stolen in a flash.

"I needed this," she says "Thanks for being who you are."

"Lilly painted the picture of my childhood. Now tell me about your family," Trey asks.

"Any brothers or sisters?"

"I have a twin sister, Maria."

He shakes his head. "No way there's two of you. Mankind isn't capable of handling that."

"Maria is in Utah. We were born in Portugal. Moved to Utah as toddlers with my parents."

"You don't have an ounce of accent. You picked up English fast."

"My father was raised in Britain, but business took him to Lisbon where he met my mother. He never did speak Portuguese, so my English is pretty good."

"So you speak Portuguese, too?" he asks as, a both turn

toward the setting sun.

"The sunset is spectacular." She shades her eyes for a better view. "Actually, I speak five languages. If you know Portuguese, you have the basics for Spanish and Italian."

"No shit? Throw some Portuguese on me," he says, thoroughly impressed.

"*Deus me abencoou com sua presenca.*" She lets the Portuguese roll off her tongue effortlessly.

He puts his arm around her shoulder. "Let me guess how that translates. 'You are a wonderful man, and I will follow you anywhere'."

"No. 'God blessed me with your presence'."

"I'll take that." They begin walking to the hotel.

Gayle grabs a magazine in the room having various tourist daytrips and is intently reading the options. Trey goes into the bathroom to scrub off the flight, the salt, and the sand clinging to his body.

An array of gels and shampoos lie boxed around the sink, and he opens several options while the shower is running.

Steam greets his face when the thick glass door is opened, and he merges with water so hot most people would jump back from it.

He welcomes the heat on his skin and is settled with his direction, not only surrounding Gayle but his decision to confront his grandfather. He rubs a handful of shampoo into his hair and leans over, letting the shower rinse the soap away. The glass door opens, and Gayle's nakedness rubs against him. A kiss is exchanged, and he empties a tube of liquid soap on her lean frame. His fingers spread the foam up and down the long legs.

The bathroom becomes a misty fog. Groping each other leads to sex on the small shower ledge.

Trey is the first dressed and at Gayle's direction reviews the day-trip picture of a massive stone bridge at the crest of a mountain.

People are standing on top of the stone arch, waving to a distant camera. The title above the photo is "Angel's Bridge."

She enters with her thick, black hair pulled back in a ponytail, and stiletto hills anchoring the cut calves into a miniskirt.

"Speaking of angels, you look perfect."

"You are a silver-tongued devil," she responds.

"I looked at the trip called 'Angel's Bridge'." He opens the magazine. "Only an hour from here. I agree, let's go in the morning."

"Mexican food first, Angel's Bridge second," Gayle says,

adjusting her hair.

"Maybe a little dancing in between?"

"Twist my arm." She extends her hand, and he takes it.

◆

The street has a lot of foot traffic leading away from the Ritz toward the center of town. Gayle and Trey walk hand-in-hand, engrossed in one another.

"Do we need an Uber?" she asks, approaching a busy intersection of traffic and horns being sounded.

"No. The bellman told me a good restaurant is only a few blocks away. Five bucks bought us a reservation."

The restaurant is full of American and Canadian tourists. The locals cannot afford the plate-pricing anytime this crowd sits to eat with their platinum and gold credit-card fare. The Cabo economy is based mostly on the tourist trade, and the high standard of expectations by visitors permeates everything from hotel rooms to golf courses.

A bottle of cabernet sauvignon is delivered to the table. The glasses touch, and the wine reveals a sharper vintage taste after their several hours on the beach.

"Why don't we plan a trip to Utah in a couple of months. I can meet your parents," Trey proposes.

"They have both passed, unfortunately, but I'm sure you would have been a big hit, especially my father. He was a businessman first and foremost." Gayle lowers her head telling the story and takes a sip of wine, as if trying to forget.

"I'm so sorry, what happened to them?" He takes her hand and kisses it.

"On a trip to visit relatives in Portugal, they were run off the road by a semi several years ago. Please, Trey, it's very painful still." A tear forms in her eye, and she leaves the table for the bathroom.

He is somewhat stunned by the turn of emotional events.

What are the odds, two people in their early thirties not having a single, living parent? He has a natural curiosity about his parents and how his life would have been had they lived. He is sure that she has the same connection.

Gayle soon returns. "Sorry for that. It's fresh on my mind."

"Don't ever apologize for losing someone close. You have every right to be upset."

"On a brighter note, my uncle is in Boston. Been my rock through all of this. He would love to meet you, I'm sure." She has regained her composure.

The meal is finished with little conversation. It is easy to see that Gayle's scars have been freshly cut, and the carefree chatter that often occurs between new lovers needs time to recharge. Trey steals several looks at this beautiful woman when she is distracted by the food or wine, and he takes inventory of his feelings.

There have been several love affairs in his life, during college and beyond, but something always jumped in the way of a long-term commitment. Gayle, on the other hand, is rapidly seeping into every pore of his body and spirit. Would he wake up in two weeks thinking differently? Right now it does not matter, the present seems to be an adventure after every step taken together.

The couple walks the sidewalk, leaning close after leaving the restaurant for several blocks. A crowd is gathered in front of an entrance to a modern high-rise building. They work around the people standing in line, and he bribes the security guard, who lets them pass to a bank of elevators. The elevator opens, and two drunk couples stumble off. Trey and Gayle get on. He hits the fourteenth floor, and the car rises quickly to the building's summit.

The door hides a huge dance floor and bar, with a deejay hammering out songs in a booth suspended near the ceiling. Unlike the restaurant, the bar is filled with locals and tourists alike. Spanish is being yelled above the six-foot speakers built into the walls on all sides. Another large tip gains a table near the dance floor with the music pounding all around. A waitress takes the drink order, and their two heads lean close in, an attempt to communicate.

Gayle's voice isn't loud enough to be heard, and Trey moves even closer. "How did you find this place?"

"Another five to the bell captain gains even more local knowledge," he reveals. "Said it was the hottest place in Cabo."

"Can't argue that." She screams above the music.

A lightly clothed woman comes by with cigarettes and cigars for sale, and Trey yells for attention. He purchases a cigar, and the lady lights it.

Gayle eyes Trey's actions. "Didn't know you smoked."

"On rare occasions. Playing golf or drinking."

"Why?" she curtly asks.

"It gives me a better buzz."

She takes the cigar and puts it out in an ashtray. "I'm all you need to get high on."

She grabs his hand and heads to the dance floor.

The next morning, Trey forces a look at his watch. It reads 9:45. His head swirls from the multiple drinks and returning to the room at 2:40 a.m. A sense of loneness flashes momentarily, and a turn to the other side of the bed confirms that Gayle is already up and moving.

On the nightstand is a note and two Tylenol. "Be back shortly with coffee and bagels."

He walks to the bathroom sink and lays the pills on his tongue, followed by tap water. The shower heats rapidly, and he lets the water roll down his neck, trying to hasten the Tylenol active ingredients.

Gayle enters the bathroom. "How do you feel?"

"Give me an hour and coffee to answer the question." He turns the water off. "Damn, you're up early. You don't have a hangover?"

"Not really. But I can help yours with the coffee."

He moves beyond the shower, towel in hand. "No hangover? That's disgusting. Thanks for the Tylenol. Going to turn out handy. What time does the Jeep arrive for Angel's Bridge?"

Gayle retrieves her phone. "Less than an hour—chop-chop!"

Trey finishes dressing and meets her on the balcony. Little is said while the coffee and bagels are consumed. Shortly they head to the front of the Ritz to meet their Mexican guide. A Jeep lettered with "Pink Tours" is awaiting their arrival.

Juan Torres introduces himself. Gayle jumps in the back seat, and Trey sits next to Juan.

"Are we the only ones headed to Angel's Bridge?" Trey asks.

"Mondays are slow this time of year. You will enjoy the day on top of the mountain," Juan answers in well-spoken English. "I have a lunch and wine for you. Very romantic."

The drive toward the distant mountain range follows the coast for the first thirty minutes, then the Jeep leaves the highway onto a dirt road for several more miles. The road becomes more rugged, and Juan shifts the Jeep into four-wheel drive to cover the last half-mile to the base of a mountain. The Jeep parks, and Trey evaluates the winding goat trail elevating above them.

"The trail starts here. Takes about thirty minutes to the top. I'll set up for lunch," Juan says, giving directions. "The food will be ready in two hours."

Trey looks at his watch. "Great, we'll be back before one-thirty."

Gayle and Trey put on backpacks and start the ascent.

118

"You up for this?" he asks, after a few steps up the trail.

"It's perfect. Beautiful day, beautiful climb," Gayle confirms, moving faster on the trail.

"And beautiful woman."

She touches her hair. "Oh, yes, pulled back hair and no makeup. Keep your eyes on the trail."

He smiles. "Why don't you lead?"

"That makes sense, then you can't see my face."

"No, so I can follow your great rear for the next half-hour."

She kicks a rock back at him. "You have learned well from Lilly."

The trail gains a sharper grade, winding back and forth along the mountainside. Gayle is relentless in the climb, and Trey is feeling the hangover come back with an increasing vengeance.

Halfway to the top, he stops. "Can we take a break?"

"Sure." She turns and walks back to him. "I'm full of energy and enjoying the climb so much. But we'll slow down."

"I feel a lot like a Billy, but little like a goat."

"Considerably more hills to climb in Boston than New Orleans." She tries to negate his lack of conditioning.

He pulls a canteen and offers it to her.

"No thanks … a little later."

He takes a big sip. A bald eagle screams overhead, flying from one hill to its nest.

"What a magnificent bird!" She follows its flight.

"He can afford to be magnificent. He flew here." He makes fun of his obvious struggles doing the climb.

"We'll slow down and take our time to enjoy the view."

"No, no. I signed on for the exercise, I'll finish it. Those fajitas are waiting below." He smiles at a laughing Gayle, and she resumes up the incline.

"Thanks for being a sport. I love this."

"What you love, I'll learn to tolerate." Trey is starting to sweat heavily following her footsteps on the trail.

Little is spoken moving along the path until the summit comes into sight. She turns, watching his slow movement to gain ground on her location.

"You could be a little more fatigued, just as a gesture of sympathy."

He is not appreciating the view as he pushes through to the top.

She starts an exaggerated panting, mocking his request.

"That sounds like an orgasm."

"Therein lies the question, fake or real?" Gayle smiles at her creativity.

"Mine is not fake, cranking over this damn mountain."

She turns and kisses him. "Neither is mine ... on or off this mountain."

◆

Juan sets the cooking utensils on a propane stove. A trip to the Jeep retrieves an ice chest and a camera with a telescopic lens.

He focuses the lens on Gayle and Trey standing at the edge of Angel's Bridge. He snaps off several photos and texts them to the couple.

Trey's phone catches the photos first, and then Gayle's cell sounds the text tone.

"I have to give Juan credit," he says looking, at the photo. "He's shooting and texting us in real time."

The ridgeline trail ends, and the stone bridge appears, leading to another mountain slope in the distance. Trey stops and takes off the backpack. For the first time, he can see the vista offering a fifteen-hundred-foot drop on either side of the natural stone bridge.

"Hold on a minute." He takes a deep breath and drinks a mouthful of water. "The bridge is awfully narrow."

"If you feel more comfortable staying here, I'll cross and be back in a few minutes." She removes her backpack and drinks from the canteen.

"No, I've made it this far, I want to finish it. Give me a minute." He sits on the backpack, resting. "When I was a kid, my grandmother took me to a park in downtown New Orleans. No such thing as a hill in Louisiana, much less a mountain. So the founding fathers built this mound of dirt in the park, fifteen feet high, to show children what a hill looks like. I got to the top. This, this fat boy pushed me off, skinning both my knees. Heights bother me ... a lot."

She offers her hand and pulls him upright. "Hold my hand. Trust me. I won't let you fall."

"What if I faint?" he asks, half-joking, half-serious.

"Come on, Trey. This is our first test as a couple."

"You mean the elevator ride last night didn't qualify as a test?" He is joking, as he does when stressed.

The two edge slowly onto the stone bridge. The wind blows their hair, much stronger than hiking the trail. Gayle does not force

Trey's movement but lets him pace the steps at his own speed. A third of the way across, she stops and holds him close. He shuts his eyes, not wanting to see the seemingly endless drop below.

"Trey." She wants him to loosen his tightening spirit.

"Yes?" he responds, with eyes still closed.

"Remember the eagle that flew overhead?"

"Sure. He has the convenience of wings."

"What if I told you, we could fly like that eagle? Would you jump with me?"

He opens his eyes but still doesn't look down. A reach in his pocket retrieves a quarter.

"Sir Isaac Newton said if you take a quarter, throw it off a mountain, and it comes up heads, that proves gravity does exist."

He tosses the quarter over the steep slope and opens his eyes to follow its drop into oblivion. After a few seconds, he looks at her. "Heads! What can I say?"

"No faith, no true love." Gayle turns, and leads Trey back to the ridge trail on solid ground.

◆

Juan takes several more photos of the two walking on the bridge and then lights the stove for cooking. A photo is texted to someone other than Gayle and Trey. Pork is placed in heated oil to coincide with the hikers' return for lunch.

◆

The walk down the mountain path moves at a much more rapid pace than the ascent. Trey leads the way and says it is all about the lunch waiting below, but Gayle is certain he was uncomfortable stepping on Angel's Bridge. It doesn't bother her. Heights are intimidating for a lot of people. What is important is that Trey regains energy and confidence as he moves lower and away from fear.

Juan is focused on the cooking and is much less engaging than on the trip out. Trey and Gayle drink a beer on folding chairs by a small fire, built in a rock pit used many times in the past.

"That was a blast." Trey winks and takes a sip of beer.

"It was easy to see your excitement overflowing." Gayle winks back.

"Going up was alright. Coming down a lot better." Trey takes a bite of the Mexican food, emphasizing the happiness of being off

Angel's Bridge.

"So, what possessed you to go on this day trip with climbing involved?" Gayle asks.

"Total honesty? Not afraid to bite off more than I can chew. Guess you read that quickly."

She raises her beer. "Here's to honesty—and overcoming fear."

The Jeep is loaded, and the three head away on the dirt road to the highway. One mile into the travel, a van is parked sideways in the road. A man dressed in a police uniform waving an AK-47 stops the Jeep.

"Get out." The Mexican speaks in broken English and points the weapon toward the Jeep. Juan immediately raises his hands and climbs from the vehicle, followed by Gayle and Trey. Several more armed men jump from the van, wrapping the three with tape and placing a flour sack over their heads. Gayle and Trey are moved to separate corners of the cargo bay, and the doors are shut. Two shots ring out behind the van, and the vehicle drives for more than two hours before stopping.

Fourteen

FOR THOSE ABOUT TO DIE

Israel Hamric pulls into a Cumberland Farms gas station in Monroe, Louisiana. Through habit, he sits in the SUV next to a bank of gas pumps for several minutes surveying the landscape. Settled with the usual movement of customers coming and going, he goes into the store, buying a Coke and forty dollars' worth of gas on pump three.

The gas pump screen reveals the ever-changing accounting and total cost toward the purchase. Once the price point hits thirty-nine dollars, the pump accounting slows dramatically and painstakingly deposits the remaining few cents into the tank.

This irritates Hamric. He sees no need for creeping to the gas finish line. His focus on the pump intensifies, trying to will the last fraction of a gallon down the tank's throat.

In that brief moment of lost background awareness, a heavy arm grabs his neck and pulls him upward. A disturbing sense of panic punctures Hamric's mind for a precious few seconds. Logic replaces the panic. It is not the law. They would approach with weapons drawn. With all his strength, Hamric squats with a large man on his back and retrieves a .25-caliber pistol from a holster buckled to the ankle. He throws the man back into the side of the vehicle and is suddenly free from the choke hold. A catlike whirl gains the advantage, and he aims the pistol at the man's heart.

"Whoa, just messing with you, Jimmy," the man says, holding up his hands.

Hamric instantly recalls it is a friend from the past. His given name is James Israel Hamric, and he grew up "Jimmy" all the way through his military days. He dropped the nickname after the Army and installed "Israel" when inducted into the murder game.

"Damn," Hamric says, redepositing the pistol. "That's a good way to die."

He takes a couple of steps in James McGowan's direction, who still has hands held in submission. He smiles. "We both got the shit scared out of us."

McGowan lowers his hands. "I just pissed my pants. You shit yours."

The Army buddies hug, having not seen each other since their second deployment in Afghanistan.

"Only a damned Indian could corral me that way." Hamric refers to McGowan having a small amount of Cherokee blood and earning the nickname "Chief" in the squad.

"Almost got me shot. You're still packing? Haven't touched a weapon since the Army."

"Old habits hard to break, Chief. You never know when an Indian might want to stalk me."

"What the hell are you doing in Monroe? Last I heard, you were in New York."

"I am still in New York. Had business in Dallas. Driving through to Atlanta for a cousin's wedding."

"Let me buy you a beer and catch up." McGowan always admired Hamric's ability as a soldier.

"Why not? I have a little time to kill."

"There's a sports bar a half-mile down on the left—Duffey's. Follow me." McGowan points west toward the interstate.

Hamric pulls onto the road, not sure why he has agreed to spend time with his old comrade. Although friendships in the military became intense, fighting side-by-side, Hamric instinctively knows past relationships should stay disconnected in his line of work. It goes against his conservative business approach and has no redeeming value, only exposure. But a couple of beers will not hurt his purpose in Monroe, and McGowan is a good guy—his last thought walking into Duffey's.

A frozen column of water wrapped in a plastic tube floats in a pitcher of beer sitting on the table. Great idea, Hamric summarizes in his mind. Must be a Southern thing keeping the beer cold. New Yorkers would never trust it, thinking it might change the beer's taste.

He looks around the bar, but his senses detect nothing out of the norm. In that short span of recon, McGowan has emptied his beer and rattled on about two of their former fighting mates. Hamric takes his first sip. McGowan pours his second beer and jumps into chapter three.

"Jimmy, I have to ask a question."

Hamric looks directly into McGowan's eyes for the first time since sitting down. "All ears."

"Why didn't you attend our ten-year reunion?"

"Working, man. Not born with a silver spoon like you and Shavers." He doesn't believe in any kind of sentimentality, much less exchanging war stories. "Don't think I was missed anyway. How many showed up?"

"Everyone that wasn't dead … except you." McGowan knocks down another half beer, as if the floating plastic in the pitcher is sucking more than its share.

"Damn. I'll be sure to make the next one." Hamric did take his commitment somewhat serious, but the shot at his ambiguous absence creates not an ounce of regret. "So how is Shavers doing these days?"

"In a wheelchair. Lost his legs when the Hummer he was driving hit an IED."

"Sorry to hear that. We had a lot in common." Hamric and Shavers grew up in New York knowing many of the same street characters. "Where's he living now?"

"Back with his mother. A whole lot of hell living in a wheelchair."

"Look him up when I get back to New York." He finishes the beer.

McGowan leans across the table. "He told me some crazy shit about you at the reunion."

"He was always a shit-talker. I have a bunch of New York stories on him, too." He pours the remaining beer into McGowan's glass, quickly realizing the pitcher does not stand a chance of absorbing warmth before it is gone.

"Told me you're a hitman, hired gun for the mob." McGowan moves back to an upright position, as if putting a safe distance between them.

"Helped my uncle once with a gambling debt. Now I'm a hitman? Wish it was true. They make a lot of money. You really believe that bravado shit-talk?" He realizes he has a problem on his hands that he did not have a clue existed.

"Man, don't know. Sorta' blew me away. I knew you were badass enough to pull it off." McGowan's eyes tell Hamric he fully accepted Shavers' story.

"Let's order some hot-ass wings and another pitcher to celebrate my promotion to hitman." For the first time, Hamric engages McGowan like their old Army days.

McGowan seems relieved. "Let's do it."

The waiter is waved over and takes a second order. McGowan relives every bullet fired in fun or struggle during their tours together. Hamric adds more fiber to numerous stories, sharing the wings and beer like long-lost brothers reunited. But Hamric sips while McGowan gulps. One is getting heavily buzzed, while the other is planning their merging fate.

Hamric understands that the hitman story would be a source

of pride for a group of fellow solders who did their fair share of killing with multiple tours in the Middle East. McGowan had earned Hamric's respect from a military perspective, but he could not eliminate a prominent Monroe citizen in the next day or so and expect his old comrade not to connect the dots.

The beer and wings consumed, Hamric pays the bill while McGowan goes to the bathroom. He writes a fake address and phone number on the back of a blank receipt, leaving his name off the paper.

McGowan returns more than a little tipsy and sits hard on the wooden bench.

"My old brother," Hamric says as he hands the paper to McGowan. "I really enjoyed seeing you again. Let's stay in touch. Here's my address and cell number."

He also slides a pen toward him. He gathers it and the paper, and writes his own address and phone number on an old receipt and hands it back. They both stand up, but McGowan on much-less-steady legs.

"Love you, my man." He embraces Hamric, like the last hug for a dying soldier on the battlefield.

"Love you, too," Hamric replies quietly.

The two walk to the parking lot, merging for one last communication between their respective cars, parked in adjacent spots.

"Can you drive alright?" Hamric asks. "More than happy to follow you home."

"Be fine. You have a long way to go. Be safe my friend."

Hamric takes two steps toward his car and turns back to McGowan getting into his car. "Left your address in Duffey's. Give it to me again. I'll write it down in the SUV."

McGowan repeats the address, and Hamric climbs into his vehicle. He retrieves the paper, and the address McGowan had verbalized matches the written one, confirming its validity. He starts the SUV and pulls out of the parking lot, but he hesitates a moment to make sure McGowan is not following. McGowan waves one last time before pulling into traffic, and Hamric returns the gesture.

He drives in the direction of the interstate while McGowan heads in the opposite direction.

◆

Hamric arrives at a Holiday Inn and taps the councilman's address into the GPS.

It is becoming dark, but he wants to circle the councilman's house to appraise the layout in anticipation for the next day.

The young woman at the Holiday Inn is attractive and smiles constantly at him during the check-in. She asks for a credit card to cover incidental charges, and he smiles back.

"I deal in cash only, my dear. My wife has shredded our credit cards. She's the spender, and I need to support her."

"Happens a lot. Enjoy the evening." The cute smile disappears.

Hamric moves online and generates an aerial view of both target addresses via Zillow. To his relief, neither lies in a gated community.

The councilman's home is located in an older neighborhood, which usually means less video from prying neighbors or businesses. Even though he feels it imperative to eliminate the McGowan issue, his professional focus is first and foremost on the councilman.

He summarizes his trip to the primary target in meticulous notes, including gas stations, convenience stores, and other security-camera-using establishments. Hamric will avoid major commercial intersections, going through and around neighborhoods to lesson the likelihood of surveillance on his vehicle.

His SUV is black, less receptive to color identification. He will steal a license plate to replace his New York tag on the day of the murders. Video is the biggest tool in the law-enforcement identification process beyond the immediate crime-scene forensics.

There will be no clues at the scene. Nevertheless, he needs to be diligent within a two-mile radius of the killing zone concerning video cameras. Hamric's paranoia is extreme. He buys a new laptop after every hit and destroys the old one.

Two days watching the councilman's house identifies who drives what and the sexual taste for young men expressed by the target. Patterns of habit are noted, final approach/exit routes defined. The second night, Hamric checks out of the Holiday Inn and unpacks a pressed Federal Express uniform. At 7:35, he dons the uniform inside the SUV, watches the sunset, and heads to the target's home. Twenty-four minutes later, he parks adjacent to the house away from the sight of anyone coming to the front door.

Binoculars view movement in the kitchen, but it is too far for a positive ID. A leisurely stroll to a small kitchen window carrying a FedEx package reveals the councilman and a young man drinking beer at the kitchen table. Hamric glances over a fence and sees no one around the pool. He walks to the front porch and rings the doorbell.

Billy Yates answers the front door. "FedEx man, welcome. I'll take the package." Billy opens the door wider.

"It requires a signature by..." Hamric looks at the package. "Mr. Reynolds."

"I sign for all his stuff. Give it here." Billy takes the package, and Hamric hands him a pen.

A .22 long-caliber bullet hits Billy Yates just below the hairline as he signs the document. The silencer, muffling most of the noise, still has a wind-piercing sound. The worthless FedEx package hits the hardwood floor, and Hamric catches Billy's body before it makes the wood.

Councilman Reynolds comes through the kitchen door with a raised voice. "What the hell is going on?"

Hamric holds Billy's limp body. "Sir, I don't know. He just collapsed. Please call 911."

Reynolds takes several steps to the slumping Billy Yates and pulls out his phone. Hamric drops the body, freezing Reynolds' thoughts and motion. He squares the .22 to Reynolds' heart and fires twice, hitting him in the chest. The second body hits the hardwood.

◆

At that moment across town, James McGowan is eyeing the six ball positioned two feet from the cue ball near the side pocket. The eight ball invitingly sits in front of the corner pocket to his right. A tap on the cue sends the six into the side pocket, and the cue ball rolls down no more than ten inches from the eight. The eight is next to hide in the the corner pocket, and James picks up the twenty-dollar bet.

A petite blonde approaches McGowan as he places eight quarters in the table slot to release the balls for the next game.

"Let's go, baby." Jeanine moves her hand to his neck and rubs it. "Tired of this place."

McGowan racks the balls. "Where do you want to go?"

"A movie ... your house, anywhere but here."

A twenty is laid on the table by one of the regulars that McGowan is sure he can beat. He hands Jeanine the twenty from the last game. "Go get us another beer and some dip. We'll leave after this round." He breaks the racked balls.

◆

Hamric backs the SUV to the gate by the pool and takes a clean-up kit inside. The bullet holes are heavily taped to stop the bleeding.

Each body is wrapped in a plastic painter's cloth, placed in the SUV, and covered by a blanket. He cleans up with a chemical solution he buys in New York that rapidly dissipates blood but will not fly by a good CSI inspection. He is hoping the Monroe police department lacks the latest tools if deciding to inspect the home surrounding the disappearance. A quick change of clothes completes the exit strategy.

◆

The predetermined route to McGowan's house is carefully driven, following all traffic laws to an extreme. This kind of patience separates Hamric from others in the business. The job is not over at this point, and he understands that the exposure of being pulled over for any reason could prove fatal.

If he is stopped by a cop, there would be no choice but to shoot the officer. That is the last resort. Killing a policeman explodes the legal attention in all directions, and making it out is next to impossible.

Hamric drives by McGowan's house, but his car is gone. He parks the truck a block from the house and waits to see if the target shows.

Hamric texts Glenn Gaylord's phone. He is Louis Fleck's brother-in-law who runs the funeral home. "Be there around 1:00 a.m. to deliver several packages."

◆

Gaylord flips ribs over in a smoker. He is agitated by the text.

Fleck and his wife are sitting in the living room talking with Gaylord's wife Sherry. He goes into the house and motions from the kitchen to get Fleck's attention.

"Need help with the ribs?" Fleck asks, guessing the answer is no.

Gaylord shows him the text from Hamric. "One in the morning, is he crazy?"

Fleck pushes him against the the refrigerator. "If Israel Hamric had been King Kong, he would still be tearing off T-Rex jaws on the island. Not only will you be sitting there at twelve-thirty, you'll bring him a rack of ribs with a baked potato. If he wants a blow job, call my sister. Are we on the same page?"

"Calm down, I get it. He's an important man." He eases himself away from the refrigerator.

"No, he's not an important man ... unless your life has more value than I think." Fleck walks back to the living room.

◆

After taking the last eight-ball shot, McGowan retrieves the twenty and walks away from the table. Jeanine greets him with avocado dip piled high on a chip. He bows low to bite the chip from her hand. She smiles as he leans on the chair and finishes crunching the mouthful.

"Where to, my gorgeous one?" he asks.

"My place. I'm not working tomorrow. We can sleep in ... make love and then breakfast."

McGowan turns his wristwatch into view. "Leave now and we can make the nine-twenty movies at the mall."

The couple walks out of the bar, not having a clue that Jeanine's day off has saved their lives.

◆

Hamric looks at his cell, noting the time, and then rotates to the back of the SUV. He cannot get rid of the nervous energy created by the bodies. Determined to circle back for McGowan in the near future, he heads for the interstate to New Orleans and the ribs waiting for him at the crematorium.

Fifteen

UP AND AWAY

Joanna Dale holds onto Chris longer than usual before he heads out the door for work. If the truth would ease out of his head and fall to the floor for all to see, the priest's prediction of heart issues was having an effect on his thoughts.

Sleep did not come easy last night. Part of it centered on his renewed contact with Jessie, but also rumbling around in his head was an ambulance ride to the emergency room with Joanna holding his cold, lifeless hand. A text from Joanna had renewed the ambulance scenario while he was parking the car at the police station: "Dr. Knox's phone number."

Chris will call for an appointment to retain peace at home—and earn a full night's sleep.

The steps to the third floor seem more laborious than usual.

One hand fondles the other before opening the door. It does not have much warmth. Placing the hand on his chin hoping to discover hidden heat does not improve the dire prospect.

Chris is aware of his new health obsession coming from, of all places, their parish priest.

The door opens to a busy and loud cop floor. Conversations about shootings, pimps, prostitutes, and sports fill the space. He feels comfortable immediately and forgets to call Dr. Knox.

Chris sits at a desk less than four feet from Bobby Rabold. They have shared the space for many years, and it has become so likable that Chris turned down an office down the hallway when promoted to lieutenant and lead detective. Rabold always beats Chris to work and fills him in on new case developments.

"Anything on the OK Corral?" Chris asks, thumbing through the countless memos that circulate from every law-enforcement agency in Louisiana.

"Not much," Rabold responds. "It was a single shooter. All the forty-cal came from the same weapon."

Chris turns to him. "You've got to be one confident sonofabitch to draw down on five gun-carrying thugs. Have to admire that. Why don't you run it up the pole with your FBI contact? See if they've stumbled onto something. Tell them we're dealing with a high-profile talent. Maybe we'll get a list of names."

"Can do," Rabold confirms. "The blade killing the old man behind the casino is strange." He hands the report to Chris.

"What do you mean strange? A knife is a knife." He glances at the report.

"The blade has a rounded edge, something like a half-moon. It's a three-hundred-year-old weapon," he says, shrugging.

"What the hell?"

"The coroner made a specific note about the high-force velocity needed to shove this type of blade into his back and through the sternum. A big man swung the weapon."

"Or the Devil?"

"Or a steroid, muscle-bound bouncer from the casino?" Rabold shakes his head.

"We're not finished putting our boot in Mr. Fleck's ass and the crew he calls friends. I've added a bloodhound to our team."

Rabold leans closer to Chris's desk. "Let me guess. A long-legged reporter with a personal interest in you?"

"That's all in the past. We only had lunch, and Jessie is fascinated about this devil case. Wants to write a story about the kid's account and maybe create needed publicity."

"Seems to work well for everybody but me." Rabold moves back to his desk.

"What does that mean?"

"Jessie writes another book, and you get laid."

Chris wads a report sheet and throws it at Rabold. "Therein lies an obvious ping of jealously. You need professional help with those kinds of feelings. I'm headed to Bourbon Street to find video on the case. Want to tag along?"

"Actually, I have a couple hours of paperwork to file. You know, covering your ass." He turns his attention back to his pile of papers.

"Keep up the good work, my man. I'll put in a word for you when the time comes."

◆

Chris parks the unmarked car in a convenient but illegal space on Bourbon Street in front of Pat O'Brian's. A cop's life is not easy. The pressure of the job never leaves deep in the gut, no matter the day or night. Parking wherever he pleases gives Chris a small power trip and makes the stomach a little less likely to implode. The humidity is thickening as spring surrenders to higher temperatures. Certainly not a surprise to Chris, taking his jacket off and throwing it in the back seat.

The best view for video footage is across the street at the Booty Trap Strip Club. Chris addresses traffic on Bourbon Street and walks over to the club. It is 11:05 a.m., the strip club is gearing up to sell their six-dollar beers and twenty-dollar mixed drinks to the constant stream of frat boys filing in for Spring Break.

A flash of his badge solicits an audience with the same child- and porno-loving manager that Fleck had visited a couple of nights before.

Chris hands Jones his card, but before he can ask the question, Jones knows the answer. Still, he plays ignorant, intently listening to the video request. His first thought is to say the video no longer exists, maintaining his so-called allegiance to Fleck. But Jones has a self-interest in preserving the status quo, and denying a homicide cop's request could jeopardize his entire porno world.

◆

Jones works the video back to Wednesday night and the timeline dictated by Chris.

"Stop it there." Chris directs.

It's tempting to tell this cop that Fleck had requested the same footage, but that, too, would move Jones out on a limb of discomfort.

"You want a still shot of the old man and kid?" he asks, with his best lip of dedication to law and order.

"The real target is the couple walking by. You ever see those two before?"

"The old man and kid have come by for leftovers many times, but the couple doesn't ring a bell. Did they kill the old man?"

Jones is wanting to appear curious, but he has almost spilled too much on the table.

"It's an ongoing investigation. A still shot would be great, I need the video, too."

"Give me a minute. Want a drink, Lieutenant?" He feels relieved Chris didn't push about his anticipating the old man was murdered.

"Diet Coke works."

Jones leads him to the bartender.

"Diet Coke for the officer. Be back with the video."

Chris sips on the Coke and runs his eyes through the prep

work needed to start the stripping day. In his early days, he roamed the strip club and bar world. Some of it was certainly the women who would do anything to get on the good side of a cop. But mostly it was the sense of power given police by the management. Free food and drinks were the least of the bribes to make the Law happy, keeping their clubs in good stead surrounding licensing and other political requirements.

A cop received VIP status by just showing up. Looking around, Chris is struck by his foolish youth on the force, and what mattered long ago now stinks, literally. He had wanted to leave after first walking in the door. Now, after recovering the video, he does just that. But the taste in his mouth does not leave with his exit.

Chris is a good cop and instinctively moves along Bourbon Street in the same direction Trey and Gayle were headed. The young couple certainly did not fit the devil profile. But it was obvious from Joe Bailly's change of expression that he saw something he did not like and immediately pulled up stakes and headed to the casino.

Several blocks into the walk, he crosses the street to a restaurant showing video cameras. He presents the printed photo to the manager.

"Ever see this couple before?" Chris asks, showing his ID.

"Not in person, but…" The manager puts his glasses on and stares more closely at the photo.

"But what?"

"A cop came by a few days ago asking to review my video from Wednesday night. This couple was walking the street on the timeline he requested."

"A cop? Remember his name?" Chris is thrown off by the realization that someone else had an interest in the case, and that someone had left the investigation hanging from a balcony rail.

"No … hold on. My assistant manager helped him with the video."

The manager disappears for a few seconds and returns.

"Jennifer, this is Officer Dale. Do you remember the police officer's name asking about the video?"

"His card is right here," She opens a small drawer in the desk used to greet customers. "His name is Anthony Cranford." She hands the card to Chris, who shows little response to the fact Cranford was working the case and suddenly turned up dead.

"Thanks. So the couple was walking east in your video?"

Jennifer nods. "Yes. What did they do?"

Chris pockets the business card and heads out the door

without responding. He continues walking east while dialing Bobby Rabold.

"Hey Chris, find anything on the video?" he asks.

"I found this young couple that appears to set everything in motion. You sitting down?"

"JFK and Marilyn Monroe?"

"Don't have a clue who the couple is, but Tony Cranford was running after the video for someone. Hours later he's hanging upside down from the banister bleeding to death."

"Bet it rebounds to Fleck's lap."

"Meet me at Tony's house at two o'clock. Maybe we can find a bridge to Mr. Fleck."

The phone pocketed, Chris sees the Marriott come into view.

No one recognizes the couple, just as Tony Cranford discovered.

Chris next heads for the Hilton's front desk, where a flash of the photo receives a negative response from the clerk.

"Need your manager here, now."

"May I help you, officer?" The manager seems sensitive to the inquiry.

"I'm investigating the murder of a police officer. Did the couple in this photo stay here?"

"Can't say one way or another, but that doesn't mean they didn't stay with us."

"I want your head of housekeeping, bellhop captain, restaurant manager, customer service—all here in five minutes."

"Yes sir." She whirls and starts calling the managers to the front desk. Within minutes, they are standing in front of Chris, including Bellhop Captain Barry, who had helped Cranford into Gayle's room.

Chris walks close to each, pointing to the photo. "A cop was killed investigating these two people. Did they stay here?"

Barry looks hard at the photo. "The lady was here for a while, but I don't recognize the man." Barry does not want a connection to Cranford, but he thinks a partial truth might save his ass.

Chris turns to the manager. "I want the registration info surrounding this woman."

"Do you have a warrant for that information?"

"Are you jerking me off?" Chris demands.

"No, just doing my job. I can't release a client's information without a warrant."

"And I'm doing my job—I'll be back with the goddam warrant," Chris fires back and leaves abruptly.

◆

Chris drives to Cranford's house ahead of Bobby Rabold. A first time over the years, but it has to do more with anger than efficiency.

The yellow caution tape still stands, a reminder of the bloodletting inside. A twist of the front door knob grants access and, in Chris's state of mind, a good thing for maintaining the door's structural integrity.

The smell of death permeates the living room where Cranford was found at the end of a rope. Chris cannot ignore the smell. He despises the fact that it will greedily attach to his clothing and travel home with him.

Not knowing exactly what he is looking for, Chris dons gloves and starts opening drawer after drawer. Rummaging through the contents, he hopes to stumble onto who hired Cranford to chase after the evasive couple.

Rabold opens the submissive door and enters.

"Sorry I'm late. Picked up the warrant for the Hilton. What are we looking for?"

"Not sure. Just trying to find a link between Tony and whoever hired him. Go to the den. I'm almost finished in here." Chris goes through yet another drawer without results, and Rabold rounds the corner where Cranford had been watching TV. Applying his latex gloves, he spots blood on the recliner. "Tony must have been killed here, right?" he shouts.

Chris leaves the living room. "Yes, he was hung after a struggle in the chair. It's apparent he was murdered there."

Rabold pulls the seat cushion off and sticks his hand deep inside.

He retrieves a small crack pipe from the depths.

"Little doubt about what he was doing," he relays, diving his gloved hand deeper into the seams.

Chris moves along the hallway to a bathroom. "The coke was all over the place. Drug habit would be an understatement. Drug dealer is closer to the truth."

He examines the medicine cabinet, which reveals the usual cold and headache answers.

"Chris," Rabold yells, "take a look at this."

Chris comes out of the bathroom. "What?"

He is handed a small piece of bloody paper with a phone number on it. "Found it in the chair."

"Hold on," Chris opens his wallet and retrieves Fleck's card. "The numbers match. He was investigating for Fleck!"

"If Tony was working for Fleck, his crew probably had nothing to do with his death."

"Maybe ... maybe not," Chris responds. "What if he found out something incriminating about Fleck? What it does is tie the old man's death firmly to Tony and Fleck. It also puts this videoed couple squarely in the middle."

"Let's go serve the warrant," Rabold adds.

◆

Both cops arrive at the Hilton. The manager has Gayle's information printed and ready after reviewing the warrant. Chris's temper subsides. It usually worked that way when a case started to take a positive spin and began to congeal.

On the way out, Rabold approaches one of the men parking cars and flashes his badge.

"Have you ever seen this couple before?"

"Sure. In and out lots of times over the last couple of weeks."

"Did you catch the man's name by chance?"

"No. Great tipper though." The young man heads to the parking lot to retrieve a vehicle.

"Hold on," Chris yells above the traffic noise passing on the street. "What kind of car did he drive?"

"A black Mercedes—a 500 SL." He disappears into the lot.

Chris turns to Rabold. "Go run all the black 500 SL Mercedes owners in Louisiana and compare their driver's license photos. Let's get to the bottom of this."

"Will do."

Chris is feeling empowered sitting in the car contemplating his next move. A decision is made to share the clearing picture with Jessie James McGaha.

◆

"Lieutenant Dale, are you calling me to fill in the blanks on the Devil case?"

"Actually, breaks are heading our way. I think it's time you meet young Emrik to boost the publicity." His voice is full of energy.

"...and start the book. Can we do it today?"

"I'll call his mother and arrange it after school. Meet me for lunch at Pearl's. I'll fill you in."

"See you at two-thirty."

◆

Chris drives the short distance to the casino to lean on Louis Fleck. It will not be easy, Fleck has been in the illegal game all his life, and standard police tactics will be blocked by a battery of attorneys. Even the FBI, with its unlimited budgets and manpower, has failed to put the man in jail, at least up to now.

Information to keep the ball rolling is the key ingredient to any investigation and, at a minimum, the goal to obtain from Fleck.

A knock on the casino door produces the towering frame of the Voice.

"Lieutenant Dale, what can we do for you today?" The man opens the door wide and steps out.

"Need to see Mr. Fleck," Chris relays.

"Mr. Fleck is not in. Anything else?" The Voice stands way north of six feet and towers over Chris.

Chris puts a hand on his shoulder. "Come with me."

The Voice pulls back. "You arresting me?"

"Not if you answer a few questions. That simple enough?"

The Voice walks down the steps with him.

"Do you know Tony Cranford?" Chris cocks his head to the side like he knows something the Voice does not.

"No, sir."

"Tony Cranford was a cop, a cop doing investigative work for you and Fleck. Someone murdered Tony over the weekend. Somebody is going to be taking a shit-bath for murdering my friend regardless of what I have to do legally to make an arrest. You understand what I'm saying?"

"I swear, don't know him." The Voice stands firm.

Chris suddenly grabs the man's hand and bends back the little finger, dropping him to his knees.

"All the patience has left my body for an extended vacation."

Chris bends the finger back more, and the Voice screams.

"Was Tony investigating the old man's death? What was he after?"

"Mr. Cranford was investigating that devil woman. Mr. Fleck thought he was next to die." He quickly abandons his loyalty under the pain Chris is applying.

"Now we're getting somewhere. Who killed Tony Cranford?"

Chris moderates the finger pressure.

"That devil woman. She came out of the ground. That's all I

142

know." The Voice realizes he has said too much.

Chris releases the hand, and the Voice moves his fingers in and out of a fist trying to recover. Chris helps him up with an extended arm.

"This will stay between us guys. Mr. Fleck will never know about the conversation. Won't get you in trouble. Now, if something comes along really important, you will give me a call." Chris hands him a card.

"Yes sir." The Voice pockets the card and returns to the casino with a sore finger and bruised ego.

Chris understands his tactics were completely out of line and is not sure why he crossed over the bridge that could very well get him fired. But the big man had shown too much attitude for his liking, and Chris wanted to make a point of who really was in charge. He had crossed the bridge and found it fun. Now, he is smiling as he walks back to the car.

◆

Jessie's eyes dance when Chris approaches the table. He leans over and kisses her cheek, eager to share the updated events. Just as Chris sits, he receives a call from Rabold.

"Hold on Jessie, let me take this." He stands and walks a few steps away from the table. "Did you match the car? Yeah, no shit? That's one helluva surprise. Good job. I'm tied up this afternoon. Go over and pay Stephens a visit." Chris returns to the table and sits in a leather chair. "Things are starting to take shape." He lays the printed photo of Trey and Gayle on the table. "Here's our devil woman."

Jessie stares at the couple. "Damned pretty devil woman."

"Her name is Gayle Kidd. The guy is Reed Stephens the Third. Ring any bells?"

"Not really. But with the 'Third' at the end of his name, it should."

"He's the grandson of the Stephens Publishing founder, Reed Stephens—the First. That large building on Broadway is the Stephens Building. A money man. He's a managing partner in multiple companies controlling interests in vending, casinos, publishing, and God knows what else. The woman is living in Boston, however. She grew up in Salt Lake City. What she's doing here with Reed Stephens is anybody's guess, but we'll have a lot more answers shortly."

"Can you connect this to Tony's death?" Jessie asks.

"Fleck hired Tony to investigate this woman. One of his inside guys told me Fleck is scared to death of her."

"She sounds more like a hired assassin than Satan. Either way, we have the makings of a great book. Do you think she killed Tony Cranford or Joe Bailly?"

"The circle is getting smaller all the time around the same group of people. Someone in that circle did the killing." Chris is sure the case is taking shape. "Let's eat. We have a meeting with Emrik and his mom at four-thirty."

◆

Bobby Rabold pulls into Trey Stephens' driveway and sees several government vehicles parked in front of the house. It is a strong FBI presence and confusing to him. He knocks on the door, and Lilly answers; a tall, young FBI agent accompanies her.

"May I help you?" Lilly asks, meekly.

Rabold flashes his badge. "Detective Rabold, here to see Reed Stephens the Third."

"Thanks, Lilly. I'll handle this." The agent steps forward, and Lilly retreats, shutting the door. "Agent Desmond, FBI. What's your business with Mr. Stephens?"

"Need to interview Mr. Stephens surrounding two homicides. One was a New Orleans' police officer," Rabold offers. "What is the FBI doing here?"

"Not at liberty to discuss, but I'll tell you Mr. Stephens is not available for the immediate future. You can contact me in the next ten days to see if the situation changes." Desmond hands him a card.

"Do you know Agent Suggs?" Rabold asks, hoping a FBI connection might generate more leeway in the discussion.

"Yeah, I work with Suggs. How do you know him?" Desmond seems to lighten his grip on the situation.

"We play golf once in a while. His wife, Silvia, is a doll." Rabold can sense an opening.

"Suggs definitely married up. I'll give him credit for his golf game."

"Look, I know you guys have a job, but so do I." He pulls out the printout of Trey and Gayle. "This woman is also under suspicion along with Stephens. Does Gayle Kidd have anything to do with your case?"

Desmond looks back to the house as if being watched.

"Okay, we're involved because Stephens and Kidd have been kidnapped in Mexico. We're not investigating any other federal

144

crimes, if that helps. That's all I can say at this juncture."

Rabold reaches out his hand. "Thanks for the help." Desmond shakes his hand and returns to the house.

◆

Chris and Jessie have sat down in Eva's living room, with Emrik and his Uncle Randy.

"Emrik, I would like to introduce you and the family to Jessie McGaha. Jessie writes for the New Orleans Times-Picayune. She has an interest in doing a story about you and your grandfather. You know, how you guys entertained the tourists through dance and music."

"How great is that, Emrik! See your name in the paper." Eva underscores the opportunity.

"Not only the story, but photos of your dancing to show off the talent I've heard so much about," Jessie adds. "Eva, do you have any photos of your father and Emrik on the street together?"

"Actually, I do have a couple pictures of them performing, but Emrik was around nine at the time … grown so much since then."

"We'll take new photos with Emrik and his Uncle Randy then blend the new and old to make the sequencing work for the story."

Chris's phone rings. "Excuse me," He walks out the front door. "Yeah, Bobby?"

"Things go from strange to stranger. Stephens and Kidd went to Mexico and got themselves kidnapped. The FBI is crawling all over his residence right now. No telling where this shit will end."

"You could tell me a UFO landed on his lawn and I wouldn't be surprised. But this shocks me. Do you think this is some type of setup? A way to disappear, live happy ever after in the Philippines?"

"From the looks of his home, he could afford it. All I know is the FBI is taking it damned seriously. The agent in charge told me to call in a week or so for an update. Those two are off the chessboard for right now, but he works for his grandfather. Let's do surveillance. Took the tag numbers for the cars parked at the house, except the Feds, to see where it all goes."

"I like that direction. I'll put more heat on Fleck and his merry band of angels. I roughed up that big sonofabitch at the front. He told me Fleck is terrified of the Gayle chick, and that old bastard is scared of nothing. You can bet he's bringing in hired guns for protection. It still could have connection to Tony's murder."

"You roughed up that big son of a bitch? That's damned impressive! You still have it. Wish I had seen that."

"Feeling it in my shoulder already. I'm getting too old for this shit … gotta' retire soon."

Chris ends the call and walks back into the living room, seeing Emrik smile for the first time. Jessie is taking photos of Emrik, Eva, and Uncle Randy. Chris watches her work the room, leading the group into exactly what to say in order to build the storyline that will eventually be published in the paper. She lacks even an ounce of the arrogance Chris sees so often in the national and local media plowing their way into an investigation. No sense of entitlement on her part. She wants only to place attention on the subject she is profiling.

He finds it hard to admit, but his emotional attachment to Jessie continues to grow.

Eva takes a tray of empty tea cups into the kitchen and places them in the dishwasher. The wall clock reads 5:24. She returns to the living room.

"We're all excited about Jessie doing a story on Emrik and his grandfather, but we need to go to church for his wake tonight."

Jessie rises from the couch. "May we attend the wake with you?"

"That's a nice gesture but not necessary," Eva says. "Thanks for your kindness."

"It would help me understand the family dynamic better. We're here for more than just a story." Jessie puts her arm around Emrik's shoulder.

"Meet us at St. Thomas Moore at six-thirty," Eva says. "We'll be a little early to greet people."

Chris stands with Jessie. They leave the house and enter the car.

"What?" Jessie asks, putting on the seatbelt and feeling something is wrong.

"I have things to do. Rabold was over at the Stephens house, and the FBI is crawling all over it."

"Did they make an arrest?"

"Both would be better off if the FBI did arrest them. It appears they were kidnapped in Mexico. If true, that's a living hell to go through. The cartels brutalize kidnap victims."

"You seem to have doubts about the kidnapping." Jessie recognizes his cop instincts.

"Who the hell knows at this point? Don't you have an insider at the FBI?"

146

"No, but my father is retired CIA. This might fall under their jurisdiction. It's worth a call."

"I didn't have a clue your father was CIA. No wonder you have that inquisitive mind to solve things."

"Don't get too excited. My dad worked behind a desk his whole career. But he does know a lot of CIA field people."

◆

The car pulls into the church parking lot, and Jessie places her hand on Chris's shoulder. "Let me out. You go do your cop thing, and I'll call Uber."

"Can't do that. I need to help this young man, too. It's your fault, making me look soft." He smiles, and she winks at him.

They sign the guest register after entering the church's main door. Father Davidson greets both with a double handshake and a low-voiced welcome. Eva, Emrik, and Uncle Randy stand next to the priest, and Eva slightly smiles at Jessie and Chris walking up the aisle. Jessie reads a tiny "thank you" on her lips.

Chris looks at his hand and wonders if Father Davidson felt a cold handshake. The hand rises slowly and gently touches his chest to confirm a heartbeat.

Joe Bailly's coffin seems diminutive in the expansive, mostly empty pews leading to the altar. In the background, surveying the casket, is a nine-foot Jesus on the Cross. Chris and Jessie kneel briefly in the front row of pews, each making the sign of the cross. Then they approach Joe Bailly, wrapped in a suit and tie that rarely graced his body when alive. An organ is played off to the side by a lady well-versed in the music, having performed this ritual hundreds of times.

After a few moments of blank staring, the two return to the second row and sit. Jessie leans over and whispers, "The man was a musician, there should be a band playing."

Chris glances at Jessie. "The funeral tomorrow will be filled with music."

Eva, Emrik, and Uncle Randy, who is carrying a clarinet, walk the aisle toward the casket. Emrik sees his grandfather lying still and motionless, a stark contrast to the man so full of life who taught him to dance. His stomach tightens and sours, a rush of emotions crushing his body from all sides, and Emrik feels his eyes dart from his grandfather to Jesus at high speed. Randy places the clarinet in the coffin next to Joe Bailly's hand, and Emrik screams, "No!" He runs down the aisle to the wooden door

147

exit and hits it forcefully, blowing through.

Chris is the first to rise and give chase, the other churchgoers' reactions slowed by the emotions already spent. Three-dozen sets of eyes watch Chris swing open the same door, feet pounding after Emrik. Eva and Randy leave their shock behind and begin running toward the exit.

Emrik slides along a metal handrail leading to the sidewalk, skipping the inconvenience of steps. The street is well-lit in front of the church, confusing Emrik's choice of direction. Chris enters the light and takes the more traditional steps in a hurry, causing Emrik to run north toward an old commercial park occupied by abandoned office buildings.

Giving chase, Chris realizes he is no match for young Emrik's speed and starts to slow, catching his breath. The lack of lung air does not inhibit his focus on the target.

"Emrik!" he yells. "Stop, son. Let's talk about your grandfather." Chris's voice reverbs into Emrik's head, and he halts.

Turning back, he sees his mother and uncle approaching the scene.

Two steps into the family reunion, a hooded figure bounds from the darkness and scarfs Emrik up by the waist. Emrik and Eva scream in unison, as if the strange sight is unfolding on a production set designed by the Warner Bros. Studio.

Extending the chase game, Randy passes Chris and rapidly gains ground on his nephew's abductor. At the point of contact, Randy grabs an arm of opportunity, but the hooded kidnapper backhands the uncle, knocking him several feet into the air.

Chris tries to catch Emrik, but the hooded figure beats him to a fire-escape on a three-story building. Jumping four feet off the sidewalk, Emrik in arm, the figure pulls down the metal ladder and ascends the three stories in what appears to be seconds.

All of Chris's senses scream disbelief in what he has just witnessed.

It is humanly impossible, yet Emrik, and this thing carrying him, have scaled the structure and disappeared.

Chris pulls his weapon. "Randy, climb after Emrik. I'll go on the other side of the building to cut them off." Randy immediately starts climbing the fire escape, and Chris turns to Jessie, who has arrived on the scene. "Call nine-one-one. Don't leave here, he may come back with Emrik."

Chris disappears around the front of the old structure as Eva falls to the sidewalk in tears. Chris shoves his size-twelve shoe through a window already cracked on the first floor. He pulls a small flashlight from the lining of his gun belt and enters the shattered window. A stream of blood crawls over his shoe to the floor, but he gives it no attention. The focused beam of light reveals a structure gutted of interior walls and a lack of any imaginable hiding place for someone carrying an unwilling boy.

A flash targets the stairwell, and Chris hurriedly makes the steps to the second floor. The same wall-less condition meets the eye, narrowing the escape route to the third floor or roof. The climb continues. Chris hears someone coming down the steps, and he lays against the wall, shutting the light off.

A voice echoes, "Chris, is that you?" Randy eases down the stairwell, feeling his way in the dark.

"Yes, coming your way. Nothing on the first two floors." Chris turns the flashlight back on, and Randy's shadowed figure is standing in the middle of the stairwell.

The two desperate men head for the roof. A quick inventory reveals only dormant air-conditioners.

"What the hell? Where has the asshole gone?" Chris asks, but only silence answers.

Both men run across the roof, heading to the adjoining building but are greeted by a twenty-foot space between the roofs.

"Noone could make that leap without falling three stories," Randy announces.

"You're right—at least not a human," Chris adds.

Blue flashing lights slam the darkness below as police cruisers respond to Jessie's 911 call.

Sixteen

THE NAKED AND AFRAID

Sweat is running along Trey's face, clinging to the cloth bag draped over his head. The musty smell of flour fills his nose.

He sneezes, making the bag that much more uncomfortable. A second sneeze only inflames the liquids inching their way to his belt, and he voices his displeasure at being treated like a POW.

The butt of an AK-47 hits his chest and rolls him over, shifting the direction of the sweat but providing even less relief than the previous upright position. Words of Spanish scold Trey's unknowing ears, though he understands the drift of their cruelty.

"Leave him alone." Gayle screams out in Spanish, and the expected retaliation for her insubordination never materializes.

A shift of his weight helps relieve the cramping in the right leg and, to Trey's surprise, the movement does not invite another blow to the chest.

They are riding in a van, driving through various changes in terrain; some highway, some obviously off-road, and all filled with broken motion caused by faulty shocks and nearly bald tires.

Trey gingerly moves a couple inches backward against the van wall, trying to reset the stiffness now covering most of his body. His wrist pushes against metal in the process, and the realization that his watch is no longer on his arm hits hard. Did the Mexicans take it, or did the watch fall off during the scuffle?

The means of disappearance didn't matter. It is not the loss of an expensive Rolex that has Trey falling into the mental abyss of despair. No, the watch belonged to his dead father, and he rarely took it off for any reason. That piece of gold jewelry was the last link to a childhood that might have been. It clung to his arm, providing emotional support for the darkness that still engulfed his heart. The blanket of warmth, providing calm over his baby crib of life for all these years, has suddenly disappeared.

The van stops and temporarily pulls Trey out of the shock.

Moisture- and stink-covered arms drag him and Gayle from the back and rudely push them to the ground. Spanish is flowing in the air, mixed with the sounds of wandering chickens struggling to survive on the hot sand and occasional bug.

A sudden rush of fresh air fills Trey's nose when the sack is removed from his head. Afraid the bag is soon to return, he inhales more than his share. He is then brought to his feet. Gayle's bag is also removed, and Trey takes a step toward her, a foolish move met with a sharp backhand for the thought. The wallet is taken from his pants, and one of the masked Mexicans thumbs through the contents, pulling out his driver's license.

Juan, their erstwhile tour guide, takes the license and places it near Trey's face while going off in Spanish. One of the cartel soldiers cuts the bindings from Trey's wrist, and he wrings his hands trying to kickstart circulation. A pen and paper are handed to him, and more Spanish is wasted on his ears.

"They want a phone number and name of the person willing to pay the ransom," Gayle tells him.

"To hell with these bastards!"

"If you don't follow directions, they have no use for us. We'll be shot."

Reality hits Trey square in the forehead. He takes the pen and writes his grandfather's name and number, although he doubts Reed Stephens would even entertain paying a ransom.

A shallow grave might well be their destination.

The landscape holds little hope of an eventual escape, either. A few scattered trees stand around a house and large barn. Other than a dusty road curling off in the distance toward a mountain range, nothing civilized meets Trey's stare. Gayle is led to the barn, and Trey is taken to the house.

"Be strong, we will get out of this together." Gayle's last words are welcomed by Trey entering the adobe-facade structure. She seems in control, while he stews in the juices of doubt, fear, and self-loathing.

Juan leads Trey to a bedroom, and a narrow wooden box barely five feet tall stares back. He points to a small door befitting a doghouse, and Trey complies by crawling in. The door is locked behind, a final signal of his incarceration.

A hundred-watt lightbulb burns at eye level when Trey tries to stand, but he quickly discovers he must lean over ten full inches to accommodate his height. He slides down the wall onto the same carpet that covers the entire cell. The heat is oppressive, but a diminutive fan mounted in the ceiling comes on, helping to keep the air circulating. Mexican music starts playing loudly.

Gayle enters the barn accompanied by two men, and when the door is closed behind, she is subjected to a strip-search and body-fondling. She slaps one of the men and receives a back-hand in the process. Gayle kicks a shin, and the men laugh at the helplessness before pushing her into a cell similar to the one containing Trey. One of the men throws her stripped clothing into the door and locks it. A myriad of thoughts rummage through her brain at lightning speed. A rooster crows from the loft of the barn, adding to the masculine insults being showered on Gayle since the ordeal began.

◆

Michael Ortiz is well educated. The first person of the Ortiz family to receive a college degree has had his life take an abrupt U-turn. Halfway through his masters program at USC, his mother, father, and younger sister were murdered by the Mendes Cartel, and it changed his focus in life to revenge.

Ortiz is a fast-rising member of the Nunez Cartel, a bitter rival to the Mendes Cartel and a way to kill with a certain amount of immunity. He has adapted to the mission well, moving from carefree college student to vicious and cruel killer with total disrespect for human life. Ortiz has received word about the Trey and Gayle kidnapping and has sent his top negotiator, Julio Varela, to push the process toward collecting a large ransom.

◆

Reed Stephens sits in front of a 75-inch TV, watching the late-afternoon stock-market results roll across the bottom of the screen.

He feels uncomfortable and angry. For the last forty hours the FBI has been living with him, waiting on the call from Mexico to establish guidelines for the ransom demands for his dumb-ass grandson and the bimbo he brought with him. He had warned Trey about the the dangers of going to that godforsaken place, and now his arrogance was going to cost the family millions.

Stephens could sense this lack of respect coming from Trey over the past year, and it mirrored the same attitude years earlier from his son.

That defiance killed Trey's father and probably would lead to his own death.

"Would you like something to eat, Mr. Stephens?" Lilly asks tentatively, guessing the answer in advance.

"No thanks ... could use another bourbon, though."

Mrs. Stephens returns from the kitchen. "Reed, you need to eat something. You're going to make yourself sick ignoring food. No telling how long this thing will last."

"Isn't that the shitty truth. I should let Trey rot in that hellhole cage."

Mrs. Stephens sits next to her husband, and her voice barely rises above a whisper. "I have tolerated your bullshit for decades … fought through your hooker days … entertained mobsters and crooked politicians so you could make one more pile of money. Trey is my child's child, and you will empty the bank account to get him back or…"

"Or what?"

"Life has simple choices, Reed. I will crack your skull open with a hammer one night when you go to sleep." She stands, flashes her eyes at him, and returns to the kitchen.

Lilly brings Stephens the drink then turns curtly around to let him stew in his thoughts, as if she knew the law had been laid in his lap.

Stephens moves to the living room, where the FBI has organized electronic equipment for recording and tracing the call.

"You ready for this, Mr. Stephens? Any questions?" Agent Desmond asks.

"No, just want to have my grandson back," he answers with a sudden new attitude.

"Again, the caller will ask for millions. Play the poor man. Demand to speak to your grandson. Proof of life is important. It's the only way we will be able to locate where Trey is. This first call, the kidnapper will not be at Trey's location."

"Understood." He sits. Twenty minutes later his cell phone rings.

All of the agents move to designated positions around the room.

Desmond raises his hand and counts backward while directing on his fingers, "three … two … one … answer."

Stephens follows instructions. "Hello?"

Julio Varela is on a payphone. "Mr. Stephens, this is your call from Mexico."

"Yes, who is this?"

"Shut up and listen. We have your grandson and his girlfriend," Varela relates in perfect English. "We will return them to you for five-million U.S. dollars. Instructions will be forthcoming."

Stephens hears the number and his heart grows cold.

"Five million? That's crazy! I have a small printing business. I can scrape together maybe fifty thousand. I want to speak to Trey

154

or there's no deal."

"Mr. Stephens, we have Google in Mexico, too. You and your grandson manage numerous companies having more than two billion in sales last fiscal year. Five million. Tell the FBI to go take a break." Varela hangs up the phone.

"Fifty-two seconds. No way to trace," Agent Haynes reports.

"You did well, Mr. Stephens," Desmond tells him. "It went as expected. Johnson, ring Google headquarters and see if they will trace any searches from Mexico about the Stephens companies. Long shot, but it's worth a try."

"Do they really expect five million in ransom?" Stephens cannot help himself with his wife not in the room.

"Not really. Typically it ends up under a million," Desmond responds As he continues giving directions. "Wallace, drive a nail in the ass of the local Cabo police for information. I'll contact the Mexican government and see who they think is responsible. Ready a team on their side to make a raid. Let's get to work."

Stephens finishes off his drink and watches all sides of his life close tighter around his neck and wallet.

◆

The small door on the wooden cell opens, and a five-gallon paint bucket filled with two inches of water is shoved into the entrance.

Trey moves on his knees toward the bucket and is greeted by hyper-Spanish and the outline of a .45 pistol. He stops and retreats a couple of feet. A small clay pot containing rice, beans, and an undercooked piece of meat is set next to the larger bucket. The door closes.

Hesitating for a couple of minutes, Trey gains enough confidence to crawl over and see the contents. The large bucket is raised to his lips and he drinks the well water. Despite the heavy sulfuric taste, he chugs the water into his dehydrated body and is left craving more. A second water mouthful releases his system long enough to start eating the food. It is the best rice and beans ever to touch his palette, and he licks both bowl and grimy fingers.

Not sure of the feeding and water privileges routine, Trey decides to save half the water for later on. After an hour, the urge to urinate begins to creep through his system. He fights it off, using all his focus. The reality of urinating in the cage or using his water bucket is seeping in, and the options make him want to throw up the rice, beans, and whatever the meat was. He hurriedly drinks the remaining water and relieves himself into the bucket.

◆

Gayle sees the door to her cell open and spots the paint bucket a couple of feet outside the cage. If she wants water, she must reach out and pull it back in. She extends both hands and begins pulling when someone grabs her body and yanks her from the cell.

Gayle knows this time would come, and she fights the two Mexicans with all her might. But they tear off her blouse and strip the jeans from her legs. She cusses them in Spanish and is overpowered in short order.

One of the attackers grabs her breasts, but the second one suddenly stops and looks to the barn ceiling. A bright light envelops the barn and pierces the many cracks in the ill-constructed wall and ceiling. Several chickens fly from their roosts in the loft, and numerous mice and rats scurry to escape the barn's confine. Both men stand and pull pistols as the light changes intensity and direction, moving across the top of the barn. The Mexicans sweat and hold still the air in their lungs. The light casts ever-changing shadows to brightness and back to dark again. The brightness dances to stone-cold silence and suddenly freezes dead center, directly over the barn.

Gayle refits the torn blouse across her shoulders. She buttons a hole or two and pulls the jeans up. The men scramble like the rats minutes earlier, and Gayle watches their trembling fear leave the barn before she takes the food and water bucket back into the cage.

Seventeen

DUELING DEVILS

Bobby Rabold places the golf ball atop the tee, steps back, and aligns his six iron. One-hundred-and-seventy yards down the fairway, the flag at the pin exposes a strong wind, blowing left to right. The swing is smooth, not quick but powerful, and the ball lands five feet from the hole.

"Damn!" Bill Suggs pats Rabold on the back. "We needed that." The "we" is a twosome playing in the team two-ball club championship. Suggs sinks the putt. He and Rabold move to eleven-under on the scorecard with two holes to play.

The two friends jump into the golf cart and tee the ball up for the next hole, a par five. Both men were high school buddies, playing golf for the Jefferson Wildcats, and both drifted into law-enforcement, Rabold with the NOPD and Suggs the FBI. Over the last sixteen years, Suggs's career has moved him around the country to four different cities, but he eventually earned the opportunity to come to New Orleans, and he jumped at the transfer back home. Rabold and Suggs love playing golf, and both are damned good at it. They rarely lose to outsiders but keep an intense competitiveness when playing head-to-head.

The round finished and the team trophy secured, Rabold and Suggs grab a beer and sit outside in the warming sunshine.

Suggs offers his mug in Rabold's direction and receives a clink of the glass in return. "Damned good golf, Mr. Rabold."

"Damn good golf, Mr. Suggs. My man, what did you find out about the devil-woman, Gayle Kidd?"

"It appears the Nunez Cartel has made a real kidnapping. What's the other guy's name?" Suggs answers and questions at the same time.

"Reed Stephens."

"Yeah, asking five mil for the ransom. Old man Stephens is a pain in the ass, I'm being told."

"Anything in her background jump out?"

"Not much. Born in Portugal. Moved to Salt Lake as a baby. Master's degree, lives in Boston now."

"What about her family? Have much on them?" He takes

another drink from the beer.

"Father was a paleontology professor at BYU. Killed in some type of school accident." He shrugs his shoulders, as if puzzled by the event.

"What the hell? Dig in the wrong hole?" Rabold is just as puzzled.

"Got me. No other details came back. One thing of note. She has a twin sister, and get this, she is confined to a mental institution."

"No way two women from the same family can look that good. Sad to hear she's being confined."

"That is blatantly sexist! I'm going to file it in my report to field command—have you fired."

"Doesn't surprise me. You'd do anything to win the club championship in September. You realize there's little chance with me playing."

"Hey, so absolutely true. But that's the kind of guy I am. No one else will look out for me … like me."

"You're FBI, and everyone knows how that works. On a less serious note, can you forward the report?"

"Yep, can do. Corresponding with other law agencies with parallel investigations is allowed. Nothing in the report required a warrant."

"Anything on Reed Stephens?"

"Old man Stephens is square in the crosshairs of our White Collar Crimes Division. The grandson doesn't seem to be knee-deep at this point, but the investigation is far from over."

"Some of your guys jumped into the mob killings. Anything on the professional talent pulling the trigger?"

"Did your CSI determine it was one shooter?"

"One weapon … one very talented shooter. We don't have a clue on who or why it went down."

"Don't know a thing there. But for my sexist and good-golfing friend, I will dig around and find out." Suggs orders another round of beers.

◆

Rabold slides into his car and looks at the golf trophy lying in the back seat. A great day all around, winning golf and clarification on details surrounding several investigative fronts.

He dials Chris Dale.

"Did you win?" Chris asks, knowing the answer before asking.

"Played well. The trophy will go on the mantle shortly."

"Damn little room left the last time I saw it. You had four hours with Suggs. What's the scoop?"

"It looks like the devil-woman and Stephens are indeed kidnapped by a cartel. But you're not going to believe this. Gayle Kidd has a twin sister confined to a mental facility."

"Crazy that a devil-woman could be kidnapped. Maybe the cartel has bit off more than it can chew?" Chris suggests. "Saw something even crazier. The kid ran from his grandfather's wake last night. I gave chase. From nowhere, this guy ... this thing, grabs Emrik and shimmies up a three story building on a fire- escape. Did it effortlessly, carrying a hundred-pound kid fighting him. Disappeared into thin air."

"Holy shit! The mother must be out of her mind with panic."

"Bobby, the more I dig into this case, the less I know. Going to the casino tonight to see what Fleck is up to. Where you headed?"

"Mind if I tag along?"

"Meet you at the station at seven. We'll grab a bite then head over."

◆

Chris makes an illegal U-turn leaving the Pizza Panz Restaurant, heading to the casino after dinner with Rabold.

"Get a ticket doing that," Rabold tells him, as if a spouse talking to a significant other.

"Might be a shootout if stopped in this frame of mind," Chris throws back, as if a cop talking to another cop.

"After eating that pile of cheese, don't understand how you could find a weapon."

"Actually, getting shot might be the answer we all need at this point."

He parks the car a full block from the casino, and the two men hesitate to get out.

"What if we pump water into the ship ... see if the rats jump off," Chris declares. "Let's tell Fleck that we've traced Tony's death to the she-devil. See what that stirs up."

"Yeah! That would put a kink in his ass. He seems to be scared of this woman to start with. Great idea!"

◆

Louis Fleck never had children, but he always liked mentoring young guys into the business. The latest project to be taken under arm is Rocky Gentile, the son of fellow mob boss Rudy Gentile. Rudy once ran the Jacksonville, Florida, crime scene but had succumbed to cancer two years ago.

Gentile sits attentively listening to Fleck's psychological profiling the clients who frequent the casino. The overall picture for those clients addicted to gambling, sex, and drugs is not pretty.

But it is predictable. Gentile watches the video monitors as his mentor points out customers and their tendencies, good and bad.

The Voice knocks on the door, and Fleck acknowledges his entrance.

"Boss, Detective Dale is in the casino to see you. Should I let him in?"

Fleck is superbly confident and likes to perform in front of others. Simply put, it is an internal belief that he is the smartest person in the room, especially when it comes to law enforcement.

"Sure, send him in." Fleck smiles at young Gentile like a conductor tapping his wand, alerting orchestra members that the music is about to begin.

Chris and Rabold enter the office carrying files. Fleck realizes pressure of some type is about to be applied.

"Officers come in, have a seat," he says, inviting them like greeting old high-school friends. "To what do I owe the pleasure of your presence?"

"Know Tony Cranford?" Chris starts in, low-key.

"Don't know any Tony Cranford. What's this all about?" He does not expect this line of questioning.

"That's the first lie. You don't get a second," Chris pulls his chair close to Fleck's desk and tosses out the blood-stained paper with the phone number belonging to Fleck. "Tony had this on his very dead body, hanging from a second floor balcony in his home … your cell number."

"That's strictly a…" Fleck is cut off in mid-sentence.

"Shut up. We know you hired him to investigate the devil-woman that Joe Bailly went into a panic mode about … and conveniently turn up dead, also."

Rabold pulls his chair next to Chris. "Here's a photo of your devil-woman and devil-man passing Joe Bailly the night he came running to you."

"Rocky, go empty a few slot machines." Fleck smiles at Gentile's leaving as if nothing is wrong, but deep in his stomach he is feeling a rising sense of panic. He did not have a clue Cranford

162

was dead and, worse, that the cops knew more than he did.

"Tony Cranford was a good cop but a bad drug addict. The FBI tells us you provided him drugs." This is a guess on Chris's part.

"I believe it's time for my attorney to get involved. You know the way out, gentlemen." He stands.

"Sit down," Chris asks nicely. "Sit!"

Fleck sits obediently, and Chris feels emboldened at the mobster becoming frayed around the mental edges.

"I don't give a damn about the drugs," Chris presses. "But I do want to find out who killed a cop and the old man in front of his grandson."

Fleck looks at the photo of Trey and Gayle. "We had nothing to do with either one of these killings. Hell, I hired Tony to find out who these two are. Why would I have Tony or Joe Bailly killed?"

"We don't have enough to rule you out. So, you better have answers coming damn fast."

Rabold places a photo of the mob killings in the restaurant on Fleck's desk. "Suddenly, mobsters are being shot in the head before eating dessert. You might be next."

Fleck rubs his chin after viewing the dead men. "Maybe we can work together on this?"

"Maybe?" Chris repeats. "Seems you have a lot more to lose than we do."

"Give me forty-eight hours, I'm running down a couple of things that will shed a lot of light on the events. I'll share them with you … if you'll share with me." Fleck knows he is vulnerable, and the smell of fear is in the room.

"Okay, what do you need from us?" Chris asks.

"Just like you, I believe the answer lies with that couple. There are non-cop ways of obtaining the facts for a conviction, but I need their names to complete the job."

Chris turns to Rabold and then back to Fleck. "Give us two minutes alone to discuss."

"Sure." Fleck leaves the office.

"Chris, this isn't exactly by the book, I don't think we should give him their names."

"The satan couple is in Mexico locked in a closet and can't be exposed to any more harm than what the cartel is willing to do. Fleck doesn't know that. We've got a twelve-year-old kid missing who I want back badly, and we both understand this is all connected."

"If we're going to throw our careers away, might as well do it at the same time," Rabold says, coming around. "Have room in Florida for a golfing partner?"

"Absolutely, but you'll have to give me a stroke a hole." Chris goes to the door and opens it. Fleck returns.

"Get your pen out," Rabold directs Fleck, and he complies. "The woman's name is Gayle Kidd. The man's name is Reed Stephens the Third."

Fleck never flinches, even though shocked when he hears Stephens' name. He understands, too well, this is the grandson of old man Stephens.

"Give me a couple of days, and we'll crack this together." An odd statement from a mobster to a couple of cops who had just made him so nervous.

◆

Back in the car, Rabold puts his seatbelt on. "Feel like I sold my soul to the Devil."

"Which devil are you talking about, the mob or Gayle Kidd?"

"I'm not sure ... which devil is the lesser of the two evils. For the life of me, I can't trust Fleck under any circumstances."

"Right there with you. Let's watch what he does tonight and have a team follow him over the next couple of days. A little insurance won't hurt."

"You did put a hot poker up Fleck's ass. Good job," Rabold says, smiling. "Any feedback on the Emrik kid?"

"No, been gone fifteen hours. The realization of what that usually means is heartbreaking. Did I ever tell you what happened to my brother?"

Rabold is surprised to hear him talking about his family.

"All these years and I didn't know you had a brother."

"One summer the family went to Destin for a few days on the beach. We didn't go on many vacations, so my kid brother and me are crazy excited. I actually have an even younger brother than David, but he was in diapers at the time. Ran all over those snow-white beaches for three days, daylight to dark. Wore my parents completely out. They got sunburned. So they decided to drop us off at the beach and went back to the motel with the baby on day four.

"I was fourteen, David twelve. My father put me in charge ... said they would be back in a couple of hours." Chris hesitates. "That happened a lot when we were kids ... it was a different time."

164

Rabold senses the guilt in Chris's voice.

"David gets caught in a riptide. It happened so fast. I can still see the panic hit him moving away from the beach. I started to swim after him. Then this older guy grabbed me, and his son jumped in.

"Turned out his son was a lifeguard, but he never made it to David ... he drowned." Chris stares out the front of the vehicle.

"Chris, I'm so sorry. That had to be devastating. But the truth is, you would have probably drowned if jumping in, too."

"His body was recovered the next day. My mother passed out when he was brought in. My father's alcoholic tendencies accelerated. He died way too early."

"Man, that's a whole lot of guilt to live with as a fourteen-year-old."

"Watching Emrik being dragged away the other night brought back all those nightmares buried for a long time. Nothing I could do to stop it. I've lived the terror his mother and uncle are feeling right now. If I have to make a pact with the Devil to get him back, it's a small price to pay."

Suddenly they spot Louis Fleck walking out of the casino and getting into his car.

"What do we have here?" Rabold asks, watching Fleck pull away from the curb.

Chris follows him at a distance, an easy task because the night is late and the streets have little traffic.

Fleck drives through a residential area four miles from the casino and pulls into the detached garage next to his home. Chris drives off to the station, the book closed on Fleck for the night.

◆

Seventeen miles away, Emrik's sight and mind are overpowered by lights changing colors into various shades of blackness and brightness. His body whirls inside a spiraling column, and he tries to reach out and touch the light, but his hands fall short in the emptiness with no contact.

Emrik feels nothing, but the motion around him accelerates to the point of making his stomach sick. Try as he might, he cannot puke to rid the sensation enveloping him. Pressure starts building on his face, pushing his features to the point of not being able to open his eyes to cry or his mouth to scream.

◆

The Rusty Nail is a popular bar on St. James Street. It empties a large amount of sliced cardboard boxes and leftover meals from the dining room around eleven-thirty every night. Dean Jones has been living on the streets for several years and can eat like a high roller if he arrives around midnight to pick through the many options in the dumpster. Jones also is aware the manager does not like anyone in his dumpster, so he must stay low in the shadows to gather the food and make a fast exit.

Thirty feet from the dumpster, Jones reviews the Rusty Nail back door and sees no sign of staff movement. He rushes in like a dog pursuing a reward. A large object falls from the darkness onto a pile of boxes. He retreats a few feet to observe before fully committing.

A sound emits from the dumpster, and Jones is convinced a raccoon has beaten him into the bend. Not to be denied, he swings a small wooden bat on the metal side to scare the intruder away.

He looks over the edge to see its effect.

Emrik hears the metal pounding around him but does not understand the strange surroundings he has fallen into. The urge to vomit remains overpowering, and he finally throws up on a pile of cardboard.

A voice meets his ears. "Kid, this is my food … get your ass out of my can."

Emrik gathers his jumbled thoughts and wipes away the meal residue on his jeans enjoyed by strangers a couple hours earlier.

Two hands on the metal bend pull him over the side and into the space of Jones's wooden bat. Jones does not need to issue any more threats, Emrik runs to the alleyway onto St. James Street. Looking around in this unfamiliar area of New Orleans. He takes a seat on a bus bench. After fifteen minutes, a bus rolls up and the door opens.

Emrik faces the bus driver. "I don't have any money, but I need a ride home. My momma is crying."

The driver shakes his head. "Get in."

Emrik still has to walk two miles to his house from the bus stop, not entirely sure how to get home from this side of town. He eventually manages to find his street and arrives in front of his mother's house. He flips over the certain rock lying the flower bed and takes the key from underneath it, unlocking the front door.

It is pitch dark, and Emrik feels guilty letting his mother down by running from his grandfather's wake. He heads into the spare bedroom and retrieves a .38 pistol his grandfather kept in the closet. Moving along the hallway, he sees his mother sitting on the edge of her bed with her back to the door, speaking on the phone.

Emrik can hear the fear and pain in her voice, talking to someone about him. He stands there, watching for a better part of a minute before she turns and notices his presence.

"My God! He's here!" Eva says into the phone before dropping it to the floor. She stands quickly and rounds the bed, approaching him. Emrik raises the .38, points it at Eva's approaching body, and pulls the trigger.

Eighteen

SICK AND TIRED

Chris Dale sits in the office of Dr. Wynn watching patients sign in and others exit the sanitary medical halls. Like him, no one is happy to be there, including the receptionist. A sign warns of dire consequences if your cell phone is not turned off, and Chris, like most of humanity, follows direction from anyone who sports a "Dr." in front of their name.

It is a large practice, housing four other doctors along with Wynn, and the traffic seems nonstop. A nurse emerges from an inner door and announces his name. Chris rises and returns her half-hearted smile with nothing that resembles one of his own.

Dr. Wynn is a busy man and forgets Chris is a cop every time he sees him. This annoys Chris. It is always Dr. Wynn's first question when he comes in. How hard is it to make a note in the damned file, he wonders.

"So, Chris, you were here for your annual about seven months ago. Has something changed?" Dr. Wynn has surprised Chris with a different question.

"A friend noticed my hand was clammy when we shook hands and said it might be due to bad circulation and might lead to heart problems."

"Yes, that could be a symptom of a circulation issue." The doctor grabs both of Chris's hands for a few seconds and then releases them.

He places a stethoscope on Chris's chest and moves it side-to-side with various points of hesitation.

Chris can feel his heart pounding in his chest as he watches the process continue. He hates anything associated with an exam or hospital.

"Relax. I can tell this is not comfortable, but we'll get to the bottom of it." He moves the stethoscope to Chris's back.

"Deep breaths."

Chris complies.

The doctor rolls a sleeve of elastic around Chris's arm to check his blood pressure. "What's your line of work, Chris?" The doctor pumps air into the elastic band, and it starts to expand and tighten around the arm. Chris suppresses the urge to swing a left hook to the man's chin and quickly lets the emotion pass. "I'm a detective."

"Right, I knew that. A lot of stress in your work, I'm sure." Dr. Wynn's standard quote when Chris tells him he is a cop.

"You could say that with a great deal of truth." Chris's standard response to the doctor's ignorance on what he did for a living.

"I don't see any changes since we last met. Probably something to do with your job. To make sure, we'll run an EKG now and then line you up with a dye and stress test next week." He makes a few notes, and Chris moves to another room for the EKG.

◆

Chris walks out of the office somewhat relieved the priest was probably wrong. Now he can move Joanna back from thinking she is married to one of the Living Dead every time he drives off to work.

He turns his cell back on and sees he has received two messages.

One is from Jessie, explaining she is at JFK Hospital, and Emrik has been admitted. The second one is from Emrik's mother, confirming the situation. Chris drives fast to JFK.

When he arrives, he sees Jessie, Eva, and Randy in the waiting room and is hoping Emrik is not in serious condition. He exchanges a hug with Eva.

"So, how is Emrik?" Chris asks before letting Eva go from his embrace.

"He returned to the house around midnight, hungry and filthy, but he seemed okay. Made him something to eat. He took a shower. Of course, I was so happy and relieved. I couldn't stop hugging him. I called Randy, and by the time he came over, I noticed Emrik seemed lethargic. Then he threw up. We brought him to the Emergency Room. We've heard nothing since then."

"Tell Detective Dale what else Emrik did," Randy urges.

Eva's head lowers, and she sits silent.

Randy turns to Chris. "Emrik used a key we hide outside to gain entrance. He went into my father's room and retrieved a pistol. When Eva approached, he raised it and pulled the trigger."

"It wasn't loaded." Eva adds with emphases.

"That's not the point," Randy declares. "If it was loaded, you would be dead."

Chris rolls his eyes. "Could be pure shock from the ordeal … not realizing where he's at … simply trying to protect himself. I

170

wouldn't put too much into it. The main thing is he's back."

"You're right. But it was a total surprise when Eva told me," Randy adds.

"Did he talk about the experience at all ... where he went, what happened?"

"No, I didn't want to press him until he was ready. This is all so overpowering," Eva says softly.

"Can't even imagine what you are going through." Jessie hugs her.

"He's a tough young man, raised the right way by you and his grandfather. He'll get through this," Chris assures.

Chris's cell rings. Rabold is on the other end. Chris takes a few steps outside the waiting room.

"Hey, Bobby."

"Tony Joseph is following our guy. Fleck went downtown to see a Madam Faith Hendrix this morning."

"What the hell is that, a whorehouse?" Chris asks, no longer surprised by anything surrounding this case.

"She does a fortune-telling thing. Maybe he needs direction from beyond the grave?"

"He's going to be speaking from the grave instead of receiving instructions when we get through with this. Listen, Emrik showed at his home last night but ended up going to JFK. I'll call you back shortly. We'll pay the Madam a visit."

"What's his condition?"

"Don't know yet. I'll keep you in the loop."

Dr. William Fortner enters the waiting room. "Mrs. Czapleski?"

Eva and the group rise at one time. "Yes, I'm Eva Czapleski."

"I'm Doctor Fortner. Your son is in stable condition, but I have real concerns. Where has he been the last few days?"

Chris steps forward. "I'm Detective Dale. Emrik was kidnapped a couple nights ago. He returned home on his own accord late last night. We don't have a clue where he was taken."

"Look, we have run every test accessible to the hospital. All the tests turned out negative, but he's still a very sick young man. I have a theory," Dr. Fortner says, hesitating.

"What's your theory?" Eva asks.

"I went through my internship in the Navy and worked at Walter Reed for several years. We had cases on several occasions with radiation poisoning. I believe he's been exposed to a nuclear power source."

Eva starts crying, and Jessie holds her tight.

"How do you treat this?" Randy asks.

"There's no facility within 500 miles that has the ability. My recommendation is to fly him to Walter Reed. I can make a call to a friend there. We might be able to evac him this afternoon."

"What will that cost?" Randy asks.

"Anything having to do with radiation exposure must be reported and investigated. It's national security, so it won't cost anything. However, I will warn you that the Feds will be all over anyone associated with the incident."

"That's a small price to pay for Emrik's health," Chris says. "What do you say, Eva?"

She stands. "Yes … absolutely, let's do this. May we see him?"

"Afraid not. If it's radiation, you could be exposed, too. I already have limited my staff's participation. I will be the only one prepping him for evac."

"Thank you, Dr. Fortner." Eva is scared but has faith in the doctor's knowledge.

"I will stay in contact after he arrives at Walter Reed. You will be able to fly and see him at some point." He turns and leaves.

"You can't be in better medical hands, Eva," Chris says. "Jessie, can we talk a minute?"

They move out of the waiting room.

"Another strange turn in the road," Jessie remarks.

"I feel like the guy that shits his pants then changes his shirt. Fleck has agreed to work with us. We'll make sure he keeps his word. We have a report on Kidd and Stephens from the FBI. I'll forward it to you. Gotta go." He turns to walk away.

"Chris," she says as he turns back to her. "Be careful."

Chris smiles. "You too. We are both waist-deep in the Twilight Zone."

The elevator is slow to respond. Chris texts Rabold on the revelation that Emrik is being flown to Walter Reed for radiation exposure.

◆

Detective Dale suddenly has a myriad of thoughts jumping sideways, bringing him all kinds of conclusions by the time he arrives at the station. He sits at his desk and reviews a number of phone messages when Rabold rounds the corner with an envelope in his hand.

He throws it on Chris's desk, and money falls out.

"Hopefully someone has come to their right mind and is willing to bribe a deserving cop," he jokes, pulling the money out and counting it. "Nine hundred and twenty ... it's a start."

"I told a few of the guys about Emrik's situation. Give that to his mother. She'll need it going to D.C. to be with the kid." He smiles.

"Actually, that's a bit humbling. Thanks for the thought. She's a good woman and can really use the cash." Chris takes two hundred from his wallet and adds it to the pile. "Let's go get our fortunes told."

◆

Madam Faith Hendrix's healing shop is off the beaten path in a poor New Orleans neighborhood. An impromptu soccer game is being kicked around on the street in this mostly residential area.

Chris pulls up and parks. The game stops, and all eyes watch the two cops approach the front door, painted rather loosely with advertising promoting the opportunity to see your life's future path.

Rabold knocks on the door, and a tall black man opens it.

"Yes, may I help you?" the man asks in broken English.

"New Orleans PD." Chris flashes his badge. "Need to see Madam Faith Hendrix."

"Come in. She will be with you in a few minutes." The man retreats into a small storefront with Chris and Rabold following behind.

The strong smell of herbs and spices takes residence in the cops' noses. The walls are lined with jars and cans, marked in English and another language neither can recognize. Some show the visible outline of dead frogs, crawfish, and baby gators floating in a solution formulated maybe hundreds of years ago.

Rabold turns to Chris and whispers, "Spooky."

Chris grins. His thought had landed on the same word walking in. A corner is filled with various potions guaranteed to promote love, sex, death, and other human destinies and emotions. Chris reads the options and shakes his head at the segment of humanity believing in this nonsensical pile of garbage and paying the asking price to change their own fate or someone else's.

A large woman with silver hair in her mid-seventies pushes aside the beaded entrance to a back room and enters the store.

"I'm Madam Hendrix."

"Detective Dale. This is my partner, Detective Rabold. Is there someplace we can talk?"

The Madam turns and walks back through the beaded entrance, followed by Chris and Rabold pushing away the strings of beads.

She mounts a small, elevated stage with a throne-like chair and sits down. Below the throne are several chairs looking up to the Madam.

Chris imagines a similar scene at the Vatican for the Pope.

"We're investigating the murder of two people, and for some strange reason all paths seem to be leading to you." He hands the Madam a photo of Stephens and Kidd. "Know either of these people?"

She peruses the photo for a few seconds. "No, never seen them before."

Rabold takes the picture back. "We have you on audiotape talking to Louis Fleck about the devil-woman in this photo. Want to change your story?" A fabrication Chris loves hearing from his partner's mouth.

The Madam's demeanor shows sign of discomfit, and Chris senses an opening.

"Mr. Fleck has used my services in the past, but I don't have knowledge about any murders."

"What kind of services?" Chris asks.

"I sell all types of potions for better love, sex..." She hesitates.

"Be specific. What did you sell Fleck?"

The Madam stares at the floor, and the room is filled with silence.

After a good twenty-five seconds, Chris jumps up, pulls the handcuffs off his belt and approaches the throne. "You're going downtown with us. Turn around."

The Madam pulls back in her seat, totally intimidated.

"No ... please, can't go to jail."

"I don't give a damn about the potion you sell guys to rub on their dicks to get an erection. What did you sell Fleck?"

"A Hell Raising," she blurts out.

"What is a Hell Raising?" Rabold asks.

"You call up a demon. The demon scares the target into changing their ways. But that was years ago. I haven't seen Mr. Fleck in thirty years, until this morning."

"Who was the target years ago?" Chris eases off the emotional push and sits back down, putting the cuffs away.

Madam Hendrix walks to a bookcase stacked with tall leather-bound books. She pulls one off the shelf and starts thumbing through the pages.

"A Mr. Reed Stephens." She looks at Chris to gain his approval.

"What year did you pull this so-called demon up?"

174

"Nineteeneighty-eight," she meekly replies, beginning to appear exhausted from the questioning.

"Are you sure this hired devil doesn't kill people?" Rabold presses.

"No! No! Never! The Devil shows the target the error of their ways … brings them to their senses."

"What does it cost to hire you and the Devil?" Chris asks.

"Ten thousand."

"You could hire a real hitman for that," Rabold adds.

"That's not the intent. You are putting words in my mouth—I swear." Madam Hendrix is feeling pressured, and it makes her unsettled.

"You've been very helpful, Madam. Just don't plan on leaving town in the near future, understand?"

The detectives move back out through the beaded entrance followed by her. Walking across the store floor, Rabold turns to her.

"What does a demon look like?"

She points toward the photo shown earlier, still in his hands. He turns the photo face-up, and she puts her finger on Gayle Kidd. "The demon starts out beautiful, but that changes quickly if the subject does not comply."

◆

Chris and Rabold sit in the cruiser while the street-soccer game continues outside.

"You believing any of this shit?" Chris asks.

"The mind is a powerful tool. If you believe something can happen, it usually does. That aside, her story does put meat on the bones. We have Reed Stephens involved back in eighty-eight, and now we have not one but two Stephens in the middle of this mess."

"Can you imagine me taking this to the PA, asking him to prosecute a Hell Raising complete with devils coming out of the ground and frogs in a bottle?"

Chris starts the car and weaves his way slowly down the street through the soccer game.

Nineteen

THE COOKOUT

Trey Stephens lies against the carpeted corner of the cell in a semi-hibernating mental state. It has been four days of solitary confinement by the cartel, and he has been let out of his cage six times to deal with a growing case of dysentery. He pounds on the side of the wall to alert the guard of the impending mess if he fails to make it to the toilet in time.

"Hey! I need the bathroom," Trey screams and pounds on the wall more frantically.

No response greets his effort, giving him the confidence to push against the small door exit. To his surprise, the door swings open, and a quick survey of the room reveals his guard's absence.

His first thought is not of escape; he is sure the guard is probably outside smoking a cigarette and would smash his head if it appeared he was making an attempt.

A dash to the bathroom avoids disaster. Trey washes his hands and face then leans on the sink, taking a deep breath of air that is substantially cleaner than what he has grown accustomed to in the cage. A lift of his shirt reveals bed sores in various stages of spread from the cramped confines and unsanitary conditions.

Trey realizes that no matter how bad his condition is, Gayle is probably dealing with more physical and mental abuse simply from being a woman—much more. This brief touch of freedom is sweet, and he makes an internal promise that he will never take anything in life for granted if freedom is ever laid at his feet again.

The extended guard absence seems odd to Trey, coming out of the bathroom. His name is Oscar, and he had introduced himself unexpectedly two days earlier when he let Trey out of the cage to abate the diarrhea. Trey acknowledged his name and tried to shake his hand. Oscar refused the hand contact but did smile at the gesture. Then he rambled in Spanish in what seemed like a nice mood, something missing since the ordeal began. After their introduction, Oscar stopped the harassing music being played constantly next to the cage, and he changed Trey's water more frequently.

Inspired by Oscar's disappearance, Trey moves toward the closed door, the single exit point from the room. He places his ear against the cracked paint and listens. The only sign of life is a large fly walking south on the door's edge probably looking for a horse that smelled better than Trey. He realizes this is a crossroads moment if he goes into other parts of the house and is discovered. There could be hell to pay. His life could become a lot more desperate for this reckless exploration.

Then the "screw it"' thought rears its ugly head. Trey opens the door leading into a living room absent of humans or furniture. Without hesitation, he heads to a small framed window spewing sunlight across the floor to gain a view of the outside world he had left behind days ago.

Oscar is talking to a well-dressed man standing beside a Lexus.

Trey guesses this must be the boss, coming to see his latest cash cows being treated worse than real cows. The two are exchanging heated words. At one point, Oscar points to the barn housing Gayle. He becomes more animated, hands flying in all directions and stomping his foot in total disrespect to something Trey could only imagine.

◆

The man driving the Lexus is Julio Varela, the man who had placed the first call to Trey's grandfather outlining the ransom demands.

Varela walks away from Oscar and calls Michael Ortiz.

"Michael, we have real problems at the ranch."

"What the hell? You deal with it," Ortiz says. "I'm doing a bunch of gardening at my house."

Ortiz watches a small CAT bulldozer crawling into the ground six blocks from the U.S.–Mexican border, excavating an expansive tunnel maze for smuggling dope and immigrants into the United States.

"No, you don't understand," Varela says. "We had a crew of six working on the project. One is left. Five ran off, scared shitless!"

"Then shut the project down and take our losses. Bury all the participants."

"It's not that simple. You need to come here and fast."

Varela knows Ortiz respects him and hopes he will do as requested.

"Very well. I will be there shortly."

Ortiz moves from the warehouse complex to several parked SUVs out front. He addresses the five associates standing there.

"We're taking a trip to the farm to check the latest Americans in custody." He turns to one of the men.

"When we get five miles out, your car will go in first to make sure it's safe for my arrival. Something's not making sense. Let's move!"

Ortiz and the others pile into two SUVs and pull away.

Varela returns to Oscar.

"Get the American out. Bring him here." Varela retrieves a Halloween mask from the car and places it on his face.

When Trey sees Oscar turning and heading to the house, he runs to the bedroom and climbs back into the cage. Soon thereafter, Oscar opens the door and waves him out with a pistol. Following directions, Trey is at the height of fear, not knowing if things have gone bad and he is about to be shot. When he sees the mask on Varela's face, he breathes an air of relief.

"Mr. Stephens, we have contacted your grandfather. He wants to make sure you're alive. If you want to stay that way, say exactly as directed during this next call. What do you call your grandmother?"

"I'm confused … not sure what you are asking," he says, as humbly as possible.

"Do you call her Grandma, Grandmother, Me-maw, or some other nickname?"

"I call her Me-maw. She raised me. I didn't want to think of her as a grandmother."

"Okay, when we make the call, you will ask your grandfather to pay the ransom or you will be killed. Right after that, you will talk about your love for your grandfather and Me-maw. Nothing else. Are we clear?"

Trey nods meekly.

Varela dials the number, and Stephens answers the phone.

"This is Reed Stephens."

Trey becomes anxious when hearing his grandfather's voice. A mental block is forming, and he tries to remember the simple instructions given only moments before.

"Mr. Stephens, I have your grandson beside me." He pushes the phone close to Trey's mouth.

"Grandfather, this is Trey … please pay the ransom or we will be killed." Trey's mind goes black, and he starts throwing up.

"What's going on with my grandson?" Stephens demands.

Varela leans the phone close to Trey's heaving stomach and

then pulls it close to his own mouth.

"That's your grandson puking. He's very sick and needs medical attention. The clock is ticking. Do you have the money ready to be transferred?"

"I can't pay the five million. Our companies are public and I would go to jail for embezzlement. I have five hundred thousand of my own funds. Release Trey and the girl."

"Trey says he loves you and Me-maw." Varela turns off the cell and waves Trey back to his cage.

Oscar returns a few minutes later, waiting on additional orders.

"Let's go talk to the girl." Varela directs.

Oscar walks to the front of the barn entrance and watches Varela open the barn door. He is shaking in a bubble of fear, realizing this kidnapping is falling apart and only the bosses will walk away in the end. The woman is evil, and even if he manages to get back home and away from the cartel, she will no doubt kill him in revenge.

Oscar nods his head confirming Varela's status as boss and follows him through the door, but immediate panic makes him turn around and exit the barn. Gayle is not in the box as expected. She stands at the back of the barn petting a goat. Two steps in, Varela realizes her freedom and turns to Oscar only to see the door closed behind him. He warily approaches Gayle. She fails to acknowledge him by looking up.

"Ms. Kidd, you need to move inside the cage before something bad happens. My men don't get much contact with a woman. They can be uncivilized."

"Am I supposed to look at you as a civilized person, standing there with a Halloween mask wrapped around your face?" Gayle continues to pet the goat while speaking perfect Spanish.

"I will have you forced back into the lockup, with bruises on your body to show for it," Varela says in Spanish.

"No you won't," Gayle says in English. "Unless you are willing to die today."

Varela does not enforce the rules within the cartel ranks. He will leave Gayle's fate to Ortiz. Considering Ortiz's current state of mind, he might kill the Americans out of spite and make Varela still pursue the ransom money with nothing left to solidify the negotiations. Varela returns to the car and addresses his emails, caring less about the fate of those on the farm beyond his own.

◆

Ortiz's lead SUV drives onto the ranch. Three heavily armed men exit and canvass the property, finding nothing out of the ordinary.

They relay the clearance code to Ortiz, who soon arrives to make quick work of the insubordination and thus return sanity and profitability to the ranch.

Varela greets his boss with a weak smile.

"What's the problem around here? Why am I not a million dollars richer off the back of these Gringos?" Ortiz points his hands to the sky, exaggerating his frustration and being overly dramatic in front of his men.

Everyone laughs at Ortiz's ongoing attempts at making a joke, their lives literally depending on how genuine their expression of laughter is. Varela understands well, the broad smile and bravado will flip into pure rage faster than his .40-caliber pistol ejects the shell casing after being fired into a man's head.

Ortiz puts his arm around Varela's shoulder. "So tell me, how close are we to collecting my ransom?"

"The guy has followed instructions to a tee. No issues whatsoever. We made the second call today. His grandfather made a counter-offer of five hundred thousand for their return."

"Then tell the old man we'll settle for seven-fifty. We'll call it a good day. Let's take a vote." Ortiz raises his hand, and all the men instantly raise theirs in unison. "See, Julio? This is how you run a business."

"The woman is another story," Varela says. "Oscar tells me she called a devil from the sky. The night came alive with the sun and badly burned several of the men. They all fled the farm."

Oscar watches and listens to the story being told about his experience with Gayle from inside the house. The fear of Ortiz runs deep into his soul, and rightly so. He has witnessed the execution of many men by Ortiz's hand, and Oscar buried their bodies behind the house in deep graves he singlehandedly dug in the tough, unforgiving ground.

Ortiz tilts his head to one side. "Burned, huh? Where is Oscar?"

Oscar's throat tightens, and his lips instantly dry his speech.

Varela takes a couple of steps toward the house. "Oscar, come out."

As Oscar opens the door, he silently prays for God to protect his family from harm.

Ortiz frowns watching Oscar emerge from the house, and Oscar sees it as the kiss of death.

Ortiz grabs Oscar around the shoulder and stares at his face and arms, like a veterinarian examining a barnyard animal for injuries. Oscar has second-degree burns over much of his upper body and face, giving credence to the story Varela has told.

Ortiz backs away from Oscar, points to him standing under the fading light, and shakes his head up and down.

"Look at this man. He has no fear. All he has is loyalty to me. I want the names of the other men that ran away. We'll hunt them down and kill their families. Come here, Oscar." Ortiz beckons, and Oscar obeys. He takes a hundred-dollar bill from his pocket and hands it to Oscar.

"You did well. Ortiz never forgets loyalty. Now, where is this diabla?"

Varela points to the barn, and the group starts walking to the rundown structure.

"This woman is about to pull a long train tonight." Ortiz and his men laugh at the threat to Gayle, and the noise echoes off the barn wall.

Oscar is feeling ten feet tall in connection with his newfound fame, but as he approaches the barn that feeling is replaced by fear. He knows not even Ortiz can save them.

Varela shoves open the barn door, and the small horde enters a dimly lit dirt floor. There is no sign of Gayle.

Oscar pulls a flashlight from his pants, goes to the cage, and opens the small entrance, but the cell is empty. The focused light covers the backside of the barn, and only a few chickens and a goat meet their view. The light is moved skyward, and they can see Gayle sitting on the edge of the loft, feet dangling back and forth in space.

"My darling, come down. Let's talk and get acquainted," Ortiz says, turning the charm on.

"I've been waiting on you to arrive. Now the fun can begin," Gayle responds, smugly.

"I cannot help but admire that much spunk." He waves two of his men to bring her from the perch.

The first man reaches the loft ladder and places his foot on the second rung. It breaks under his weight. The next seven rungs on the ladder disintegrate, nails popping from the sixty-year-old wood.

Suddenly, an intense beam of light blows a hole in the roof and spotlights the gang below. Each man instantly looks at the light and desperately tries to protect his eyes from the rapidly expanding pressure in his head. Ortiz and the rest fall hard on the dirt floor and writhe in agony, like a group of cockroaches sprayed with Raid.

182

Gayle slides down a rope hanging from the loft and, for a moment, watches them struggle. She lingers while Ortiz's body decomposes into a pile of ashes.

The goat gently moves to her side, and Gayle exits the barn, leading it out of harm's way. Then the entire barn bursts into flames as she approaches the house.

Trey sits up in the cage, hearing the door to his room open.

"Trey, are you alright?"

Trey has not heard his name in days from Gayle's smooth voice, and he cannot comprehend how to assess its meaning. The small door opens, and Gayle's face meets Trey's gaze. But he thinks it is a cruel dream.

"Trey, come out. We can leave," She realizes he is stunned seeing her smile. "I love you, come with me."

Trey crawls through the hole and meets a hug from Gayle.

"What about the guards?" he asks, looking at the open door to the living room.

"It's okay. They left." She tries to give him the confidence to leave the house.

They find the key fob for the second SUV lying in the cupholder in the console. Gayle moves behind the wheel, but Trey stands beside the open passenger door watching the barn collapse under the weight of the blaze.

"Trey, jump in. The fire might attract attention. We have to get on the road."

"What the hell happened?" he asks, sliding into the vehicle and turning to meet her stare.

"It's a long story. Oscar befriended me. He stopped the others from molesting me after the first day. Not sure I would be alive if he didn't step in and take charge of their disgusting behavior.

He gave me his pistol and left the farm, afraid what the boss would do for stopping the ongoing rape."

Trey looks back one last time, and the old barn has fallen flat back to the Earth, causing the high flames to subside. His hand moves across the dark cab and finds her hand.

"Thanks." he says in a low voice.

The SUV hits a bump and rises sharply on the winding road then settles into following the contour in a calm manner. A rabbit runs parallel to the beam of the headlights, and crosses the road just ahead.

"For what?" Gayle squeezes his hand.

"Saving my life. I don't think my grandfather would ever pay a nickel to ransom us out." He firmly believes this to be true.

"It doesn't matter now. We're headed home," Gayle assures.

"I'm so sorry. This is all my fault. We should have never come to Mexico to begin with. Please forgive me." His head shakes at his own decision-making and self-interest.

"Nonsense," Gayle says, stopping the SUV. "I wanted to come the moment you mentioned the trip. We're the victims. This experience will only make us closer."

She leans to him and kisses him passionately.

The SUV is put in gear, and the night and dust pass under its wheels.

"Can't wait to take a shower and touch you," Trey says. He has no clue how Gayle saved his ass. It only reaffirms what a complete woman she is.

"That thought helped me live hour-to-hour," Gayle says, visibly smiling in the dashboard light. Trey leans back in the seat, physically and emotionally spent.

Twenty

THE SHADOW CREEPS

Israel Hamric is frustrated with his employer, Louis Fleck. It is against all protocol to contact the person who hires you to kill a target, even if he has a secondary target next on the list. As the professional, Hamric is supposed to wait on subsequent instructions. This rule is not a time-honored tradition, generated decades ago by the Murder for Hire union. No. Electronic surveillance by the Feds is so sophisticated that any communication now engenders extended risk.

Hamric changes the burner phone weekly and posts the new number on a dark website. The number is scrambled in sequence, and the employer has the code breaker. Fleck is well versed in how to call him, but so far has not.

The lack of direction is not a complete negative, however. Hamric has been paid in full for two jobs. Worst case, he leaves town for another hire and owes Fleck a target to be named later. If Hamric is completely honest, the lack of contact has more to do with another round of sex than taking care of the second target. Patience has always been a stable weapon in his makeup when tracking a target, but his thirst for sex lacks the same characteristic.

This planning gap for Hamric's schedule has pushed a desire to clean up the potential exposure James McGowan represents.

Hamric arrives at McGowan's house shortly before 11:15 a.m. and circles the block, soliciting any movement at his home. The carport is absent a vehicle, and Hamric moves away from the house to avoid suspicion. Parking a strange vehicle in a neighborhood for any length of time is asking for trouble.

Hamric drives toward downtown to eat and pass the time until dark, when McGowan will probably be home. This enables him to take the final step, covering his trail while in Louisiana.

The cell rings, and he answers. "Yes?" Fleck is on the call.

"Sorry for the late response. Our friend has been out of town and unavailable." Fleck, even using throwaway phones, never talks specifics.

"My vacation is about over. Ready to come back to work,"

Hamric answers.

"Can you meet at my office at three tomorrow to discuss your return?"

"That fits my schedule perfectly. See you then." Hamric places the cell in a cupholder and pulls into Duffey's parking lot.

The wings had grabbed his attention when having lunch with McGowan, and now he wants a reboot. A grin graces his face when he enters the restaurant, thinking about the good food he has discovered there. But that smile slides away quickly when he rounds the corner heading to the restroom, and sitting in a booth with two other men is James McGowan.

McGowan waves to gain Hamric's attention. It wasn't necessary. "Jimmy, what the hell? Have a seat."

He does as requested and offers his hand to the new faces that have suddenly placed a major stumbling block in his plans.

"I'm Israel. How did you guys get stuck for lunch with James?" he jokes, sliding next to McGowan.

"I'm Danny," one of the men responds. "This is Seth." They both shake hands with him.

"You must go way back with James. He never buys lunch," Seth comments.

"He says his name is Israel," McGowan says, "but he'll always be Jimmy to me—we fought together in Afghanistan," he adds, proudly.

"Thanks for your service. Man, that was, and still is, a brutal war." Danny offers his hand a second time.

"Thought you would be back in New York by now." McGowan looks at him and props his hand under his chin inquisitively.

"Actually, I wanted to see you again. A friend of mine in New York has received a patent for the ride-share industry, and I'm going to invest in it. Thought you might want to do the same. We'll talk later. I don't want to bore your friends."

Seth speaks. "I would like to hear about the patent."

"Yeah, don't keep it to yourself," Danny adds.

"Okay, there's a big issue going on with Uber and LYFT. Women are jumping into the wrong vehicles and getting mugged, raped, and even killed."

Seth interrupts. "I read in The Wall Street Journal where Uber paid out more than two hundred million last year in lawsuits. This is a big issue."

McGowan jumps in. "A woman in New Orleans was picked up by a guy saying he worked for Uber in a bar—he killed her."

Hamric resumes. "My buddy invented a screen mounted

on the passenger side of a vehicle. The screen flashes out the rider's name and customer's confirm number. It can be seen fifty feet away from the car. Even a drunk can make the right decision about jumping into the back seat or not."

"That would help customers identify their Uber ride in crowded places like airports or sporting events," Seth adds.

"Exactly." Hamric shakes his head in agreement. "I'm buying into the company. Thought it might be the right move for you, James."

McGowan nods his head in confirmation. "I want in. Will he take ten thousand? I don't have a ton to invest."

"Me, too," Seth adds.

"You can get a lot more than ten thousand out of Seth. He's loaded," McGowan concedes.

"Not my company, but I've known the guy since high school. Let me see what he would take for an investment." Hamric is relieved he can give McGowan a sound reason for suddenly returning to Monroe and looking for him.

Seth hands Hamric a business card identifying him as an attorney. "Please forward the prospectus. I have a real interest, and several in my firm would, too."

"Let's order some of those hot wings and beer," Hamric says. "Maybe we can get James to buy lunch."

"Maybe," McGowan adds with a wink.

Hamric leaves Monroe a second time without tidying up a perceived problem. There would be no third time.

◆

Hamric parks in front of the casino a few minutes before 3:00 and calls Louis Fleck.

"Parked in front," he announces.

Fleck grabs his file and joins him in the vehicle.

Detective Tony Joseph spots Fleck getting into Hamric's SUV and retrieves field glasses. He quickly writes down the tag number, vehicle color, and make. Joseph presses the binoculars closer to his eyes and adjusts the distance vision. The driver of the SUV cannot be seen well, but he finds it interesting the man is in the backseat, while Fleck sits in the front on the passenger side.

Fleck hands the file to Hamric and stares straight ahead. "The woman's name is Gayle Kidd. The man's name is Reed Stephens the Third. I don't have an address for her, but Stephens' address is listed, and where he is, she will be close by. The target is the woman. I prefer to keep Stephens upright, if possible. We do a lot of business with his company and don't want to jeopardize that opportunity."

"Not an issue. Will handle her. Anything else?"

"The two are in Mexico now but should be coming back tomorrow, according to Stephens' grandfather. A Mexican cartel kidnapped them and they've just been released. The Feds are involved … all over Stephens' home for a few days." Fleck knows if he does not paint the full picture for his hired gun, he would soon be lying in a box at his brother-in-law's funeral home.

"I'll let the scene cool before taking on the target. I need a few days of recon anyway. I'm staying at the same hotel. Send over a woman tonight at nine."

"A different woman?" Fleck asks.

"Loved Mercedes, but you can surprise me."

Fleck opens the door of the vehicle and retreats to the casino as Hamric drives away. Joseph grabs his handset and calls dispatch.

"Dispatch." A man's voice answers.

"This is Detective Joseph, Badge forty-one seventy-two. Got a New York tag to run. 'W' as in Wayne, 'T' as in Tom, six-one-four, 'Z' as in zebra, four-seven."

"Got it … hold please."

"Sure." Joseph is not expecting much on the tag but thinks it is worth a shot.

"Registered to a Rainman Corporation in Delaware. No outstanding warrants or traffic infractions."

"Thanks for the help." Joseph sets the radio on the seat, thinking about a company New York tag conveniently appearing in a meeting with Louis Fleck. He makes a few more notes and sits back, waiting for Fleck to show his face again.

◆

Mercedes does her last routine on the stage at 6:15 and collects her tips before changing into street clothes. Like all strippers, she hates working the afternoon shift, dancing in front of frat boys with flat wallets. She leaves the casino expecting a better night, physically and financially, when she meets Hamric at 9:00.

A short drive to a residential area, and the small apartment over a garage she calls home, has her head filled with thoughts about returning to Dallas to live with her sister. She is tired of the lifestyle and yearns to do something beside hooking and stripping. Six more months is her goal to save money, make the move away from this degrading game, and find a man to father some kids.

Mercedes drives the last block to a narrow alleyway providing a rear entrance to the apartment. A hot shower and something to eat will ready her for the night. But standing in the alleyway blocking her entry is a young woman hovering over a baby carriage and frantically waving Mercedes to stop. She gets out, anticipating something is very wrong.

The woman looks at her. "My baby isn't breathing! Can you please take me to the hospital?"

"Sure. Let me help you into the car." She moves to the carriage to help with the child, but no baby stares back at her.

Mercedes turns to run the alley and escape the setup. Immediately, a long blade plunges into the middle of her back. The trunk of her car is opened, and she is rudely thrown into the darkness. The carriage is pushed to the side of the alley, and her car is parked next to the garage.

The make-believe mother goes into the apartment, takes a shower and dresses in one of Mercedes' many outfits. Makeup is meticulously applied, and the mirror reflects a beautiful woman filled with darkness and evil.

◆

Hamric sits on the edge of the bed watching the Knicks being kicked in the head by the hated Celtics. A firm knock on the door distracts the bloodletting momentarily. He reaches for his watch sitting next to the hotel phone, and it reads 8:20. He likes a woman who respects his time and comes early. A closed left eye allows the right one to view through the door's peephole and frame a tall, well-built woman wearing a Lone Ranger mask.

Hamric instantly loves the look of the sexy lady standing in front of him dressed to mystify. "Come in. Let's have some fun."

"I intend to." The masked lady with the stunning figure walks in, carrying Mercedes' bag of sex toys.

Hamric shuts the door and retreats to the edge of the bed. "Love the mask ... adds to the intrigue."

"That's not all you're going to love," The woman lifts her dress and pulls a joint from a garter belt. "Mind if I smoke?"

"Only if you share." He lights the joint for her, the woman takes a pull, and hands it back to him.

"What's your name, mysterious one?" he asks, as he inhales deeply.

"Whatever the hell you want it to be. A more important question is, how do you like your sex? Hot and sticky or fast and furious?" The woman slides out of the dress and stands next to him totally nude.

Hamric takes one more drag off the joint, his eyes painting up and down this portrait of a perfect body standing before him. He puts his hands around her waist and moves her body toward his face.

"All of the above," he answers.

◆

Hamric is a night owl. It is 2:00 a.m. and he is watching "Hangover" on HBO, but his mind keeps drifting back to the sex with the masked lady hours before. Damn! The woman was good at her craft, and the two moved from the bed to the dresser and back. Virtually every piece of furniture in the room had suffered action in or on it, to the point where someone started pounding on the wall to quell the noise.

It was obvious that Fleck's reputation for a stable of highly qualified women, if anything, was understated. Then a knock on the door created an optimistic thought of round two in the immediate future.

Hamric gladly jumps to greet the masked lady. Instead, two uniformed cops meet his portal view through the door. This does not push him into a panic mode. It is not the first time cops have interrupted one of his business trips. The .40-caliber pistol used on the mobsters was dumped, and the .22 used in Monroe could not be traced when the bodies were cremated.

He opens the door. The two uniformed officers and Detective Tony Joseph, flashing his badge, pour in.

"Israel Hamric, I'm Detective Joseph. Mind if we take a look around?"

"Unless you have a warrant, get the hell out." He tries to shut the door, but Joseph puts his shoe against the base.

"Just so happens we have one of those." He hands him a warrant, while the officers start turning his room inside-out.

One of the officers comes out of the bathroom and whispers in Joseph's ear. The two return to the bathroom and, tucked under the sink and hidden by several rolls of toilet paper, is a blood-stained knife.

"Don't touch it. Cuff him and read him his rights," Joseph directs one of the uniforms. "And put your damn body cam on when you read the rights."

He walks into the hallway and makes a cell call. "Get CSI down to the Marriott. We need to impound two vehicles. Have a body in one."

Tony walks back into the room as Hamric is being cuffed.

"What the hell are you talking about? What murder?" he demands.

"Mercedes West. Officer, help Mr. Hamric put his clothes on before taking him in."

◆

Chris Dale's back and shoulder have been bothering him since he dropped the Voice to his knees at the casino. He makes a stiff walk to the bathroom and retrieves a bottle of ibuprofen from the medicine cabinet. He washes down three tablets with faucet water, and he heads back to bed, deep in thought about golf in Florida after retiring.

At a distance, Chris sees the phone screen on the nightstand light up, announcing an incoming text. Usually a dead body is attached to any text received at 3:00 a.m. He slowly walks to the kitchen, turns on the light, and gains access to his glasses sitting next to the computer.

Bobby Rabold has already acknowledged his receipt to Detective Joseph about the arrest of Israel Hamric and the body of Mercedes West in the trunk of her car at the Marriott. Chris simply returns the text to Joseph: "Got it. Be in shortly."

A second text comes from Rabold, and they decide to meet at the jail at 5:00 a.m. He writes a short love note to Joanna and jumps in the shower, not to wash clean but to pour hot water on the shoulder and back.

◆

By the time Chris arrives at the jail, the ibuprofen has kicked in, and his step has an artificial and temporary flight of energy. This newfound spark has not altered the rusting mental state of late-night job requirements.

Sitting on the other side of the oneway glass is Jimmy Israel Hamric, sharing a pissed-off attitude with Chris Dale.

"So, who the hell is this Hamric character that yanked my ass out of bed at four in the morning?" Chris asks.

Rabold examines a file and responds. "We received a tip that a body could be found in a vehicle at the Marriott and that Hamric is the one that stabbed her. Joseph found the body of Mercedes West in the vehicle and a bloody knife in Hamric's room."

"How utterly convenient. So, who is trying to set this guy up?" Chris takes a sip of coffee and looks at Hamric through the glass.

"Hamric met with Louis Fleck yesterday afternoon in front of the casino. Tony Joseph ran his plates. A New York guy that just happens to have a file on Reed Stephens and Gayle Kidd in his SUV. The guy is a hired gun ... has all kind of weapons in his vehicle."

"Well, our Mr. Fleck was using his forty-eight hours wisely. Hard to kill two people kidnapped by the cartel in Mexico."

"Called the FBI," Rabold continues. "Kidd and Stephens are due back today. This dead Mercedes West we found is a stripper for Fleck. Hamric may have killed her." He shrugs.

"If this guy is a professional, he doesn't kill for sport. Too bright for that. Who would pay for a stripper to be killed. Fleck? No way in hell he kills off a revenue stream. None of the pieces fit together."

Chris stands up. "Let's go receive the cold shoulder from Mr. Professional Hit Man."

They walk into the interview room, and a stoic Hamric meets their introductions with an air of indifference.

"Mr. Hamric ... what name do you go by? Jim? Israel?" Rabold asks.

"Israel is fine." Hamric leans back in the chair against the wall.

"So, you're out of New York. What brings you to New Orleans?" Chris asks.

"Visiting an Army buddy."

"What's his name?" Rabold inquires.

"That's not important," he replies. "I want an attorney. We all understand how the game is played."

Chris stands. "Give Louis Fleck a call, I'm sure he'll come running with an attorney. But watch your back in jail, Fleck's reach is far and wide around here."

He and Rabold start to leave, approaching the door.

Hamric stops them. "Someone framed me with this girl's murder. I don't have a clue who or why."

Chris turns. "What's your relationship with Fleck?"

"I was told he had world-class women for the right price. This Mercedes chick came over to my room several days ago. We had

194

sex. I haven't seen her since last Thursday. I'm a business guy. Call my buddy, James McGowan in Monroe. I spent a few days with him about a stock buy in New York."

Chris and Rabold return to their seats.

"The guy in the next hotel room says you were bouncing off the walls last night. That had nothing to do with Mercedes?" Rabold asks, pressing the issue.

"No, Fleck sent me another chick last night, a mystery woman. She wore a mask. We had rough sex, but she walked out of the room around nine-thirty."

"How did the bloody knife end up in your bathroom?" Rabold asks, leaning forward.

"The masked woman must've planted it. Why would I kill Mercedes, put the body in her own car next to the hotel, and leave the weapon in my bathroom? No one is that dumb, no one."

"Why are you carrying so many weapons?" Chris asks.

"It's more than a hobby. I have a license to sell wholesale firearms. Go find my wallet, check out my license to carry and permit to sell."

"We'll do that. And we'll try to get you transferred to the county jail. It's safer than the city lockup." Once again, they get up and start to leave.

"One last question. What's your relationship with Reed Stephens and Gayle Kidd?" Rabold asks.

"I have connections in New York that have international reach. Louis Fleck ask me to help free them from the kidnapping in Mexico."

The two detectives leave the interview room.

"You get the feeling our buddy, Israel, starts with a small fiber of truth and weaves the perfect response?" Chris asks.

"Oh, he's good. Damn quick on his feet. Some of his shit could check out, but not sure which ends in the truth or the toilet column."

"It would be ironic if he was a hired professional charged with a murder he didn't do. This is a setup, pure and simple. Have you ever seen an anonymous tip with a more perfect sequencing?"

"No, tips like that tend to be vague," Rabold answers. "Maybe name-dropping or change of behavior that triggers suspicion. The tipster knew too much detail. Whoever called it in killed the girl."

"Let's assume Hamric is a hired killer. Now that he's in jail, that should really pucker Fleck's ass tight. His forty-eight hours are up. Let's go pound him for more answers." They head to the

Fleck's residence to push him out of bed.

◆

Mrs. Fleck stands in the kitchen with a glass of apple juice, watching the squirrels run the sides of a giant oak tree in the front yard. A black squirrel soon makes an appearance, and she has named it Boston Blackie, after the old TV series. All of the squirrels scamper toward the tree's top when Chris and Rabold approach the front porch.

"Louis, are you expecting someone this morning?" Mrs. Fleck takes several steps to a glass-enclosed back porch where her husband is reading the paper.

Fleck moves to the kitchen, paper in hand. "Hell no."

The doorbell rings, Fleck goes to the kitchen window and spots the unmarked car he recognizes belonging to Chris Dale. "Go upstairs and clean something," Fleck orders, and his wife obeys.

He opens the front door. "This can't wait until I get to work?"

Chris hands Fleck a bag. "We brought you a coffee and croissant. Be nice."

He walks in, and Rabold follows without an invite.

"Beautiful home, Louis. Those strippers must pay off for you," Chris comments sarcastically.

"What the hell couldn't wait for a couple of hours?"

"One of your casino young ladies, Mercedes West, bled out in the back of her car trunk last night. We arrested your hitman for killing her."

"What hitman?" Fleck demands.

"Let's go sit on your porch. The coffee is getting cold," Chris says.

Fleck is acquiring a sinking feeling in his stomach as he walks to the back porch. The cops are painting a bad picture. If any of this is true...

"We know you have met with Israel Hamric on several occasions and gave him a workup on Reed Stephens and Gayle Kidd. The guy is a professional from New York." Rabold sets the file on a table in front of Fleck.

"Hamric must have been bored last night and decided to carve open the stripper you sent over. You going to eat that croissant?" Chris asks, reaching for the bag. Fleck shakes his head, and Chris starts eating it, seemingly without a care in the world.

"You asked for forty-eight hours to provide answers. We're waiting," Chris adds, chewing on the bread.

196

"Look, I don't know much about this Hamric guy. He likes women. We provided him one on a couple occasions," A last-ditch effort to put distance between him and Hamric. "Reed Stephens hired me in the late eighties to help break up his son's romance with a black woman. I went to Madam Hendrix to buy one of her spells. Joe Bailly introduced us. Told me it would work—guaranteed. Something went wrong. Reed Stephens Junior, the black girl, Stephens' wife. All killed. I'm just a middleman in all this trying to make a buck."

"Accessory to murder could land you a manslaughter charge," Chris notes, trying to add pressure.

"Is this the so-called Hell Raising?" Rabold asks.

"Yeah," Fleck admits.

"So who killed Bailly?" Chris asks.

"I don't know. Bailly was convinced that Gayle Kidd was involved in the Hell Raising. Someone sent her to kill everyone connected to the first one. None of it makes sense to me. That's why I hired Tony Cranford—to find something out about this Kidd woman."

"Do you expect us to believe any of this shit?" Chris stands, hovering over Fleck.

Fleck looks up at him. "No, but it's the truth. That's all I have … the truth."

Twenty One

BLIND MAN'S CUFF

Jessie McGaha slows the car, eases up to a red light, and stops at the entrance to Louis Armstrong New Orleans International Airport. A reach into her purse retrieves an envelope, which she hands to Eva Czapleski.

"What's this?" Eva asks.

Jessie drives through the now green light. "Chris Dale and his cop buddies wanted to help your expenses in D.C. Several staff members at the paper added to the fund."

"I don't know what to say." Tears start to form in Eva's eyes. "Thank you. I'm overwhelmed with the generosity. What wonderful people you and Mr. Dale have been to my family!"

"Chris is a special man. Now go and take care of Emrik. Bring him back to all of us." Jessie parks in front of the Delta Airlines terminal, and the two women embrace before Eva disappears inside.

◆

Jessie drives to the Sunset Grill and takes a table with a view of the front door. The habit of watching people coming and going had started in her early days of journalism. She began trying to extract mood changes and see what the public's attitude reflected when different kinds of stories made the headlines. It was not based on anything scientific but more of a longstanding habit of reviewing facial expressions and trying to gauge happiness. A bit of jealousy always reminded her of that elusive solicitation of happiness whenever she witnessed it.

Chris, as usual, is late for their lunch. Jessie is the one waiting for him to arrive on most occasions. Maybe someone in the crowd would see her face light up in a short burst of happiness when Chris walks through the door. Probably not, because only Jessie seems to care about facial expressions.

Jessie has always prided herself on a fierce independence, especially when it comes to the men in her life. But Lieutenant Dale has her number, and she has always compared whomever she is dating to him. It did not take an excessive amount of commonsense to see how unfair it was to her male friends and, more important, to herself taking radar readings and comparing the results to a married man totally out of reach on a regular basis.

Not that Jessie has not tried to break the bond. She drifted off several times with other men to fill the Chris void. But inevitably it circled back to the cop and his never-ending mysteries to be solved. Perhaps it was the standard she loved to bear, that of loving something that could never be hers.

Chris walks through the door and, true to form, Jessie feels better. An extended stare at the menu makes Chris have to work to find her, a small win in a bigger game.

"Sorry, I'm late."

"You're always late. Nothing new."

"But worth it. We have so much breaking in this case your head will spin." Chris sees the waiter approaching. "Crown and Coke—and lime."

"Ice tea is fine, thanks." Jessie takes out a pen and pad for notes. "By the way, I dropped Eva off at the airport. She was very grateful for the help."

"I hope Emrik comes out of this alright. Those two have been through a lot."

The waiter sets the drinks on the table. "Pepperoni pizza work for you?" Chris asks.

"Sure," she nods. "So, what other pieces to the puzzle have you added?" She takes a sip of tea.

"Thanks," Chris hands the menu to the waiter and redirects his attention. "Fleck led us to a Madam Hendrix, a voodoo priestess over on Beverly. She sold old man Stephens a Hell Raising demon to stop his son from having an affair with a black woman back in the eighties. Something went wrong. Stephens the son, his wife, and the woman were all murdered."

"Perhaps something didn't go wrong. Maybe those people were supposed to die?"

"Interesting direction. You could be right. Fleck believes Bailly and Cranford were murdered by a new Hell Raising for revenge. I don't hold with any of this voodoo horseshit, but you can hire individuals to hurt other people."

"I could be a woman scorned and go see Madam Hendrix about my ex-husband and his new girlfriend. I'll need to work up more details about a revenge package."

"You are a devil of sorts." Chris offers his drink, saluting the idea.

200

"I talked to my dad about what happened to Emrik and his grandfather. It piqued his interest."

"Do tell! What's his CIA-based assessment?" He leans in closer.

"He thinks his opinion doesn't count. But a colleague involved in paranormal activities is going to be at his cabin in Arkansas this weekend to fish. Dad invited me to bend his ear. Wanna' take a couple days off and drive up?" She is hoping he will make the trip with her to give them open space to share, and running around in Arkansas would create a sense of freedom they cannot find in New Orleans. Such is the plague of having an affair.

"Sorry, no way right now. One of Fleck's strippers was murdered last night. I'm up to my ass in bodies. It would be fun, and I'd love to meet your father."

Chris does have an interest in driving away with Jessie, with the job pressure bursting his pipes. But he does not understand what she is trying to tell him.

Jessie does not allow her disappointment to reveal itself. Emotional misdirection has been an asset for years.

"Another murder close to Mr. Fleck? He seems connected to all the mishaps in this case."

"I detest who Fleck is and what he does. But I can tell when a man is scared. Fleck's backed into a corner of fear."

The waiter brings the pizza. Chris grabs a slice and offers another to Jessie. She turns it down with a halfhearted smile and looks at her watch. "Gotta' go … pressed for a deadline."

A kiss to Chris's forehead is followed by dropping two twenties on the table.

"I'll get this. Take care of your writing." Chris offers the money back, but she blows him another kiss and heads out the door.

◆

Jessie walks onto the main floor of the newspaper and sits at her desk. She opens her purse, and a shuffle through the contents produces a compact case. The tiny round mirror reflects a little tea residue on her cheek. She grabs a Kleenex from the desk and wipes it away.

"Be a big girl, Jessie James McGaha. Be a big girl." She grabs the purse again and throws the compact to the bottom.

"What did that compact do to you?" Stony Fetter, Jessie's editor, appears and sits on the edge of her desk.

"It has a mirror that says too much about myself."

"Sounds like a woman thing. You need a little conflict in life. Things are too perfect for you."

A slight smile finds Jessie's face. "My 'life' and 'perfect' together in a sentence? Where did you stumble on that?"

"You have me as a boss. The rest is infinitely small. Where's my story about the young man that flies from building to building?"

"Actually, he's at Walter Reed ... radiation poisoning. Hopefully, the story will have a happy ending. In the meantime, my piece on his kidnapping will be in Sunday's paper in two weeks. I'm waiting on the results from Walter Reed to complete it."

"This kid has gone through hell and back. What can I do to move the dialogue along? I believe it has national interest."

"I have a meeting with a person in Arkansas this weekend to confirm a couple of suspicions. I'll be gone until Monday."

"Alright, kiddo. Keep your receipts for the expenses. Report to me the moment you return." Fetter walks away.

Jessie flips up her laptop and begins writing her current Sunday column about a Louisiana swamp man who makes his living bagging giant alligators. Strictly a filler piece to buy time until she can connect the dots on the Hell Raising story and start a series laying the outline for her sixth book.

The photos of the large gators being trapped and harvested make her stomach uneasy. She loves animals but understands that in Louisiana the story will have widespread interest and probably be syndicated by the widely circulated information portals. Part of the job, she reminds herself, writing about things that make her feel uncomfortable yet still doing it well.

◆

Jessie submits the alligator story to Stony Fetter for editorial review then clears her desk and slips the computer in a case. A look around the floor reveals people she has known for years, all hurrying to make next week's deadline, a timeworn process that starts ticking the moment you complete this week's column or story. Charles Manson be damned, she thinks. This is the real Helter Skelter, and she loves the pressure. Maybe Fetter is right. Her life is not all that bad, and he is a great boss.

◆

The drive to see Madam Hendrix weaves through the poorer subdivisions of New Orleans, away from all the tourist destinations

202

maintained by city inspections. A mattress rests on the street, and Jessie drives around the mystery. How anyone could lose such a large object so haphazardly?

She parks the car. There would be no tourist finding the Madam's address easily. It is a hard concept to swallow, how the Madam could stay open working with only locals.

A knock on the screen door fails to receive a response, and Jessie mouths a less-than-strong, "Hello ... anybody here?" The wooden door is invitingly open behind the screen door, so she enters the screened-in porch, repeating the question she spoke at the entrance. Still nothing meets her solicitation, and she starts to reverse her actions and leave.

Then she hears something inside, making her turn around and enter again. A frantic cat rushes past her feet, leaving her to view and smell all of the jars of floating animals. This is what the alligator-tanning buildings must smell like.

Yet another "hello" gains no response, and now she stands in the middle of a room overpowered by the thought that Louisiana must be filled with crazy, animal-killing individuals.

The beaded doorway leading to the back room beckons, and Jessie enters. A brief moment of disbelief greets her stare, now anchored to the two dead bodies lying less than six feet from her. Stranded in time by the argument between what she sees before her, and the mental block telling the brain it is not possible, she freezes.

Jessie moves her dulled wit back into cognitive thinking and turns rapidly back to the beaded doorway. Her heart pounding, a stiletto heel trips on the wooden floor, and she falls forward. The surrounding shelving seems to come alive with motion, real or imagined, making her fight for air and sound footing all the way out to the car.

Jessie's eyes never leave the front entrance as she raises her cell to face level and finds Chris's number.

"You miss me?" A typical Chris response on speaker hits her at the wrong time.

"Chris, I'm at Madam Hendrix's place. Two bodies have been hacked to death." Her voice is hyper, and Chris reads it instantly.

"Exactly where are you now?"

"In my car out front."

"Okay, pull away and keep me on the phone. Drive to a busy parking lot."

"Leaving now." Jessie's nerves settle considerably hearing Chris take over.

"Did you see anyone else?" he asks. He understands how traumatic witnessing a murder scene for the first time can be.

"No. I thought I heard something after discovering the bodies, but it could have been my imagination when running out. This is just awful!" She pulls into a convenience store. "I'm at a 7-Eleven, about a mile away."

"Stay in your car. Let me call this in. I'll come to you in a few minutes after we clear the building." He ends the call.

Jessie sets the phone on the seat and tries undigesting the bloody vision but to no avail. A knock on the window sends her sideways toward the passenger side, grasping to retain air in her lungs. A twenty-something man holding a can of car wax tries to talk the window down for a sale's pitch. Jessie returns to the full upright of the driver's seat. Using hands and head, she frantically waves him away. The young man moves to another car being filled with gas.

Jessie finally succumbs to the seatbelt bell, ringing its warning since jumping in the car at Madam Hendrix's. After a circling look around the 7-Eleven parking lot, she slips the belt in place, and the bell stops complaining.

She retrieves the phone and calls Fetter.

"Hello?"

"I was doing some investigating on Emrik's case. I've walked into a crime scene with two bodies."

"No shit? Take any photos?" he asks excitedly.

"No. I called the cops."

"Have they arrived yet?"

"Nope." Jessie knows where this is leading.

"You're a reporter. Go take pictures before the cops can turn it upside down."

"Okay."

Against every instinct in her body, Jessie drives back to Madam Hendrix's.

◆

Jessie sets the cell to photo and snaps a couple of shots of the front of the building and then enters. A photo of a small gator stored in a jar clears her through the product room. The beads hanging from the top of the door leading to the bodies now seem to her like the Berlin Wall in its heyday. A final flash of adrenaline, and she breaches the beads to witness, a second time, the carnage on the floor.

204

Steadying her hand, a look through the viewfinder squares the bodies. More photos clicked. A kneel nurtures one more frame, until all journalistic professionalism suddenly leaves her thoughts.

The barrel of a pistol inches down to the back of her head. "Don't move or I'll blow you away." The voice is deep and determined.

Jessie's predicament confirms the ridiculousness of the advice Fetter issued from the safety of his office. It freezes her.

"Stand up. Put your hands behind your back, and walk backward toward my voice," the cop directs, and Jessie complies.

Though being handcuffed, she feels greatly relieved. "I found the bodies then called Detective Dale. He's headed this way."

"Why are you taking photos?" The cop asks, turning her around to face him.

"I'm a reporter for the Times-Picayune. It's what we do." She realizes the moment the sentence leaves her mouth it sounds like pure BS.

A second cop approaches, and the first gives direction. "Take her to the back seat of the car. We'll obtain her story after we clear this place."

◆

Jessie sits in the squad car, becoming more claustrophobic by the minute confined by the cuffs. The dripping sweat shrinks the back seat, a reminder Jessie agreed to a really stupid suggestion that turned into a really stupid action. As is his creed in life when it comes to Jessie, Chris shows up forty minutes late after her incarceration and finally sets her free.

"Why did you come back to the scene? A less-experienced cop might have shot you." Chris hands her the cell confiscated an hour before.

She rubs the tenderness settling in her wrists. "I don't know. I just want to get the hell out of here."

She gets in her car, starts the engine, shifts into reverse, and leaves Chris standing beside the squad car holding the cuffs.

Twenty Two

FLY BY NIGHT

Eva Czapleski rides the escalator to baggage claim at Washington's Reagon National Airport and sees her name printed on a board. A young man extends his hand, and she shakes it.

The man produces an ID, and Eva leans low to view. "I'm Agent Willis with Homeland Security, here to take you to Walter Reed. Let's get your luggage."

"Thank you. Do you know how my son is doing?"

"I'll leave the reporting to the physicians at the hospital. I do know the team working with Emrik is one of the best in the world."

The ride to Walter Reed is anxious and slow for Eva in thick traffic. America's monuments roll by in the distance, gaining little attention in the silence of the car.

Once at the hospital, Eva goes through extensive documentation page-by-page, enough to satisfy government processes but try anyone's patience, much less a mother not seeing her son in five days. A final signature graces the last page, and Eva passes the paperwork under a thick glass barrier to a non-smiling, head-shaved Army officer.

Eva drifts over to a vending machine and buys a cup of coffee. In the background, through a window, she sees the top of the distant Washington Monument. Agent Willis works on his phone, exchanging emails and texts to several colleagues while Eva sits nursing the small cup.

Then Willis approaches her. "Ms. Czapleski..."

"Please call me Eva."

"Eva, you are checked in at the Essex across the street. Just go to the sixth floor in the hospital. The lobby is connected by a walkway. Your luggage is in the room."

"Thank you. I intend to stay with Emrik tonight. I may go over to take a shower later."

"Well, not sure if you can actually enter his room tonight. But the doctor will be more specific shortly. We have a team that needs to meet at eight tomorrow morning for additional information, then you will be free to stay with Emrik all day. Go to the Lincoln Room in the hotel at seven-thirty. We'll have breakfast ready."

Willis extends his hand for a second time. "See you at seven-thirty."

"I'll be there." Eva watches him move away along the hallway then returns to the cold coffee.

She looks around the empty visitor's sitting room, wondering where friends or relatives of patients staying in the hospital must be. At this major military medical facility, surely she could not be the only one waiting to see a loved one.

Dr. Edmond Rivers arrives from an adjoining wing. He has been focusing on a file, reading it with each step. A wave of an ID hanging around his neck, and the double doors open to the visitor's room.

"Ms. Czapleski ... did I pronounce that right?"

"You did better than most. I'm Eva," she responds, with a slight smile.

"I'm Dr. Rivers, head of the team treating your son. Please, let's talk."

He sits next to her.

"Emrik is doing much better, but he's not out of the woods yet. He has been exposed to radioactive material, and I suspect microwave poisoning, too."

"Microwave? I don't understand."

"Like radioactive particles, microwave substances can be found naturally in the earth and enhanced through electronic devices. In larger doses, it is fatal. Emrik has been exposed, but to what degree we can only estimate."

"Is he going to be alright?" Eva asks desperately.

"I'm comfortable in saying yes, but you will need to watch him closely over the next few months and alert us if his symptoms return. What he went through would probably kill you or me. But his youth and physical fitness made a big difference."

"Can I see him?"

"He's in an induced coma for the rigorous treatment schedule. Tonight you can see him through a glass, but tomorrow he will be awake, and you can be in his room—though no closer than five feet."

Rivers stands. "In a couple of days, you can probably take him home."

"Thank you so much for what you have done to save my son. We lost my father before all this happened. I'm not sure I could handle losing Emrik, too."

208

"He's a strong young man. You should be proud." Rivers walks to the soldier sitting behind the desk and points to Eva then returns to her side.

"Corporal Gonzalez will take you back to Emrik. I'll see you tomorrow."

Eva follows the corporal through a maze of hallways and doors, each requiring a lock to be cleared. Finally, Eva can see Emrik, and she puts her hand on the glass panel separating the two. She glances skyward and says a prayer for the boy's body hooked to many wires and tubes, looking helpless in his sleeping state. Eva wants to hug and kiss his face, but that would have to wait. She leaves, looking forward to the next day.

◆

The hotel, unlike the hospital, is full of individuals going and coming. A hot shower washes off the film of travel, but the tension is impervious to the water and soap dripping to the tile floor. Eva's sleep has been intermittent at best since her father's murder, and this night the time between the alarm being set and going off at 6:30 a.m. seems like seconds. Her body demands more and does not want to rise. The demand is ignored.

Eva opens the door to the Lincoln Room at 7:20, and four men are seated around a table, strewn documents lying within grasp. Agent Willis smiles at a distance and approaches Eva, while the other three do not move from their discussion.

"Good morning, Eva. Did you sleep well?" Willis asks.

"Yes, slept well." Eva follows Willis to the table, and the other three finally turn their attention to her.

"Eva Czapleski, this is my boss at Homeland Security, Michael Thompson. This is Agent Flint with the CIA and Major Sherbrooke with the Air Force Tactical Services." Willis goes through the introductions like bringing a stranger to a company Christmas party.

Thompson motions to Eva. "Please, have a seat. Don't let this bunch intimidate you. It's standard procedure anytime a radioactive incident occurs. For obvious reasons, something radioactive is a serious threat to the country. This brings out investigative eyes from several levels of the government."

"I understand … anything to help," Eva responds.

The door opens, and several waiters bring in breakfast. The communication shifts to the mundane.

"You live in New Orleans? Where do you work?" Thompson asks with a smile.

"I'm an assistant manager at Swain's, a restaurant," Eva responds, not sure where this is leading.

"Are you married?" Thompson glances at a document to verify the questioning.

"No, divorced. What does that have to do with anything?"

The waiters leave, and everyone but Eva takes a bite of food.

"She's right, stupid questions," Flint asserts. "What I've been told is your father and Emrik had a street act, and your father was killed in front of Emrik. Correct?"

"Yes. Emrik ran from the murderer and got away."

"He wasn't abducted at that point?"

"No. The abduction came several days later at my father's wake. Emrik was emotionally charged and ran from the church in the middle of the service. We gave chase. Then this man grabbed him. Climbed up a building and disappeared."

Sherbrooke leans forward. "Your son is how old?"

"He's twelve."

"Approximately what does he weigh?"

"Hundred, maybe hundred-and-five pounds."

"What did the man look like?" Flint inquires.

"It was dark. He wore a hoody." Eva finally reaches for a piece of toast and takes a bite.

"Who besides you witnessed the abduction?" Sherbrooke asks.

"My brother Randy; Chris Dale, a detective, and Jessie McGaha—she's a reporter for the newspaper."

Sherbrooke continues. "When you say he climbed the building, was it a stairwell? A fire escape? What do you mean?"

"It was a fire-escape, but ..."

"But what, Ms. Czapleski?" Flint asks.

"He carried Emrik like he was a box of Kleenex. It was fast, effortless."

The men make their notes as Eva explains the circumstances.

"When and how did you get Emrik back?"

"Emrik returned to the house on his own, late the following night."

"This is important," Flint says. "Has Emrik described what happened to him the thirty hours he was gone?"

"No, he became sick and threw up. We took him to the hospital."

"Ms. Czapleski, there's a good chance a terrorist group could be involved with the abduction," Flint continues. "We need your permission to place Emrik under hypnosis to find out more about what happened to him."

"Why would a terrorist group have an interest in my son? He's twelve years old!"

"That's why we need to dig deeper. Emrik was exposed to bad things, and we need to find out who and why."

"Will it hurt, Emrik?"

"Absolutely not. He'll be interviewed by a doctor, an expert in the field. In and out ... an hour at most." Flint moves a document across the table and provides a pen for Eva to sign.

She scans the document and looks up at Flint. "Can I see him first?"

"Yes, it's our understanding you will be with him today after he's brought out of the coma. We'll do the hypnosis tomorrow, giving you a full day with him."

Eva looks over to Willis, wanting confirmation.

"It's the best thing to ensure Emrik's safety and yours in the future," Willis confirms.

Eva takes the pen and signs the document. Within minutes, she is heading to the fourth floor and nursing the same tasteless coffee sampled the night before. After three hours-plus of watching HGTV and home renovations in four states, Dr. Rivers returns to the waiting room.

"We took Emrik out of the induced coma, and he ate some solid food. It's a good sign when his appetite is already back. Let's go see your son." His smile is returned by a nervous Eva.

Traveling the hallway maze now has some familiarity for her, but the twists and turns still bring confusion. She concentrates on the white smock of the doctor and doesn't let her curiosity drift to the open rooms and various medical issues as she moves past the gray walls.

Issued a cloth-and-plastic mask outside Emrik's door, clumsy and excited hands finally make the alignment right between her ears and nose.

Emrik's face is red, free from the intubation, and he issues a smile when Eva walks into the room. She smiles back through the tears dampening the mask.

"Emrik, it's Momma," she says, embarrassed from so much clothing clinging to her head.

"I know." Emrik's response is direct and to the point. It fills Eva's heart. She takes a step toward him, but Rivers raises his hand as a reminder.

"A little later you can hug him."

"I can't be close right now, tomorrow will be better." Eva

explains.

Okay," Emrik says. "Why are you crying?"

"Because I missed you ... I love you."

"Can I have some ice cream?"

Eva looks to Rivers. "Think that can be arranged. Have a seat, Eva. Enjoy Emrik. I'll be back later, but keep your distance."

He leaves the room and is met by Flint and Sherbrooke in the hallway. The three walk away in deep conversation.

Soon thereafter, Emrik has finished his serving of strawberry ice cream and falls asleep. Eva does not mind the needed sleep taking away his voice temporarily. It will make him stronger and bring him home faster. A text from Jessie asks about Emrik. Eva types two long paragraphs about the experience and how well he is doing. The women exchange their relief and returning happiness.

Eva stays with Emrik until after 6:00 p.m., when Dr. Rivers asks her to leave for some needed rest for both of them. Emrik's energy waned as the afternoon flew by, but his spirit and smile gathered strength. Eva is now full of optimism about taking him back home and into a regular routine soon.

Heading to the hotel, Eva sees Willis rising up from a lobby couch and approaching.

"How is Emrik doing?" he asks sincerely.

"Great! I spent the whole afternoon with him. He's tired as expected but excited to see me."

"A couple follow up questions, if you don't mind."

"Sure." They both sit on the couch.

"Did Emrik seem any different today ... anything out of the ordinary?"

"No, not really. Low energy yet responsive." Eva leans back in the couch. "Is there something I should know?"

"Dr. Rivers says his cognitive skills are fine ... that's good. We're trying to see if his personality has deviated any."

"So far, so good," Eva answers.

"Have there been any breakthroughs surrounding the murder of your father?"

"Not aware of any. You need to communicate with Detective Chris Dale of the NOPD. He's handling the case." Eva wonders why these questions have any value concerning Emrik.

"The hypnosis for Emrik will be at nine in the morning. Would you like to attend?"

"Absolutely! If it has to do with Emrik, I want to be there." She moves forward on the couch in a more protective posture.

212

"Then meet me here at eight-thirty. We'll go together. Thanks for working with us. We'll get to the bottom of all this."

Eva tilts her head slightly and nods. Willis walks away, and she moves to her room, not having a clue what hypnosis could pull from her son that is not already known.

Randy calls her cell to check on Emrik, and brother and sister talk for thirty-five minutes.

◆

Emrik's eyes grow wide as a loud noise originates behind the bed. A turn to find the source is limited by the electronics connected to his arm and chest. His heart-rate monitor jumps up and down on the screen, fear replacing sleep. The plasma bag hanging next to the bed starts to shake side-to-side and violently falls to the floor. The walls start to crumble and fall on top of Emrik.

Eva sits straight up in bed, shaking. The dream about Emrik disturbs her deeply. She wants to run to the room and take him away. In her mind it is a premonition of doom and a spiraling-out-of-control cycle, set in motion by the hypnosis.

◆

Agent Willis is on the phone when he sees Eva leave the elevator and head in his direction. He notes that her walk and demeanor are different from the previous day.

"Agent Willis, I want to call this hypnosis thing off." She moves close to the agent's face.

"Eva, what has changed in the last few hours?"

"That's not important. I don't want Emrik subjected to the interrogation. Call it off!"

"It's not an interrogation. Nonetheless, give me a minute to see what I can do." Willis walks a few steps away and makes a call.

Eva watches his actions and hears the subject being discussed, but she has no clue whom he is talking to. The phone goes back into his pocket.

"I'm afraid it can't be called off. You already signed the release."

"He's my son. You're going to run over my wishes like a truck."

"Ms. Czapleski, this is a national security issue. My orders come from the top. Do you still want to witness the hypnosis? I assure you, I have no say in the matter."

"Yes," Eva says sullenly, realizing the discussion is over.

"We need to go, now." Willis turns and heads for the elevator with Eva close behind.

◆

They enter a small room with an elongated window overlooking an operating facility. Several strangers in suits are seated, but no introductions are made. Eva believes her sudden lack of cooperation might be the reason the others remain strangers.

The fact that she is seeing an operating room makes the process even more ominous. Several chairs have been staged in front of the small room that normally serves as a training stage for medical students and doctors enhancing their trade from around the world.

The men from the CIA, Air Force, and Homeland Security who had interviewed Eva the previous day enter the operating room along with Dr. Wang, a high-profile hypnotist from Harvard. The agents sit in a semi-circle facing the back of Dr. Wang's chair, with a video camera mounted six feet off the floor to record the proceedings.

Eva is anxious about Emrik, and this is heightened when Dr. Rivers brings him into the room and seats him in front of Dr. Wang. Willis looks at Eva, but she is oblivious to him.

Rivers kneels low in front of Emrik, and Eva can tell the doctor is genuine in his caretaking of her son.

"Emrik, you are the center of attention for some fun today. Would you like that?" He smiles.

"Yes, I like fun." Emrik's voice is barely heard on the intercom in the small room, so one of the strangers increases the volume of the speaker.

Eva moves to the edge of her chair.

"Okay, let the fun begin," Rivers says. "Dr. Wang will give you directions. Pay close attention to him." Rivers moves back, and Dr. Wang leans forward in his chair, pulling out a red-jeweled coin from a pocket.

"Emrik, I want you to concentrate on this coin as it moves side-to-side. If you feel sleepy, that's just fine." Wang begins moving the coin rhythmically, back and forth, ten inches in front of Emrik's eyes.

Eva is starting to feel some relief watching the two doctors professionally administer the hypnosis. It appears simple and non-threatening.

"Emrik, we want to go back to the night you were grabbed by

214

the man that took you up the fire-escape. Can you see the man that took you away?" Wang keeps moving the coin in a pendulum motion, and Emrik's eyes follow it, rapidly opening and closing.

Now Emrik leans his head backward, and his eyes are open wide. He answers the question with a simple, "yes."

"Where did the man take you, Emrik?" Wang asks, now pocketing the coin.

"We jumped building-to-building then went straight up high."

"What do you mean 'high'? Where did he take you?"

Emrik points skyward. "In a plane."

Wang looks at a script prepared earlier by others. "What did you do in the plane?"

Emrik stands and rotates on one foot like a figure skater pirouetting at a rapid pace. Round and round he goes, making a very athletic move and finally stopping in front of Rivers.

"Were you ascending to the plane, Emrik?" Wang questions.

"Yes."

"Going in circles?"

"Yes." Emrik seems to be reliving the experience.

"What else did you do in the plane?"

Emrik walks to CIA Agent Flint, grabs the pen he is using to take notes, and stabs the pen into the back of his own neck behind the head. Emrik stands still, the pen protruding from the base of his skull.

Everyone jumps to their feet in the small room, and Eva screams in horror. Rivers immediately rushes over to pull the pen from Emrik's neck, but Wang raises his hand to stop him. Rivers halts in his tracks.

"What else happened in the airplane, Emrik?" Wang asks the final question.

Emrik looks around the semi-circle of men, choosing someone to participate in the playacting. He again walks to Flint and motions him to lean forward. Flint looks at Wang, and Wang nods his confirmation. Flint leans forward, his jacket and shoulder holster carrying a .40-caliber pistol falling away from his chest in the process.

Emrik suddenly grabs the pistol and shoots Flint in the head. Eva passes out cold, banging her head into a front-row chair during the fall.

Twenty Three

THE DEVIL AMONG US

Chris Dale opens the door to the station, and Tony Joseph's desk is the first one he passes. A half-empty box of donuts sits in full view. Chris reaches to help himself, watching Joseph finish a conversation on the cell.

"That'll cost you," Joseph says, suddenly.

Chris takes a bite then opens the box and starts to put the donut back.

"Okay, you called my bluff. Keep the damn thing."

"How's our killer doing? Talking anymore?" Chris asks between mouthfuls.

"No, moved him over to county myself. He's retained Lawrence Goldman as his attorney.

"Big-dollar representation. Could he really be a business guy in the scheme of things?"

"He's a hired gun. But we both know he didn't kill the stripper."

"So damned true. Could you buy crème-filled next time?"

"Thought you had a heart problem?"

"Who told you that?" Chris asks, fully aware the source is Bobby Rabold.

"You can trust me," Joseph says with a grin. "I wouldn't dare spread anything so personal."

"Why I tolerate this lack of respect is beyond me," Chris says, half-joking and half-pissed.

He walks to his desk and sits hard in the seat. Rabold looks over from his paperwork. "What's wrong?"

"Did you tell Tony I have a heart problem?"

"Didn't say a damned thing to Joseph. What kind of partner do you think I am? I did tell Lee, so he must have mentioned it to Tony."

Chris knows it is the cop way, and nothing would change it.

"Have Stephens and his girlfriend come back from paradise yet?"

"Back in town yesterday. I'm going to see them in twenty minutes."

"You're a worthless friend but a good cop." He speaks like a cop would.

"Take that as a compliment ... as a good cop. I've been digging through the files on the Stephens killing back in eighty-eight. The assigned detective was Marc Bone."

"I know Marc. He retired a couple of years ago ... told me he was going to focus on catfish farming. Can't see him doing something that crazy."

"I called HR. Don't know if he's messing with catfish, but he lives on a farm twenty miles out, close to I-Ten. Thought we might pay him a visit after we interview the devil-woman."

◆

Chris and Rabold pull into the long driveway leading to Trey's home.

"The publishing business must be pretty damn lucrative," Chris notes, opening the car door in front of the mansion.

"He's not yanking down a cop's salary," Rabold retorts.

"Hell, a cop's salary wouldn't pay for the landscaping." Chris notes the rolling, detailed yard and turns his attention to the front door.

Lilly answers the door. "May I help you, gentlemen?"

Chris pulls his badge out. "I'm Detective Dale. This is Detective Rabold. We're here to see Reed Stephens."

"I'll get Mr. Stephens for you." Lilly dislikes the law but is not surprised by their visit.

The ceiling in the entryway flows upward twenty-five feet to a second-floor balcony. Both cops take in the expansive opulence more as a byproduct to the investigation than envy.

Trey soon appears, thinking the visit is about the kidnapping.

"Officers, come in," he says, leading them to the den. "Would you like something to drink?"

"Bottled water, thanks," Rabold responds.

"Make that two," Chris adds.

Soon, Lilly returns with the water.

"I gave the FBI a detailed description of the events in Mexico. I assume they shared the information with you."

"We're not here concerning Mexico," Rabold says. "We're dealing with a series of murders, and all roads seem to cross paths with you and Gayle Kidd." He opens an extensive file and lays it on the coffee table.

"What are you talking about? Who's been murdered?" Trey's throat is suddenly thick with anxiety, knowing things have been

218

done in the name of the company that could put him in jail for life.

Rabold thumbs through the file and points to the photo of Trey and Gayle passing Emrik and his grandfather on Bourbon Street.

"Do you know the old man playing the instrument?" he presses.

Trey looks intently at the photo. "No. I don't have a clue who he is."

Chris leans in. "His name is Joe Bailly. He knew you and Ms. Kidd, and he turned up dead within an hour of when this photo was taken. Joe was so scared of you he ran to a mobster named Louis Fleck for protection. It didn't help him any."

Lilly stands close to a wall outside the den, listening to the conversation.

Rabold moves the papers around in the file and retrieves a graphic photo of Tony Cranford's body hanging from a rope in his home. "This is what happened to a fellow police officer investigating Bailly's murder. See the pattern forming?"

"We have several more bodies piling up, all connected to the same subject—you."

Trey shakes his head in disbelief. "This is all bullshit. I'm walking down the street and suddenly turn serial killer?"

"Where is Gayle Kidd? We need her perspective," Rabold demands.

"Lilly?" Trey yells out.

Lilly knocks a vase over sitting on the end table next to the wall but catches it before hitting the floor. She gathers herself, walks quickly to the kitchen, and then answers, "Coming." She rounds the corner.

"Lilly, please bring my phone from the kitchen. It's on the charger," Trey instructs. He turns back to Rabold and Chris. "Gayle is staying in a suite behind the house."

Lilly returns with the phone, and Trey texts a note to Gayle, requesting her appearance.

"What's your relationship with Ms. Kidd?" Chris asks.

"Business. She's writing a book our company is publishing shortly. The rest is none of your concern."

"It's all our business," Rabold shoots back. "The next time we come by, we'll have a search warrant for your home, the company, and your grandfather's house."

"We're dating. It went personal pretty quick," Trey explains.

"How long have you known her?" Chris asks.

"Couple months." Trey is regaining composure, now understanding the cops have leverage.

"Doesn't it seem strange all these murders and your kidnapping happened after you met her?"

Rabold continues the barrage, not letting Trey catch a breath. "Your mother and father were murdered, a known mobster with ties to your grandfather arranged a Hell Raising. This started the carnage back in the late eighties. Are you still going to protect old Mr. Stephens at the expense of your parents?"

Trey's mind is flying in many directions, and the questions started to fester when the file was laid on the coffee table.

Gayle Kidd enters the room. The introductions are brief and obviously strained coming from Trey. The questions rain on Gayle with prejudice, and she answers in much the same kind of dumbfounded mystery as Trey. The murder scene of Madam Hendrix and her assistant grace the table. Gayle recoils in horror at the vivid details revealed.

The meeting's intent is shock and awe. Throw Trey and Gayle in the fire pit and watch them try to climb out to follow their reactions.

◆

Chris and Rabold return to the car. "What do you think?" Chris asks.

"Way too much innocence being spit out for my liking. There's a dead rat in the wall somewhere. Sooner or later the stink will drive the truth out in the open."

"Think you're right. Let's see where the stench leads us." Chris hands over his phone. "Call Marc Bone to make sure he's home."

The call runs through the bluetooth speaker system, and Bone answers the phone.

"Hello?"

"Marc, this is Chris Dale. How is the catfish going?" Chris drives toward Interstate 10 as they converse.

"You finally retire from the force?" Bone asks.

"No, investigating a cold-case murder. Have a few minutes to catch up?"

"Sure. About to fry some catfish. Hungry?" He always liked Chris.

"Sounds great! Bobby Rabold is with me."

"I feed nineteen acres of catfish. Plenty to go around."

"Be there in twenty minutes or so, depending on traffic." Chris takes the phone from Rabold.

"Never had catfish before," Rabold confesses.

"Fried catfish and hushpuppies. You're in for a treat." Chris steps on the accelerator and moves along the interstate, ignoring the speed limit.

◆

Chris drives up to a recently painted blue house with white trim, and a porch extending around all four sides. A tall, slender man is working an outdoor kitchen built under the eave of the porch on the east side. The catfish is boiling in oil and fills the air as Chris and Rabold climb the steps.

"You old Billy Goat," Chris yells, approaching Bone. "Does the fish taste as good as it smells?"

"I cook only good things. You, on the other hand, will eat anything."

Bone and Chris shake hands. "This is my partner, Bobby Rabold."

He extends his hand. "You must be exhausted carrying Chris around on your back all the time. Want a beer?"

"My back is sore. I need a beer."

"Help yourself. All brands in the refrigerator." He points to a built-in unit under the counter, while he tends to the hushpuppies roiling in a deep fryer, along with french fries in an adjoining fryer. "So, what the hell brings you out to these boondocks?"

Rabold begins. "In eighty-eight, you were the investigating officer for the murder of Reed Stephens and his wife." He takes a sip of beer. "Do you recall the case?"

"My name ended up on the report, but I was not a detective at that point."

"What was your level of involvement on the case?" Chris asks.

"I was a street cop. I received a call about a body out by the Clemens Cemetery. It was Halloween, so I figured it was a fraternity prank. But I found a black female dead next to a car, hacked to pieces. Inside the cemetery, we found Reed Stephens. His body was in the same condition."

Rabold opens a file he has brought with him. "You discovered Helen and Reed Stephens in a cemetery ... not at their home?"

"The girl was not Stephens' wife. I can't remember her name, but it wasn't Stephens. They died in the cemetery. Lemme see that report." Bone takes the file and starts reading. "That sonofabitch!"

"What sonofabitch?" Chris asks.

"Captain Hitchens. At the last second, he jumped in the

middle of things, which we all found odd at the time. That's not my report. I swear."

"Isn't that interesting. Hitchens is dead, so we'll never know who bought him off," Chris says.

◆

Trey walks with Gayle in silence to the bungalow behind his house. The emotions are now thick and sticky in their world, gone from idyllic to absurd in a matter of days. Once inside, Trey goes to the refrigerator, grabs a beer, and looks at Gayle.

"Beer?" he asks.

Gayle shakes her head.

He opens the bottle, tosses the cap in a nearby wastebasket, and joins her on the couch.

"It's time for a talk. What do you know about the insanity we just witnessed?"

"Nothing. I swear on my father's grave. I have no idea who these people are, much less their connection to each other. What about you? Do these crimes have anything to do with the company?" she asks, jumping from defense to offense.

"No, but we'll get to the bottom of it. I swear."

"Could your grandfather be involved?" She takes his hand in hers.

"That would not shock me at all." Trey kisses Gayle's hand.

Twenty Four

BLOODY MARY

Chris and Rabold drive back down Interstate 10, full of catfish and a new set of legal issues to investigate. Filing a false report on any case, much less a murder investigation, would be grounds for dismissal and jail time. Yet Hitchens had taken Marc Bone's case file and changed a wide range of details to shift focus away from someone who could afford to buy off an NOPD captain. Solving the old crime could confirm the identity of those responsible for the recent waves of murder and destruction.

Chris's cell goes off. Jessie's name appears on the caller ID.

"What's the latest?" Chris says, answering. "What? No way in hell! Hold on. Lemme put you on speaker. Bobby's riding with me." He taps the cell to bring the conversation alive on Bluetooth.

Rabold turns to Chris and asks in a low voice, "Who's that?"

"Jessie," he whispers back then talks aloud to the car's microphone. "Tell Bobby what you just told me."

"Eva Czapleski called. The CIA tried to place Emrik under hypnosis. It went terribly bad. He shot one of the agents!"

"How did he get a gun?" Chris asks, shocked at the turn of events.

"I don't have a clue. Eva was hysterical on the phone, even under sedation. She rambled on and on about them arresting Emrik for murder. Chris, can they arrest a twelve-year-old? I can't imagine what Eva is living through at this moment."

"It's rare for a kid that young going on trial for murder. But the Feds have far more legal power than local jurisdictions. What do you think, Bobby?"

"You did confirm he was hypnotized when it happened?" he inquires.

"Yes. Eva watched it occur. She signed the authorization to do the hypnosis but wanted to back out at the last minute. They refused and went ahead anyway."

"I think if Emrik was induced into hypnosis, he couldn't be legally responsible for actions as a result," Rabold says. "That's speculation on my part. You should call PA Mike Broadaway and get his opinion."

"I like that idea," Chris responds. "Jessie, call Eva back in a couple of hours. Get as much information as possible. I'll call Broadaway in the morning. Hopefully, he can give us a direction to follow."

"Thanks," Jessie says. "This is too much for Eva piled on top of what she has endured the last month." She ends the call.

"That's a lot to digest on top of the catfish," Chris quips.

"But Broadaway will know what to do," Rabold adds.

Chris suddenly feels confused about his line of action, one of the few times in his career.

"Hope so. I'm going to get an interview with old man Stephens. Want to ride along?"

"Sure," Rabold answers.

"Let's try for Thursday. Tomorrow's Joanna's birthday. I'm taking the day off."

"Okay, Thursday." Rabold agrees, opening the file on the Stephens murder.

A text pings Chris's phone, and a glance confirms it's from Jessie: "Come by the house at 5:00. I want you on the call with Eva."

A look in Rabold's direction shows little notice of the text. Chris stares at the interstate in front of the car, and an eighteen-wheeler is the only vehicle in sight several hundred yards ahead. His focus returns to the phone, and he taps a simple response: "Sure."

A sudden sense of excitement pushes the police cruiser past the truck at a high speed.

◆

Chris parks the car in Jessie's garage. She always leaves the door open for him. He pushes the wall switch, and the door grinds and complains toward the floor. Chris, not sure why, always watches the door's slow-motion effort. Maybe his conscience is sealed with the door's descent.

He knocks on the kitchen door, which is locked, to gain entrance permission. The familiar voice anoints the entry. "Come in."

Jessie sits at the kitchen table where numerous files and notes are scattered about, just like her newspaper desk. Chris smiles at the system only she understands, but she doesn't reciprocate the look and flash her very white teeth. Instead, she pens more notes in a busy, two-fingered grip, trying to fit together a sense of story logic.

226

Chris walks over and pulls out a chair, careful not to break the concentration he has seen before. He does not sit down.

"Want something to drink?" Chris finally asks.

Jessie looks his way, not surprised by the ease Chris navigates in her home. "Make one of your Crown and Cokes for me. No lime." Her head and pen redirect downward.

Chris pours two half-full glasses and holds them under the ice-maker, which drops cubes into the black liquid. He brings them to a chair and sits.

Jessie reaches for a glass and takes a sip. "Thanks."

Chris follows her lead but takes a bigger sip. "The pressure piles on. How're you handling it?"

"Not well. Deadlines and writing I can work through. Up close, watching people being destroyed, is eating me alive. It used to role off my back. Why has that changed, Chris?" Her eyes are dark and haggard, an easy read for him.

"The old premise that bad things happen to good people is true. What this sorry-assed job has shown me is bad things happen to all people. We walk around waiting for the hammer to fall. It's only a matter of time."

Chris finishes the C and C, feeling Jessie's pain crawl across the table and slide into his drink. He wants to go over and place his arm around her but remains seated. The distance can't be traversed by him.

Jessie draws a deep intake of air. "Let's call this poor lady. You're the cop, you do the talking. I'm worthless at this point."

"Dial her up and put it on speaker."

"Hello?" Eva's frail voice barely seeps through the phone. Jessie increases the volume.

"Eva, I have Chris Dale with me. It's a bad time, but Chris knows far more than me on the subject and can help you." She moves the phone onto the table in front of Chris and stands by his side.

"Thanks, I'm way over my head right now with grief, sitting in this hotel room not having a clue which way to turn."

"You're not alone in this, we're going to fight through it together. Where is Emrik, now?" Chris asks.

"He's back in the hospital room. I saw him briefly after the incident."

"Did he remember any of the events during the hypnosis?"

"No, his demeanor was like it never happened."

"That's good. How did he obtain the weapon?"

"Emrik was asked about his experience when kidnapped. Said he flew off in a plane. Then he took a pen from the CIA guy and

227

stuck it in the back of his neck and..."

"Wait! What?" Chris interrupts. "Emrik stuck the pen in the agent's neck?"

"No, Emrik stabbed himself. I screamed to wake him up, but Dr. Wang let Emrik continue. He approached the agent again— he took the agent's gun and shot him."

"How would Emrik even know how to operate a weapon like that?" Jessie asks.

"CIA people have no safeties on their weapons. They've got hair triggers. It wouldn't take much pressure to fire it. I have the same thing for my sidearm," Chris explains.

"What do I do now?" Eva asks.

"You need legal help. My personal opinion is the Feds can't do much to a twelve-year-old under their induced hypnosis, but I'm not an attorney. I will be talking to our prosecutor in the morning to pose that question. Hang in there. We'll find a way out of this."

"Thanks so much for caring about Emrik," Eva says, ending the call.

"What do you think?" Jessie's eyes have come back to life. She moves over and leans on Chris.

"I'll know a lot more tomorrow. I'll keep you in the loop."

Chris rises. The thought of sex is in his head, but he knows it won't be happening here and now.

Jessie hugs Chris. "This is important, thanks."

Chris smiles, kisses her on the cheek, and leaves to watch the garage door reverse the process. It always seems to rise slower on the way out.

◆

The bed is empty next to Chris, confirmed by rolling over and eyeing Joanna's usual sleeping position and seeing no one. The night flew by. Chris slept deeply, the heavy thoughts from the last few days escaping his dreams, and fortunately, altering the late-night nervous trips to the bathroom to urinate.

He rises and unzips the gym bag he carries to work containing a change of clothes and shaving kit. He unwraps a Rolex watch box hidden inside and places it next to the shorts Joanna has laid out for him. Joanna is anything other than a high-maintenance woman, but Chris had wanted to go overboard for her 50th birthday. When he asked where she wanted to celebrate, in typical Joanna fashion she chose a trip to a park overlooking a lake and picnic. What she didn't know was a dinner at Houston's tonight would be his arranged end to a special day well-deserved. The biggest decision for Chris will be when to give the watch to Joanna, in the park or the restaurant.

◆

If the truth would lie naked beside her, it would reveal that Joanna has been dreading this impending birthday since the one she marked last year. The depression emerged when she began thinking about the approaching milestone and that inevitable mail from AARP. Being married to a cop, drifting in and out of her life on a daily basis and never straying far from death, including his own, certainly has not helped rounding that Big Five-oh corner.

New Orleans was her birthplace, but so many local changes for the worse were making their plans to retire and move to Florida seem too good to be true. Joanna is a giver, and Chris is a taker. These facts gave her a comfort zone she cherished, and the thought of it all being taken away lived in her head daily.

Joanna pulls into the driveway and grabs several plastic bags of groceries, including sandwiches for the picnic. Going to the park and having Chris by her side does feel good—birthday be damned.

She opens the kitchen door, and Chris is standing by the refrigerator on the phone. He grabs a pen and writes a note on one of the 3x5 cards she keeps for the daily activity schedule. Internal panic sets into her thoughts. That dreaded call where he kisses her and takes off to attend to someone bleeding on a floor is probably their picnic destiny.

A smile crosses her lips in his direction, and a slight crease on his lips meet her effort. It's what she does to cover the hurt.

Chris ends the call and smiles widely. "Happy Birthday, lover."

"Thank you. Work?" Joanna bleeds the answer before he issues the verdict.

"Of course." He walks over and takes the bags from her motionless grip, placing them on the table. "But I'm one text from being yours."

He kisses her in a sexy way, and she does everything in her power to keep from crying. She turns away and installs the groceries, hoping the emotional vulnerability is not revealed.

Chris sits at the table, oblivious to the rollercoaster ride he creates in the mere discussion of a phone call. He touches Jessie's name on the text menu. He is sending her an attorney's name in D.C., Jim Young. Young is a former classmate of PA Broadaway and partner in a high-powered firm that hates the Feds. Emrik will be well-represented if charges are brought against him.

"Done," Chris proudly announces. "How about a Bloody Mary to kick this birthday thing off properly?"

Joanna feels a large weight fall off her shoulders, the one from digging around in her rose garden all day, waiting for Chris to return from a body count only to have him walk away to a second crime scene and leave her alone again.

Chris makes a great Bloody Mary, an inheritance from his bartending father. It is Joanna's favorite drink. Searching for the various ingredients, Chris moves around the kitchen, light on his feet and energy focused.

Amazing, but he leaves the dreaded cell turned off through the drink-making process for the first time in their marriage, and Joanna goes into the bathroom, hiding the tears she can no longer contain. Put back together, Joanna takes a drink of the best liquid to ever grace her lips. Two sips into it, she circles the table and sits on his lap, wrapping her arms around his neck. Not entirely sure of the reason, Chris finally senses the impact of the moment and pulls her close.

Twenty Five

BAILING WIRE

Israel Hamric walks the metal-framed floor from his county cell down a series of steps to a common TV area, where thirty other prisoners are milling around. This is not his first experience in jail. An illegal-weapons conviction in Pittsburgh required seven months of a one-year sentence, compliments of a DA who could not touch him for a murder.

Hamric is frustrated and, more ominously, angry for what he perceives as a setup in the stripper stabbing. The only person in a position to make this happen is Louis Fleck. Adding insult to injury, Hamric has been in lockup for five days and received not a single ounce of contact from Fleck. It is too late for a reconciliation at this point.

An older inmate walks up to him and sits a couple of feet away. Hamric is constantly on guard, day and night, in any environment, especially in a jail full of people who have nothing to lose and will kill a fellow inmate just to add to their reputation.

"What do you want, old timer?" Hamric asks, anticipating something beyond a social visit.

"Is it true what they say about you?"

"Depends on who's saying it. Godzilla been talking to you?"

The old inmate laughs. "Must be true. Y'all badass and such."

"You're a veteran behind bars. It pays to be a badass, don't you think?"

"Wilkes, over there," the old man nods toward a large man playing checkers thirty feet away, "says you're a mob killer."

Hamric is not surprised about a rumor about him or anybody else in the cage. But the source can't be explained or revealed. It seems to originate from an all-knowing jail Wizard, rarely wrong in the rumor-mongering trade.

"Bare hands, that's the preferred method. A little more personal. Tell Wilkes he's square on the money." He winks, and the old guy walks back to the checkers game.

A guard approaches him then turns away without a directional sound uttered. He understands to follow, an unwritten rule of obedience in such places. Several clearance points and un-locked doors later, he enters a small room, where his attorney, Lawrence Goldman, is texting on his phone.

Goldman slides the phone in a briefcase. "How are they treat-ing you?"

"It's jail. It's suppose to suck."

"This is what will happen at the arraignment." Goldman starts his usual spiel of court procedure, but Hamric holds his hand up, stopping him.

"Don't want legal lectures from you. I know the codes better than ninety-percent of the attorneys wearing Ferragamos. Your job is to get me out of here."

"If … and that will depend on which judge presides, if you get bail on a murder charge, we're talking heavy seven figures. Can you post that kind of cash?"

"The bail will be met. Can I be placed on house arrest in my New York home, with an ankle bracelet for tracking?" Hamric has a plan in mind that depends on the restrictions imposed by the court.

"I can push for that, but letting you go out of state is doubtful. Renting a house in the parish may be the only option." Goldman quickly suspects Hamric is not the usual run-of-the-mill business-man caught up in bad circumstances.

"Do you have a good PI for investigating this bullshit charge?" he asks, calming to a certain degree.

"Two of the best. Don't want them coming here to interview, though. What you say to them can be used by the state. Let's get your bail in place, then we can attack the charges. Sit tight for forty-eight hours. I'll try to rush it through." Goldman stands and offers his hand.

"Let me have your pen and something to write on." He takes what Goldman offers, writes a name and number on it, and hands it back.

Goldman eyes the writing and places the paper in his pocket. "What do you want me to say to Shane Appleton?"

"Shane is my uncle. He'll know what to do when he hears the charges. Fill him in on the bail and date of release when you get it."

◆

Shane Appleton goes into the back door of his pawn shop where longtime assistant manager, Rudy, is negotiating the value of a

234

watch with a customer. A strange number appears on his cell phone, and the theme song of "The Good, the Bad, and the Ugly" ringtone announces the incoming call. Shane loves Clint Eastwood and lets the ring continue, creating a mental movie flashback before answering.

"This is Shane. How may I help you?" Most of his cell calls involve the pawn shop.

"Mr. Appleton, I'm Lawrence Goldman, attorney for Israel Hamric."

"What's the charge?" Appleton asks, instantly understanding.

"Murder."

"Where are you located?" He has asked this question before.

"New Orleans. The bail hasn't been approved yet."

"Text me a competent real estate broker for a possible house rental, and give me the bail amount ASAP. Anything else?"

"I'll be in touch," Goldman responds and ends the call.

Appleton walks to the main floor of the pawn shop and sees Rudy is in heavy discussion with the now-belligerent customer.

"What kind of watch is it?" Appleton asks. He rarely gets involved with his staff when haggling over a transaction, but he wants the guy gone.

Rudy slides the watch over the counter toward him. "It's an AP, has mechanical issues."

"What does he want?" He flips the watch over to examine.

"Twenty-five hundred. I've offered fifteen."

Appleton turns to the customer. "It'll cost me at least two-fifty to get the watch ready for sale if you forfeit. Seventeen hundred, take it or leave it."

The man knows the negotiations are over. "I'll take it."

"Wrap this up and come to the office when you are through." He heads to his office, and soon Rudy joins him.

"What's up, bossman?" Rudy has worked in the shop for seven years and senses something is not right.

"Going out of town for a few days. Leaving tomorrow. Do we still have that forty-cal with the laser scope?"

"I'll get it cased up with a box of ammo for you. Going to Detroit?"

"Close. New Orleans. Thanks." Rudy leaves pursuing no further details.

Appleton opens his wall safe and extracts two forged passports and a driver's license for a Dean Wellington with Hamric's photo. He places the items in a briefcase.

◆

Appleton's day is busy. Trips to Hamric's home and three bank safe-deposit boxes yield nearly eight-hundred thousand in cash and nearly a like amount in fine-cut diamonds and gold coins.

Appleton, having power of attorney for Hamric, notifies Bank of America to transfer his stock portfolio of three-million dollars to Appleton's account. This is done to prevent any state or federal agency from freezing Hamric's assets, and providing runaway money if necessary.

The next day, Appleton is packed and driving south to New Orleans. When Hamric needs him, Appleton will drive to Hell and back. Hamric once saved him from a direct trip to Hell in his gambling days.

◆

Louis Fleck is beside himself in fear. The assassin he hired to eliminate Gayle Kidd is being held in jail for murdering one of his top-producing strippers. Fleck is not sure if Israel Hamric did the killing, but his offensive tactics to protect himself are turned inside out, and individuals associated with the old Hell Raising are acquiring toe tags in the morgue.

The Voice has only been to Fleck's home once in three years, and that was to help remove carpet from the second floor being replaced by hardwood. Since Hamric's arrest, Fleck's panic is pulling the Voice tighter into the inner circle of trust, and now he is receiving the biggest endorsement possible by going to a private meeting away from the casino.

Fleck watches the Voice walk to the front door, but he has mixed emotions about overloading him with lifesaving expectations. On the other hand, Fleck's options are running thin, causing him to hit the panic button. He opens the door before the Voice arrives on the porch and walks him to the back yard.

Fleck turns to the Voice next to the detached garage then puts a hand on his shoulder in a rare moment of affection. A thrill circles his back and crawls to his neck rapidly.

"I need you to do a job for me. A bonus of three-thousand dollars is riding on it." Fleck takes his hand away from the man's shoulder and looks around the tree-strewn back yard, expecting a cop to jump out from one of the black oaks and place him in cuffs.

"Won't let you down, Boss." The Voice wants desperately to

236

prove his worth, and that opportunity is standing in front of him.

Fleck pulls a small square of paper from his wallet and turns it over. "This is Reed Stephens' address. The next couple nights, I want you to follow him to find that Gayle Kidd demon. See what their habits are. Don't do anything until I give you the word on when and where to kill her."

"What about Stephens?"

"Right now, I don't give a shit … kill them both. Listen, this is a recon to figure out the best place to get the job done. Don't go off half-cocked on your own. Talk to me in person. No phone calls between us until this is all over."

The Voice isn't sure what "recon" means, but he is confident he is about to take a giant step forward in the organization.

"One more thing…" Fleck says, hearing a neighbor slam his back door a hundred feet away. He goes silent for a moment then lowers his voice. "Do you have a clean gun?"

Fleck can recognize the confusion on the Voice's face. "Non-traceable … no registration number."

His lack of response reveals the answer.

"Come with me. I have a pistol you can use." They go in the back door. He produces a weapon and hands it to the Voice.

Fleck watches the big man return to his car and feels even less confident than when the Voice had arrived not twenty-five minutes earlier.

Twenty Six

CHECK UNDER THE HOOD

Eva Czapleski sits in the waiting room of one of the biggest law firms in the nation's capital. Inlaid wood trims the vaulted ceilings, and cut glass welcomes your entrance to a major player in the most legally documented city on Earth. Eva is physically and mentally exhausted, fighting for Emrik in a strange town against people who seem to hold a royal flush in every hand.

This is about to change.

The receptionist is kind to the frightened woman, offering her coffee, water, and danish pastries to pass the time. Eva has lost eight pounds during the D.C. stay, on a frame already too thin. Pressure is coming from all sides, some of it with good intentions, some not. The manager at her restaurant has been encouraging on one hand while asking when she is returning to New Orleans on the other. Eva understands that her boss's workload has doubled since her absence, and she knows she would be asking the same question if the situation were reversed.

A good-looking young man leads Eva to a boardroom overlooking the city's K Street corridor, but she is too weary to take in the view. She is more concerned about the dress she has worn three days in a row. The dress, full of wrinkles, is the only thing suitable to wear because she had left New Orleans in such a state of stress and confusion. Now, focusing on such a small issue helps to hold off her panic about Emrik.

Jim Young enters with a serious demeanor on his face and a file. He lays it on the twelve-foot-long table for Eva to examine. She manages a faint smile while flipping it open on the polished rosewood surface.

"Relax, nothing is going to happen to Emrik other than returning to New Orleans with you shortly," Young says, offering his hand. She takes it and begins to cry.

His hand is a warm and giving grip, but Eva cannot stop the tears. He offers a hanky, and she wipes her eyes continuously for the next couple of minutes. Young is patient and allows Eva the freedom to vent some of the pent-up emotion she has carried for weeks.

"I'm sorry. I've never felt so alone in my life. Emrik is everything to me." Eva smiles again, a slightly larger expression.

Young's confident voice floats through the air to her ears. "We've gone through the report and reviewed the video. It's a tragedy, but Emrik is not responsible. The Feds would be fools to file any charges against him," he assures.

"Why do you say that? It's the government. They have unlimited powers."

"Beyond the fact that they induced hypnosis on a twelve-year-old—a process you tried to stop at the last minute—what happened to Emrik in the kidnapping is something the Feds don't want exposed in a trial." Young's confidence is slowly seeping into Eva's demeanor.

"I don't understand about the kidnapping. What are the Feds trying to cover up?"

"This abduction has all the markings of a real UFO encounter," he explains. "Emrik's contact with radioactive material. The multiple witnesses, including a police detective, watching your son being taken by someone or something defying physics in the escape. Hundreds of so-called UFO abductions occur around the world every year. Less than one percent meet the criteria Emrik's has demonstrated."

The door opens, and Randall Specks, Young's partner, enters and is introduced.

"Good timing, Randall. Tell Eva about the upcoming announcement."

"Eva, are you familiar with Project Blue Book?" Specks asks.

"To be honest, no."

"Blue Book came along back in the fifties. It was commissioned to study UFO phenomena. Everything about the program was top-secret, even reports gathered and studied by the highest military officials. Our military brass had two goals, to disprove visitation from other planets but at the same time make sure the unexplained objects flying around in our airspace didn't originate from a Russian military complex."

"Like the 'X-Files' on TV?" Eva asks, her eyes beginning to reveal understanding.

"Exactly, but on a much larger scale," Specks explains. "Blue Book commanded a large budget to finance its operation, but defunding in the eighties closed the operation down. We have a source in the Pentagon telling us a new Blue Book-like program has been under way for several years. Here's the key. The government is going to announce the program's existence and release UFO footage in the next few months."

"So what does this have to do with keeping Emrik out of trouble?"

"For lack of a better term, Emrik is their prized student, a link to something suddenly very important. We do have a downside, however. The Feds will want more from Emrik..."

"We're comfortable you will have control of his accessibility," Young interrupts.

Specks lays a document on the table. "This will garner Emrik's freedom."

Young's phone chirps, like a bird in a nest receiving a worm. "Speaking of the devil, the friendly Feds want our presence to start the negotiations. Let the games begin."

◆

The limousine passes through the guard post at the entrance to Walter Reed and proceeds to the front door of the building housing Emrik. Specks gets out on the passenger side, and as the law firm's driver rounds to open the rear passenger door, Young turns to Eva. "Let us do the talking. If you are asked a question, please glance my way before answering."

Eva smiles and nods affirmatively. For the first time since this nightmare began, she feels a sense of control and is no longer worried about the wrinkles in her dress.

They enter a meeting room that seats about thirty people around a large central table. When Eva and Young enter, fifteen individuals are already seated, among them a dozen solemn faces with various military uniforms, none of them present in the observation room during the hypnosis. No introductions or friendly chit-chat permeates. Nevertheless, Eva feels confident. Young pulls her chair out from the table for seating, demonstrating he's a gentlemen.

Young begins the conversation. "My client would like an update on her son's condition and when she can take him home."

"It's a little more complicated than that, counselor," Michael Thompson answers.

"No, it's the start and end of this meeting. If you have something to add in the middle, have at it." Young sounds stoic and adamant.

"The CIA wants to charge Emrik with murdering one of their high-ranking officers," Thompson counters.

"A tragedy to say the least, but putting a twelve-year-old under hypnosis against his mother's wishes? I don't think that would sit too well with a jury, particularly when over three-quarters of this country doesn't trust the government to pave the road in front of their house. So stop the pandering and give this woman an update on her son." Young leans back in the chair and folds his arms.

Thompson turns to Major Sherbrooke and exchanges a few low words.

"Emrik has been cleared to fly in the next couple of days," Thompson says, relaying the thoughts between the men. "But we need more cooperation from Emrik and his mother before we can release him."

Specks answers. "If we agree to more interrogation—and that's a big 'if'—we need a release from any and all charges surrounding what has transpired and anything that may occur in the future."

He slides two copies of a document across the table toward Thompson, who waves to the other end of the table. Two government attorneys take the document and leave the room.

"What more do you want from this family?" Young asks. "You have left them dazed and in shock."

"We need to put Emrik under hypnosis again," Sherbrooke asserts.

Eva places a hand over her mouth and inhales a rush of air, attracting attention from everyone at the table..

"You must be out of your collective minds," Young says sternly. "That's never going to happen after what the child has been exposed to." He places his hand on Eva's shoulder.

Admiral Jessip stands. "This is non-negotiable. Tell them, Major Sherbrooke."

"Tell us what?" Young stands up. "And it better be a damned good story."

Sherbrooke looks at the admiral as if caught grabbing the wrong female's derrière at his boss's party. "After Emrik shoved the pen in his neck, for precautionary reasons we gave him a modular MRI. We found what we suspect is a microchip about the size of a pencil dot. We are performing further analysis to attempt to determine its functionality … if any."

"So this foreign microchip placed in Emrik's body could possibly alter his behavior? Do something like fire a weapon unconsciously?" Young asks.

"We don't know what it's capable of doing. Our scientists need to dig deeper. Ms. Czapleski," Thompson looks at Eva, "your son might be subject to a subsequent abduction. We can provide protection through the U.S. Marshals service, but we need another session with Emrik to explore what and how this came about."

Young and Specks exchange glances. "Let us discuss in private. May we get our release today?" They stand, and Eva joins them.

Jessip rises as well. "No, not without another session. Otherwise, the government's position will be to pursue a murder charge."

"Noted." Young says and leaves the room with Eva and Specks. They head to a small office at the end of the hall.

"I think it's a bluff," Specks says, shutting the door behind him.

"It's not a bluff," Young counters. "Their backs are against the wall with this microchip they found. It's up to you, Eva. We'll defend Emrik pro-bono, no matter how this thing goes."

"Is he telling the truth about another abduction?" Eva asks, her confidence once again retreating.

"Government lying is an art form. But common sense tells me U.S. Marshals' protection would be a valuable asset for your family. One more hypnosis and you can head home with Emrik—the bottom line that really matters."

"Emotionally, it scares me to death," Eva says. "But I need to take my emotions out of the formula and look at the long-term consequences, pro and con." Eva stares at a shelf of books on the far wall and then back at Young. "Let's do it, so I can take my son home."

"Alright, I'll tell them to schedule the hypnosis for tomorrow morning. Meanwhile, try to rest. You'll need to be strong for Emrik." Young walks out of the office and heads back to the boardroom. He soon returns with the signed release protecting Emrik from any prosecution.

◆

Eva walks through the hotel lobby numbed by the previous activity and watches the elevator reduce the floor numbers, counting backward to the lobby level.

"Ms. Czapleski?" A woman's voice comes from somewhere behind her, pronouncing her name perfectly. Eva turns but cannot identify the voice's origination. Then an early thirties lady raises her hand and advances to the elevator area.

"Ms. Czapleski, I'm Brooke Davenport of the U.S. Marshals service." She reaches into her coat pocket and reveals an ID, which Eva views with little enthusiasm. At this point, she has no interest in federal agency staff members, even one sent for protection. But when Davenport pushes her hand out, Eva shakes it, wondering how much further things will be intruding into her life.

"Please call me Eva." Her Southern upbringing has always made manners a priority, regardless of her need to shower and crawl into bed as soon as she returns to her room.

"May I buy you a cup of coffee?" Davenport offers.

Eva unconsciously steals a glance at the arriving elevators and the several individuals walking out the open doors.

"It's just an introductory thing. My son is nine, and I would like to find out about Emrik. What a great name! How did you come up with it?" she asks, trying disarm Eva by bringing Emrik into the conversation.

"Okay, we can talk, but I need to go to bed early." Eva does not want to shut the door on this woman's kindness, despite being near exhaustion.

The two women sit in the hotel restaurant, and the first thing Davenport hands Eva is a photo of her son, Hunter. Eva matches with a picture of Emrik, and they discuss the boys as if at a first-time PTA meeting. Davenport makes notes on Emrik's likes and dislikes, the story behind his grandfather's death, and how they arrived at this point at Walter Reed.

Eva feels a kinship with her immediately, and an hour into their conversation a sense of calm returns along with a newfound energy. So much so that Eva keeps on talking until ten o'clock, when Davenport finally breaks it off.

"I'll see you in New Orleans in a couple of days. We'll work on the scheduling so I'm not in your way on a daily basis. The idea is to blend into your life while still providing a sense of security," She rises and hugs Eva. "Can't wait to see Emrik do his dancing. I understand he's quite the talent."

"He's certainly a ham when it comes to it. Yes, see you in New Orleans."

Eva goes straight to bed, bypassing the hot shower but feeling more confident about the future.

◆

Attorneys Young and Specks flank Eva in the observation room waiting for Dr. Wang and Emrik to appear. Eva touches the side of her head, fingering the four stitches in her hairline still sore from the previous session fall. Nothing at this point is going to make her feel better until she is on a plane headed home with Emrik by her side.

Dr. Wang walks into the empty operating room hand-in-hand with Emrik and sits him on a chair next to an easel and whiteboard. Wang soon begins swinging his jeweled coin inches from Emrik's face. A sense of innocence or familiarity allows Emrik to be led through the hypnosis process silently with no resistance. Eva has enough anxiety to cover any shortage on Emrik's part.

Deep into his mind's inner thoughts under the spell of the coin, Emrik looks different to Eva. His eyes do not roll back in his head like the hypnosis produced previously. Emrik appears fresh and wide-eyed, as if getting on a swing set at the park surrounded by other kids.

"Emrik, let's go back to the plane you flew on when you were abducted. How many people are on the plane with you?" Dr. Wang inquires.

Emrik holds up three fingers.

"So three people are present?"

"Yes." Emrik swings his feet back and forth sitting on the chair.

"Are they nice people, Emrik?"

"No!" Emrik practically shouts. "They hurt me."

"Where did they hurt you?" Wang looks at a paper and makes a note.

Emrik rises from the chair and stands next to him, pointing to the back of his neck.

"Anyplace else, Emrik?"

Emrik's hand rises to his eyelids, and fingers pull the eyelashes upward, revealing a wide-open look.

"Your eyes were examined?"

"Yes."

"Emrik, can you draw what these people look like?" He hands Emrik a marking pen and leads him to the whiteboard.

Emrik's demeanor changes dramatically. His back stiffens, and he eyes the board like a highly trained and gifted Disney artist sizing up a cartoon character to be transformed onto a canvas. With incredible speed, Emrik's hand works the marker back and forth. First he outlines a figure and then rushes through extreme detail on the face and, ultimately, body markings and shape.

Emrik's work stuns far more than Eva's eyes.

Twenty Seven

SKINWALKER RANCH

Jessie has always loved the people of South Louisiana, and there seemed to be endless stories about the quirky Cajun land, unique in the United States. But she has also made several trips to Arkansas to see her father, and the scenery took her heart by storm. The flat geography of Louisiana starts changing to hills and valleys soon after crossing the Arkansas line, making the drive a refreshing visual of distant hilltops and a feeling of heading into the sky.

An hour short of Michael McGaha's cabin on the White River, Jessie stops at Carter's Diner, perched like an eagle's nest on a sheer cliff, providing a view of another set of mountains twenty-five miles distant.

Jessie, being afraid of heights, makes her way slowly to a table next to the floor-to-ceiling windows, weighing uncomfortable thoughts against the breathtaking view. By the time the iced tea and apple pie arrive, the distant scenery has pushed the fear of falling two-thousand feet to the valley below to a far corner of her memory.

"Anything else, honey?" the middle-aged waitress asks in a Southern accent. She seems genuinely interested in the answer.

"No, thanks. The view and pie are perfect," Jessie responds.

The waitress writes a note on the bill and lays it on the table. "Glad to share the view with another outsider on their way to someplace moving at a much faster pace."

The apple pie was good—no, damned good in Jessie's estimate when it met her lips. To hell with Chris Dale, Jessie thinks, cursing under her breath and imagining that his view today is probably over a pile of bodies back in New Orleans.

Beyond the view and apple pie, the reason Jessie stops at Carter's is to buy a large bag of homemade peanut brittle, which Michael McGaha loves.

Jessie grew up in a loving home, but her mother was oppressively strict and had laid out a clear path for her, from boyfriends to what Jessie was going to study in college. Like many teenage girls, she rebelled and fought constantly with her mother over each directional push and other minute details. The final straw came over Jessie's wish to become a journalist. But her father had put his foot down, siding with her on the career choice. As a result, Sylvia McGaha did not speak to her daughter throughout her college freshman year, and even though things moderated by graduation, the shunning left a bitter taste in Jessie's mouth and moved her even closer to Michael. Sylvia passed away with breast cancer six months before Jessie's first book was published. Jessie was convinced she died thinking her daughter was a failure.

◆

Jessie drives across the bridge transversing the White River, one of the best fisheries in the world for German brown and rainbow trout. Michael spent his career in D.C., and Jessie knew his retirement would be far away from crowds and close to fly-fishing.

She turns onto a gravel road winding up a steep incline, Michael's cabin comes into view, neatly perched and surrounded by oak trees filling out with spring foliage.

Getting out of the car, the air smells clear and sweet. Jessie hears the White River's restless churning as she approaches the empty carport. Her father's absence isn't alarming. Only extreme winter weather would keep him from walking the shoals in waders, casting a lure created by his own hands.

Settling into a recliner on the back porch, she takes in the view of the river below, white water rushing over large rocks, and pools of calmness lying under the chaotic motion. It has always been easy for her to understand the hypnotic attractiveness the river provides in both sight and sound. Leaning further back in the recliner, Jessie's stress flows away, and her muscles relax. When Michael approaches, She has fallen deeply asleep.

"Jessie!" Michael rounds the cabin corner with Wallace Spence, a fellow longtime CIA staff member. A hand on Jessie's shoulder brings her back to reality.

"You enjoying the river?" He smiles at the sight of his daughter awakening.

She quickly gathers her senses and hugs him. "Sorry, didn't even realize I was napping."

"Jessie, this is Wallace Spence, a good friend—a pretty decent trout guy, also."

Jessie shakes his extended hand. "Call me Skip. Your father is angry because I just caught the biggest brown in three days."

"Pleasure to meet you. So, you had a good day on the river?"

"Skip had a great day. Used a sorry store-bought Mepps spinner he found in a convenience store to catch a four-pound brown. That will cost him."

"I'm sure the price will be steep," Skip counters. "I've heard so much about you, Jessie. It's certainly my pleasure."

"I assume my father has held you captive the last couple days. He knows two things very well, fishing and me." She kisses her father's cheek, appreciating the attention. "So, where is my dinner? Still swimming in the river?"

"Michael is conservative when it comes to his pet trout. We released everything today, including my big German. He did let me take a picture, though." He shows her his prized catch.

"Wow, beautiful trout!" She turns to Michael. "I drove from New Orleans for fresh fish. You let them go?"

"In a sense of full disclosure, we've had trout the last three nights. I thought we'd crank up the grill for a few burgers. But we'll catch lunch for tomorrow. Is that a compromise worth having?"

"That's such a government response. Like the rest of America, I will have to suck it up and like it." Her comment makes both men laugh.

"I'll start the grill," Michael says. "Skip, can you grab a beer for everyone?" He moves to the grill that has cooked a thousand meals but looks like he bought it yesterday.

"Sure." Skip opens the back door and retreats into the house.

Jessie notices that Skip opened the door without a key. "Dad, you don't lock your doors when going off fishing all day?"

Michael pours lighter fluid on the charcoal, and the flames jump in response to a match tossed onto the mixture. "Jessie, this isn't New Orleans. People respect property around here."

A deer and her fawn tentatively approach the sizable garden, now showing the bean sprouts Michael had planted several weeks earlier. Skip walks out carrying three beers.

"Skip, flip that far-left switch. Thanks."

Jessie is in awe of the deer walking close to the cabin and starts taking photos on her phone. "They are so beautiful."

The doe extends her head over the fence and starts eating the new sprouts.

Skip hands Jessie a beer. "Those are Michael's pets, also. The fence is electric, but he turns it off for the deer to eat."

"Really?" Jessie turns away from the deer to her father placing patties on the grill. "You let them eat your garden?"

"Only Maxine receives that kind of access," he explains. "She has a baby to feed."

"Maxine, huh? You never cease to amaze me, Dad." She holds her beer high in salute to the doe and her fawn. "To Maxine and the next deer generation on the White River."

Michael takes a large sip of beer, sets it on the table, and turns back to the burgers. "I do draw the line when my tomatoes start coming out, which will be in a couple of weeks. I won't share those."

"Principles, must admire a man having those kind of principles." Skip says, winking at Jessie and earning a smile in return.

Jessie watches the doe nip the beans as she eats a cheeseburger, and the fawn obediently trails step-for-step waiting his turn for the milk, soon to be accessible when mother finishes her own meal. The river and deer overpower Jessie's visual senses, further distancing the emotional upheaval back in New Orleans. Another beer, and the feeling of being on a different planet settles neatly in her mind. As darkness begins to hide the river's sight but heightens the sound, Michael builds a fire in the pit, and Jessie shares her story behind each of her published books. Skip urges her to unseal the hidden secrets behind the murder cases; how they were solved and what eventually happened to the survivors left behind to rebuild their lives.

It becomes a night about Jessie's talents and, even though self-centered in tone, Michael and Skip keep the fire and questions blazing to prolong the process. Jessie feels good. For a change, it is all about her.

◆

Michael wakes Jessie at 6:15 the next morning to a breakfast ready for consumption. The sun is just waking, too, and Jessie is not sure about the eagerness shown the night before to join them on the river, even though the pancakes are worth the early rise.

Michael clears a bacon strip from his plate and turns to her. "I have another set of waders and rod if you want to fish."

"No, that rod-whip thing you do has never worked for me. I will enjoy the river and watching you catch my lunch." She smiles large.

◆

The drive is slow and deliberate, covering the last mile of dirt road and avoiding large rocks that seem to grow from the rutted trail, driven countless times by men clothed up to their chest in rubber.

Michael and Skip remove their gear from the truck bed while Jessie edges close to the fast-moving water, trying to see what lunch might look like. Silver flashes come and go in the rising sunshine-drenched stream. She remembers her father describing schools of small trout reflecting the light, released into the river by the Game and Fish Commission. The bigger fish lie in wait at ambush points in the deeper pools, not wasting their energy on exploration.

The two men spend an inordinate amount of time, in Jessie's mind, talking lures by the truck, when fish seem to be lurking behind most rocks. Both men come to a negotiated decision on the tools needed for the appropriate trout response. Skip heads downstream, and Michael walks the road in the opposite direction. Jessie trails Skip at a distance in his pursuit of the bigger trout catch between him and Michael. Having fished alongside her father, Jessie understands the concentration required to be successful and does not engage in conversation.

The trout suddenly cooperate. Skip catches three rainbows in six casts, while Jessie videos the process and gives him a thumbs-up for the action. An aggressive brown bows the rod and threatens to break the four-pound line. He tries to maneuver the large fish through the boulder-strewn channel, and man and fish alike are successful early in the struggle.

Jessie is happily engaged in the process, following the action on her phone while maintaining balance walking the grade-changing bank. The brown makes one last energetic dart downriver but gives in to Skip's skill and the hand net. The six-pound-plus trophy will be the catch of the day. Jessie stops the video, claps for the success, and quickly snaps several photos before he releases the big German brown.

Skip climbs out of the river and reviews his once-in-a-lifetime trout skirmish on Jessie's phone. Jessie receives a hug from him for capturing the priceless event and sharing the private moment in person. Like every fishing-crazed individual in history, he wades back into the freezing water convinced an even bigger brown is about to make a debut. The fishing slows after the intense action, letting the conversation echo across the water.

"So, Michael tells me you have an interesting storyline for your next book. Want to share?" He continues casting the free-flowing line on the nine-foot rod, but his focus has clearly shifted.

Jessie is warming to the attention and welcomes the

opportunity to merge closer on a personal and professional level. As with any good writer, she vividly paints the portrait of the personal relationship between Emrik and his grandfather, and what fate dealt them. Ten minutes into the narration, Skip stops fishing and wades to the bank, now drawn into the intricacies of the multiple homicides and the conjuring of evil forces seemingly instigating the sequence of events.

Skip is totally engaged and asks pertinent questions as the two walk back to the truck. Michael is setting up the Coleman stove to cook the rainbows next to the White's beautiful water.

The thought of preparing the equipment and fish for the frying pan comes to a sudden halt as Jessie explains what happened in D.C. with Emrik's shooting of a CIA officer. Both men deny knowing the victim personally. Both are convinced his rank and position in the agency was near the top, meaning the report of the abduction and radiation Emrik suffered probably went to the White House for discussion.

"I didn't know someone in the agency was killed," Michael says.

"It all happened in the last few days. I'm not sure of Emrik's legal status, yet."

"That will be an interesting turn of legal wrangling," Skip adds. "I've never heard any case even close to those circumstances."

"Dad said you might have experience at the agency that could shed light on the case." Jessie raises the subject she had driven from New Orleans to discuss.

"Maybe, maybe not," Skip answers vaguely.

Jessie pulls out her phone. "May I record your thoughts?"

He shakes his head in the pristine air. "No. Sorry, but I have a pension to protect."

"Skip, you and I go way back. There's nothing off the record you might add?"

"Well, I've seen things that might be connected—but those events can't show up in a book."

Jessie puts away the phone. "I've become close to Emrik and his family. If you have something that would help them get through this, I'd be grateful. I don't want anything else negative happening. It won't appear in my book."

"Strictly off the record, right?"

"Yes, off the record."

"In 2007, I led a nuclear-response team investigating an incident in Utah. A group of paleontologists found a T-Rex skeleton in a dig. Three of them died from exposure to a radioactive source.

In fact, the entire group suffered varying degrees of..."

Before he can finish, Jessie jumps in. "Was any of the paleontologists named Kidd?"

"To be honest I don't remember the names. I'll go back to my notes and let you know. The dig was on a five-hundred-acre stretch known as Skinwalker Ranch. An area with a reputation of crazy-assed things happening back to settler days. The locals won't go near it."

"So this group of bone-hunters dug up radioactive material?" Michael asks.

"No, the dig site was clean. We did find radioactive emissions, including microwave, in a series of caves more than a half-mile away. The survivors all swore they were abducted by UFOs."

"Just like Emrik?" Jessie asks with a half-question/half-fact.

"Just like Emrik," Skip repeats.

"Damn! That's beyond belief," Michael says. "How did you guys respond from a scientific standpoint?"

"Hogwash was the official response. To be honest, I thought the same thing. The assumption was the diggers explored the caves and suffered illusions from toxic shock."

"But something tells me you don't believe that."

"Well, following scientific protocol, we measured atmospheric conditions for radioactivity by firing rockets up six-thousand feet to sample the air. We found a high degree of contamination. A scary set of conditions, but that was the least of our issues..." He hesitates and starts removing the waders. "Are we going to eat trout or whistle Dixie?"

"No way in living hell you're not going to finish this story," Michael demands.

He looks at Michael and finishes pulling off the waders. "You know exactly how serious the agency can be. We could lose more than our pensions if this leaks out. You willing to bet everything on knowing what we found?"

"Dad," Jessie interjects, placing her hand on her father's arm. "I don't want to go any further. It's not worth it."

"My daughter has given her word to not use the information, and in spite of the truth that should be exposed, she is a person of extreme integrity." He puts his arm around her shoulder, and Jessie has to summon all her strength not to begin crying uncontrollably.

"We spent four months onsite firing rockets," Skip continues, "and drilling two-hundred-foot holes in the ground. The locals were right, the place scared me more than working years in the Middle

East chasing terrorists. Our instruments continuously failed. Hell, we couldn't even keep batteries charged and functional. After the second series of rockets launched, we started seeing objects appear in the sky. It was as though the rockets were acting like a dog whistle for UFOs. We documented their appearance with telescopic photo equipment. When we sent it back to Langley, all hell broke loose. Deputy directors flew in, not believing until seeing with their own eyes what was happening around a rocket launch. The Navy brought in F-18s to give chase, but the UFOs simply blasted out of sight. Then we'd launch another rocket, and they reappeared. It was cat-and-mouse shit—and we turned out to be the mouse."

"So forget science," Michael says. "What does your gut tell you?" He and Jessie lean against the truck in anticipation.

"Do you remember Dr. Telly Frombort?"

"Einstein, the guy we called Einstein?"

"Yeah, the smartest person I have ever been around. He spent twenty-two days with us watching, scratching notes, rolling those fat joints. One night I'm trading drags on the dope, and I asked him the same question. He takes a deep hit and looks at the night sky. 'Those are highly developed creatures from another world,' he said, 'stopping at Earth to refuel with atomic energy. We are nothing more than lab rats, something to experiment on, something to see how the human race reacts.' Then I asked him why won't they interact … expose themselves, beings that have nothing to fear if so superior. He smiled that crooked grin of his and said. 'When you stop to fill your tank with gas, do you have an interest in the rats running around the sewer beneath your feet'?" He pauses as if throwing the question out to get a response.

"That's frightening," Jessie says, her mind now working in high gear.

"As I'm digesting those thoughts, Einstein throws the conversation into a totally new direction." Skip looks into Jessie's eyes and continues. "He says, 'I have a parallel theory. What if the Devil exists but not in the Biblical sense?' Now Einstein is talking way above my head, and I asked him to qualify. He went on. 'Having far superior technology, they could program humans to do evil things then track the outcome of tragedies as a control mechanism.' What he said hit me so hard I retired ten months later to get away from any more realities. Do you know what makes Einstein's theory so powerfully truthful?"

"What?" Michael asks with a furrowed eyebrow.

"If mankind found inferior life on another planet, we would do

the same thing."
  He lays the waders in the back of the truck.

Twenty Eight

I NEED SOMEBODY

Trey eats his breakfast in total quiet. Lilly instinctively knows his mood has been pressed to the brink of exploding, and she hurriedly moves out of sight after depositing eggs and bacon on the table. The ill-gotten mood is fed by multiple sources of doubt and disgust. What rolls around in Trey's head playing bumper pool comprises facets of love, betrayal, need, calamity, and loss of control. All scrambled like the eggs staring back from the gold-scribed plate.

His grandfather had wanted him back at work the day after returning from the Mexican kidnapping, but the doctor overruled the old man. Since his flight hit the tarmac in New Orleans, his relationship with Gayle has been distant and contorted. Only days removed from their walk on the beach and intense physical attraction, a shroud of doubt has fallen on them. Trey does not want to face up to the negative reality between the two at this moment; he has larger concerns awaiting at Stephens Publishing.

◆

The drive to the office has Trey feeling mentally neutered, like a drunk going home after a long bar night on autopilot.

"Trey, welcome back ... so good to see you." Gabby smiles large when he enters the reception area.

"Good to be back, thanks," he says, returning a forced smile.

The elevator seems slow arriving on the ground floor to take Trey upward. Maybe it knows this isn't going to end well. Cindy, the old man's secretary, sits like a sentinel outside his office and is surprised to see Trey's approach.

"How are you feeling, Trey?" she asks, not hearing the sanitized answer she expected.

"Like I want to punch a hole through the wall," Trey informs, moving past her desk and opening the patriarch's door without formally giving notice in the matter. Cindy rises from her chair while Trey disappears into the office closing the door.

Stephens, on the phone, hastily excuses himself and hangs

up.

"Trey, coming back early. That makes me happy."

"I need the truth," Trey says, his expression one that his grandfather has never seen before. "What did you do to my parents?"

"Why would I hurt them? One happened to be my son." The old man knows this moment would be coming sooner or later.

"You have the full story. Stop the bullshit or I'm leaving the company."

Stephens slumps deeper into the large leather chair and suddenly seems frail and diminutive, the reality ready to pound him into the corporate sewer drain. His beloved company could not afford to lose Trey.

"I've always tried to protect you from an ugly truth about your father, but you're leaving me no option."

"I'm a big boy—try me."

"Your father was having sex with a black woman in a cemetery when he got killed. He was going to divorce your mother and move off with that whore, leaving Helen and you for that piece of trash. That's the truth. I'm tired of covering it up to save everyone's perception of my son." Stephens suddenly feels emotional relief, despite not painting the full picture of his involvement.

"So, you had Louis Fleck murder my father because you couldn't stand him being with a black woman. Did you kill my mother, too?"

"No, that's crazy talk." He stands, backbone fully restored. "This is your father's doing, not mine. I don't have a clue who killed them."

"You know more. Better think long and hard or you can take this company and shove it up your ass." Trey rises, approaching the old man's desk. "You're through running all aspects of my life, including who I date." He starts for the door.

"Just like your father."

Trey turns. "What's that suppose to mean?"

"That woman living at your house is evil, and you're too blind to see it." Stephens sits back in his chair, understanding these words could completely unravel what little is left of the relationship with his grandson.

Trey realizes if he does not leave now he will do something extreme to the old, hollow-looking man staring back at him with his evil eyes. He slams the door on the way out.

◆

The Voice had watched first Lilly and then Trey leave the house hurriedly. He feels certain the property has no other eyes to see him jump the fence and move his six-foot-six frame across the yard to the house. Having been told to scout the situation and report to Fleck before taking action, he is determined to explore the lay of the land. He had made that determination after he Googled what "recon" meant.

A stop at the edge of the garage allows a breath of restored air to enter his lungs as he continues to the front porch. Jumping fences will do that. Looking through windows periodically, the Voice photographs and circles the property, still unsure what to look for but focused intently in the process.

◆

Gayle has been tapping the keys on her MacBook, trying to keep her mind on writing and ignoring the large fracture in the relationship with Trey that seems to be expanding. Other than bringing her lunch yesterday, Trey's noticeable absence and lack of communication are striking at her heart. Although determined to give him space, she frequently walks to the front window of the bungalow and looks to the house, something that gives her a small shred of connecting.

This time, she spots a large man conspicuously walking around the property. The sight is definitely out of the norm, and it plants a sense of fright in her stomach. The Voice, completely unaware of most things in life, has no clue his picture is being taken when circling the pool and peering into a picture window.

Gayle follows the peeping giant, clicking her phone's camera as he disappears around the side of the house and eventually returns to his car. The phone yields several excellent photos, and Gayle calls Trey, trying to determine whether the strange occurrence is trouble or not.

◆

Trey is driving fast toward home, daring law enforcement to pull him over. The ringing phone captures his attention momentarily, but he quickly turns it off when he reads Gayle is on the other end. He has no desire to interact with anyone at the moment. He turns off the cell's power, trying to restore a sense of control. Gayle has forwarded her photos of the trespasser; Trey, however, has put the world on ignore.

The Mercedes stops just short of the back wall in the garage, and Trey makes no effort to shut the garage door. Rather he opts to kick at the kitchen door to force his entrance. The door is unyielding, and after numerous black shoe imprints and bruised toes, Trey opens it, pissed at the sound construction. The grandfather clock watches Trey abduct a canister of Scotch from the liquor cabinet and take a large drink, ignoring decorum. He heads downstairs to the shooting range, canister in hand.

A .40-caliber pistol riddles the imaginary outline of his grandfather on the cardboard thirty feet down the range. Reloading the gun and the Scotch in his mouth, thirteen more shell casings hit the carpet next to his feet. Trey rips the earphones off and checks for the fourteenth live round properly chambered and ready to be fired. He swallows the canister's last bit of Scotch and throws the crystal container against the wall, shattering it on impact. Trey places the silver barrel of the pistol in his mouth and sits down in a chair to weigh the consequences.

It takes great strength to blow the back of your own head off. Weak people rarely commit suicide, but Trey is not weak. One more drink would give him the necessary bravado to pull the trigger, but the source lies shattered. His fingertip laced tight against the trigger, a slight pressure will quickly end the need for love and quell the thoughts of being abandoned as a baby.

"Trey, are you there?" Gayle's distant voice inquires.

He suddenly removes the pistol from his mouth and answers, "Yes, be right up."

He places the .40-cal in a wall-mounted gun case, but the lock lies next to a lamp unused for the moment. Trey wipes his face clean of the useless tears and tries to regain composure as he ascends the stairs to the living room. The Scotch overtakes the adrenaline-fueled rage running through his body only seconds before.

"Are you okay?" Gayle asks, never seeing Trey so disheveled.

"Had it out with the old man today. I sucked down a couple Scotches to celebrate." He takes a step in Gayle's direction but stumbles under the influence. She catches him.

"You should have called me. I would have celebrated with you." She leads him to the couch and sits next to him.

"Turned my phone off," Trey informs, slightly slurred in the delivery.

"Let's get you to bed." She helps him to his feet and moves to the bedroom. She undresses him, but he refuses to lie down.

"I need some water," he says.

"I'll get it. Please look at this photo. The guy was looking in your windows today." Gayle hands Trey the phone and leaves the room. When she returns, Trey is lying on the bed passed out.

◆

When Gayle returns to the bungalow, she pulls Chris Dale's business card from her wallet and calls him.

"Detective Dale, this is Gayle Kidd."

"How may I help you?"

"I took photos of a man sneaking around Trey's home today. I just forwarded them, do you recognize him?"

"Hold on," he says, calling up the photos. "I'll be damned! That's Herman Dailey. He works for Louis Fleck at the casino off Military Trail. What exactly was he doing?"

"He was circling the house and taking photos close to the windows. Basically a peeping Tom. Is he dangerous?"

"Could be, I'll pay him and Fleck a visit and let you know what's going on."

◆

Dailey, aka the Voice, had shared the recon photos with Louis Fleck but received a cold shoulder. It was an upsetting moment, and Fleck told him to stay away from the home because it was probably equipped with video. Make the hit after dark when Gayle and Trey drive away from the property. With an hour left to darkness, Dailey goes home to eat before returning to the tracking assignment.

At the end of his third sandwich, Dailey's cat, Tubby, runs to the kitchen door wanting out. One more mouthful of potato chips and he complies with the request. Tubby hurries past the garage in haste, and Dailey follows him a couple of steps into the backyard. Out of sight for a few seconds, the cat cries out for help in the bushes and goes silent.

Dailey rapidly turns back to the kitchen, goes to the living room and grabs a shotgun from behind the couch. A pump of the handle places a twelve-gauge shell in the chamber. He walks hurriedly to a bookcase and retrieves a Bible with a cross and rosary lying inside. After kissing the cross, he sits in a corner surrounded by the approaching dark. He lights a cigarette and takes a long drag then exhales the smoke, his bravery rapidly conceding to the unknown.

A distinct sound of footsteps is slowly planted, one after

another, on the second floor overhead. Dailey stands, watches the ceiling intently, and takes two steps directly under the movement, but the ceiling becomes silent. New footsteps shortly form a pattern, and he points the shotgun at the ceiling and fires twice. Wood and plaster fall from the suddenly large holes decorating the living room. The second spent shell is ejected amid the quiet, and he backs next to the picture window, anticipating someone coming down the stairwell at the other end of the room.

Suddenly, something crashes through the picture window behind Dailey, hitting him in the back. In absolute panic, he rushes forward to the kitchen and out the back door, falling on the patio steps. From the concrete, he fires a shotgun blast into the open kitchen door and pulls himself up using the shotgun as a crutch.

A large figure moves fast and rounds the corner of the garage. A blade hits Dailey in the center of the chest, knocking him backward to the ground. Blood fills his mouth, and Daily struggles to inhale in a desperate need for air.

◆

Bobby Rabold and Chris Dale have visited the casino and received an audience with Louis Fleck. In spite of the dread suddenly engulfing Fleck about Herman Dailey's incompetence, and the possibility of being arrested on the spot for accessory to murder, the detectives must leave armed only with conjecture. No related facts about Dailey's strange appearance at Trey's house were be pinned on Fleck for the moment.

As the two detectives drive away from the casino, Chris asks Rabold, "What the hell do we need to haul Fleck in on murder charges? He's knee-deep in this shit."

"It's all circumstantial," Rabold answers. "Mike Broadaway would take a two-minute look and toss it back in our faces. There's only one way to break this case. We need someone from the inside to back our facts and connect them to Fleck. I have an idea. We both know the hired killer sitting in jail didn't kill the hooker."

"Yeah … go on."

"Let's make him a deal. Turn state's evidence against Fleck and get immunity. We'll have Fleck on a murder-for-hire rap, and he goes to jail, dying there."

Chris thinks for a moment. "I like it. You're onto something. Also, I've frazzled Dailey into giving inside info before. Let's squeeze him tonight."

"I'm in for waterboarding, and if that doesn't work we can rely on your own torture techniques."

Chris laughs. "Should have never admitted what I did. You'd turn me in to Internal Affairs for a donut."

"You obviously don't know the depth of our friendship. It would take a dozen crème-filled. Don't ever sell me short again."

◆

Chris parks the cruiser in front of Dailey's small, two-story house, and both cops immediately see the broken picture window. Weapons drawn, they approach the scene cautiously.

Chris turns to Rabold. "I'll take the front. You cover the back."

"Done." Rabold walks toward the house and disappears around the side .

Chris approaches the picture window, but the interior is dark, and nothing stares back through the shattered pane.

"NOPD! Coming in! Police!" Chris screams at the front door. He turns the doorknob, but it is locked. He returns to the broken window and enters, again shouting, "Police!"

Chris switches on his flashlight, which outlines a dead cat on the floor covered in glass. He moves the light to the stairwell and heads to the second floor, finding nothing but an unmade bed, scattered dirty clothes, and shotgun-blown holes in the hallway floor. He returns downstairs and cases the kitchen, seeing the door open and Rabold approaching.

"The big man is dead, stabbed like Bailly at the casino," Rabold relays as Chris holsters his pistol.

"Nothing in the house except a dead cat. Herman went down swinging. Looks like a gun battle in there," Chris relates.

"I'll call it in." Rabold takes out his phone.

Chris walks to the back of the garage, where he finds Daily dead, lying in a puddle of blood with his eyes wide open. Chris leans over and closes the dead eyelids gently. "Wonder what you saw, big man ... I wonder."

The lab techs, ambulance, and officers arrive in short-order.

Chris turns to Rabold after walking the other investigators through the scene. "I'm headed back to the casino. Want to come play?"

"Hell, yeah," he answers.

Twenty Nine

CHANGE IN ATTITUDE

Israel Hamric waits impatiently in the county jail's release-holding cell. The bail, set at two million, has been posted by Shane Appleton, his uncle, but the process started four hours ago and has been stalled by an internal issue of unknown origin. This helps Hamric's anxiety not a bit. Getting out expands his options and places him in a position to control fate. Jail, and the loss of control, eats at the mental threads until death or insanity stops the feast for many serving time. Hamric feels this plague spreading after only nine days behind bars.

A guard finally leads him to a changing room to disrobe the orange jumpsuit and reclaim civilian status with a shirt and blue jeans. Signing for his personal items, Hamric walks out into the sunshine, sporting a newly minted GPS tracking monitor firmly gripping his leg.

Hamric hugs his uncle, each man glad to see the other.

"We have two hours to make the rental house and meet with a cop before this thing blows up on my leg. Let's get some seafood."

"I could go for lobster," Appleton responds, climbing into the car. "Where to?"

"A restaurant named North Water. Give me your phone." He enters the name in the GPS program. "It can't be too far." He sets the phone in the cupholder. "How was the trip down?"

"Not bad. I stayed one night in Savannah and took my time. How do you feel about the charges?"

"Pure setup. I'm about to have a short conversation with the guy responsible," Hamric says curtly.

◆

The men pull up to the rental house after eating a pair of two-pound lobsters and clams over a bed of pasta. Detective Tony Joseph gets out of an unmarked unit and joins them on the front porch.

"Cutting it close, Hamric." Joseph pans the house and

Appleton, sizing up both.

"Lobster. It was calling me after nine days in the can." Hamric wants to smash his face but deals a sarcastic grin instead.

"Who's your new roommate?"

"That's my Uncle Shane. He loves me, unlike you."

"At least he's not a hooker," Joseph shoots back. "Let's get this over with."

Appleton opens the door, and Joseph goes room-to-room casing the place and soon returns.

"Put your leg on that chair," he directs.

Hamric lifts his monitored ankle onto the chair and pulls back the jean pantleg.

Joseph checks the monitor tightness with his hand, uses a tool to activate the electronics, and stands back.

"Like hairy legs, Detective Joseph?" Hamric spouts off.

Joseph straightens up. "No, but you'll start liking them soon enough."

"You know the rules. Go thirty yards outside either door and the monitor is activated. We'll revoke the bail and you'll return to jail. One more thing. You can be visited any hour of the day or night to verify your compliance." He leaves the house and drives away.

"Do all these Louisiana cops pretend to be standup comedians?" Appleton inquires.

"I egged him on … should have kept my mouth shut. Nothing to be gained by pissing these clowns off. Let's go out front to talk."

Hamric heads to the swing hanging from the ceiling on the front porch and sits on the wooden slats. After a push off the wooden deck, the swing moves gently back and forth. "Have to admire Southern people. Ever see one of these in Brooklyn?"

"No, you need a mint julep to make the picture complete."

"A beer will have to do. How far are we from Fleck's house?"

"I clocked it, one-point-two miles. Not much of a jog for you."

"Weapon?" Hamric asks, pushing off the deck to keep the swaying going.

"Brought a forty-cal and suppressor. Also carrying my personal twenty-two as backup, but I don't think my carry license is good here."

"The license is fine if haven't been charged with a weapons violation. Good work, and thanks for your help. I'm in deep trouble without you."

Appleton shakes his head. "What you did for me can never

be repaid. I'd be in a shallow grave in Jersey if not for you. On another note, I transferred your stock portfolio to my account. But the Feds can still take it from me if you're convicted or skip bail. I can convert it to cash and order my manager to fly down with it."

"That's an option. We can plan around it if need be. Meantime, the Yankees are about to play Boston. Let's go inside and watch some ball."

◆

The Yankees are losing in the bottom of the seventh when Appleton goes to the kitchen to retrieve a couple more beers. On his return, he notices a police cruiser parked on the street and two cops walking to the front door.

"That didn't take long," he says, handing a beer to a seated Hamric.

"What are you talking about?"

"Two cops are headed to the door."

"Can't be checking on me this quick." Hamric sets the beer on the table and starts for the door, opening it just before Chris and Rabold make the porch.

"Mr. Hamric," Chris says, climbing the four steps. "Getting settled in?"

"Detective Dale. You couldn't stay away. Want a beer?" He opens the door, letting them in.

"Not on this trip. Can we have a word, alone?"

"Shane is my uncle. You can talk in front of him."

"Unless he's your attorney he can't be involved in this."

Hamric turns to Appleton. "Better take a walk."

Appleton strolls past everyone and continues out the door and down the sidewalk.

Rabold turns off the ballgame and joins Chris sitting across from Hamric.

"So, what's this all about?"

"Laying out a hypothetical," Rabold asserts, "if this guy comes to New Orleans from New York, hired to eliminate a threat from Gayle Kidd for Louis Fleck, but didn't actually kill the threat..."

"And would turn state's evidence against Fleck for said murder contract," Hamric says, finishing the sentence.

"Exactly." Rabold adds.

"The next question this man from New York would ask, if here, is will a trumped-up murder charge be dropped in exchange for his cooperation?"

Chris jumps in. "It's a hypothetical that will have to be run by the PA. Let's just say for discussion purposes that the man walks."

"The man from New York might have an interest. No jail time is the only deal willing to be made."

"Let us talk to the PA. Then you can relay the offer to the man from New York." The detectives stand up and leave.

On Appleton's return, Hamric replays the conversation.

"They really want this Fleck character if offering full immunity … seems too good to be true," Appleton responds.

"It would change our plans completely. That old bastard will die in jail, and I go back to New York a satisfied man."

◆

Chris drives five minutes toward the station when his cell rings. "You're not going to believe this. It's Mike Broadaway," Chris relays to Rabold then answers. "This is Detective Dale."

"Broadaway here. I need you in my office. ASAP."

"On my way," Chris answers and places the cell in the console.

◆

The two detectives walk into the parish office building and alert the receptionist that Broadaway wants to see them. Barely sitting in the waiting area, Broadaway's assistant appears, and the cops follow her to a corner office.

Broadaway is on the phone and agitated as they enter. "I don't give a damn about decorum. Get it done. We both have a job to do." He hangs up.

"I don't need Robin here," Broadaway says, referring to Rabold, "just Batman. Detective Dale, go to the conference room. A CIA agent wants your time about this Bailly case. Detective Rabold, go write some speeding tickets. Go!"

Chris looks at Rabold then back to Broadaway. "We need a few minutes of your time on the Bailly case. It's really important."

"I'm going to a city council meeting in twenty minutes to kiss *their asses* about budgets. Dale, don't keep the CIA waiting. Rabold, you have exactly ten minutes to kiss *my* ass. That's how it all works."

Chris heads to the door, and Rabold stays in front of Broadaway.

◆

Victor Mirontshuck knew he was going to be an intelligence officer in the seventh grade. His entire educational process pointed to the sciences, law, and psychological behavior. He graduated at the top of his class at Columbia—but just to make sure he added a master's degree to the resume. Much to his dismay, the agency wasn't hiring at the time due to a series of government budget cuts, so he went to work for the West Palm Beach police force for three years before the CIA came calling.

Mirontshuck doesn't dislike local cops; he was one. Chris on the other hand, doesn't like interacting with any federal law enforcement.

Chris enters the boardroom expecting a buttoned-down, dark-suited, short-haired government robot. Mirontshuck is all of those, just not a robot. Although walking the company line on most issues, he challenges what he considers outdated thinking and takes a stand against it. One of those challenged subjects is the government's past "ignore button" on UFOs.

Mirontshuck spent his childhood next door to Dr. Edgar Dean "Ed" Mitchell, a former astronaut and the sixth man to walk on the moon. Mitchell captained Apollo 14 and spent his post-astronaut days trying to force government, and other countries, to open their eyes to the fact that overpowering data prove UFOs are visiting various radioactive fueling points around the planet. Mitchell wanted the whole world to know.

Mirontshuck spent countless hours listening to Mitchell's arguments, supported by hard evidence in many cases. Mitchell was a lightning-rod for controversy, and as a result people throughout the globe brought him video, photos, and other items surrounding the UFO issue.

The two cops shake hands, drawn together by the oddest of circumstances. All created by events centered around a twelve-year-old boy.

"Detective Dale, I admire your work," Mirontshuck says, having reviewed Chris's arrest record and determined he is a good cop.

"That kind of flattery buys one question answered." Chris smiles, and his urge to flee the room subsides.

"I'll keep the flattery coming, if that's the case."

"So, what does the CIA want from this cop about the Bailly murder?"

"Not hard to figure out. Mr. Bailly's death was a tragedy, but what happened to his grandson Emrik is the true point of my investigation."

"Sorry about the your colleague's death in D.C., but I can

assure you Emrik does not have an ounce of evil in him."

"The shooting was intentional, but it wasn't committed by a conscious action. Let's back up before the shooting. You were there when the abduction occurred. I've read your case file, but please let me hear it from you."

Chris goes back to Bailly's viewing and Emrik's dash from the church, and the subsequent chase that ended in Emrik being yanked up the fire-escape.

"Would you mind taking me to the scene of the abduction?"

"Only if you buy lunch for my partner and me." Chris is beginning to like this young man.

"I believe the agency can afford it. Let's go."

"Meet you in the parking lot. Give me ten minutes with Broadaway and my partner."

"I'll see you downstairs." Mirontshuck leaves, and Chris finds Rabold sitting in the waiting area.

"What did Broadaway say? Do we have something to work with?" Chris can tell from his partner's expression things didn't go well.

"He won't give immunity, but he'll reduce it to second-degree manslaughter. A five-year sentence. Probably out in three."

"We'll see how Hamric reacts. We can only play the cards dealt," Chris says matter-of-factly. "The CIA guy wants to have lunch and then go by the abduction site."

"This should be entertaining."

◆

Two cars drive to the church, and the men walk the sidewalk toward the abandoned building. Mirontshuck is busy photographing the path of the chase, asking questions as they progress.

"May I call you, Chris?" He seems too polite when compared to other Feds Chris has encountered in the past.

"Sure ... been called worse."

"My old cop days in West Palm were brutal, getting my balls busted by fellow officers."

"Should have known you were a cop. You're too nice a guy for a Fed."

"Agency arrogance gets you nowhere. Unfortunately, most of the intel officers with attitude have never driven a beat, sat all night on a stakeout, or worn the same clothes for forty-eight hours investigating a murder. Chris, where were you standing when Emrik was grabbed?"

Chris positions Rabold as Emrik, and backs away thirty feet. "I couldn't catch Emrik and screamed for him to stop. He did. We talked for a few seconds, and he started back my way when this guy came out of the dark and grabbed him by the waist. Headed straight for the building and up the fire-escape."

"Are you sure it was a man?" Mirontshuck asks, taking additional photos.

"Had a hoodie on ... maybe five-eight or five-nine. You know what? I assumed he was a guy because of the speed and strength. I'm guessing Emrik weighs a buck ten. That would've been a pretty strong woman. Emrik's uncle got knocked backwards when he caught up with them. The uncle is a big man. Nah ... had to be a guy."

"Don't let your preconceived ideas of strength stand in the way. I have video from Russia showing a woman beat down three Army specialists ... that's equivalent to our special forces... then make her escape. So, where did this guy come from that plucked Emrik up?"

"It was dark. I was concentrating on Emrik. He came from that direction." Chris points to an empty lot across the street.

"Chris, you're a trained observer of people and actions, unlike civilians. Think back. Did you see any motion from the corner of your eye before his appearance?"

Chris looks at the empty lot and back to Mirontshuck. "No, I don't believe there was any movement. He just appeared."

"So he fell from the sky?" Rabold jokes.

"Maybe," Mirontshuck answers, not joking.

He walks to the fire-escape. The ladder is hanging a foot from the cement. "Was the ladder in this position?"

Chris moves closer. "No, the ladder was raised well off the ground." He pushes the ladder skyward, and it moves six feet above Chris's extended hand.

"Did this guy sit Emrik down and then jump for the ladder?" Mirontshuck asks, taking still more photos.

"It was unbelievable. Holding Emrik, he jumped at least six feet off the ground and pulled the ladder down then shot up the fire-escape with incredible speed. I know it sounds crazy."

"That is crazy," Rabold adds.

"Wish it was crazy. I've see things far scarier. Then what?"

"The uncle climbs up the fire-escape after them, I break in the front of the office building and work my way to the top floor."

The three men head to the roof and look in all directions.

"What the hell? Where could he go carrying the kid?" Rabold

asks.

Mirontshuck points to a building twenty feet away across the street. "He jumped to the next building."

"Sorry, Victor," Rabold challenges. "I call bullshit on your premise."

"What to bet lunch on it, Bobby?"

"You're on ... prove it."

Mirontshuck leads them to the second building, breaks into the front door, and the three follow the stairs to the top. A walk across the finely grained gravel makes a crunching sound on the flat surface.

Mirontshuck points to skid marks in the gravel, five feet from the building's edge. "That's where he landed, Emrik in hand. If you want to research the next two buildings, you'll find the same skid marks where he touched down."

"Sonofabitch! What the hell are we dealing with?" Rabold's voice now has a tone of fright.

"Yeah, what are we dealing with?" Chris adds volume to the question.

"Let's go to lunch. You deserve some answers." He heads toward the stairwell.

"What kind of food blows your skirt up?" Chris asks.

"Anything, as long as oysters Rockefeller are on the menu."

"That only covers ninety percent of the restaurants in New Orleans. What do you think, Bobby?"

"Blue Point Crab is less than ten minutes ... great oysters."

"Blue Point it is," Mirontshuck agrees. "I'll follow you."

◆

Once seated in the restaurant, Mirontshuck relays his past relationship with Ed Mitchell and his focus on UFOs in the CIA. Chris and Rabold sit silent, shocked to the point of not even asking questions.

After ordering food, Rabold finally asks, "Doesn't the CIA work in a cloud of mystery? Why are you being so open?"

"Several reasons. One, as law enforcement you need to know what you're facing. I won't sugarcoat it. Real danger is close by. Two, we work closely with Homeland Security. In the next six or eight months, HS and the Navy will be releasing a number of amazing UFO videos showing things the public has never seen before. Several federal agencies will be briefing the world, admitting we don't have a clue what we're dealing with.

"That's a major change in attitude," Rabold says, somewhat stunned.

Mirontshuck's cell rings, and he looks at the caller ID. "Excuse me, I have to take this." He gets up and starts to the front door then stops in his tracks and returns to the table. "Sorry, it's an emergency. We'll catch up shortly." He hustles out the door and disappears.

"Damn! Thought we were about to be painted the full picture," Rabold laments.

"Must have been really important. He gave up the oysters," Chris quips as the food is laid on the table."

"We're getting stuck with the bill," Rabold counters.

"What's this 'we' you make reference to? You lost the bet." Chris slurps down an oyster.

Thirty

ALONG COMES MARIA

Jessie McGaha's mind has festered with thoughts while driving back from Arkansas to Louisiana. If UFO technology and the beings targeting mankind are a reality, there is an unlimited range of human actions that could be affected. Jessie believes the "if," but the "why" keeps rebounding from one side of her brain to the other. Is this just another Pavlov's dog experiment, replacing the dog with a man and digging deeply into human experience and response? Jessie has developed extensive crime-solving abilities, and she now regards this thing as an absolute truth—what is going on is the ultimate crime.

A nervous excitement, spawned by both awe and fear of the unknown, fuels the debate inside Jessie's gut when pulling into the driveway of Stony Fetter. Her editor had said he didn't want to wait until a new workday to obtain the full story she heard from her father's CIA friend.

Fetter meets her at the door, no knock necessary. "Come in. You have my undivided attention." He leads her to the den.

Jessie sits at a round table used for extended chess matches between Fetter and his grown son, Seleck. The chessboard has Civil War soldiers, North against the South, a tribute to his intense love of history. He removes the board and sits across the table, ready to absorb.

Fetter's wife comes into the room. "Jessie, good to see you. Want some tea?"

"That would be great, Estie. Just had a long drive. Thanks!"

She walks to the kitchen feeling good about her deep Southern ways.

"I don't think you're going to be happy with the parameters laid out by my source," Jessie tells him.

"Off-the-record comments?" he asks in a disappointed tone.

"I gave my word, and I won't breach it. Now, I need your word. Will you honor it?"

"You give me no choice. Yes, you have my disappointed word. It won't go beyond my ears."

Estie soon returns with pound cake, stopping long enough to hear Jessie outline Skip's experiences at Skinwalker Ranch. She heads to the kitchen and soon reappears with a tray of hot tea, sugar, and cream, which she lays on the table. Patience is the center of everything Estie does, but Fetter stands up, losing what little patience he has left in his body.

"The Feds have real proof aliens are buzzing around our planet interacting with mankind? They expect me to sit on the biggest story in world history? What kind of journalist am I to let this slide off in the darkness?"

"A silent one—you gave your word," Estie answers, before Jessie can throw it back in his face. "Go on Jessie, what else did the man say?"

"The rest of the day my father, Skip, and I discussed why advanced beings have any interest in doing this. Control? Scientific study? What's in it for them?"

Estie takes a sip of tea. "Entertainment, maybe? Wouldn't it be fun to witness how people react seeing the Devil face-to-face—or who mankind actually thinks is the real Devil. Everyone has some element of superstitious thought in their makeup. The aliens are reenforcing our own inner fears. Wouldn't surprise me if Mothman or Bigfoot came to life via the aliens."

Jessie looks at Estie in disbelief. "That's so simple but, damn, it makes sense. What do you think, Stony?"

"Being from Pennsylvania, I did several stories on Mothman and the people connected who are all-in believers. What Estie says does seem conceivable. The real question for me is how do we move beyond the CIA to define the story and not divulge or incite your original source?"

"I might have the answer," Jessie says. "I received an FBI file on Gayle Kidd's family in Utah. She, her father, and her twin sister were part of the Skinwalker Ranch contamination study. Several members of the paleontological dig were abducted like Emrik. Maybe it's time for a trip to Utah?" She looks to Fetter for confirmation.

"I can't leave before tomorrow morning, and you're not going without me."

◆

While Estie washes the teacups, Jessie retrieves the FBI file from the car to find the phone number of Jana Kidd in Utah. In a quick call, she confirms her willingness to communicate about her husband's death. And three minutes after Jana agrees, Fetter reserves two seats on a flight to Salt Lake City the next day.

◆

The flight is uneventful, and Jessie watches the snow-capped mountains rush by until the plane touches the tarmac at Salt Lake City International. "Did you bring a jacket?" Fetter asks as the plane taxis to the jetway escape.

"No," is her uneducated answer.

"My bad," he says apologetically. "I've been to Salt Lake several times and know it's cold even in late spring. We'll buy you a jacket. Maybe we can actually visit the Skinwalker Ranch, adding a true backdrop to the story."

The rental-car paperwork completed, Fetter takes possession of the key while Jessie waits for the luggage. The short drive into the city from the airport is a scenic contrast to New Orleans, with the Wasatch Mountains rising to the east and the vast namesake lake at their back.

"What time are we meeting with Mrs. Kidd?"

"One o'clock ... we won't have time for lunch," Jessie responds, as he plugs the Kidd address into the GPS.

A Target Store conveniently appears at a shopping center, and Jessie buys an inexpensive but functional jacket. The dry air is crisp, and the coat makes Jessie realize how cold the walk to the rental-car terminal made her feel. Renewed by warmth, she smiles at Fetter, returning to the car.

"What makes you so happy?" he asks, smiling back not sure where the joke is coming from.

"You can't bitch about my expense report this time."

"That I have to concede."

◆

Jana Kidd lives in an apartment complex on the outskirts of downtown, and the traffic is minimal en route. The complex is well maintained and large. The GPS takes them to a building on the far side of the property, sitting at the base of a two-hundred-foot hill casting a large shadow over the three-story garden apartments. The sun has risen in the sky, slightly diminishing the shadow when Jessie knocks on the door identified by the number 317. A wreath is still hanging from Christmas. A diminutive, elderly lady answers the door with a pretty face.

"Mrs. Kidd, I'm Jessie McGaha, and this is my editor, Stony Fetter. May we come in?" Jessie tingles at the thought of pushing beyond the CIA info and obtaining a story she can write about.

"Please come in," Jana Kidd says in accented English. "We have so much to talk about." Jana has been reclusive over the years, but she welcomes the company, no longer embarrassed by the strange circumstances that made her a local celebrity after the abductions.

Family photos line three walls in the living room showing the twin girls in various stages of youth, doing everything from soccer to horseback riding.

Fetter and Jessie follow Jana, hoping the photos will help paint a picture.

"Your girls are so athletic and beautiful," Jessie says as they all sit at the kitchen table.

"Both played sports through high school," Jana explains. "Would you like a blueberry muffin? I made them this morning."

Fetter beats Jessie to the answer. "That would be great. It was a long flight."

"Coffee or tea?"

"Just water for me," Jessie answers.

"Water is fine, also," Fetter adds.

Jana retrieves two bottles of water from the refrigerator and places a pile of muffins on the table in a brightly colored bread bowl with matching plates. Jessie thinks back to her grandmother's actions in Florida, matching the hospitality years ago.

"So, you want to write a story about my husband?" Jana asks. "He was a brilliant man, a professor at BYU."

"Can you tell us about the circumstances leading to his death?" Jessie begins, taking a bite of muffin.

"At Skinwalker Ranch, the Feds were drilling holes all over the place—I'm not sure why. They found a T-Rex bone and by Utah State law had to bring in a paleontologist to investigate. Mario took his graduate students, including both our girls, to commence the dig and get the T-Rex out of the ground. After that, I'm not completely sure what happened. I was told by an Air Force major the dig hit a pocket of radioactive material, killing Mario and two other graduate students. Maria was never the same. They flew her off to Walter Reed for three weeks to recover. A reporter told me UFOs abducted them, but I don't know what to believe anymore."

"Was the reporter local or national?" Fetter asks.

"She worked for The Salt Lake Tribune. Came out a couple times to see me. Nice lady."

"What's her name?" Jessie asks.

"Della St. John, but it won't do you any good."

"Why?"

"She was killed by her worthless husband. He blew her away with a shotgun three months after the incident."

Jessie and Fetter sit silent for a moment, stunned by the revelation.

"Where is Maria these days?" Fetter finally inquires. "Does she live in this area?"

"Maria, my poor baby, she has been institutionalized in Ogden for years now."

"What's the name of the facility?" Fetter asks.

"Water's Edge."

"Would you mind if we borrowed some pictures of your family? They will help to put faces on the story."

"That would be fine," Jana responds, rising from the table. They all head to the living room. "Take all you want."

"Oh, we won't need to physically take them," Jessie explains, taking out a pro-grade digital camera to photograph several pictures on the wall then finishing with a live shot of Jana. She seems excited to be part of the storyline, Jessie thinks, even though the details had never crystalized in her mind.

◆

In the car, Fetter and Jessie each make a few notes before committing to a plan.

"It's a start," Fetter says. "I'm not surprised Jana has been left out of the detail loop—it's always the same old coverup. Let's have lunch, you drop me off at the Trib for research and a chat with the editor. Ogden is a little more than an hour away. You go visit Maria Kidd. My guess is she knows a helluva lot more than her momma."

◆

A pastrami burger from Crown's and, two hours later, Jessie drives into the Water's Edge parking lot. The facility is stoic in its appearance; manicured and recently painted.

Jessie walks to the door, eyeing the bright colors and Utah landscapes framed along the walls. Not a bad place to be stored if that's your fate, she thinks.

A uniformed nurse sits at the desk, guarded on both sides by locked doors accessing the facility.

"May I help you?" the nurse asks, hers lips turning up slightly in a faint welcoming smile.

"Yes. I'm here to see Maria Kidd." Jessie explains.

The smile instantly leaves the nurse's face, and she taps out a code of unknown keys into the computer. "May I see your ID?"

Jessie retrieves her driver's license and hands it over. A few more keys are squared up, and the gatekeeper looks back to her.

"Sorry, you're not on the authorized list."

"I'm her sister, and I flew across country to visit. You can't give me a few minutes?"

But Nurse Ratched is not in the mood for sentimentality and turns the computer screen in Jessie's direction. "Here is a photo of Ms. Kidd's twin sister. You are not her sister."

"May I talk to a supervisor?" Jessie asks, summoning the best authoritarian face she can muster.

"I am a supervisor. You can leave of your own accord, or I will call security."

Jessie turns, incredulous to the wall being thrown in her way, and walks out the door. On her way to the parking lot, a black orderly walks up the sidewalk and checks her out, grinning. She stops in her tracks and whirls back to the orderly, now moving away.

"Sir, excuse me … sir." Her voice rises louder, spitting out the second 'sir'.

The man turns back in her direction, suddenly excited about the attention he is receiving. "What's your name, little lady?"

"I need a little help. I need to see a patient, and that little bitch at the front desk turned me away. Can you help me see Maria Kidd?" Jessie flashes a perfect smile to romance the request.

"Strict rules around here. Walk with me." They head toward the parking lot, the orderly taking long strides that Jessie has trouble matching. He stops a few car-rows deep. "Getting in won't help you."

"Why?"

"Maria left a couple months ago. She was the strangest case we ever had here."

"Go on," Jessie prods him.

"Nothing's free in life, little lady. I'll need a hundred." He looks at Jessie for several seconds, waiting for her reaction. When there is none, he becomes inpatient and starts walking back to the facility.

"Hold on." She digs five twenties from her purse and hands them over.

"Everyone in the hospital was scared to death of her," the

orderly says, pocketing the cash. "She could make things fly through the air and pop your ass if anyone tried to make her do anything she didn't want to do. Once, Maria got in a fight with one of the orderlies. He was found dead at his home. Head bashed in."

"How could she hurt someone outside the facility?"

"Cause the bitch came and went when she wanted to."

"You just let her out anytime she wanted?"

"We had no control. She would disappear from her room. Be gone for days and reappear in bed one night. Security didn't mean shit. Then she got out, but the security video showed nothing. We have cameras on every hall and stairwell. The bitch disappeared and reappeared whenever she wanted. The whole staff hopes she stays gone." He turns and strolls away.

◆

Jessie walks into the Marriott City Center and finds Fetter sitting at the bar writing notes, a Scotch next to his elbow. A handful of peanuts keep his left hand busy while the right one does the writing.

He sees her approaching and rises, giving her a hug. "Helluva day. Want a drink?"

"Helluva day is an understatement, and yes, whatever you're having, double for me." She drags a tall chair close and leans on the bar.

The bartender sets a double Scotch and a new bowl of peanuts between them. It take only a second or two for Jessie to draw the Scotch down severely.

"What did Maria Kidd have to say?"

"When she stops riding her broom, I'll get an interview. She left a couple months ago."

"Broom?"

"I bribed an orderly. He told me Maria could make objects fly at the staff. She literally came and went, invisible to their video surveillance." She finishes off the double Scotch and orders another.

"No shit? That's one hell of a talent. Do you believe the guy?"

"Yes. He didn't know why I was there, but he was genuinely scared of the woman. What happened on your end?"

"Half-dozen articles surrounding the event and subsequent UFO sightings. Great photos, but none of it made AP or any of the nationally syndicated publishers. The editor will let us use all the material if we give credit. Best news of all?" He raises his glass. "Tomorrow morning he'll drive us to Skinwalker Ranch. A film crew is shooting a documentary there."

Jessie meets his glass in midair. "To my bright, and generous editor!"

"I like the bright part. When did I become generous? The jacket must be really warm."

"When you approve my hundred-dollar bribe of the orderly," she says, grinning.

"You're lucky I'm full of Scotch and have an interest in the Pulitzer." He is not joking on either count.

◆

Three double Scotches normally knock the lights out for Jessie, but she realizes the story unfolding around them is special and gigantic in the history of journalism. A Pulitzer Prize might not be too far-fetched if solidifying proof of the UFO connection. The biggest question, though: What will be the price for revealing the truth?

Hot water pours down Jessie's back, and she leans against the tiled shower wall, soaking heat deep into the pores. Tiredness seeps into the body paralleling the heat's comfort, and she turns off the water before sleep attacks her upright stance. A towel gently rubs off the wetness, and her framed outline starts to become clear in the moisture-laden mirror only four feet from the glass door. Turning for a second towel to wrap her hair, she sees a tired expression staring back and decides teeth-cleaning can wait until morning. But pangs of guilt reverse the laziness, and she engages her electric toothbrush.

Jessie dons a hotel bathrobe and moves to the bedroom. A knock on the door shifts her thoughts to Fetter, probably too excited to bed down early. She opens the door, and Maria Kidd stands three feet from her, making comfortable fatigue suddenly turn into panicked fright-and-flight mode.

Her next thought is to slam the door and call Fetter, but Jessie's body is frozen like a forgotten popsicle stuck in the back of a second freezer in the garage. Kidd steps forward, hand extended, a smile of dominance written across her beautiful face. The cold fingers wrap around Jessie's throat, pressure applied, and the true understanding of complete hopelessness engulfs all Jessie's senses as her body is lifted off the floor.

"You seem like a smart woman. Death has a way of lowering

that IQ into the grave. Back away, while you still can." Kidd's fingers drop to the door's edge, and it closes in front of Jessie's upright, rigid figure.

Seconds pass and Jessie can't fathom what to do, scared that Kidd would open the door again without her permission. Now free of death's grip, she goes to the bed, sits down, and calls Fetter. Tears fill an extended run of bedside Kleenex while she relates the event to her equally shocked editor.

"We should call the police," Fetter tells her. "This needs to be reported."

"No, they'll make a report and drive away not understanding what we're dealing with. Nothing will come from it."

"Okay, in the morning you go to the newspaper for more research. You'll be around a lot of people and should be safe there. I'll go to Skinwalker Ranch with Bill. Then we're out on a plane tomorrow night. Want me to sleep on the couch?"

"Thanks, I'll be alright. Go to bed, we have a long day tomorrow."

◆

The morning finds Jessie and Fetter in the hotel café. She is stirring a coffee cup laden with far more cream than usual and barely touching the omelet and bacon sitting on the plate. He is finishing his pancakes and looking at her going through the motions.

"You need to eat. You can't take her broom away without a full stomach."

She barely smiles at him. "Only you could make that analogy."

"Thanks, I'm a practical man."

Fetter receives a call that a Jeep has driven to the front of the hotel and is awaiting him. He finishes a glass of orange juice. "Want to meet, Bill?"

"Sure." She stands as he lays cash on the table.

Outside, a tall man steps out of the black Jeep and offers his hand. Under normal circumstances, she would soak in his rugged looks and slender frame.

"Bill Jackson. A pleasure to meet you."

"Jessie McGaha. Thanks so much for your help."

"I've been hearing about your writing talent. Want to live in Utah and work at the Trib?"

"Whoa … whoa! Don't be so brazen, Bill." Fetter steps between his prize reporter and the editor.

"We'll talk later." Jessie responds, thinking she wouldn't live in

Utah if they gave her the newspaper.

The two men drive away, and Jessie runs to the rental car, closely inspecting the back seat before opening the door. The drive to the Tribune features excessive speed and frequent reference to the rearview mirror, looking for the dark-haired monster. Jessie arrives and goes in to meet the associate editor.

◆

Fetter is glad to be riding in a Jeep with four-wheel drive, though the dirt road leading to the heavily guarded front gate of Skinwalker Ranch is a bit rough on his kidneys. But the place can not be accessed otherwise. Two paramilitary men carrying AR-15 rifles and sidearms halt their advance.

Jackson explains the editorial interest he and Fetter have in the ranch, and that solicitation is forwarded by radio. A positive answer rebounds, and the two are escorted to a compound consisting of several buildings and an old barn.

"Not sure what I expected, but this place is underwhelming," Fetter says, rolling out of the Jeep.

Three members of the production crew plus two scientists greet the two men with an open attitude. The reason becomes obvious quickly.

"We're filming a documentary airing on the History Channel in late 2021. It will be a weekly one hour series. Anything you can put in print will promote the show," the producer, Jayson Mansion, explains.

Trent DeLaney, head of the research group, jumps in. "The Feds left the property several years ago. Now we have a chance to do our own studies. You guys know much about the history?"

Fetter wants desperately to give the CIA version of the events he heard from Jessie, but he plays dumb and defaults to Jackson giving the local history. The group knows about the deaths at the T-Rex dig, but they seem oblivious to the many dangers still facing the production crew.

A tour of the facilities is more impressive inside, revealing a well-financed operation. Expensive electronics abound, including seismic, radar, and atmospheric measuring devices for radiation and microwave energy. Sightings and radar recordings support the stories of heavy UFO activity.

"Can we have a copy of the UFO photos and findings?" Fetter asks.

"We'll bundle all the research to take on your way out."

DeLaney is eager to deliver anything that will stir an interest in the new show. "If you brought a camera, you can take a UFO picture for yourself."

Jackson lowers his backpack and removes a digital Nikon and a large, extended lens for the shoot. "Don't leave home without it!"

◆

A two-vehicle convoy takes the men one mile into the property, and a chainlink fence mounted with barbed wire guards a launching pad. Preparations are made, and a countdown sequence is started to launch a rocket high into the cloudless sky.

"Get ready," DeLaney advises. "When the rocket hits six-thousand feet, within thirty seconds several UFOs will appear."

Jackson focuses the camera and takes a couple of distant pictures for practice. Video and still-camera imaging equipment is pointed skyward by the crew in anticipation of the rocket's ascent.

Earplugs are issued, and after a countdown the rocket is sent toward the heavens. Within a few seconds, the first rounded vessel positions itself directly over the streaking projectile. All the cameras catch the UFOs appearance, and to the amazement of Fetter and Jackson, two more UFOs station themselves ninety degrees horizontally from the first craft. All three objects hover at around ten-thousand feet. The action lasts more than two minutes, and suddenly all three UFOs disappear at breathtaking speed and agility.

◆

While the two editors are watching the rocket's red glare, Jessie is being introduced to several writers at the Salt Lake Tribune who have connections to the story about the Kidds, the T-Rex dig, and the subsequent deaths. Her investigative instincts kick in, and Jessie's attention is refocused from the terrifying Maria Kidd encounter to uncovering facts. A writer asks Jessie to lunch along with two others, and she accepts.

It is a comfortable environment, a small restaurant located a couple blocks from the Tribune, surrounded by peers of her trade. The people of Utah are generous with their time, and they listen to the contrasts in newspaper styles. Each staff member eagerly absorbs different techniques to refine his or her skills.

Jessie's appetite returns.

Fetter calls her mid-meal about the UFO photos, and Jessie's spirits are lifted. The trip could indeed provide many answers outside the stand-down instructions from the CIA stories she heard in Arkansas.

Reentering the first floor of the Tribune, Jessie excuses herself for a restroom break. The facility has four stalls, and the sudden lack of people in her midst gives Jessie a more cautious attitude. One by one, she looks beneath the stall doors to see if anyone is present. The restroom is empty.

Jessie retires into the privacy of a stall and locks the door behind. Disrobing her pants and panties, she sits on the toilet when the outside door is opened. A woman wearing stiletto heels taps her way to the sink and starts washing hands. Unconsciously, Jessie stops breathing, fearing it will expose her existence.

The heels strike the granite floor, and something tells Jessie the woman is looking under the closed stall doors, just as she did minutes earlier. The shoes click to the stall next to her and the door is opened, but the woman finds it empty. The distinctive red soles of Christian Louboutin stilettos move to her stall. Jessie's eyes close in anticipation. It is obvious something bad is about to happen. The thought of pulling up her pants and fighting never transpires in the dread of the moment.

Eyes tightly closed, her fate is beyond her control. The door is pounded with great force and swings open. Expecting a merciless kicking by the red-soled heels and embarrassingly dying with her panties around the ankles, she opens her eyes to whatever the soulless devil is about to deliver.

The restroom is suddenly empty.

Thirty One

FARE THEE WELL

Chris and Rabold park in front of Hamric's rental property and walk to the house, hoping the manslaughter plea offered by PA Broadaway will be accepted. A life sentence is the alternate possibility in a tough Louisiana penal system, something that should make the deal a little more appealing. At least, that is the thought shared by the two detectives.

What they do not know, however, is that Hamric never intends to stand trial for the Mercedes murder.

The conversation is cordial among the three, and Hamric nods his head, giving false hope of turning state's evidence against Louis Fleck. The last comment by Hamric is a promise to contact his attorney in New York to weigh his options then get back to them in the next couple of days.

While this façade is being built, Appleton has been taking photos of Fleck's house, giving Hamric an eye-level view of all the options to take out the target. The two men sit at the kitchen table discussing those options.

Appleton points out several features on and around the house. "The home is most assuredly equipped with an alarm system. The question is, does it have motion detectors?"

"He'll be sleeping on the second floor. I can bypass the alarm by cutting through a window and not opening it. But if there is a motion detector, it would go off and that old bastard will be armed before I can make the bedroom."

"I may have an answer, though it's not without risk."

"I'm not averse to risk," Hamric counters. "What's your idea?"

Appleton uses a pencil to point out a tall oak growing close to the side of the house. "You can climb this tree to the second floor roof," he says, moving the pencil to a skylight on the roof. "Cut through the glass here and rope down to the second floor. Most people don't install motion detecters on the second floor."

Hamric smiles. "Let's go with it ... makes a lot of sense. Good work! Then how do I travel to my bungalow in Indonesia?"

"We fly you to L.A. on a private jet. Homeland Security is really tight now, flying into Hawaii by private plane, but I've gotten you a fake passport and driver's license for a ticket on a commercial carrier to Maui. From there, you're on a ninety-foot yacht run by a Japanese crew to Indonesia. We'll cash out your stock, and my manager will bring it here tomorrow by private plane."

"My stock less five-hundred grand for you," Hamric says emphatically.

Appleton holds his hand up. "No way. I owe you my life."

"And now, I owe you mine. It will pay for your boy's college, and I don't want anymore discussion. Set this in motion immediately. I'll take care of Fleck tomorrow night and fly out a couple hours later."

Hamric has always planned to pay for his nephew's college education, and the time has come.

◆

Detective Ron McConnell arrives at the station before 7:00 a.m. and goes to his desk in the Evidence Room. He sips on coffee while working the computer nonstop for three hours. McConnell was a college-trained engineer-to-be, but he left school early to help support four younger siblings and a single mother struggling to pay the rent.

McConnell's meticulous focus and calm demeanor have made him a damn good detective. For the first seventeen years of his service in the NOPD, he roamed the streets chasing bad guys and putting them behind bars.

All that changed six years ago when his wife Jill passed away, and he asked for a transfer to Evidence Maintenance. His exacting nature flourished in the new assignment, and he quickly turned the system into one of the best-run evidence facilities in the country.

McConnell tidies the evidence-extraction paperwork for the court appearances the next day. He moves into the high-security locker room, where he pulls and bags various corresponding weapons and drugs to be put on courtroom display. Parish officials will pick up and sign out evidence starting at 3:00 p.m., keeping McConnell's system running like the lines of patrons at a Disney World amusement ride.

Depending on the caseload, McConnell leaves the station between 4:30 and 5 o'clock. Going home is the usual destination except on Wednesdays, when he drives to the cemetery to place flowers in front of Jill's vault also housing four generations of his family.

McConnell's habits are predictable; most bright, linear-thinking people walk the same line. A stop at the local Winn-Dixie garners a chicken sub, a six-pack of Coors, a package of assorted nuts, another of Reese's Miniature Cups, and a dozen roses.

This Wednesday, McConnell walks across the cemetery grounds to a bench and sits thirty feet from the vault's entrance. His routine is set, rain or shine. There he eats the sub and drinks two beers. A fox squirrel named Rusty, because of his red-tinted tail, climbs down from a nearby tree and approaches without caution, waiting for McConnell to share the pecans and peanuts. Rusty, aggressive after months of familiarity, jumps on the arm of the bench and barks a demand for the reward.

"Rusty, it's not nice to be yelled at." He opens the bag, lays a pile of nuts in the palm of his hand, and extends it to the squirrel.

Rusty crams nut after nut into his bulging jaws until the hand is empty. Then he scampers off, only to return in minutes to repeat the process. McConnell meanwhile enjoys the rest of his sandwich and beer chaser, happy to have company in a lonely place and time.

He has finished the first beer and is drinking the second when a bright light escapes numerous crevasses in the vault. He stares, doubting his eyes.

McConnell sets the beer on the bench and walks to the vault door as the light gains intensity. Suddenly, everything becomes dark. He pulls his .38 from its holster and inserts a seventy-year-old skeleton key in the lock. It clicks its surrender and releases the unknown hell brewing behind the door.

Following his police training, McConnell quickly opens the door and jumps into an explosion of light and chaos, blinding him. An odd-shaped figure screams and runs across the stained floor. Ron opens fire, getting off four shots before silence returns to the cemetery. Light intensifies around his comatose body, which is dragged across the floor and out the vault's entrance.

McConnell wakes fully clothed in his bed, doubting everything around him. The .38 is neatly tucked in the shoulder holster, giving him a limited feel of comfort and familiarity. He rolls out of bed, notices four beers and a bag of Reese's Miniatures lying on the dresser top.

He extracts the .38 and removes the clip, seeing that four bullets have been fired. Then he slides the clip back in place. Concentrating on the absent shells brings no sense of closure; when and where did he fire them? An awkward confusion emerges in the foggy thought, and regardless of the gifted engineering focus,

McConnell cannot shake the feeling of complete lack of control.

He walks to the closet and retrieves a suitcase, packing underwear, socks, and an overnight grip containing a toothbrush and toothpaste. He starts for the door, placing a warm beer under his arm. Compulsion suddenly changes that thought. He sets the Coors on the dresser and grabs the Reese's instead. The reflection in the mirror confirms it is Ron McConnell, but an assessment of the strange actions is bewildering.

◆

McConnell drives to the police station and seems to be following established habit, except it is in the middle of the night. The Evidence Room is dark, but determined to follow a prearranged path he flips a light switch and turns his computer on. A few strokes of the keys, and the inventory list comes into view. He moves deep into the bowels of the storage facility, opens a box containing plastic explosives and detonators confiscated in a plot to blow apart a Jewish Community Center.

McConnell spends the next two hours unwrapping the Reese's cups, neatly cutting off the chocolate tops and forming the plastic explosives into an identical shape. He then puts the chocolate tops on the explosive material and rewraps the branded Reese's foil around each candy bite. The top half of the candy sack is filled with regular Reese's cups, but the bottom half has enough explosives to blow a plane out of the sky.

The mental picture driving his activities is a distant, endless tunnel. Each step in the process is encouraged by endorphin dumps into his brain and like a heroin injection, he does not want to lose the artificial high.

He tapes a detonator to the back of his metal-framed belt buckle. Then he drives to the airport and boards a plane for a midnight flight to Los Angeles. Flashing his detective badge at the ticket counter, he buys a seat under the guise of picking up a prisoner for extradition in Hawaii. McConnell knows airport security will not let him bring the .38 on board without federal papers authorizing the prisoner pickup, so he leaves the pistol on the floorboard of his car.

Gate security fails to check the Reese's cups being carried onboard by an NOPD detective. Not surprising. Who doesn't like Reese's? He texts Chris Dale about his sister's sudden illness in Dallas and his intent to be back at work in three days. Chris acknowledges and offers his thoughts and prayers to what he thinks is a McConnell family emergency.

◆

Shane Appleton takes a set of watch tools from a leather case and picks the locking mechanism on Hamric's ankle monitor that has been limiting his movements.

Hamric rubs the suddenly free ankle and vigorously scratches the calf that has been breaking out in a rash since the confinement.

"Damn! That's almost better than sex, peeling out of that contraption."

"Don't look at me with those loving eyes. Just doing my job."

Hamric straightens his watch from the back of his arm. "Four more hours and I'll be on my way to L.A," he says happily. "But first things first. A little conversation with Mr. Fleck is in order."

Appleton opens a gym bag and lays out the tools Hamric will need to take care of Fleck.

"Hold on. Let me darken the front lights of the house before we get started." Hamric leaves, and returns rubbing his hands together. "The only thing that can throw a wrench in the machinery is a cop visit at two a.m."

"Think you have bought a little time with Detective Dale. We've only had one visit in the last forty hours."

"If a cop checks in, are you prepared to shoot him?" Hamric asks.

"That's why I brought the .22. I won't let you down."

"Give me the .22," Hamric demands.

Appleton hands over the weapon.

Hamric firmly grips it leaving a nice set of fingerprints, and sets it on the table.

"Wear gloves, and dump the gun outside of Louisiana on your drive back to New York."

The two men pack their tools of the trade, anticipating a long night of decision-making, using a skillset honed in the art of killing and getting away with it.

◆

Louis Fleck has a bladder problem. It matters not when he stops drinking liquids in the evening; the bathroom will still call two or three times a night. Not happy even when things go well, Fleck hates the routine of two hours sleep, fifteen minutes at the toilet,

293

then repeat.

Fleck sits on the side of the bed trying to decide whether to go to the bathroom or steal another thirty minutes of sleep. His wife Marie turns in his direction.

"Are you alright?" she asks, a genuine gesture from a woman who loves an undeserving man.

"Go to sleep," Fleck fires back, a gesture from a man who cares nothing about the woman who has shared his bed for thirty-two years.

He gets up and walks the familiar path to the bathroom, night-lights lining the hallway like an airport approach. The return trip to the bed is halted three steps into the hallway by the barrel of a .40-cal, pressed against the back of Fleck's head. He raises his hands as a result.

"Move your ass." Hamric's voice is slightly altered by the ski mask surrounding his face and, for the moment, Fleck has no clue who is giving him directions.

"Do you know who you're messing with?" Fleck asks quietly but bluntly, trying to leverage a tiny advantage under the circumstances.

"Tell me." Hamric has heard this worthless threat before, and is amused by the answer.

"I run this town. I'm the mob, and your ass will be hunted down if you don't get out right now."

They enter the bedroom, and Fleck's wife screams.

"Shut the hell up!" Fleck directs, and the screaming ceases.

Hamric flips the light switch on and throws a roll of duct tape on the bed.

"Tape her hands and feet," he orders, and Fleck strips the tape off, wrapping several layers satisfying the demand.

"Take the cash. It's in the closet wall safe." Fleck realizes the man holding the gun is a professional.

"Show me." He stands five feet from Fleck.

Fleck now comes to the conclusion the gun-carrying stranger is Hamric, meaning this is big trouble.

The walk-in closet is large, and Fleck leads his assailant to the back corner. A few turns of the dial and the safe opens, containing twenty-four-thousand dollars in cash and numerous pieces of high-end jewelry.

"Hamric, I'm sorry ... what?"

Fleck's forehead is pinpointed by the red laser light. Hamric fires the weapon, and the body drops instantly to the carpet. He empties the safe and returns to the bedroom, listening to Marie

Fleck crying uncontrollably.

"It's okay. I did you a favor." He walks to the bed, and every step causes an increase in sobbing. He places a glove-covered finger to his lips, and Fleck's wife finally eases her crying. More tape secures her to the bedpost, and a final piece covers her mouth. Hamric leaves.

◆

Ron McConnell rents a car in Maui and drives around the city, finding a Walmart where he buys a burner phone, wiring, hammer, and a nine-volt battery. He visits a steak house and orders a T-bone and lobster for supper.

The sun is setting when McConnell pulls into a private marina and watches several crew members readying a ninety-foot post boat named Fare Thee Well.

Forty minutes later, he has wired the pile of Reese's Cups with the phone, battery, and detonator. He removes the hammer from the Walmart plastic bag tucked under his suit jacket and makes his way to the boat. Upon boarding, Ron flashes his badge.

"I'm here to inspect your vessel. Please bring your crew members to the deck." All cops understand that tone of voice and a strong pretense of authority garner both attention and obedience.

The Japanese crew instantly comes to attention after the boat captain shouts out directions, and the four sailors look straight ahead, waiting on their next set of orders.

McConnell walks in front of the four men and sees that the captain packs a sidearm. "Let me see your license for this firearm."

The captain disappears below deck, and returns with his license-to-carry and paperwork from the State of Hawaii. McConnell pretends to read for a few seconds then hands the paperwork back.

"Stay here. I'm going below." He walks past the men and heads under the deck. As he starts down the stairs, one of the sailors says, in Japanese, "For a cop, he stinks."

Three of the crew start snickering, and McConnell stops his descent, not understanding why the crew is laughing. The captain dresses down the sailor in Japanese then bows toward him.

In the main cabin, McConnell removes a seat cushion, places the Reese's package deep in the back of the couch, and replaces the cushion. Wasting another few minutes using the bathroom, he returns to the deck, where the crew has not moved a muscle.

"You run a clean boat," he says to the captain and receives yet another bow of submission.

McConnell walks back to the rental car, unwraps a handful of the nonexplosive Reese's cups, and eats the miniatures.

◆

When Ron McConnell had boarded the commercial airliner in New Orleans, Shane Appleton was driving Israel Hamric to a private airport twenty-four miles east of the city, parking next to a Lear Jet.

In many ways, Hamric feels relieved about dropping off the grid and putting the hitman's lifestyle to bed. There are no redos in the murder-for-hire game. Sooner or later something goes wrong, and you either spend the rest of your life in prison or the target kills you.

Appleton had bought the bungalow under a fake corporate name three years earlier, and Hamric made three trips, finishing it to his exacting demands. The landscape around the house is remote, located as it is in a beautiful mountain range on one of the country's six-thousand inhabited islands.

Hamric arrives in Maui and rents a car using the fake driver's license. After a trip to the suburbs and an isolated dog park, he takes a shovel and digs up a five-gallon paint can containing a .40-cal. pistol and a disassembled AR-15. In addition to a stack of cash, the container yields four-hundred rounds of ammunition for both weapons. Hamric had buried the cache over a year ago, anticipating this exit day. He assembles the AR-15, loads it, and places it in the car.

The twenty-minute drive to the docked boat Fare Thee Well is made calmly by Hamric, not going even a tiny bit above the speed limit. This kind of patience is a natural part of his personality. Tonight, however, he is eager to board the boat and start the final leg of the journey. Things have gone right down the center of a plan he had formulated and put on the rails over three years earlier.

The dock comes into view, and he sees the boat being readied to launch. He carries several bags of money along with his weapons and clothes up on the deck.

"Permission to come aboard?" He gives the captain immediate respect, and the crew takes note.

"Welcome aboard." The captain takes the bags and stows them below, though the AR-15 continues to hang from Hamric's shoulder. The captain goes through a launching checklist and receives process confirmation from the crewmembers by radio. The men, moving in numerous directions above and below deck, appear confident.

The salty sea breeze increases at the bow as the Fare Thee Well eases away from the dock. Hamric feels like a kid on Christmas morning. He cannot stand still and moves next to the communications tower to smell the air and feel the taste of freedom.

◆

McConnell has been watching from his car all the movement on the Fair Thee Well and figures the man wielding the AR-15 is Israel Hamric. It does not matter. His job has not been one of discretion but of execution. The cell is set for a three-minute detonation, and he activates the program. The phone's clock begins counting down. When falling to zero, it will create a massive explosion, killing all aboard, including the monster that Rusty the fox squirrel had described in detail.

The boat clears the first buoy and increases speed to the open sea. The cell reads 2:20 and decreasing. McConnell is detached from the event and has little anticipation. He is ready to fly back to the mainland in the morning and visit both Jill and Rusty.

From the upper deck, Hamric can hear two crew members below suddenly break out in laughter. Knowing the strict adherence to custom and orders, he walks inside the wheelhouse and asks the captain what the laughing is about.

"We had an inspection a couple hours ago, and the cop had a bad odor about him," the captain responds.

Hamric instantly understands. No inspection would be performed this time of day to a docked boat. He screams, "Turn around, fast! Go back to the dock." He runs below to the living quarters, frantically opening drawers and closets, throwing objects in the air looking for a bomb.

At the 1:18 mark of the countdown, McConnell sees the craft turning back to the dock, outlined by the brightly lit lights on the bridge. The boat is running at full speed and he leans forward in disbelief. The clock face reveals forty-one seconds to detonation.

The captain has no clue why Hamric seems to be going crazy, but he follows the orders of his charter and speeds toward the dock. Hamric reappears on the deck, now pacing back and forth. Then he runs to the rear of the Fare Thee Well and stands at the stern ready to jump. The cell hits zero, and the bomb blows the deck upward in a giant fireball.

McConnell watches intently as the boat burns. The flames build, and the Fare Thee Well sinks within minutes.

Thirty Two

STRAIGHT SHOOTING

Gayle Kidd decides to run a few miles in early afternoon to clear her head, trying to reset her thinking about the book and handling the relationship with Trey. Running has always been mind-sharpening for Gayle, and hitting the pavement is a quick fix. A regenerative tool since her track days in high school.

The neighborhood jog follows her usual circular route, and the stride is longer than usual, trying to outrun a feeling of being followed. The only revelation coming to Gayle at the end of the fast-paced workout is that Trey is a much bigger subject in her mind than the book. Something she did not think possible just a few months ago, her professional life is taking a back seat to the personal one. Love will do that. It is the only justification she can wrap her mind around to make sense.

Opening the front gate to the property, Gayle is diligent in reconnecting the electronics and wrought-iron framework together. The privacy that had seemed so comfortable was shattered with the late Herman Dailey's intrusion the day before. She walks around the back of the house and sees Lilly emptying a vacuum cleaner into a soon-discarded plastic grocery bag.

"Hi Lilly, how is Trey doing?" she asks, walking to the extended wooden deck.

"That boy is scaring me. Since you laid him in bed last night, he's been up once to pee and drink water. Went straight back to sleep about two hours ago. Seen him drunk plenty, but this is crazy. Maybe you should go check on him."

"Not sure. He seems upset with me, and anyway I need to work on my book."

"Come here," Lilly summons.

Gayle moves closer to Lilly.

"Do you have feelings for Trey?"

"Yes. I'd be lying if I said differently."

"Then get off your pretty little ass and grab hold. What the hell is wrong with you?"

"I hate to impose myself on Trey. Guess that's stupid, huh?" She squints her eyes, having nothing to do with the sun beating on the deck.

"Trey has two issues," Lilly counters. "One, he's a man, and two, he's been spoiled rotten by most everybody in his life—including me. He's used to being chased, know what I mean, girl?"

"I'm getting there. Shred my ignorance."

"He needs you to take control. He's looking for a beacon of light like you. Don't sit on the sideline and let this fall apart." She finishes emptying the vacuum.

"What would you recommend I do?"

"Go to his room right now, push him out of this woe-is-me sleep. I'll make lunch, then you both go out tonight. Dammit, be a young lover again."

Gayle has had a soft spot for Lilly since their first meeting, and now she heads inside to follow her advice. Trey's head is buried under two pillows, and it scares her momentarily. She removes them, and he repositions himself, still asleep.

"Trey, time to eat something. I'm worried about you." She pushes the hair away from his face and his eyes open.

"I'm fine. A couple more hours' sleep is all I need." His hand moves to her face and moves her hair back to uncover the perfect set of eyes looking at him in concern.

"I'll make a deal. One more hour of sleep, and we'll eat on the deck."

"Deal," he says, and buries his head back in one of the vacated pillows.

"One hour," she reminds him, leaving the bedroom.

A glass of wine greets her on the kitchen table, and she sits beside it.

"Is he coming off that roost of his?" Lilly asks.

"I gave him one hour. He'll be down to eat. Thanks for this, Lilly. He is special to me." She begins sipping the wine.

"Don't thank me, young lady. I've seen too much bad stuff to let this fall apart. Grab all you can. Always someone ready to take it away."

"Want to talk about those bad things? Sometimes it helps to share."

"Just an old black lady. Things happening years ago. No one cares, anyway. All dead now. Only alive in my memories, and when I'm gone it's like nothing happened at all. I have one more suggestion, Miss Gayle," she says, smiling.

"What's that?"

"Go take a shower and put a little perfume on. Dress in something with a short hemline. You have one hour until the food lands on the table." Lilly takes a bottle of olive oil from the cabinet.

302

"Good idea," Gayle responds, leaving the table.

She opens the door to the guest house, and something seems wrong. The MacBook Pro containing countless hours of words she has been crafting into a best-seller is lying at the end of a small daybed. She has been doing most of her writing on a desk sitting in front of a large picture window facing the back deck of Trey's home. When she left the room earlier, the laptop was plugged into a charger. She is certain she had followed that routine before the run; unless the computer has suddenly grown legs, it should not be where it is.

Gayle's response is one of extreme caution. Buoyed by Lilly's lecture, she grabs a knife on the kitchen counter and moves along the hallway. She opens the bedroom door, and an inspection under the bed and in the closet reveals nothing out of the ordinary. A quick check of the bathroom likewise yields little to fear.

She goes to the front door and locks it. Then she contemplates all the wild things in her life since arriving in New Orleans. She takes a quick shower and dons a cute sundress. She spends time applying her makeup, spraying a generous amount of Tom Ford Black Orchid on her arms and neck. One last mirror framing makes her feel ready, and she goes out to the back deck carrying a small clutch.

Lilly is setting the table and sees Gayle approaching. "My, my! Ain't you a doll-baby. That'll wake up his sleepy ass."

"Did I tell you how much I love you, Lilly?"

"So many love me ... hard to keep count. I'll refill that glass of wine and bring it out shortly."

The May sunshine is a perfect compliment to a lunch on the deck overlooking the swimming pool and a yard full of flowers opening wide to the light and bees. Trey arrives showered and shaved, something Gayle is sure has Lilly's fingerprints.

"How are you feeling, Trey?" she asks, brandishing her dentist-perfect smile.

"Better than last night. Thanks for rolling my drunk ass into bed."

Lilly sets a beer in front of him and places the wine within hand's reach of Gayle then returns to the kitchen.

He offers the beer in a salute. "To a little more sober approach."

"Hear, hear! she exclaims, agreeing with the sentiment then laughing.

"What's so funny?"

"We're saluting sobriety with a drink. Kinda' hypocritical, don't you think?"

"First time hypocrisy has ever tasted good," he quips.

The clutch purse comes to life with a phone demanding attention.

Gayle retrieves the cell and answers. "Hello?" Her head moves sideways in a negative response. "Really? Poor man. Do you know who did it?" A few seconds go by with her listening intently to the call. "Thanks for keeping me in the loop," she returns the phone to the clutch.

"What was that all about?"

"There was a guy here yesterday morning taking pictures," she replies, taking a sip of wine.

"Why didn't you tell me?" Trey looks totally surprised and irritated.

"I tried to, but that's not important. I called Detective Dale and sent him a photo of the man. He knew him." She pulls the cell out again and shows Trey the photo. "Detective Dale found the man murdered last night."

"Damn, that's beyond spooky!" His mind instantly goes off in several directions, including his grandfather's accusation that Gayle is evil.

Lilly brings a bowl of pasta and hot bread to the table then quickly retires to the kitchen. Gayle serves the pasta.

"Yes it is. After my run earlier today, I found my computer moved to the bed. But this guy obviously didn't have anything to do with it."

"Did you lock the door?" Trey asks, taking a bite of the bread.

"I don't have a key, and to be honest I never felt threatened until now. Do you have a key?"

"Sorry, I should have given you one. That aside, what the hell is going on? Do you have a clue?"

"Ever since the kidnapping, all has spiraled out of control. I don't comprehend any of it. The only thing I know for sure is … I'm in love with you, and I'm simply empty when you're not around." She reaches out, and his hand meets hers halfway across the table.

"I feel the same way. We'll get through this and move on with our lives."

The food and talk move from the strange events and fear to a light banter and more hand-holding. For the first time in their relationship, Gayle and Trey openly discuss their love. It feels, and tastes, good for two people struggling emotionally to understand their fiercely independent natures now merging.

After two hours drenched in the sun and love, Gayle has a

suggestion. "Why don't we go out tonight, get something to eat, and go dancing?"

"A date night?"

"A date night. I think so," Gayle confirms. "Can I get a key and do a little more writing today?"

Trey leaves to retrieve a key and returns shortly. "Can't believe I didn't give you one."

"Fess up. You wanted twenty-four-hour access."

"Let me walk you over and check out the guest house."

"That would be welcomed." She takes his hand again, and the two walk the stone-lined path to the back of the property. After checking out the cottage and finding nothing amiss, he gives her the key and starts to leave. She kisses him and leads him to the bedroom. More writing of *Hell Raising* will have to wait.

◆

Late afternoon is approaching. Trey runs to the main house full of spirit and ready for a change of clothes. He and Gayle are headed out for an evening of fun, something missing since their first night in Mexico.

Gayle finishes refreshing ahead of Trey. She opens the back door and walks to the kitchen, where Lilly sits drinking a bourbon and 7UP.

"You going out tonight, Lilly?" she asks with a wink.

"You never know what Lilly has up her sleeve. May be something really big." She returns the wink.

"God bless you. Have fun." She hugs her.

"I'm sure, you and Trey will have a lot more excitement than old Lilly," she says, fixing another drink.

Trey slips a .38 into an ankle holster and buckles it down. His feet are light in movement, and the steps are covered easily to the kitchen, where he hugs Gayle.

A faint knock on the front door is noticed by Lilly, not the engaged couple. She opens the heavy wooden door and Trey's grandmother appears, out of breath and crying. Trey hears the commotion and rounds the corner. Seeing Lilly helping Mrs. Stephens to the couch, he immediately reads her distress.

"What's wrong, Me-maw?"

"It's your grandfather. He slapped me. Threw my phone against the wall. He's lost it, threatening to shoot himself." The small woman is truly terrified.

"I'll take care of this. It'll be okay." He starts for the kitchen door and Gayle follows.

Mrs. Stephens screams out, "Don't hurt him, Trey—please! He's been crazy since you got kidnapped."

"I won't hurt him. We'll talk this out." He and Gayle head to the garage.

"Should I call the police, Trey? He could hurt himself or you."

"No, he's a stubborn old bastard, but he won't hurt me. I'll be back shortly. Save me a dance." He drives away.

◆

The car moves through the Stephens driveway with caution. Trey is not sure what awaits, but he doubts his grandfather is dangerous to anyone other than his wife.

Parking at the front door, he starts to get out but realizes the .38 is tethered to his ankle and removes it from the holster, placing the pistol on the passenger seat. He is thinking his temperament toward his grandfather right now might make him do something foolish. Better not have that option.

The front door is ajar, and Trey moves into the house. Every light seems to be on.

"Grandfather? It's Trey, where are you?" He repeats the words every few steps, but the large house is silent except for his voice and footsteps.

He searches the second floor rooms, one-by-one. He opens doors, shouts words, and shuts them. He is feeling increasingly nervous going through rooms and expecting his grandfather to jump from the next door opening, gun in hand. The master bedroom at the end of the hall is next. Trey approaches carefully, takes a deep breath, and opens quickly. A spotless room and made bed are the only silent rewards.

The third floor finds him moving at a faster pace, wondering why he jumped at rescuing the old bastard. Finishing off the top floor, he reaches for his pocketed cell and realizes in haste he had left the phone at home.

"Dammit to hell!" he shouts to a house that cares nothing about his frustrations.

He heads for the stairway, and a sudden revelation sparks a suspicion. Did his grandfather know about all the secret passages in the house, like he did? If that is the case, he has unlimited places to curl into a fetal position and hide.

The stairway seems to be lined with countless steps, moving

down from the third floor to the first, and Trey's heart begins to accelerate along with his feet. A last peek into the expansive kitchen and he is bent on leaving the old fool to his self-destruction. Then, in the far corner, the open door to the basement is staring back. He is stuck deciding about going dancing with a beautiful woman or trying to help his petulant grandfather.

Something comes over Trey during this split-second decision. Maybe it is guilt or an unexpected pang of selflessness, but for whatever reason it becomes his fate. He walks to the basement door and down the steps.

Unlike the rest of the house, the basement lights are not on. Trey flips the switch at the top of the stairway and descends into a decaying smell. He has not been in the basement since a child, and he does not recognize the old home's metamorphic and cryptic death going on beneath his grandmother's feet.

A large concrete wall has been built since Trey's childhood adventures as a pirate. The wall has eaten much of the storage space once so abundant. An uneven hole has literally been pounded into openness by a sledgehammer and other tools lying around the hole's entrance.

On Trey's last visit, Me-maw said his grandfather was pounding in the basement, but that lent no clue why the structure was built to begin with. What in God's name was his grandfather hiding behind that wall? And why, suddenly, did he decide to reopen it?

A nine-volt flashlight lies next to the sledgehammer, welcoming Trey to witness the secret. Bravery begins quickly losing the mental battle when moaning from a helpless man creeps out of the hole along with an increasing smell of decaying death.

Trey grabs the flashlight, flips it on, and leans low in the crawl space, making his way to his injured grandfather. The wall is three feet thick and requires a few seconds of knee-and-hand progress to breach the hole. He stands in the dark space beyond the wall. The flashlight reveals nothing but a dirt expanse surrounding his initial survey, and no grandfather in sight. He takes a few more steps inward, and his eyes adjust to the dark depths. A side-to-side sweep with his light only leads to more confusion, but Trey is sure he heard some type of cry for help before entry.

Several more steps and Trey almost falls into a crevice in the ground, twenty feet across and thirty feet wide. The flashlight tries to feature the bottom of the crevice, but its beam is far short of discovery. Trey grabs a rock the size of his fist and throws it into the gaping hole, listening for it to hit bottom. The rock disappears without ever hitting anything solid. Trey can't imagine how a hole this deep could be built under any house without the use of major equipment.

One more circle of the flashlight kills any additional thought of his grandfather being stranded in this creepy structure. As he turns for the escape route, a blast of light fills the once-dark cave, emitting from the hole and to the point of temporarily blinding Trey. He clamps his hands over his eyes, trying to adjust to the sudden brilliance.

The light dims, and beyond the hole stands a giant, bear-like man, face hidden by a Grim Reaper's Halloween mask. His right hand shifts the grip of a three-foot machete in a round and round motion.

Trey dives for the exit space and scrambles just short of the basement side. His left foot is grabbed and the long blade slices across the shoe, piercing the skin through the leather. The confined space saves his foot and life. A roll on his back and Trey kicks the caveman from hell flush in the face-mask, buying precious seconds.

Desperate to escape from the basement, he makes it halfway up the steps when a large hand surrounds his ankle. The fall on the stairway knocks him out cold. Seconds or minutes go by, but Trey has no recollection of time. He rises from the base of the steps and touches an expanding lump on his forehead, proving the nightmare was real. The bear-man is not in sight. Thankful but still frightened, he takes the steps three at a time, ascending to the first floor.

He bursts into the kitchen and starts for the front door but stops in his tracks. Standing between him and the car is the bear-man, now advancing to his side of the kitchen.

Trey pulls a steak-knife from a wooden block and moves to the back of the kitchen. A dumbwaiter serving lift in the wall is his only escape route, with the bear-man meticulously circling the kitchen island. Lowering a shoulder gains entrance to the lift, and he reaches out to finger the kitchen wall for the switch to move him skyward. A massive hand latches onto his fingers and begins to yank him from the wooden box. With his free hand, Trey stabs the arm trying to rip him from the box, and his own hand is released.

A flip of the electric switch and the box jumps upward toward the third floor. The box bounces rapidly from the kitchen level, but immediately slows to a nerve-wracking, inch-by-inch progression. Passing the second floor gives Trey a chance to start breathing again, but six feet from the third floor the box stops, suspended between floors. The claustrophobic box starts being dragged downward back toward the second floor by a pair of muscled arms.

Trey understands death awaits if he cannot escape the dumb-waiter, which is rapidly seeming more like a coffin. Three adrenaline-filled kicks against the door and it shatters. His body barely clears the tunneled wall, and he grabs the elevator rope above, starting a hand-over-hand climb to the third floor servant opening.

He swings the rope to the opening and grips the sidewall. He jumps onto the third floor hallway but hears heavy footsteps running the stairway to his floor. The second bedroom down the hall has a hidden tunnel he found as a child. He runs to the closet and slides the panel back, climbing in.

The newfound relief is short-lived. He makes his way to the first floor in a series of escape spaces, surrounded with two-by-four studs and old wooden paneling. But the bear figure and his machete have found his route, barreling down on Trey amazingly fast through the maze.

He heads to a bedroom on the first floor, clearing it only a few feet ahead of the bear-man, crashing ever so closely behind. Trey begs a desperately needed second wind and rushes through the front door, jumping into his car. The bear-man grabs the passenger side door and opens it. Trey raises the .38 and fires shot after shot. Five bullets penetrate the face and chest, and the giant stumbles backwards and falls.

Trey starts the car and races the driveway for the safety of his home and to the people that love him. He will need all the love they can muster.

◆

Returning to his house with torn clothes, numerous scratches, and a bloody foot that Lilly cleans, medicates and bandages, the injuries are the least of Trey's surprises. He has shot and killed someone who attacked him, but the biggest mystery still remains. Where is Mr. Stephens? Me-maw is hysterical, and the night has just begun. Gayle calls 911, and the police head to both residences.

Gayle brings an icepack to Trey sitting in the den, and he rotates it between the back of his neck and his forehead.

"Can't believe this," he says, leaning over in obvious pain.

"This guy was big as a bear. I ran all over the house trying to get away from him."

"I'm so sorry, baby. I should have gone with you. I could have helped," she responds.

"You don't understand, there was no fighting this guy. He would have chopped us to pieces with that machete," Trey asserts, trying to paint the picture. "Can you get a couple Tylenol? My head is killing me."

Gayle leaves and returns a few moments later, offering a bottle of water and two tablets. The doorbell rings in the background, and soon Lilly rounds the corner with two police officers and Detective Rolando Silva.

Silva produces a recorder and listens to Trey's sequence of events. He stops the recording after hearing that the elder Mr. Stephens was not at the house and missing.

"Excuse me," Silva says while retreating to the kitchen. "I need to order an APB for Mr. Stephens."

He returns and resumes the questioning. "You shot this man, with what weapon?"

"A thirty-eight snub-nose revolver. It's in my Mercedes out front."

Silva turns to the uniformed officers. "Go to the car and bag the weapon."

"Why are you doing that?" Trey asks, bewildered.

"It's procedure for every shooting. How many times did you fire the weapon?"

"It holds six. I think it was emptied but can't swear to that." His headache grows more intense as the process extends beyond what he considers a reasonable time.

"The guy kept coming at you. The first few rounds didn't stop him, or did you miss early?"

"He opened the car door. It was point-blank. I don't think many shots missed."

The questions continue for another twenty minutes. Trey's patience is stretched, and physical exhaustion is taking over.

Detective Silva receives a call, again moving to the next room for private communications. He returns to Trey.

"Detective Dale is on his way. I have enough for now. Thanks for your cooperation." Silva starts out of the house. He whispers something to both officers then retreats to his car.

Trey stands and leans over, kissing a seated Gayle. "Going to take a shower and knock some of this stink off me."

One of the officers moves in Trey's direction. "Sir, Detective

Dale will be here shortly to ask additional questions. Please stay down here."

"Alright. I'll put the shower off for a while."

"Can I get you something else?" Gayle asks, seeing that Trey is at his limit and wanting to make him comfortable as possible.

"Orange juice would be wonderful ... thanks."

Lilly returns. "Your grandmother is finally resting. I've never seen her so terrorized about your grandfather."

"After what I saw, I'm not optimistic—but would never tell her that."

Gayle brings the OJ, and Trey takes a sip. Lilly rises and turns to them.

"We all better do a lot of praying. He's an obstinate old bastard, but that lady upstairs is lost without him." She disappears into the depths of the house.

◆

Chris Dale pulls into Trey's driveway next to Detective Silva's car and joins him in the front seat.

"Rolo, what's Stephens story?"

"Says an unknown assailant jumped him when he entered the house looking for his grandfather. The stranger chased him from one end to the other before he made his car and shot him with a thirty-eight."

"He didn't see his grandfather at all?"

"Nope ... adamant about that."

"Do you believe his story?"

"He's bruised all over. Has a nasty cut on his foot. He's definitely been in a fight and seems scared about the encounter. He did say something that didn't make sense. He said the guy came from a deep hole behind a concrete wall in the basement. Does the story match with the scene?"

"In some ways, it matches. The house does show signs of a chase and struggle, but we have one rather major discrepancy. The guy laying on the driveway with five gunshot wounds is old man Stephens. He blew away his grandfather."

"Damn! Didn't see that coming. How do we handle it from here?" Silva asks.

"Take him to the station in cuffs. Run a gun-residue test. Take photos of the injuries ... drug tests. Don't know how he can defend it. No other weapon found on premises. Got the thirty-eight?"

"Bagged it."

"Did he change clothes?"

"No. He's sitting in the den waiting on you. Want me do a financial search tomorrow to see what the grandson receives to cash-out the grandfather's death?"

"Great point. Work with Bobby Rabold on that. Now, let's go hand him the wonderful news." They move out of the car.

◆

Gayle and Trey sit close on the couch waiting for Detective Dale to complete the process so they can go to bed. The grandfather clock ticks off eighty-nine more minutes before he enters the room.

"Lieutenant Dale, good to see you," Gayle says, offering her hand.

Chris smiles slightly, ignoring her hand. "Just a point of clarification before we wrap this up, Mr. Stephens. You didn't see your grandfather at any point tonight?"

"No, did you find him? Is he okay?" Trey asks, rising from the couch.

"I'm afraid not. The man you shot in the driveway is your grandfather. Detective Silva, read him his rights. I'll meet you at the station in an hour or so." Chris walks out of the den and in the background is an all too familiar sentence.

"You have the right to remain silent, anything you say, can and will be held against you."

◆

Chris Dale's thoughts are not converging on a central theme of who, what, where, when, and why as he returns to the scene of the crime. He runs the routine on every case, but this one does not seem so nearly defined as the facts accumulate.

As he arrives, the lab boys are finishing up, and Mr. Stephens' body has already been removed. The large pool of blood is noticeable under the bright lights, mounted like a movie shoot positioned around the murder scene.

Chris walks into the house and to the kitchen, and sees the dumbwaiter opening. He looks upward in the vacant hole. A flashlight marks the box's appearance above the second floor. The light flashes downward, and Chris notes the wooden door has been knocked off its hinges, lying at the bottom of the shaft.

A tech walks by on his way out. "Did you find any weapons?"

Chris inquires.

"Nope," he answers and keeps moving.

Chris moves to a small closet in the corner and retrieves a broom then returns to the dumbwaiter. His cell takes a photo of the broken door, and he uses the broom to flip the door over. The flashlight outlines a steak knife and blood on the blade. He takes two more photos and heads out the front door, but the CSI truck has left.

A return trip to the kitchen and he opens the door to the basement, making his way step-over-step, descending the stairway. The concrete wall and carved entrance stands in front of him. At least part of Trey's story holds water.

Removing his jacket and tie, Chris kneels low to the floor, searching the strange hole in the wall with his flashlight. The large expanse of dark space gives little detail to the penetrating light. He crawls in and the same decaying smell meets his senses, a warning to all not to enter.

Getting off his knees to an upright stance is harder than he wants, but he is determined to find out what triggered the events. The cave-like room is much larger than he imagines, outlined by swinging the light wall-to-wall at eye level. Five more feet into the concrete prison and he notices the large, in-ground hole and tries to understand the function. A structured hole under a prominent citizen's house, and a supposed monster of a man crawling out of its depths, fails to pass any sort of sensibility test.

Having seen all he cares to, Chris crawls back out to the basement and puts his jacket on, tucking the tie in his pocket. Three steps from the top of the stairway, a brief, bright light emits from the bowels of the Earth like the flash of a camera. He freezes and turns toward the source, not understanding where the flash came from. A decision to investigate is incubating in his mind, but he does not return and challenge fate.

Thirty Three

CAVEMAN

Brooke Davenport, the U.S. Marshal assigned to guard Emrik upon his return to New Orleans, parks next to an expansive baseball facility with four games being played simultaneously. She is here to see Emrik play in a Little League game. Dressed in jeans, she displays a more comfortable attire than the usual marshal protocol. Arriving in the park early, she walks the various fields, making mental notes of exits and the general demeanor of the crowd going and coming.

Twenty minutes into her surveillance, Eva and Emrik appear, heading for the number three field and joining his teammates wearing Braves uniforms. Eva sees her and waves her to the third-base side of the ball diamond. Emrik moves onto the outfield and starts throwing a ball to several other players, very much in his element.

"Brooke, how is New Orleans treating you?" Eva asks above the loud voices amplified by the many player actions, all within a few hundred yards.

"I've certainly had much worse location assignments. I've heard from your brother that Emrik is a really good center-fielder."

"From his mother's perspective, I'm a little biased," Eva says, smiling. "But yes, Emrik is damn good. His granddad played minor-league ball with St. Louis, so he has it in his genes." Her smile is natural and at ease since her ordeal in D.C. is over and having Emrik back in a familiar routine.

It does not take long for Davenport to see that Emrik has the gift. He hits a home run in his first at bat and makes catch after catch in the outfield. The Braves have a lot of talent, and the game moves out of hand quickly, evoking the ten-run rule in the fifth inning.

Eva receives a call as the players are exiting the field. "Yes, I'm busy right now but will see if I can work it out."

Emrik joins the ladies, and Eva gives him a hug.

"Great game, Emrik. I'm Brooke Davenport."

"Thanks." Emrik is used to hearing the accolades.

"Emrik, Miss Brooke works with the U.S. Marshals Service. She's here to make sure nothing happens to you again." She hands him a five-dollar bill, and he starts off toward his teammates to grab a hot dog. As he leaves, Eva gives him a directive. "Not too long with the boys, I have to be at work early this afternoon."

Emrik kicks the dirt. "Aw Mom, c'mon. We won!"

"How can I help?" Davenport volunteers.

"Thanks, we'll work it out." Eva does not want to impose, even though she has built up some trust with the marshal.

"I'll take him home if that helps. It's sorta' my job anyway."

"You just have to take him to the house. My brother will be home within the hour."

"Very easy assignment," Davenport says, smiling.

"Emrik, come here," Eva demands, and he returns. "Miss Brooke will give you a ride home. I'm headed to work. Whatever Miss Brooke says, you listen, understand?" He nods and runs off with his teammates.

"Go to work," Davenport assures. "We'll catch up tomorrow. He'll be home when you return."

"Thanks so much." Eva hugs her in a typical Southern way and leaves.

Davenport places Emrik's bat and other ball equipment in the trunk of her car while the parking lot clears out. As she leans against the back of the vehicle, Emrik arrives and asks a pointed question.

"You're a U.S. Marshal. Is that like being a sheriff?"

She stands up straight. "Like a sheriff, but instead of working in one city like New Orleans, the marshals work in all fifty states. We even go to other countries to chase bad guys."

"So, where's your gun? Can't be a sheriff without a gun."

"Good question," She raises her foot to the bumper and pulls up her jean pantleg. A nine-millimeter pistol is tucked inside a holster and strapped to the ankle. "Sometimes my weapon is on the ankle, sometimes it's under my jacket. Depends on what I'm wearing. I'm always armed."

"Except when you sleep?"

"When I sleep, the weapon is under the pillow next to me."

"Not the pillow you sleep on?" Emrik asks, fascinated with the topic.

"No, not under the pillow I sleep on. That would be a little dangerous, not to mention uncomfortable for your head. Hop in Emrik, we'll head home."

He jumps in the front seat and buckles his seatbelt. Davenport drives away from the lot and taps Emrik's address into the GPS on the dashboard of the rental car.

"What did you do?" Emrik asks, watching her complete the process.

"Well, I put your address in the computer, and a satellite in the sky takes the information. It gives me directions how to drive to your home. See? The satellite wants me to turn right at the light. It will take us directly to your house."

"I've been on one of those satellites." He says matter-of-factly.

"Really, did you see it on TV?"

"No, I rode one in space." Emrik pulls a baseball card out of his pocket and places the accompanying gum in his mouth.

◆

While Emrik chews his gum, Jessie McGaha and Stony Fetter sit in the newspaper's boardroom with a production crew discussing the next steps in placing their series of stories on the street. Photos, newspaper articles, and reams of other material lay on the fifteen-foot cherrywood table.

"What we have is a load of dynamite with the fuse lit ready to go off. The question is how do we launch and allocate the material over several weeks?" Fetter asks.

Lee Jenson, VP of circulation, offers a direction. "If you want the big boys jumping on the story early with syndication, better not lead off with a bunt single."

Jessie looks at Jenson. "Explain your plan so even I can understand it."

He stands. "The grand slam is the abduction of the young man by an alien spacecraft. Is he willing to say he flew in space?"

"I watched his abduction take place. His mother has relayed his experiences. I'm comfortable leading with that."

"Other witnesses?" Jenson inquires.

"An NOPD detective and other relatives."

"There's your intro, and the syndication networks will come running." He sits down.

Fetter stands. "Okay, we need to align the story sequencing and photos to build interest throughout the series. Save the UFO shots for the last two stories. Questions?"

Heads shake around the table, and staff members file out.

Jessie approaches Fetter. "It's the weekend. Emrik should be working Bourbon Street. I'm going over to shoot photos with his uncle playing and him dancing."

"Perfect," he endorses, as she starts for the door. "Jessie, you won't leave me when this story breaks?"

"Better work on that raise you promised ten months ago, boss-man." She disappears out the building.

◆

Jessie drives to Bourbon Street and sees Emrik and his uncle working their music and dance one block from O'Brian's. It is Saturday night, the tourist crowd has parking stacked several blocks off Bourbon, and Jessie finds herself leaving the car in a less-than-desirable neighborhood. She takes a hurried inventory of camera, flash, and purse while walking away from the car, wasting little time in the trouble zone.

The photos start eighty feet away, and the dancing/playing duo have no clue they are subjects of a camera focused on them. Jessie has taken countless pictures, but she inherently believes these will be the most viewed photos she will ever take. Every few steps, she employs a new angle and different lens, bringing Emrik's motion-filled dancing, often airborne, into frame.

Jessie is completely immersed in the process and does not notice being stalked. Standing across the street from Emrik, working her final flight of photos, Jessie's arm is grabbed and turned abruptly around. Her state of mind was already fractured in Utah, and she screams at the top of her lungs. Bourbon Street's opulent, over-the-top style of booze, drugs, and sex swallows the scream and throws it to the curb without a single ear turning in her terrified direction.

"Calm down," the arm-puller says to Jessie. But the words have little effect as she rips away her arm and jumps back, falling in the street. Her expensive Nikon hits the sidewalk, and that alone is reason for panic.

Brooke Davenport extends a hand to help Jessie up, but the offer is snubbed. Then she grabs the camera and inspects the damage, which is minimal.

She pulls out her U.S. Marshals badge and flashes it. Jessie is not impressed, dusting the less-than-sanitary Bourbon Street grit from her jacket.

"Why are you taking photos of that young man dancing?" Davenport demands.

"Number one, I'm friends with Emrik and his mother, Eva. Number two, I'm a reporter doing a story on Emrik. Who the hell are you, coughing up a badge that can be bought at any pawnshop on the strip for ten dollars?"

"I'm Agent Davenport with the U.S. Marshals. I've been assigned to protect Emrik. Sorry if I startled you, just doing my job."

"Well, I'm doing mine, and by the way, I can take photos on a public street anytime I want to. Before you go grabbing anyone else, better weigh the circumstance more professionally." She takes a photo of Davenport to prove a point.

Jessie had intended to interview Emrik and his uncle about their performing routine, but she is shaken by the altercation and walks away to her car. By the time she sits behind the wheel, little of her anger has abated. Jessie is level-headed and rarely blows her cool, but Agent Davenport never should have touched her. The situation cannot be pushed away in her mind completely, and it begins to fester for good or bad.

The cell in her purse rings. She answers, not looking at the number. It is Chris Dale.

"Jessie," how was your trip to Utah? Any UFO shots?"

"Actually smart-ass, we did take photos of real, live UFOs."

"No shit? Have to see those. I have something that will blow your skirt up and help the book-writing," he says excitedly.

"Talk to me," she demands.

"Too much over the phone. Meet me at old man Stephens' house tonight. There will be a CIA guy with me. He's a government expert on UFOs. I'll text you the address."

"What do I say to Mr. Stephens on why I'm showing up?"

"Don't worry. He's in the morgue. His grandson shot him five times. It's a crime scene. Be there in an hour."

"Uh ... okay ... see you in a bit." She tries to digest what she has just been told while shoving the phone in her purse and temporarily losing her anger at the Davenport.

◆

The yellow tape waves from side-to-side, wind-aided in front of the Stephens home. Jessie feels uncomfortable driving toward the front door and into the middle of a homicide scene. Chris's police cruiser and another vehicle are parked off to the right, short of the garage. Jessie pulls beside the cruiser.

The house is large and detailed in luxury. Jessie wonders what would possess a grandson to shoot his grandfather. It certainly was not due to an argument over Oxycodone in a trailer park.

She enters the open front door and hears voices. She follows the sound to the kitchen, where Chris and Victor Mirontshuck are covering ground she can only guess at.

Chris's eyes light a smile on his face when she rounds the corner.

"Jessie McGaha, meet Victor Mirontshuck."

They shake hands and, in somewhat of a surprise, Chris hugs her.

"Jessie's is a damned good reporter and noted author. Victor is a CIA officer, the government expert on UFOs." Chris seems giddy to her for some strange reason.

"Pleasure to meet you, Jessie. I've heard so much about your reporting skills,"

"Chris exaggerates at times, and this is one of them. How do you spell your last name for the record?" She does not want another off-the-record conversation with anyone from the CIA.

Mirontshuck looks at the floor as if disgusted. "I don't know how to spell it. At least that's what I told my father in the fourth grade. I have to refer to my business card to make sure." He hands her his card. "You witnessed the abduction of Emrik, I believe?"

"I did. We watched Emrik ripped off the street." She instantly likes this CIA man's self-depreciating humor.

"I would appreciate some time the next couple of days to gain your perspective."

"That can be arranged. I have a lot of questions you can help me with, I'm sure." She gives him her business card and adds a friendly, come-on smile. Chris recognizes her patented move on a man and changes the subject.

"Catching you up on the crime, Jessie, Trey Stephens claims a large man wearing a mask came after him in the basement with a machete, and he made it to the kitchen. He stabbed the man and jumped on the dumbwaiter, right here." Chris moves over to the dumbwaiter and aims a flashlight high into the tunnel where Jessie and Mirontshuck can follow the action.

"He's the grandson, right?" she asks.

"Yes. Trey crawled into the dumbwaiter and headed to the third floor." Chris knows the details after spending hours with Trey in interrogation.

"Did you recover the knife?" Mirontshuck asks.

"We did. It had blood on it. We sent it off to the state for DNA analysis."

"A wild guess, but you'll find a match in CODAS."

"Hope you're right. It would help prove how much of Trey's story is true."

"It won't help the case," Mirontshuck counters. "It will only make it more confusing."

"Why do you say that?" Jessie asks, awed by his investigative skillset.

"Let's get the results back, and we'll have a subsequent discussion." He smiles as if he has a secret.

"This stranger chased Trey downstairs from the third floor and out to his car, where Trey pulled a thirty-eight and shot him dead. Then he left, called the police, and when we got here..."

"The body is his grandfather laying out front," Mirontshuck says, cutting off Chris and filling the blank.

"Exactly ... how did you know that?" .

"I've seen it before. But that's not important now. You mentioned a walled-off area in the basement. Take us to it."

Chris leads them to the basement and points to the hole in the thick concrete wall. Without hesitation, Mirontshuck turns a flashlight on and enters on all fours. Chris does the same, and Jessie follows, not sure what in the hell she is crawling into but a willing participant nevertheless.

Jessie clears the entrance, and two flashlights are moving in different directions, adding to her confusion. Mirontshuck flashes the light downward, and his profile is visible along the edge of the chasm. Walking toward his light, Chris grabs Jessie by the waist and stops her forward motion.

"Sorry, can't get too close to the hole. You're dead if you fall in."

"Thanks," she responds. "What is this thing?"

Mirontshuck's voice comes out of the dark. "It's a necropolis ... a city of the dead."

She looks over the edge seeing nothing but darkness below the inept light both men are forcing down the throat of the hole.

A flash of Mirontshuck's camera records the crater's surface, followed by two more pictures deeper into the hole. Jessie is angry not bringing her camera to document the exploration.

Mirontshuck turns to them." Let's move out of here, what you're seeing is real danger. I'll explain later."

Jessie is the first to emerge from darkness, followed closely by Chris and then Mirontshuck. The group ascends to the first floor, and they keep walking until all are standing by the vehicles.

"So what is this 'city of the dead' thing?" Jessie asks.

"Necropolis is an ancient Greek word for underground burial sites. Paris and Rome have miles of such tunnels filled with skeletons and human remains. Eight years ago, the Egyptians found a small pyramid and excavated it. They asked for our help because a crevice similar to this was found below it. Strange light emitted from the hole. Eleven of the digging crew and archeologists were killed by crazy, unexplainable events. Some of our engineers went in. The thing collapsed and killed seven more. Keep your men away from here. The whole damn house might be sucked into a giant sinkhole."

Chris looks back at the beautiful home and turns to him. "According to his wife, old man Stephens spent weeks pounding into the concrete, and it's obvious he wanted to get behind the wall. What was he trying to do, let something out of the hole?"

Mirontshuck looks first at Jessie and then to Chris. "My educated guess? He was trying to make something go back into the hole, not the other way around."

Thirty Four

HOGTIED

Victor Mirontshuck drives off the Stephens property, leaving Jessie and Chris alone.

"Well, that was one crazy-assed conversation," Jessie quips, watching the taillights disappear out the gate and onto the street.

"When Victor showed up on the doorstep the other day, I knew after a few minutes he could be an asset for both of us," Chris says, proud of making the connection but a little defensive seeing Jessie flirt with the man, even on a subdued level. "Want to find something to eat?"

"Not interested in food," she replies. "But I could use a strong drink."

"How about Davey's Locker on Commerce?"

"Meet you there." She climbs into her car, taking one last look at the home of tragedy having many paths leading back to her.

Davey's Locker is one of the oldest bars in a town whose residents know a lot about drinking and are extremely judgmental about where it is done. Being around a long time means the ownership is doing something well, and the brand does not waver. Davey's serves double shots in all mixed drinks and charges a single-shot price. Almost as important, their burgers boast three patties on an exaggerated bun, with a pile of french fries stuffed on top of the patties.

Two things patrons rarely leave Davey's with: an empty stomach and driving their own car. More Ubers and taxis are called to Davey's on Friday and Saturday nights than any bar in New Orleans.

Chris arrives ahead of Jessie and does what cops are good at: sitting in a corner booth usually saved for VIPs. The place is rowdy, an annoyance for talking and listening. This is disappointing to Chris, but Jessie is happy to have an active crowd around her providing insulation from the bad things that have happened to her while alone.

They order drinks, and Chris raises his voice above the noise. "Tell me about Utah."

A hangover of ill will is attached to Jessie's thoughts about

Chris, making it hard to flip a switch and feel as though all is well.

"Met your devil-woman's sister," she says, welcoming the double bourbon laid close to her hand by the waiter.

"Really? What's she like?" Chris asks, starting to sip his double Crown Royal.

"A real bitch ... nearly choked me to death."

"Tell me more. Maybe she's the real Devil." Chris has never seen anything in Gayle Kidd that makes him think she could hurt someone.

"You know, Chris, it's not really important. I'm tired of talking about all this bullshit. I just want to have a couple of drinks..." She glances at the menu. "And have one of those french-fried burgers. I always wanted to try it."

"We can do the burgers," Chris says, waving for the waiter. "Maybe you should talk to Gayle Kidd. I don't think she's violent."

Jessie watches the hustle of food and drink being distributed in all directions and feels good about being home. She had flirted with Victor back at the house. It was unconscious and playful, but Chris did get jealous. That, after a second double, is circulating round and round in her head, creating a sense of pleasure. And the one thing Chris said touched a vein in her reporter's heart: talk to Gayle Kidd and see if she can add to the storyline being created for national headlines.

"Text me Kidd's number. I'll do an interview about her boyfriend's charges of shooting his grandfather." She attempts a first bite of the oversized burger, looking even larger in her smallish hands.

Chris retrieves the cell, quickly taps Gayle's contact information, and forwards. Then, looking at Jessie, he starts laughing.

"Damn! I don't know who has the advantage in your death match with the burger, but right now I wouldn't bet on you." He reaches across and wipes a large amount of ketchup off her cheek.

She looks around and sees several other customers in the same messy battle and realizes she is no exception. Her mouth is simply not big enough to bite through the four inches-plus of buns, fries, and patties.

"Do I look bad as I feel trying to eat this?" she asks, taking another swipe with a couple of napkins.

"It's not your finest hour. I'm being nice." He displays his stained mouth as if immune. She lets him wear it, not wiping away any of his ketchup ignorance or his man-sized ego.

Now she is enjoying the burger beyond the taste and chases it with a second double-shot. Chris, despite his clumsy attempt at being a friend and part-time lover, has broken through her veiled attitude of being emotionally hurt by his indifference on many occasions in the past. Maybe it has something to do with the double drinks, she thinks. No, it is feeling safe around Chris, and right now that is worth its weight in french-fried burgers at Davey's Locker.

◆

After their meal, Jessie had asked Chris if he wanted to go home with her, and of course he agreed. Shortly after arriving at the house, however, it is not to be. The on-again, off-again love affair must skip another beat when Bobby Rabold calls with a real murder mess on his hands. Chris kisses Jessie, both displaying ketchup-stained clothing, and leaves her house destined for a date with CSI.

He parks on the street in front of Louis Fleck's house. Going through the front door he can smell the reek of death, an old companion recognizes all too often. The second floor is buzzing with activity, nothing exceptional when dealing with a double homicide.

Mrs. Fleck is hanging over the side of the bed, tethered by duct tape to the post. Rabold emerges from the closet and sees Chris kneeling close to her body.

"Fleck is in the closet, a gunshot to the forehead."

"Is he tape bound?" Chris asks, standing up.

"No. The safe is emptied."

"I don't see a wound on his wife, how long have they been dead?" Chris walks to the closet and sees Fleck's open, blank eyes staring at the ceiling.

"The housekeeper found them a few hours ago. The coroner thinks it's been at least forty-eight hours. Mrs. Fleck didn't have any visible wounds, but the housekeeper says she was a diabetic. The guess right now is when the perp taped her to the bed she couldn't get loose and died of toxic shock. We'll know more after the medical exam."

"Can't say I'm surprised," Chris says. "Being in the line of business Louis Fleck pursued, it was bound to happen sooner or later."

"Everyone associated with this Hell Raising bullshit is going down."

"That could be it, but I guarantee there was forty ... maybe fifty thousand in that safe, and God knows how much jewelry."

Detective Mike Lee walks into the room. "You have to see this." Chris and Rabold follow him to the third floor.

A rope is hanging from the skylight that has a gaping hole cut in the glass.

"Sonofabitch, this is not amateur hour," Rabold says, flashing his light up to the fractured pane.

Chris looks at Rabold. "Israel Hamric."

They rush to the cruiser and drive to Hamric's rented property. The house has a light shining in the second floor bedroom, but they both understand what the score is before knocking on the door and receiving no answer. Instead, they kick in the locked door, and with weapons drawn they clear the house room by room. It is empty of any evidence that Israel Hamric ever resided there.

"I'll call it in," Rabold says, walking to the front porch.

Chris ponders the next move in this giant chess match before walking outside and approaching his partner.

"Not going to believe this," Rabold says. "Wilcox came by to check on Israel this morning and reported the AWOL to the state police and FBI."

"Why the hell is Wilcox checking on Israel, and why didn't anyone bother to tell us he's missing?" Chris frets, obviously pissed about the lack of communication in his own department. "We need an APB on that uncle of his, too."

"Did that a minute ago. He's probably back in New York without a clue Israel has gone someplace. Just a guess."

"A damn good guess, I'm sure."

◆

As Chris drives away from the vacated house and calls Jessie, he knows two hours have passed and he cannot be sure she is even awake.

She answers. "Who is dead now?"

"Louis Fleck and his wife. Conveniently, Israel Hamric has jumped bail and left town."

"The professional?"

"Yeah, and he's got at least forty-eight hours on us. He could be halfway round the world by now." He knows catching a man who has probably prepped for this day for years will be difficult to hunt down, even by the FBI and the U.S. Marshals. "You still up... want me to come by?"

328

"I made some hot tea, trying to stay awake. Better get here fast." Jessie knows too well Chris loves sex, and inviting him to come over means she does not want to disappoint. Besides, she thinks, it is not exactly bad having him around the house for a couple more hours, and truth be known she enjoys the sex.

Chris hits Jessie's garage door opener and steps out of the car, waiting patiently for the door to make its ascent. As the last few feet of wood panels creak and settle into final position, Chris hears a loud bang created by something large hitting the ground. Pistol in hand and flashlight on, Chris moves around the side of the garage but sees nothing moving the entire length of the building.

A walk around the garage and into Jessie's backyard spots nothing Chris can use to verify the source of the noise. What or who created the commotion must have jumped the six-foot vinyl fence before he made the corner. He returns to the raised garage door, hits the down button, and watches it fall back into place.

Chris is fearless about his own safety and a great partner to have as a fellow cop. In his early days on the force, he served countless arrest warrants and was always the first to break down the door and rush into the unknown with armed felons on the other side who were not exactly happy about the intrusion.

He is not sure what Jessie has experienced over the last couple of weeks chasing the same murder mysteries he is pursuing, but he can tell she is scared and needs his help. Something definitely was in her back yard, and he does not think it was two raccoons fighting over trashcan scraps. On his way into the kitchen, Chris has an apologetic mood and is determined to make Jessie understand he is on her team moving forward.

He finds her lying on the couch sound asleep, the teabag hanging in water having cooled from a high boil earlier. Chris anticipates sleep is needed and goes into the bedroom, pulls a blanket stationed at the bottom of the bed, returns, and places it over Jessie. She never moves, even when he kisses her lightly on the cheek.

Going through the kitchen, he sees a notepad and pen on the counter. He writes: "I'm here for you. Love, Chris."

◆

Jessie does not stir off the couch until after 9:00 Sunday morning, and only when her bladder demands relief. She sees the note, which strikes a chord. Chris has never mentioned love in any form during their relationship, and now he has displayed it, twice. It is not one of those turning-points kind of things. But it does show that Chris cares, and right now it means a lot.

Jessie goes to the bathroom and brushes and gargles her way free of the bad taste left by the onion-filled burger-mountain she had consumed, partially, last night. A hot shower brings a new sense of purpose, and she calls Gayle Kidd. Contrary to Jessie's thought before the call, Gayle seems eager to meet and talk about Trey and what is going on.

◆

Jessie rings the doorbell and Lilly answers.

"Here to see Gayle Kidd," she announces in her best reporter voice.

"You a cop?" Lilly asks abruptly.

"No, a reporter with…" Before she can complete the sentence, Lilly tries to shut the door but a tennis-shoe-covered foot stops the closure.

"I have an appointment," she insists.

Lilly opens the door slightly. "I'll confirm. Move your foot."

The door closes, and Jessie is left on the porch, her eyes taking in the landscaping. A couple minutes go by, and Lilly opens the door, poking her head out.

"Go around back, you'll see a cottage. Ms. Gayle is there." Lilly shuts the door rather abruptly.

The next door Jessie approaches is opened before she knocks, and for a few seconds she can't move her mouth or tongue. Knowing that Maria and Gayle Kidd are twins does not prepare Jessie for the reality of seeing a clone of the woman who had nearly choked her and finished it off with death threats.

"Jessie McGaha, I'm Gayle Kidd. Come in." She turns and heads inside.

Jessie follows, gathering herself with each step, determined to be a reporter and stop the fear.

"Coffee?" Gayle asks, as Jessie sits on the couch.

"Black, please … no sugar."

Gayle pours two cups and returns.

"Beautiful property." It is not the first thing she wants to say, but it comes out anyway.

"Yes, Trey is generous and lets me share this part of the property while writing my book."

"I have published five books. I'd love to read it when you're

330

finished."

"My first, but I have done a lot of newspaper and magazine articles." She changes the subject. "You said you have interest in doing something on Trey?"

"I do. It seems to me something is wrong surrounding the circumstance of Trey's arrest. I have strong contacts on the NOPD, and things don't add up."

"He's innocent. He would never harm his grandfather. He was raised by his grandparents, and they were business partners."

"But partners do have disputes. Anything radical in their relationship?" Jessie asks, falling into her reporter mode.

"One needed the other. I can't say all was perfect, but that doesn't exist on a business or personal level anywhere."

"I can't argue with that," Jessie responds. "I will be upfront with you. I went to Utah and met your sister and mother. I have a professional interest in the story. You and Trey caught my attention surrounding the murder of Joe Bailly."

"My mother is a saint. How is Maria doing? We don't communicate anymore."

"Why is that?"

"Very personal between us. Let's move back to Trey. What do you need to paint his true portrait?"

"Has he had a bail hearing? I'm assuming being a high-profile businessman with no criminal background he'll be out on bail soon."

"His hearing is on Tuesday. Our attorney believes he can be home on bail this week."

"I would like to come back and take photos of you both - during an in-depth interview. I want to paint the picture of a New Orleans businessman's success story. If this thing goes to trial, local exposure will help frame public opinion."

"I'm sure Trey would be open to that." Gayle smiles, and Jessie is overtaken by her sheer beauty.

"Having a loyal woman by his side will enhance the public persona."

"I suppose that's true. Loyalty is hard to find." Gayle finishes the coffee and offers to take Jessie's empty cup. Both women rise.

"By the way, how is the young man getting along?" Gayle inquires, heading to the kitchen with Jessie behind, who is thrown off by the question.

"What young man are you referring to?"

"You wrote a story about Joe Bailly's grandson dancing after his grandfather was murdered."

"That would be Emrik, a tremendous young man. He's doing fine, but he's been through a lot after the abduction."

"He was abducted? That's horrible! Trey and I were abducted in Mexico. It was pure hell."

"Emrik's abduction is way outside the norm. It was done by a UFO." She carefully studies Gayle's expression to see if anything hits home.

"Really, how do you know that?" Gayle asks, with a sense of innocence.

"I was with him when it happened. He suffered a high degree of radiation exposure and spent ten days at Walter Reed Hospital in Washington. Didn't the same thing happen to your family?"

"I'm sorry for Emrik. Those things have a way of reappearing later in life. My family has been decimated by the incident, but it's in the past and I want it to remain that way. Thank you for helping Trey. He's innocent." She walks to the door signaling the interview is over, and opens it.

"Thanks for working with me. The story is important to both of us. By the way, please mail me your book when you finish. I can give you publicity advice to help the promotional side." She hands her business card to Gayle and walks out and toward the front yard.

Lilly stands on the back deck, a glass of wine sitting close by. She tracks Jessie's stride away from the cottage and takes a sip. Jessie notices, thinking it odd that the housekeeper seems to have more control of the residence than most people in her position.

Thirty Five

BAD MAN RISING

The bright, moonlit night outlines many objects moving on the bay at the salt water's command. Having been blown clear of the Fare Thee Well, Israel Hamric sits in the sand, dizzy and disoriented, as the shallow water washes on and around his body. He places a finger in his right ear to clear any water clinging to the eardrum, and he repeats the process for his left ear. Neither action clears his thinking or his ears; the explosion has left him deaf.

An arm from a crewmember washes onto the beach ten feet away, rolling back and forth as if still functioning. This brutal fact of death shoves Hamric's memory into hard reverse, making him relive the explosion in that remote bay off Maui.

He tries to stand but can manage only to crawl free of the water on hands and knees. After several minutes of painful maneuvers, he stands, burdened with the bent-over appearance of an eighty-year-old.

Taking inventory of any other adverse effects beyond the lack of hearing, he discovers a wide array of cuts, bruises, and three fingers broken on his left hand. A touch of his head reveals the left side has little hair, badly singed in the fiery blast.

None of this is good, but better than having his arm float on someone's beach in the next few days. He slowly makes his way back to the rental car, opens the door, and receives a badly needed bit of luck. The keyfob is still on the dash and ready to start the car. His slide under the steering wheel is deliberate and painful, but after a few seconds of gathering strength he finally drives the short distance to the water.

The headlights point at the gentle, rolling sea, and he has a clear vision of what can be salvaged. Thirty yards off shore is a familiar floating bag containing seven-hundred-thousand dollars in cash. He wades out, swimming the remaining distance despite pain in every joint and brings the bag back to the shore. Staring at the money he had assumed was lost minutes before, he tosses it in the trunk and takes one more look at the sea for valuables.

Scared someone has reported the explosion, Hamric drives two miles from the beach on a dirt road that eventually intersects with pavement. He parks the car off the roadside and for the next three hours, watching for some type of responders coming to investigate the explosion. But to his amazement, none appear.

At daylight he drives back to the beach and finds a suitcase of clothing floating in the gentle surf, but the other two bags of money and bonds have not surfaced. The valuables must have sunk, still inside the Fare Thee Well. Hamric drives fifteen miles to a cheap roadside motel, checks in under an assumed name and pays cash, falling asleep naked after removing the still-wet clothes.

At 3:20 the next afternoon, a woman knocks on the room door to make the bed, but he does not hear her. The door's opening motion catches his eye, however, and his reaction time is stiff and in slow-motion. The woman walks in, catching a broadside view of his nakedness trying to move to the bathroom. He smiles to mediate the awkwardness, only to receive a quick about-face and slammed door. A hot bath regains a little of the lost mobility but proves temporary.

The cobwebs are slowly clearing, and as they do, Hamric turns angry and short-tempered trying to regain his mental and physical strength. Whoever did this, it was a highly sophisticated hit, and he wants to tear out the tongue of the responsible party. He knows it could not be his Uncle Shane. That leaves Gayle Kidd or the mobsters working for Louis Fleck. Regardless of his own personal safety, he will have his revenge.

The local Hawaii TV stations have not reported the explosion, giving rise to Hamric's optimism of recovering additional resources from the wreck. Another positive: his hearing is slowly returning, hour by hour, and he is intent on contacting Shane Appleton in New York.

He drives around the vicinity and eventually finds a Target store where he purchases a cheap laptop. He logs onto his email and sends a one-word message to Appleton: "NEED." This predetermined signal tells his uncle to hack into the Dark Web and communicate via an encrypted phone number.

"Are you settled in?" Appleton asks him.

"You need to shout into the phone. My hearing is greatly reduced from the boat exploding under my feet."

"Where did this happen?" a shocked Appleton inquires.

"Shortly after boarding. I'm still in Maui. I'm banged up and happy to be alive."

"Do you need money?"

"Recovered some of the money. Going to dive for more. Listen, I need transportation to New Orleans. Can you make the arrangements?"

"You know I will. But maybe you should complete the trip westward and let the thing go."

"No, people are going to pay, even if it costs me everything. We'll talk again in twenty-four hours. I'll send you the code to a new phone." He hangs up and heads out again.

Hamric finds a dive shop on the ocean, buys scuba gear, and loads it into the car. On the way back to the motel, he passes a chiropractor's office in a strip mall and stops. His back has been slow coming around, and he wants to accelerate the process.

The session is painful, but when Hamric exits the office he has regained some of the lost mobility. A drive back to the bay draws some new perspective. Looking over the water, he realizes how close he had come to death.

His thoughts shift. Maybe his quick temper is leading him down a road of self-destruction, and for what? The opportunity to set sail for his bungalow, leaving New Orleans in the rearview mirror, is by far the easier choice. He makes a pact with himself to take a few more days to regain his health then make a decision based on logic. The business path of dealing out death for money has never been ruled by emotion, and he should not let his wounded pride and body do that now.

Hamric dons the wetsuit and enters the water, not sure what awaits him. Only a few hundred yards offshore, the Fare Thee Well lies at a tilted angle, a massive hole on its port side, and much of the wheelhouse missing. The Maui water is clear, and the boat is resting in twenty feet of water, making the dive an easy one. A six-foot bull shark rolls in and out of the hull, seemingly bored and looking for something to do. Hamric has dived in many places around the world and is aware the bull shark is aggressive and not to be messed with.

He circles the boat close to the bottom and makes a large financial discovery. He places a leather pouch containing diamonds in a net webbing attached to his belt. This is the good news. The bad side of the equation is the pouch was in a larger bag of bonds and other precious jewelry no longer present. It is evident the explosion blew apart the bag, and unless it stayed within the Fare Thee Well's hull, the sea has claimed another greedy man's bounty.

Circling back to the port side and the bull shark nowhere to be seen, Hamric swims into the vessel. Body parts from several crew members have been picked at continuously by creatures of all sizes. For most people an unsettling sight, but not

Hamric. Encouraged by the valuables already found, he pushes the Japanese parts away, contorts his body around the jagged and sharp edges of fiberglass, and continues searching.

He finds no more of his bags, but wrapped stacks of hundred-dollar bills litter what is left of the main cabin floor. When he surfaces, he brings a .40-caliber pistol, which he will clean and oil to make functional.

Hamric's mood has been uplifted by retrieving a large amount of the cash and other valuables, a financial disaster if lost. A second stop at the chiropractor's continues the healing and pushes him closer to a sense of neutrality about his next moves.

He walks into a Waffle House with the laptop under arm, delivering the coded time and phone number for his uncle to call. Then he concentrates on the waffles and bacon sitting on the plate in front of him.

Suddenly, Hamric catches a man in the corner staring at him, rapidly lowering his head when the eyeing is returned. This act, even if inadvertent, is a challenge to his safety. He eats the waffles with one hand and places the pistol on his lap. He has not made it this far in his profession by not taking minor incidents seriously, and he continues to watch the stranger's every move from afar. It could be mistaken identity, but having the deck of a boat blow under you will heighten your sense of doubt about anybody's intentions or character.

The man leaves his table and the restaurant, and drives away. Hamric notes that the blue Toyota is probably a rental and the man is not a local. He will not discount anything as coincidental at this point, and he makes mental notes about the stranger's features, how he is dressed and carries himself. He finishes the waffles and bacon, but they have lost their taste after the encounter. He leaves a nice tip for the waitress, and she is genuinely thankful as she watches him leave the restaurant.

Hamric drives to the motel, takes an extended shower, and then jumps on the phone with his uncle.

"Feeling better?" Appleton asks.

"Somewhat. Hearing's not completely back, but it's definitely returning. Got a plan?"

"If you're hellbent on going back to New Orleans, I recommend flying to Cancun then boating over. Flying into Louisiana is far too risky."

"I can tell there's something else on your mind."

"I think you should board another boat heading west and leave all this revenge shit in the rearview mirror."

338

"Duly noted, and to be honest I'm leaning that way. We'll get it going one way or another shortly," Then Hamric says something he has never spoken genuinely. "Thanks for all your help. Love you, my man."

"Love you, too."

◆

Ron McConnell had sped away from the Waffle House after being spotted by Hamric. Apparently, the bomb had not done its job. He watched Hamric rise from the water at a distance, afraid to finish him off without a weapon. McConnell is aware of the man's reputation and had realized a fistfight could very well lead to his own death.

To complete his mission, he now needs a weapon and heads to a gun shop to purchase one.

A buzzer rings, announcing McConnell's presence at Gun World, bringing Geoff Sands from the back room.

"May I help you find something?" Sands asks, for the eighth time this morning.

"I'm sure you can. I have a crazy situation on my hands," McConnell says, placing his detective's badge and driver's license on the counter. "I'm in Maui to pick up a prisoner for extradition to New Orleans. I checked my forty-five with the luggage on the way out, and the airline lost the bag. Airline protocol will not let me escort the prisoner without a weapon, and I have to leave tomorrow."

"Thought I'd heard it all, but that's an original. What are you wanting, another forty-five?"

"A Smith & Wesson forty-five if you have one," McConnell says, smiling and proud of the fiction Sands has swallowed.

Sands walks along an extended counter, unlocks a glass case, and retrieves a .45.

"Got the forty-five hollow-point?" McConnell asks.

"Sure do." Sands stops, pulls a box of .45 cartridges from the shelf, and places the weapon and bullets within his reach. McConnell grips the gun to check its weighted balance and starts to load it.

After two go into the cylinder, Sands raises his hand. "Whoa… can't do that in the store, against the law."

"Sorry. Makes sense. Do you have a range to test fire it?" McConnell counters quickly.

"Sure, down that hallway and to the left. Go fire it while I do the

339

paperwork."

"Okay," McConnell answers and starts toward the range.

"All I need is your federal authorization paperwork for prisoner transportation to complete the sale," Sands demands.

"Left that in the hotel. Let me test-fire the forty-five and I'll bring it back," he says, trying to buy time.

"Sorry, I can lose my license if you don't have the paperwork. Hawaii law makes you wait ten days to take the weapon without proper papers—I don't make the rules."

"Neither do I." McConnell points the .45 at the man's chest and fires a single shot, knocking him against the wall and killing him instantly.

He hustles out the door, drives away armed and determined.

◆

Hamric sleeps very little under normal conditions. His mind is always racing ahead of his life and laying out the next steps. It is obsessive, a comfort zone that keeps him sharp, exercising the demands he places on his mind and body. Focusing on what is right for the long term, he has decided to stick with his original plan and start his life anew in the Indonesian bungalow.

The morning finds Hamric doing a light jog along the ocean, something he had thought would be impossible while crawling onto the beach five days earlier. Sunshine drenches the jog, and Hamric is sure this day will be repeated many times when jumping off the next boat that his uncle is working to send his way.

A shower removing the sea salt and sweat, Hamric dries off and changes into a jogging suit for his next trip to the chiropractor. The bags containing his money stays within arm's reach at all times, and he loads the valuables into the trunk. Knowing a rental car has a lot of keys in circulation, and disappearing valuables have plagued tourists in Hawaii for years. He breaks off the trunk key in the slot. A trip to the car dealership two days earlier got the lock changed, and the new key only Hamric has in his possession.

He parks the car in front of the chiropractor and walks inside, a small office window framing his parked car from the waiting area. He positions an issue of Sports Illustrated near his face, an eye focused on the prized trunk. He is led to a room while McConnell parks behind the office and walks to the front.

McConnell has come to understand criminals and their behavior over a long career, and he thinks Hamric meets the profile of a murderer and thug. He has come to Maui to dispose of this trash and keep the community safe. When the office door opens, a bell rings alerting the staff. He approaches the receptionist and solicits the pricing structure for treatments.

Every good cop learns early in his career to read from the opposite side of the desk what is printed or written and pointed backwards from his direction. That information shows there is only one patient being treated currently, and he is in Room D.

McConnell sits in the reception area and pretends to read the literature. When the receptionist answers the phone and engages with giving directions to the office, McConnell enters the treatment area. He heads to Room D, his hand wrapped around the Smith & Wesson tucked in his belt.

Hamric, meanwhile, has fine-tuned every aspect of his actions, regardless of the circumstances or surroundings. Whenever he walks into an office environment and is assigned a room, he demands a change in location at the last second. Now, he sits on the edge of the bed in Room C. The office doorbell has told him someone entered shortly behind his check-in.

McConnell opens the door to Room D, pistol drawn and ready to fire. The room is empty until Hamric places his .40-cal at the back of McConnell's head.

"Drop the gun, and take two steps forward," he demands, and McConnell complies.

Hamric pockets the .45. "Down the hallway and out the back."

The two step into the alley, and he recognizes the blue Toyota.

"Keys," he directs, and is handed the keys.

Hamric takes the barrel of the .45 in hand and smashes the butt against the base of McConnell's skull. He immediately drops to the ground.

An hour later, Hamric throws a glass of water onto McConnell's face. He comes to, looking at a distant vision of the ocean, his hands taped to the steering wheel. It takes him a few moments of mental adjustment to understand that the car is perched precariously on the ledge of a sheer hundred-foot drop to the rocks below.

"So you're a New Orleans cop. Who sent you here to kill me? Who is your boss?" Hamric asks in a calm voice.

McConnell tries to pull away from the steering wheel, but it is quickly evident that Hamric holds the discretion on whether he lives or dies. He settles back into the seat, resigned to his fate.

"You have a choice in the way you die," Hamric says, leaning into the driver's-side window. "Smell that gasoline at your feet?"

McConnell looks down and sees and smells the splashed gas. Real panic starts to set in.

"Now, if you don't tell me who sent you, I'll light the gas and let you burn to death. We both understand what the last forty seconds of your life will be like. Or, I can push you off the cliff, and you'll be dead the moment you hit the rocks. Which is it going to be?" He flicks a Bic lighter and moves it inside the window, burning close to McConnell's face.

"I report to Chris Dale, but this wasn't his idea. My life has been over for years. Shove me off the cliff, and do me a favor."

McConnell surprises Hamric. He has placed many men in life-or-death circumstance to gain information, and invariably they beg and plead to live. McConnell has his reasons to throw in the towel, but Hamric will never know why.

"Who sent you, someone else in the police department? You have twenty seconds before the smell of your own burning flesh chokes you to death."

"You won't believe anything I say. Go ahead and burn me." He challenges Hamric like no other person he has ever faced in similar circumstances.

"Try me. Who sent you?" Now he is actually admiring the balls of this stranger sitting in the front seat of a car full of gas and on the edge of a cliff.

"Rusty sent me," McConnell says, looking directly into Hamric's eyes.

"Who the hell is Rusty?" he asks, pulling the lighter away and leaning closer to McConnell, making sure he hears every word correctly.

"A squirrel in the cemetery. I've been feeding him for years and he told me to kill you."

"Are you a comedian? That's your answer? A squirrel in the cemetery told you to kill me?" He takes a couple of steps backward to gather his thought beyond dealing with a man crazy as a loon looking at him.

"I knew you wouldn't believe me. Rusty has been talking to me for six years. The light came from the sky and told me who and what you are. Rusty is right, you are a murderer." McConnell stares straight ahead in defiance, his story told, and the truth giving him a sense of satisfaction.

Hamric's memory drags up David Berkowitz, the Son of Sam killer who terrorized New York City in the seventies by creeping up to unsuspecting couples in parked cars and blowing them away. When caught, Berkowitz told authorities he was given

342

directions to do the killings by a neighbor's dog named Sam. Now he is talking to the same type of psycho, someone who thinks a squirrel named Rusty told him to kill him.

Hamric paces back and forth, realizing the cop next to him really believes that a squirrel gave him specific instructions. People facing certain death steadfastly reveal the truth, and McConnell has spoken the truth. Now, Hamric has lost the ability to torture the man. A squirrel, and some kind of light, have blinded him to the point of chasing Hamric over four-thousand miles, trying to kill him not once, but twice.

Something far larger than Ron McConnell and Israel Hamric is in play, and a determination to find the truth is now engrained in Hamric's head beyond the simple emotion of revenge. He walks to the passenger side door and opens it. He grabs the gearshift, puts the car in neutral, and pushes it off the cliff.

One last look at the the car's resting place on the rocks below and Hamric walks away. Two hours later, he requests his Uncle Shane to arrange a trip back to New Orleans. The bungalow will have to wait. There is a lot of cleaning up to do, and the quicker he can begin, the sooner he can retire.

Thirty Six

GONE BOY

Gayle Kidd has been parked in front of the county jail for more than an hour waiting for Trey to be released on bail. She has moved the radio dial from one side to the other looking for credible country music, but it is not to be. It was not a surprise she could find no country station in Boston, but New Orleans? She settles on a jazz station while anxiously awaiting Trey's appearance.

A large, razor-wired gate begins sliding, expanding the opening gap, but for a moment no one appears from the inner reaches of the prison to give Gayle an indication who is walking out of the sixteen-acre cage. Then she spots Trey's attorney and, a couple of steps behind, Trey follows. The two stop outside of the gate as it slides back shut, and Trey listens intently to Wayne Treble.

Gayle notices Trey has lost considerable weight and thinks she will be happy to sit him in front of Lilly's cooking. Trey shakes hands with Treble, and they depart in opposite directions. Gayle opens the door and meets Trey ten feet from the car. They embrace at length, with Trey not wanting to let her go, and Gayle excitedly complying.

"Just wanted to smell your hair. Does that freak you out?"

"Whatever you want to hug is fine with me." She offers him the car key and starts for the passenger side of the Mercedes.

"No, please, you drive. I don't want to think about anything." He circles the car and hands the key back to her.

Getting behind the wheel, Gayle can see Trey is deeply depressed, and it certainly is easy to understand why.

"Have you talked to Me-maw?" he asks, lowering the jazz music as if hurting his ears.

"Lilly did. I understand she has flown to see her sister in Jacksonville. I'm sure she's aware you would never hurt your grandfather."

"I've gone over the event countless times in my head. There's no way my grandfather was in the house when I arrived. We had a lot of problems over the years, but I could never hurt him." He stares straight ahead, not exchanging any looks coming from Gayle.

She reaches over and takes his hand. "We'll get through this.

Somebody set you up. It's that simple. You have a good legal team, but we also need a private investigator to jump in the trenches and uncover the dirt."

"You're right, this whole thing started with that mobster, Fleck. He's neck-deep in this shit, and my grandfather used him numerous times over the years for all kinds of things—illegal things." Trey seems to be gaining energy.

"A reporter for the Times-Picayune wants to interview you and learn your side of the story. I think it would really help from a public perspective to give her access to you and the family."

Trey looks in Gayle's eyes for the first time. "That makes a lot of sense. Maybe I can have her come over in the next couple of days."

The Mercedes drives into the garage, and Lilly meets both before opening the kitchen door.

"Did you miss me, Lilly?" Trey smiles ever so slightly, walking into the kitchen.

"You damn right! I didn't have a single soul to yell at. Looks like you missed me and my cooking. Got a skinny white ass now. We'll go to work on that in about two hours. Making your penne alla vodka and lemon chicken. Start you off with clam chowder and apple pie for dessert. That'll put pounds on those bones of yours."

"You have no idea how wonderful that sounds," he says. "Thanks, Lilly." He and Gayle walk to the den, where he opens the liquor cabinet and pours a stiff Scotch.

"Want something to drink?" he offers.

"No, I'm feeling high having you home. Enjoy the drink. You've certainly earned it."

He sits on the couch close to her and begins rubbing her leg gently. "Damn, I missed you!" He salutes her and takes a sip.

"I have been pretty lost without you, too. But you're home now."

"The system is going to try and take me away from you. Please don't let them." In response, Gayle kisses his cheek.

"Don't worry about me. I'm here for you. I don't run from love."

Trey drinks the Scotch empty then lays his head in Gayle's lap and closes his eyes. She rubs his face with gentle fingertips, admiring his handsome features as he sleeps. She wants him to be happy and is sure she is the key.

◆

A half-hour later, Lilly summons Gayle and Trey to the veranda overlooking the pool, where they find the table loaded with the dishes she has prepared. Gayle can see Trey's self-esteem returning as he jumps into the meal like it was his last.

"Prison food wouldn't be too bad if not so bland," he pronounces, as Lilly walks to the table with a bottle of champagne in an ice bucket.

"Don't tell me you're going to sit there and compare my food minus the spices to that garbage you ate behind bars?" she barks then dashes off to the kitchen to drop the apple pie into the oven before he can respond.

Trey watches her exit, and he and Gayle burst out laughing.

"So wonderful to be home and in control of the household," he quips, taking a forkful of the pasta.

"You deserved that. She protects her turf, especially the food around here."

"God help me with you in her corner. I have as much control behind bars as I do home."

"Maybe it's time to open the champagne and talk less about the service or food around here."

He pops the champagne cork and pours two tall glasses full. Gayle leans close to him and kisses him.

"To our love," she says, clinking glasses.

"To my love of you," he responds, taking a large drink. "Didn't have any of that in the cage."

"You couldn't find love in the cage?"

"Well, one guy made me a lot of promises."

She shoves him away playfully. "Bet he doesn't have what I'm wearing tonight."

"That's a sure-fired truth." he refills the glasses. A scowling Lilly delivers an oven-baked focaccia bread hot to the table. The evening slides by in a drinking and food haze.

◆

Gayle wakes with a headache and finds Trey not in bed. She knows better than to mix wine and champagne, but the evening was filled with great energy, and she did not want it to stop. On her way to the bathroom, Gayle sees the nightie she had taken off last night in a striptease for him. It brings an added energy to her step.

Downing several Tylenols, Gayle throws on shorts and a sports bra then heads to the first floor looking for Trey. Neither he nor Lilly can be found. She decides to go to the cottage and work on her book.

Heading for the back deck, she hears several pops coming from the basement gun range. She drifts down the stairs to see Trey sitting at a table parallel to the range, headphones on and firing a pistol from an awkward angle. On the table is a hand grenade, which shocks her senses.

"Where did you get that?" she asks, watching him fire two more shots at the target. She places hands over her ears to shield the sound, not waiting on an answer.

Trey removes the headphones and looks her way. "What did you say?"

Gayle points at the grenade," Where did that come from?"

"Actually, that belonged to my grandfather. He was an Army captain in Vietnam. He brought home a live grenade and a dud used in bootcamp training."

"Is that the dud?" Gayle questions, keeping her distance.

"I stole both my freshman year at LSU. I don't think he ever noticed they were missing. It's not dangerous unless you pull this pin." Trey grabs the grenade and puts his finger through the circled, metal pin.

Gayle jumps back at the thought of Trey setting off the explosive, but he removes his finger and lays the mini-bomb back on the table.

"Not going to blow us to hell. You're the best thing I have going in life." She walks to him and hugs him. He kisses her, placing the grenade and pistol on the top shelf of the gun case, closing and locking the door.

"I had this crazy-assed fraternity brother named Jeremy. There's one of these do-anything bastards in every fraternity. One year, we flew to Fort Lauderdale for spring break. We were all stoned. We went out on the motel balcony, and several girls from Auburn screamed at us to jump onto their balcony. It was a four story drop, but Jeremy never hesitated. He flew off the railing and nearly fell to the ground, hanging on with one hand from their railing before finally climbing up."

"That was crazy. Did you jump?"

"Not enough dope in all of Mexico for me to do that. But looking back, I did something just as stupid." He glances at the grenade in the cabinet then back to Gayle.

"It involves that grenade?" she asks, her eyebrows raised in anticipation of the answer.

"Jeremy was suicidal, but at twenty no one thinks they can actually die. We got drunk one night, and he decided to play

Russian Roulette with the two grenades in my room. Idiot me, I complied. I put the two in a pillowcase, and he pulled one out. We didn't know if it was live or not. Half a bottle of Jack Daniels later, he pulled the pin, and we put hands over ears like it would stop us from being blown to pieces. Twenty seconds later, I realized God had mercy on my stupidity. Jeremy wanted to do it again, fortunately I drew the line." He looks off in the distance, as if seeing something or someone.

"What ever happened to Jeremy?"

"He went through law school and turned into a fine attorney in Mobile. Then he blew his brains out four years later over a break-up."

"Let's move you away from the grenade and guns." She grabs his arm and leads him upstairs.

◆

Jessie McGaha is busy typing on her MacBook Pro in her office cubicle when Stony Fetter leans over the carpet-lined partition that separates her from several fellow reporters.

"You have Emrik and his mother coming in to look over photos for the second installment of his story at three o'clock, right?"

"That's correct. Where's your mind going with this?"

"Why don't you invite Trey Stephens and Gayle Kidd to the office around three-fifteen for their interview, and we'll introduce them, going and coming, so-to-speak."

"You want to see Emrik's reaction to the devil-woman?"

Fetter nods slowly, as if contemplating. "Yes, that's the plan."

"Your plan doesn't pass the ethical smell test in my opinion."

"Have that covered. Let Emrik's mom know you have an interview with Stephens, then inform Gayle Kidd that Emrik will be here if they would like to meet him. Didn't Kidd mention Emrik in your interview the other day? If either party doesn't like it, nix the meeting."

"What angle do I give Eva Czapleski for letting Emrik see Kidd and Stephens, old Sage Master?"

"It might help with the investigation of her father's murder. There's no danger to anyone in the office with thirty people around, including security. Now go set it up." He leaves.

Jessie leans back in the chair and reaches for a cold sip of coffee. If she can sell both parties, it might be an interesting meeting. She warms the cup with more coffee, and she calls Eva first.

◆

Fetter is on his cell phone, sitting in his office overlooking the Mississippi River off in the distance, his feet up on the window sill. He moves the swivel chair away from the view and back behind his desk when Jessie knocks on the wooden frame of the open door. He lays the phone on the desk.

"You better be bringing gifts, Miss McGaha. That was the lieutenant governor I shut off for you."

"The meeting is a go," she tells him. "Better let security know what's going on at three."

Fetter stands. "For the record, I like you better than the lieutenant governor. Have Willis order pizza for the floor. It's going to be a good day."

◆

Eva Czapleski watches Emrik eat a peanut butter sandwich at the kitchen table and marvels at how fast he is growing. Four months from his thirteenth birthday, Emrik is already taller than Eva's five-feet-seven frame.

Emrik's father, James, had left New Orleans after their divorce two years ago to work on the oil pipeline in South Dakota being constructed from Canada. James is six feet four, leaving little doubt Emrik is going to be a tall man. Her ex had been back twice to see Emrik around Christmas, but his extended absence did not seem to bother his son. James helps Eva financially from month-to-month, something greatly needed and appreciated. When Emrik smiles, Eva can see a lot of James's face come into view. Not a bad thing, she thinks, watching Emrik eat a second sandwich.

The doorbell rings, and standing on the other side is U.S. Marshal Brooke Davenport. Eva lets her in.

"Come in, Brooke. Hungry?" Eva asks, walking to the kitchen.

"No thanks. I had a late breakfast. How's my all-star doing?" she asks, exchanging high fives with Emrik.

"Eating me out of house and home," Eva replies. "I guess that's what happens when you have a growing boy. Something to drink?"

"Yes, please. I'll have a water." Eva opens the refrigerator and hands her a cold plastic bottle. "What's on the agenda since school is out, Emrik? More baseball?"

Emrik sets his sandwich on the plate. "We play twice a week

350

through June. Then we have an all-star team that travels in July and August."

Eva moves next to Emrik and rubs his hair. "Oh yes, the traveling team. They went as far as Little Rock and Mobile last summer."

"Wow, impressive! What's going on the next couple of days?" Davenport asks.

"Going downtown to the Times-Picayune this afternoon to pick out photos for the next editorial. Can you go with us? Trey Stephens and Gayle Kidd will be there also."

"You realize Stephens is out on bail for shooting his grandfather. I'd advise you to stay clear of them."

Eva walks to the living room, and Davenport follows. "I know what you're saying. But the paper has security, and you will be by our side. Maybe Emrik can recognize someone who chased him that night. It could help in my father's case."

"You're the boss. You understand my consternation on the meeting?" Eva nods. "I'll follow you and make sure all goes smoothly. Are you going to work after the meeting?" She smiles to give Eva a sense of safety and confirmation.

"Yes, could you bring Emrik home?"

"Sure. I might even get us a couple of milkshakes on the way back," Davenport says, returning to Emrik.

"Emrik loves strawberry shakes. Thanks!"

◆

Jessie feels nervous. Stony Fetter has no blood going to his brain when it comes to newspaper reporting and thinks everything is fair game. What if Emrik freaks out seeing Kidd or Stephens? Of course, that's exactly what he wants. In the back of her mind, Jessie does, too. The two slices of pizza sitting on her desk are missing a couple of bites.

Two security guards exit the elevator and walk into Fetter's office. Jessie follows to brief them and explain what might go wrong. It does not seem all that dramatic to the security team or to Fetter, so Jessie cools down a bit.

The boardroom is laid out with photos of Emrik and his uncle, and Jessie makes a test run on the tape recorder. She can only wait until someone shows to start the process, and with luck she will receive good feedback, something worth its weight in gold for any journalist.

Trey and Gayle are the first to arrive. Jessie introduces them to Fetter and three other team members. Gayle seems more energetic and open to Jessie than during their first meeting at the cottage, but Trey is distant. He is a match for Gayle when it comes to looks, and Jessie can see why the two have hooked up. The paper's photographer snaps numerous shots of the couple and then takes several solo of Trey.

Jessie leaves for her desk knowing Eva and Emrik will soon be coming out of the elevator and, if the truth be present, they are priority one. Emrik is the first out of the sliding elevator doors, and Eva follows with a woman closely behind her. Jessie recognizes the woman as the one who knocked her into Bourbon Street while she was photographing Emrik. She does not regard Marshal Davenport's appearance as a shock, considering she has been charged with protecting Emrik. On the other hand, Jessie does not like her snooty attitude. Now she is here, in Jessie's domain, a place she does not want to share with her.

"Jessie, this is Brooke Davenport."

"We met the other night while I was shooting Emrik. Welcome to the Times-Picayune, Brooke," she says, practically grinding her teeth. "Follow me to the boardroom."

Jessie opens the boardroom door and realizes this is the moment of truth. She moves to one side of the central table, seating Emrik, Eva, and Davenport.

Fetter stands, and introduces the other side of the table. Jessie watches Emrik closely when he mentions Gayle and Trey, but his expression never changes. He seems content to be in their presence. Jessie returns the honors, and introduces everyone sitting with her. When telling the room about Brooke Henderson and her capacity, Gayle Kidd's expression changes to the negative, and Jessie notes it.

Fetter then moves Trey and Gayle to his office and on the way out, Gayle leans close to a seated Emrik.

"Emrik, I'm so proud to meet you. We have many things in common." She turns to Eva. "You have raised a brave young man. Please let me have a few minutes before you leave the office today."

Eva shakes Gayle's offered hand. "Thanks so much. He is special in my eyes. I'm sure we can spend time with you today."

Gayle turns back to Emrik, shakes his hand, and coincidently Jessie touches the chair where Emrik is seated. She feels some sort of low-frequency vibration exchanged between Gayle and Emrik and conveyed through the metal armrest of the chair. It is like a charge of static electricity, and it makes Jessie pull her hand free of the chair. But Emrik only smiles as Gayle walks out.

Jessie is not sure what to make of the phenomenon and pretends it did not happen for the moment. Leading Emrik and Eva to the vast array of photos, she listens to suggestions from Eva as they inspect the images. After twenty-five minutes, the preferred photos are chosen, and Eva checks her watch.

"Jessie, I need to leave for work. Brooke will run Emrik home. "Thanks for all the coverage on Emrik. You're too kind to my family."

Eva kisses Emrik on the cheek and hugs Jessie. She leaves the building.

Jessie leads Davenport and Emrik to the receptionist area.

"Like some water or coffee, guys?" she asks.

"No, I think we're fine," Davenport answers. "We're going for a milkshake after we leave here."

"Let me check on the interview. It shouldn't be much longer. Thanks for sticking around." Jessie opens Fetter's office and disappears.

Davenport grabs Emrik's hand. "Let's get that strawberry shake, big guy."

She and Emrik move to the elevator.

A few minutes later, Jessie returns, and the receptionist reveals that the two have left. She heads back to the interview, feeling confused. There, she sees Fetter shaking hands with Trey and Gayle. "Thanks for coming in," he says. "We have enough to get started, but we'll probably need a follow up conversation. Jessie will contact you for the arrangements."

"We appreciate putting our side of the story out," Trey answers. "When do you think the story will hit the paper?"

"Typically ten days from the final interview. We'll place it in a Sunday edition to maximize the circulation."

Jessie walks Trey and Gayle to the reception area, and Gayle immediately notices Emrik's absence. "Did Emrik leave?"

"Yes, Eva had to go to work, and Brooke left soon afterward with Emrik."

"You don't know me, Jessie. But I'm telling you; Brooke Davenport is evil and a threat to Emrik's safety." Jessie notices Gayle's concern on her face.

"She's a U.S. marshal, here to protect Emrik. What are you talking about?"

"She's not a U.S. marshal. Do your homework and warn Eva before it's too late."

"Okay, I'll follow up," she confirms. "I actually had my own run-in with her a few nights ago.

"Promise me, please."

"You have my word."

◆

Gayle and Trey walk to the parking garage and climb into the Mercedes.

"What the hell was that U.S. marshal bullshit?" He looks at her as though she is a stranger.

Gayle lowers her head for a second and takes Trey's hand. "I haven't been completely truthful about my life with you."

"Then it's time to start right now. I'm so deep into you, I deserve the truth."

◆

Jessie sits hard on the contoured chair in her cubical, cell phone in hand. Fetter looks in over the partition. "Did you notice anything between Emrik and Gayle? I did."

She raises her hand, stopping the conversation. Her cell call is for Chris Dale. "Hello?" he answers.

"I'll be in my office when you can talk." Fetter walks away from the cubicle.

"Chris, have something really important," Jessie begins.

"You miss me, many people do," he retorts.

"Please do this for me. Confirm the status of a U.S. marshal named Brooke Henderson out of D.C." She is sitting on the edge of her chair.

"No, I can't assess Fed files. You sound rattled. What's going on?"

"I had Gayle Kidd and Emrik in my office today. This supposed U.S. marshal is providing protection for Emrik, but Gayle Kidd swears to me she's a fraud."

"And she might do something to Emrik?"

"Yes ... maybe ... I can't fathom where to go from here if you can't do it."

"Let me call our favorite CIA man. He can access any Federal agency staff member. I'll see if I can obtain a file and a photo of Marshal Brooke Henderson."

"Thanks. I appreciate it," she says, breathing easier.

"I know." Chris ends the call, and Jessie heads to Fetter's office.

After an extended conversation about the kinetic energy she sensed when Gayle shook Emrik's hand, Jessie packs up her laptop and grabs her purse. It has been a stressful day. She stares at her phone and checks email. So far, nothing appears from Chris. It is 6:20, and the traffic will still be a PIA going home. But a tall glass of wine awaits, and alcohol will help the escape from tension.

The elevator door opens to the parking deck, and Jessie takes long strides walking to the car in the back of the garage. The deck is empty, but something always seems unsettling about making the car safely in the evening when she leaves the office. She rubs the key fob twenty feet away, and the door lock clicks upright. Opening the door, her cell pings the presence of a new email, and Jessie locks herself in before reading.

The message is from Chris and has a file attached. She opens the PDF, and it features a thumbnail photo of Brooke Davenport. She enlarges the image, and a rush of fear slides up her back. It is not the person in her office today. In fact, the real Brooke Henderson is black.

Jessie calls Chris, but he does not answer immediately. "Call me ASAP," she says to his voicemail system.

Next, she calls Eva, and it ends in the same result. "Call me immediately, Eva. It's an emergency."

Jessie starts the car and screams the tires loudly, the sound bouncing off the closed-in walls. Traffic congestion is annoyingly slow despite her attempts to dart in and out of the lanes on her way to Eva's house.

Eva is checking in a late truck delivery of seafood and is not carrying her cell phone. Staff rules mandate all phones be placed in personal lockers before going on the floor. As the last dolly of lobsters is put in refrigeration, the manager approaches.

"Eva, you have an emergency call about Emrik at the reservation phone."

She rushes to the front of the restaurant and grabs the phone.

"Eva, this is Jessie ... Brooke Davenport is not a U.S. marshal. I'm on my way to your house right now."

Eva drops the phone and heads for her car.

◆

When Chris finally calls Jessie, he explains he was in a meeting with the PA that he could not ignore. "Jessie, is that your marshal?"

"The woman is an imposter, and she has Emrik. I'm headed to Eva's now. Chris, I'm so scared."

"I'm on my way but will get a black-and-white there ASAP. Do not go near that house. Park down the street. Understand?" he says, sternly.

"Yes ... yes, please hurry!"

Jessie drives past Eva's home showing no sign of life. She parks two doors away, leaving her engine running. She is trying to think through the situation, but her thoughts are moving too fast, eliminating cognitive thought.

"Take a deep breath, Jessie, and calm down," she lectures herself.

She stares at the cell phone, as if an app existed telling her what to do.

"Gayle Kidd," she suddenly says out loud and taps her number. The call goes to voicemail. "Gayle, call me please. You are right about Brooke Davenport."

A black-and-white cruiser arrives at Eva's home, and two officers start for the front porch. Jessie moves forward, parks behind them, and jumps out.

Both officers turn and walk toward her, hand on guns.

"Stop! Who are you?" an officer directs.

Jessie instinctively holds her hands high. "I'm Jessie McGaha. I called Chris Dale, and he called you. He's on his way."

"Okay, stand back while we check the exterior," the taller officer relays.

He goes to the back of the house, and his partner heads to the front door and knocks. No response meets his effort, and he looks into the windows.

Jessie takes a couple steps forward. "Can't you go in?"

"We can't break-in without a warrant. But I don't see any movement inside."

Just then, Eva's car slams into the driveway, and immediately behind her Chris drives up, lights flashing. The taller officer returns from the back of the house, shaking his head.

Eva runs to the door, unlocks it, and the two policemen go inside. Chris moves Eva away from the front porch, and the three wait for the search to be completed. Eva calls Brooke Davenport but immediately is placed in voicemail.

The two officers approach Chris. "It's all clear, Lieutenant. No one inside."

Chris calls the station to get Emrik's photo out on the street. He then calls Bobby Rabold. "Call the FBI and the U.S. Marshals.

Emrik has been taken by a Brooke Davenport pretending to be one of them. My guess is the real Marshal Davenport is dead somewhere in D.C."

Eva and Jessie burst into tears hearing the dire reality that Emrik has again been abducted.

Thirty Seven

TOMB AND GLOOM

Chris Dale closes the laptop on his kitchen table, having little interest in the off-season trades going on in the NFL. Nearby, Joanna slides two eggs and hash-brown potatoes onto a plate and sets it on the table in front of him. As with most long marriages, Joanna reads her husband well and spots the agitated symptoms quickly.

"Want some toast, Chris?" she asks, unwrapping a loaf of bread and expecting a "yes."

"No thanks, this is fine." Chris takes a forkful, his mind miles off in thought.

Joanna re-wraps the bread then walks behind Chris, rubbing his neck. He lowers the fork and leans back into the spontaneous massage. Usually he barks at Joanna that he has no time for such things, but now he reacts with the pleasure of a puppy being petted.

"You don't sleep but three hours a night. You're up and down a dozen times. Chris, can you share what's going on? I've seen it all by now." She continues to rub his neck.

He breathes deeply, really wanting to talk. But letting his wife see his raw, naked emotions right now is a hard decision. Since the drowning death of his brother years before, Chris became a man in his actions and mind, even though physically he was a young teenager. He regards showing weakness about anything as chipping away at his self-confidence; a tough thing to admit, especially to people who depend on him.

After a minute of welcome rubbing, Chris takes Joanna's hand and leads her to the chair next to him.

"I always hesitate bringing you into my job. There's no need for both of us to suffer."

"Chris, I don't know all the details of what you go through, but I'm not ignorant to what police work is. I do watch the ID Channel, you know." Joanna grins at her own joke.

He returns the smile. "Maybe I should watch it, too, 'cause right now I'm at a loss about what to do. I don't always have the answers, but at least I used to understand what path to walk to gain a better perspective and align the investigation. It's the only edge beyond technology a good cop has putting the pieces together."

"Has Emrik's second disappearance tripped the loss of control?" Joanna asks.

"Well, yes and no. It sounds crazy. All this mayhem is connected, however. The common thread eludes me. The Feds are crawling all over New Orleans, and it makes our department look like Keystone Kops. A deputy commander with the U.S. Marshals asked me why this kid has been abducted twice under my nose. I didn't have an answer. If I said we think it's little green men from Mars, they would lock me away as insane." Chris is spilling his guts, and Joanna absorbs every word.

"What did you tell him?" She holds his hand tighter.

"Something that lawmen understand: mob wars, professional hits, jumped bail, drugs, gaming. Now he's pissed 'cause he's missing a marshal that we all realize is dead, so he thinks I'm incompetent." He shakes his head in disbelief.

"Chris, you're not incompetent. You have solved hundreds of murders. This guy is pushed against the wall losing a man. He wants to lash out."

"He starts to walk away, stops, and looks me in the eye. He says, 'something is way sideways in this case'. I say, 'spit it out', getting pissed at myself. He says, 'nine times out of ten, boys are taken for ransom, unless it's domestic'. I says, 'well, it's not domestic abuse, and this woman has no money for ransom'. He says, 'get smart, Lieutenant Dale'."

Joanna rises and kisses him on the cheek. "You will prove him wrong. You're a gifted cop and a great husband."

"Thanks for listening to my tale of self-pity." Chris puts his jacket on and heads out for the office, not comfortable with peeling away some layers for Joanna.

◆

Chris sits at his desk, rolling through the endless reports the department generates. The reports go to the captain after Chris reads them and signs off. New Orleans has one of the highest murder rates in the country to begin with, but things have accelerated beyond the norm in the last few months. Getting behind is easy, so Chris has carved out two hours each morning to clear the deck. He takes the paper trail seriously. It ascends the chain of command, and his signature guarantees authenticity.

Bobby Rabold has spent most of the night shuffling between the FBI and U.S. Marshals on Emrik's abduction. Large coffee in hand, he parks at his desk, retrieves a Snickers from a drawer, and takes a bite.

"You have another one of those?" Chris asks.

Rabold finds a letter-opener, slices off a last third of the candy bar, and tosses it on Chris's desk.

"Never too early to start on the sugar," Chris says, taking a bite, Rabold nods in agreement. "Any movement on the case?"

"The FBI tracked the fake Brooke's phone. It was headed west on I-Ten, so I called the Texas State Police to intercept. They found the cell taped to the back of a Walmart truck. I can't imagine what the driver thought seeing four cars with troopers surround him, guns drawn."

Detective Lee approaches, carrying a file. "I have something you won't believe."

"You have absolutely nothing that would surprise either of us at this point." Chris brags.

Lee drops the file on Chris's desk. "We received a hit on CODIS from the DNA on the Stephens knife. A Robert Mayer. Long Rap-Sheet in Texas. Convicted of killing a couple in Austin in twenty-oh-seven."

"How did he get out of jail to chase the grandson around the house?" Rabold asks.

"He's not in jail. He was executed in twenty-eighteen."

"Sonofabitch! The CIA guy predicted a surprise about the DNA," Chris announces. "Take this report to Ron McConnell and have him file it under the Stephens case."

"I was in Evidence yesterday. McConnell hasn't returned to work in more than a week." Lee walks away.

Chris checks his cell phone about his last communication with McConnell and finds nothing beyond his trip to Dallas. He taps in McConnell's number, the phone rings and the call is directed to voicemail.

"Bobby, something is wrong with Ron McConnell. I'm going to check on him." He puts his jacket on and starts to leave.

"Don't have anything to lose but sleep. Lemme go with you."

◆

Approaching the front door, newspapers from the last ten days are randomly scattered on the porch. Rabold heads to the mailbox standing next to the street and opens it, finding it full of mail.

Chris turns the doorknob and finds it unlocked. The home's interior is neat and organized; not a shock to Chris. He heads to the first bedroom and sees nothing out of place. The hallway leads to the master, and he suddenly senses something wrong. A six-pack of beer has two missing cans on the dresser. The bed is made but ruffled, as though someone slept on top of the covers.

Chris walks to the kitchen and Rabold is rummaging in a cabinet.

"Anything unusual?"

"Only this." He swings open several doors, and neatly organized are dozens of empty bourbon bottles. The last cabinet is loaded with full bourbon bottles.

"You know McConnell better than I do. Is he suicidal?" Chris asks, struck by the large amount of booze apparently consumed.

"Jill's death hit him hard a few years ago. He has no family other than a sister, to my knowledge. If Ron was going to kill himself, I have a good guess where he would do it."

"Where?"

"Jill is buried in the Saint Jude cemetery. He goes there a couple times a week. 'Bout two miles from here."

"Let's go."

◆

The cemetery is situated on a rare, elevated plateau that once housed a fort in the War of 1812. The McConnell vault sits on a rise of property, and Chris guesses the family has owned it for generations, occupying such a prominent location.

Numerous old-growth trees surround the McConnell burial vault. Chris is not sure what to expect walking to the front of the concrete structure adorned with sculptured angels, hands pointed skyward.

The metal vault door is wide open.

Both cops know it makes no sense for such a private family surrounding to be so accessible. Chris turns his flashlight on and enters, followed by Rabold. Several coffins have been displaced from their in-wall mountings and thrown on the floor, exposing the deteriorating bodies.

"What the hell happened here?" Rabold asks, walking to one of the turned-over metal coffins and noting the damage.

Chris flashes the blackened floor and walls with the light. "Looks like someone turned a flamethrower loose in here."

Although plenty of dead are in the vault, Ron McConnell is not among them.

◆

Jessie McGaha had tossed in and out of the bed the night of Emrik's abduction. She was forced to leave Eva's home by the FBI establishing their base operations, anticipating contact with the kidnapper. A shot of vodka and two sleeping pills only accelerated her anxiety. At 4:10 a.m., she had texted Gayle Kidd a plea for help in finding Emrik. At 7:15, no response greeted Jessie's pleas. She left one more message on Gayle's voicemail at 8:05.

Now, Jessie is wondering if Gayle herself might have been kidnapped. Why in the name of sanity would she ignore Emrik's dire circumstances? How could anyone turn their back on such innocence?

Five minutes after leaving the last voicemail, Jessie drives to Trey Stephens' house and parks on the street in front of the estate. Determined to face Gayle with questions about Emrik, she will not let a gate stop her. Her plan is to follow Gayle leaving the property and confront her. It seems to make sense to her fractured thinking and current lack of focus.

The gate opens within a few minutes, making her heart pump faster. But she sees it is Lilly driving away. She notices the gate takes almost thirty seconds to slide back into position. Her cell phone pings, declaring a text arrival. It is from Chris asking about a lunch date. She ignores it.

A metal-on-metal unlocking sound alerts her the gate is opening again, and she starts the car in anticipation. Trey drives out in the Mercedes, but Gayle is not with him. She turns off the engine, pulls the key from the ignition, and quickly exits the vehicle, heading for the gate. Trey's tail lights disappear as his car takes a right, one block in the distance. She hustles through the now-open gate.

Straight to the cottage door, Jessie knocks on it with force. A second knock, and Gayle is standing in front of her.

"Come in." Gayle says politely, although politeness is the last thing on Jessie's mind at this point.

"You know what's going on with Emrik?" Jessie asks, making her way to the living room behind Gayle.

"I did receive your message, but I can't get involved. It's complicated." She turns away from her, looking at the back of Trey's house.

"It's complicated? That's your answer to a twelve-year-old's life being destroyed? Let me tell you something, Miss Kidd. My paper has a whole lot of reach in this town, and I will do everything in my power to insure Trey Stephens is put down like a rabid dog if you don't help me with Emrik."

"I'm sorry. Trey is livid with me. I wasn't forthcoming on what happened to my family in Utah. He has demanded I move out, breaking things off."

"Then you have nothing to lose by helping Emrik. Tell me how we get him back." Her eyes flash with determination.

"I don't have the answer you're looking for. No magic words will free him. The FBI is useless in getting him back. All government agencies are worthless." She sits on the couch and Jessie becomes lightheaded, placing a hand on the couch, feeling for a spot to land on.

"Are you okay?" Gayle asks.

Jessie sinks to the couch, temporary blinded by the emotions welling out of control.

Gayle hurries to the kitchen and retrieves a bottle of water. Jessie takes a mouthful and leans back.

"So, what's going to happen, Gayle? What's going to happen to Emrik?"

"They won't harm him physically. It's a mental-control process he will go through. An abduction is done to alter normal thinking. An endgame is behind it."

"I don't follow what you're saying."

"There's always a plan behind each action taken. When Emrik shot the CIA officer, that was not an accident. It was a message to the Feds to stop jumping into our world and do not go public with what you know." Gayle raises her eyebrows, trying to see if Jessie understands.

"Then will Emrik be released soon?"

"My guess is yes, but don't expect a sweet, innocent twelve year old to return. Some type of action will be performed sooner or later ... and Jessie..."

"Yes?"

"The target will not see it coming. Emrik will have to pay the consequences." Gayle lowers her head in sadness.

"Did this happen to you, Gayle?"

"I won't go any further. Now, please leave." She stands and walks her to the door. On the way, she notices that Gayle is packing her belongings.

"What are we're dealing with?" Jessie demands, stepping away from the front door and turning back to Gayle.

"Be afraid Jessie. You're about to find out." She closes the door and retreats to her packing.

Thirty Eight

EMBRACING DEATH

Trey Stephens pulls a nice pair of slacks up to his waist and buttons it down. A look in the full-length mirror in the large, walk-in closet reveals a loose fit and weight loss. He tucks a dress shirt inside the pants and tightens it in place with a belt. He thumbs through a dozen sport coats, chooses a dark-blue jacket, and slides his arms into the sleeves. A slender figure stares back from the mirror. It feels good to dress in fine clothes after what he has been through. A lot of changes are coming in his life, and Trey thinks he can shape them.

Today is important. A meeting with his legal team at 10 a.m. will give him a look into their defense strategy. At 1:00 p.m., he is headed to Stephens Publishing for an audit review with an outside CPA firm, and the internal Stephens team headed by Neal Jenkins, the CFO. Jenkins has always been one of Trey's biggest supporters, having wanted to see him run the company three years earlier.

Lilly greets him in the kitchen, nose in air, unhappy about him kicking Gayle "to the curb," as she described it. Not that he wanted to disconnect completely from the relationship, but right now all sides are closing in from a legal and business standpoint. He needs unfiltered air to breathe; the hard decisions will be coming at a high velocity.

"Good morning, Lilly," he says neutrally, hoping to gauge her attitude.

"It's not much of a good morning, Mr. Trey Stephens."

"Why is that?"

"You know why. Stop being a bigger dumbass than you already are." She sets an egg-and-bacon bagel on the table.

"Let me ask you something. Suppose we reverse our relationship for one minute. Instead of me being the boss, you are."

"Lordy, lordy. You finally have come to your senses. Go on and on, if you will."

"If you came down the stairs this morning, expecting a nice breakfast experience and, out of nowhere, I called you a dumbass, what would you think of me?" He leans back in the chair, taking a bite of the bagel sandwich.

"Now, I'm the boss?"

"Yes."

"You are the one cooking breakfast?"

"Yes."

"When I came down, you would be kissing my ass. I wouldn't break up with Gayle Kidd. Therefore, I'm not the dumbass." Lilly nods her head emphatically, fully convinced she has taught Trey a lesson.

"Miss Lilly, sometimes you make too much sense." Trey finishes the bagel with a glass of apple juice, kisses her on the forehead, and leaves the house.

◆

Trey's legal representation has locations in nineteen cities and is one of the top lawyer groups in the country. A young lady leads him to the boardroom. By his educated guess, she is interning for the summer. Her toned legs have not fully adjusted to the three-inch heels, and he watches her attempt to be professional with each uneasy step. He wants to say something encouraging, something about going from college and Converse sneakers to big-time legal billing. But nothing his wit can conjure seems to fit.

"Water or coffee?" the young face asks, opening the boardroom door.

"No thanks," is all Trey can summon, though he suspects his bleached-white smile will give her something to think about.

Two of the partners, John Davis and Raymond Collins the Third, seat themselves across from Trey. Both fully realize his defense will result in a large, six-figure invoice, and therefore they are glad to see him and discuss his case.

The meeting is laborious and too long in Trey's view. Not that he fails to understand the seriousness of the charges. But having internalized his innocence so deeply in his psyche, he has no doubt that a jury will acquit him. But it is not only the tedious legal direction being laid out that distances Trey. It is also his change of direction about Gayle. It might very well be "dumbassed," as Lilly elegantly put it. All of it slow-roasts his thoughts.

One new item did stand out in the meeting. The lab results from the knife he used to stab the assailant did not reveal his grandfather's DNA. Instead, it belonged to a convicted felon. Surely, that revelation will have an impactful influence on the trial.

◆

368

Trey leaves the law office tired but excited as he heads to Stephens Publishing. He walks into the lobby, rides the elevator to his office, and receives greetings from the staff. The office smell immediately gives Trey a sense of homecoming. Gabby is busy on the phone, and the view from the reception area gives him a returned feeling of power. Stephens Publishing is his company now, something he has wanted since running down the hallways on Saturdays when his grandfather took him to the office at age nine.

He opens the bathroom door in his office and washes his face in the marble sink. Perhaps only symbolic, Trey feels cleansed of the old and welcomes the new. A return to his desk feels natural, like glancing in the rearview mirror driving on a highway.

Gabby rings him that Gayle Kidd has entered the first floor and is on her way to the elevator.

Trey's good feelings about Stephens Publishing suddenly dissipate. They redirect to the beautiful woman arriving on his floor, as she did months ago, dressed in business attire and stiletto heels. Maybe Lilly is right, he thinks. Maybe it is time to swallow his pride. Maybe it is time to leave behind the fact of his parents' murder. Perhaps he should likewise leave behind what he has learned about Gayle's family and move forward together. Suddenly, only one thing matters to him. It is time to discard the bad history and build a new future together.

Those stiletto heels click toward his office and, for the moment, Trey has mended the distractions that made him withdraw from her. She takes two steps inside the office, a look of helplessness haunting her face. Then she turns away and moves back out the door. Trey jumps from the chair and follows. He sees her enter the stairwell at the end of the hall and gives chase.

"Gayle, wait up!"

She ignores him and ascends the stairwell to the roof deck.

The roof door shuts ahead as Trey climbs the stairwell, taking two steps at a time. Stepping outside, the sunshine temporarily disrupts his vision. He loses sight her, making no sense of her actions. As his vision adjusts, he sees her move to the far side of the roof and climb onto the building's ledge. Her black hair whips back and forth in the accelerated wind as she stands a hundred feet from the street below.

"Gayle, come down!" Trey pleads. "Let's talk."

She ignores him, standing immobile on the precipice. Trey slows his steps moving to the ledge, afraid his rapid approach might make her do something irrational.

"Please come to me. It's too dangerous." He stops a few steps from where she stands.

"Trey," she says, "I love you."

"I love you, too. Get down, please. Let's drink a glass of wine and talk." He extends his hand.

She lifts her hand in his direction and beckons. "Take my hand and prove you love me."

He moves closer to the ledge and their fingers touch.

"You know I'm afraid of heights. Jump down, please!" he implores.

"Come to me, just for a moment. Then we'll go home and make love." She smiles, and he is wanting to believe.

She suddenly drops her hand, emphasizing the disconnect, and turns back to the expanse of buildings and concrete below.

Trey looks around the roof, not sure what to do. It is all on him now. If she falls, it will destroy his life. He climbs onto the ledge and stands next to her. She takes his hand.

"You do love me!" Her eyes come alive with excitement.

He can't stomach to look down, where tiny cars and even smaller people are going about their lives. The danger is near and real, he closes his eyes pretending that a fate only inches away does not exist.

Her lips meet his, and he feels alive with hope. Both her arms surround his shoulders in a deep embrace. Then, slowly, her arms retreat. Trey opens his eyes and watches her hands extend to his chest. She pushes gently at first, a frightening tease. The pressure builds and Trey loses his balance. A realization of death's embrace fills him with an electric bolt of terror. He screams on the way to the sidewalk below.

◆

Chris Dale stands in the shade of a large tree thirty yards from the McConnell family vault watching the CIS team go in and out, dressed like astronauts on Mars. The cell phone rings.

"This is Dale."

"Lee here. Stephens' grandson was murdered this afternoon."

"Hold on." Chris yells for Bobby Rabold to join him, and he sets the phone on speaker. "You have to hear this. Go ahead Lee. What happened to Trey Stephens?"

"He was pushed off the Stephens building by Gayle Kidd. Fell a hundred feet to his death."

"How do you know it was Kidd?" Rabold asks.

"Two people taking a smoke break across the street saw a commotion on top the building. They said a woman pushed him. Building security cameras showed both going to the roof at the same time."

"Is Kidd in custody?" Chris asks.

"No, she has disappeared."

"Send a black-and-white to Trey's estate. She is staying in a cottage out back. I'll be there shortly."

"Let's go," Rabold insists.

"No. Stay here until CSI is finished. Get a ride to the station and go home. You've been awake for thirty hours and need to sleep. I appreciate the help, but go to bed—that's an order." Chris heads to the car and leaves.

Rabold is tired. He always feels the need to jump in headfirst to keep the department moving forward. He walks to the vault entrance and flags down a tech. "How long until you wrap up?"

"Thirty minutes, max. By the way, that is human blood on the floor, but something strange happened here."

"Explain 'strange'."

"Well, plenty of burnt flesh on the floor and walls, most from the deceased bodies in the vault. It's something you see in a lightning strike. The problem is, we can't find an entry point to create the power and heat necessary to displace the flesh."

"So, what happened?"

"Looks like highly advanced laser heat, strictly a guess on my part. That kind of tool is sophisticated military." The tech goes back into the vault.

"Crazy-assed techs, living in a different world," Rabold says to no one. He heads to a nearby park bench to sit.

Chris was right about one thing, he thinks. He is crashing rapidly and deeply feels the need for sleep. His eyes feel heavy and he dozes off briefly, leaning back on the bench despite the hardwood reception.

Then something feels strange, and he fights off the sleep allurement momentarily to understand what is happening nearby. Barely opening his eyes, Rabold sees a fox squirrel jump on the bench and, without fear, scamper over and sit on the palm of his hand. The squirrel pushes his fingers wide open with its nose and paws, trying to find something. It dawns on him the red-tinted squirrel is searching for food.

"Sorry, my man. I don't have anything to share." He tries to pet the animal, but it hops on the bench arm and barks a demand for food.

"Damn! You must be kin to Chris Dale." He smiles at the thought.

Thirty Nine

THE RANSOM PAID

Trey Stephens' iron gate greets Chris Dale in the cruiser. Pulling within ten feet, Chris parks the car and pushes the intercom button, demanding communication. A second punch to the button brings Lilly's voice on the speaker.

"May I help you?"

"This is Detective Dale. Open the gate immediately and leave it open."

"Yes sir."

The gate's mechanics moan into action, Chris returns to the vehicle and drives to the house. Lilly opens the front door and watches Chris quickly move past her.

"Is Gayle Kidd in the house?" he asks.

"No sir. I think Ms. Gayle left yesterday. What's going on?"

Two squad cars enter the gate, lights flashing, and park behind Chris. Three officers rapidly deploy and join him as he walks back outside.

"You two search the main house," he points and directs. "You come with me."

They go to the cottage door and knock loudly.

"NOPD. Open immediately," Chris demands.

Silence meets the demand. He kicks the door twice and breaks the latch. The cottage is empty, and Chris notices two packed suitcases. He hears "all clear" over the radio from the main house, and repeats the phrase concerning the cottage. Returning to the main house, Chris enters and sees a wide-eyed and frightened Lilly standing in the entryway.

"I want a cop in this house and one stationed in the cottage all night. Move those squad cars down the street and out of sight. Questions?" He looks to the officers to gain responses and sees confirmation. "Okay, move your asses into position and stay off the radio unless Kidd is spotted."

Chris turns to Lilly. "Sorry for the intrusion, it's an emergency. Gayle Kidd is the prime suspect in the murder of Trey Stephens."

"Dear God, what happened?" Lilly asks, stunned.

"Not at liberty to say, other than to confirm Mr. Stephens is deceased. "If you have any communications with Gayle Kidd, you must relay them immediately to me. Do you understand?"

"Ye...yes sir. I will. Can't believe Mr. Trey is gone." She moves to the couch in shock.

◆

Gayle Kidd sits in a Starbucks on the outskirts of New Orleans, computer open and fingers quickly working the keys. A look to the window reveals a police black-and-white parking. She tugs on her baseball cap, pulling it farther down on her forehead as the two officers enter. Paying no attention to her, they order two coffees and leave. Several more minutes of typing and she stops to read the manuscript, makes a few corrections, and sends the document in an email.

She walks to the bathroom, pulls a lipstick from her purse and precisely applies the red stick to her lips, adding the final stroke of perfection to her face. A step back, and the mirror reflects a beautiful woman straightening a light jacket on top of her jogging suit. Satisfied with the look, she returns to the chair and smiles at a young black teen wiping off the adjoining table.

"I have good news to share with you," Gayle says, motioning the teen over. "I hit the lottery today, and I'd like to make your day as special as mine."

"Really?" The young man's eyes grow wider.

"Yes, but first, could you use a new computer?"

"Is this a joke?" The teen cannot believe his own ears.

"No joke. Write this down," Gayle directs.

The teen pulls a pen from his apron. "Go."

"120189MYTIME. That's the password. To access, put in gaylekidd@bostonglobe.net. Got it?"

The teen reads it back perfectly and is beyond excited.

"There is one catch to the free computer. You can't tell anyone here at Starbucks about receiving it, okay?"

She places the MacBook Pro in the carrying case. "Where are you parked?"

The teen points across the street.

"Let's go to your car." They walk out to the parking lot, and he opens the trunk. She places the case inside, and then the teen closes the lid.

"One last thing." Gayle empties her purse of $340 and hands the cash to the young man. "What did I tell you? Not a word about anything to the staff." The teen hugs her in tears.

"What's your name?" she asks.

"Treylon ... Treylon Jones."

376

"My name is Gayle Kidd." She places a finger on her lips to signify silence.

Treylon zips his lips and runs back to Starbucks.

◆

Gayle drives for thirty-five minutes hoping law enforcement will not identify her car. If she is cornered, she knows a bloodbath will ensue. But the trip attracts no unwanted attention, and she pulls close to the gate of old man Stephens' estate and eases the car near the metal framing. Pressing her foot on the accelerator, the gate bows inward and breaks open, allowing her advancement to the front door.

She slides out of the seat and looks at the rambling opulence that Trey's grandfather had built and died for. A tear uncontrollably forms and gathers speed on its way down to her chin. No need to wipe the moisture off. It is far too late to anguish in guilt or self-loathing.

The front door is not locked, as she knew in advance of arrival. Inside, she clicks a flashlight on and follows the beam to the door leading to the basement. A moment of hesitation in the kitchen, as she pictures Trey's desperation to escape the intruder by climbing into a dumbwaiter, now ripped from its cables.

No matter what happens from this point forward, she promises not to shed another tear.

Down the stairs she moves, making almost no sound in her running shoes. Not a planned approach, but Gayle will take any advantage that falls her way. That advantage slides by the wayside quickly, as a light suddenly escapes from the basement cave's entrance, somehow anticipating she is only a few feet away from the jagged opening.

Gayle steps lively into the mouth of the lighted hole, ready to take on the challenge of her life and win. The musty crawl into the light causes her heart to beat faster, not in fear but anticipation.

The cave's interior walls are coming to life. Shadows refract the light pulsating from the deep hole, now boiling with energy. Gayle places a hand over her brow to lessen the blindness and make visual sense of all the motion defending the target she has come to face.

A voice emits from the backside of the light. Gayle instantly recognizes the sound she has heard since birth but still can't pinpoint the source.

"Good to see you, Sis," Maria Kidd says, stepping from the

moving shadows.

"Wish I could say the same, but what the hell, I'm here … Sis."

"Glad you made the decision to participate. You have been missed by all of us." Maria watches Gayle take steps around the gaping hole of light, getting closer to her. Maria matches her movement but in the opposite direction, keeping the same distance between them.

"If you're so glad to see me, why don't we get face-to-face?" Gayle stops walking and awaits the response to assess the options facing her.

"You're way too angry right now. No need to make this about you and me. Much bigger goals await." Maria stays out of reach.

"When you killed Trey, you made it about you and me. It was easy. Trey thought he was saving me from a fall to my death." Gayle starts walking and so does Maria, keeping the cavernous hole between them.

"You would never return with him in your life. We both know that."

"I've served long enough. Let me go, and release Emrik to be a normal boy."

"Sudden self-righteousness? You can't just walk away, fall in love, and live happily ever after."

"What's the bottom line? I'm tired of running and constantly waiting for the other shoe to drop."

"Emrik will be released with no strings attached—if you go through a new indoctrination program. Come back and play. Simple, actually."

"Sure you don't want to come hug your sister to cement the deal?"

Maria smiles. "You look good tonight. Let's keep it that way."

"I'll do this. I have nothing to live for now. But you better be looking over your shoulder from this point forward. Your time is coming." Gayle jumps into the hole of light, falling faster and faster while rotating at an increasing rate.

◆

Jessie McGaha has been alerted by Chris Dale about Trey Stephens' death and that Gayle Kidd is the suspect. Reflecting on the connections she saw surrounding Gayle, it was somewhat a fitting end to the string of confusion and chaos originating with the death of Joe Bailly. After all, Trey and Gayle were the reason Bailly confided to Louis Fleck that the devil-woman had come back to town.

Maybe Gayle is the Devil, Jessie thinks, and if she was capable of killing Trey, no one is safe from her murdering ways. It feels like a just conclusion to all the deaths attached to this wheel of rotating mystery.

In mid-afternoon, Jessie receives a text from Chris about having dinner, but she declines. Victor Mirontshuck has asked her out, and the date is set for 7:00. Jessie is excited about going out with Victor. He is attractive and carries the CIA flag for UFO studies, which certainly adds to the intrigue. Several emails ping their arrival, but Jessie is tired of work. She packs her laptop in the carrying case and slips out of the office early.

After arriving home, Jessie pours a glass of cabernet sauvignon from Caymus Vineyards and slips into a hot bath. The wine was a gift she samples only on special occasions, a case received from her father on her thirty-fifth birthday. The wine splurge has little to do with the impending date with Mirontshuck. No. Jessie just wants to feel good about herself and where she is in life at the moment, and nothing speaks louder than Caymus Vineyards.

Mirontshuck is fifteen minutes early, a refreshing change from Chris Dale and his lateness. Jessie offers him a glass of the Cabernet, and he accepts.

They talk for thirty minutes about Jessie's book on the UFO phenomenon before leaving for the restaurant. He seems interested in her thoughts and has paid attention to Jessie's point of view. The evening cannot have started out any better, and the banter between the two lasts several more hours over French cuisine.

◆

While Jessie shares her evening with Victor Mirontshuck, Emrik has watched a baseball game on TV between the Atlanta Braves and Philadelphia Phillies. Ronald Acuna Jr., his favorite player, has gone three-for-four, including a stolen base. The game has kept Emrik's mind occupied for a few hours, but he wants to go home and see his mother.

Davenport has told Emrik that Eva is in danger and both need to be sequestered in separate locations for their safety. Emrik had stopped believing her the second day, even though Eva told him to mind her. He did not want to disappoint his mother, but Emrik has grown tired of being nice and is determined to go home.

At 2:00 a.m., as Emrik watches Davenport sleep in an

adjoining bed, he sneaks to the bathroom, putting his jeans and shirt on. He is not exactly sure who this woman is, but he has figured out she is not a friend of his family and could very well hurt him or his mother.

Davenport's pistol is under the pillow she is not sleeping on. Emrik eases the weapon free and heads to the door, with only two locks between him and freedom. He slides the deadbolt easily, but moving the second lock wakes her.

"Stop, Emrik!" she shouts, reaching for the pistol but finding nothing under the pillow.

Davenport jumps to her feet, but Emrik is far too quick and flees to the sidewalk of a residential area. She chases him out the door for a short distance, but she is aware Emrik has the capability to fire the weapon. She jumps into her car and drives down the street, hoping to spot him and talk him back into her custody.

She grabs a cell phone from a console pocket and taps a number while looking side-to-side for a glimpse of Emrik.

"Emrik has escaped. It's my fault."

"Stand down," a male voice instructs. "Gayle Kidd is back in the fold. You'll get an order to release him tomorrow. Get back to D.C., ASAP."

◆

Emrik has worked his way across town riding the bus system and notes the strange vehicles parked around his home. Thinking the gun might get him into trouble, he stashes the weapon in a treehouse built months earlier. The pistol is now a weapon of comfort for him, and he is determined not to be left defenseless again.

Eva is ecstatic about Emrik's return, and the FBI questions him on the details surrounding the kidnapping. He tries to sleep after the long ordeal, only to suffer a headache that will not disappear.

The FBI leaves the next day.

◆

Jessie has enjoyed her evening with Mirontshuck, but she is by no means ready to jump into bed with any man after one date. A kiss on his cheek and he drives away, and she waves goodbye from the front window. She then goes to the bedroom, undresses, and preps for bed. Reflecting on the evening, she texts him and thanks him for a special night.

She sees several emails newly posted and cannot resist a

peek to see who sent them. She drops her phone on the bed and rushes to the computer after seeing one from Gayle Kidd. She reads it, in awe of the revelations and torn between disbelief and excitement. Gayle has profiled her UFO abduction as a teen, the altering of her mental capacities at the hands of the abductors, and the dedication to their direction for years. Meeting Trey changed her outlook and redirected her focus back to herself, away from the fraud and abuse being perpetuated on mankind for experimental and scientific study.

Gayle is adamant that the recent wave of murder and destruction in the New Orleans Hell Raising must be planted squarely on the shoulders of her twin sister, Maria. She also has promised to detail what happened to ignite the 1988 Hell Raising and subsequent events leading up to and beyond Joe Bailly's death. All is laid out in her book attached as a file. The only missing piece of the puzzle is who ordered the recent Hell Raising as retribution for the '88 event, something Gayle claims she does not know.

Gayle is evasive about her own fate, and Jessie has an intense desire to find out where she is and why she sent the email. One reason: She recognizes the last-rites tone of a fellow writer. But Gayle has not mentioned suicide, and Jessie does not want to believe she is dead. If the email is a suicide note, where is the body?

One last thing Gayle has made perfectly clear. She wants Jessie to take the file and complete the book, exposing the UFO intrusion into people's lives. That request, however, has come with a warning. Their reach and power is terribly wide and long, and exposing their existence and intent will have consequences.

Jessie starts reading the *Hell Raising* manuscript, and it puts fear into her thinking page after page. A truth emerges a couple of hours into the story. If Jessie writes the book exposing the UFO intrusion, it will change the course of her life—for better and worse.

Forty

PANDORA'S BOX

The night has come and gone slowly for a sleepless Jessie. Caught between the pain of truth and fear, she finally understands the enormous story staring her in the face and the sacrifice she would most assuredly have to make in exposing it. Regardless of that truth and consequence, she must alert Chris about the email from a suspect in a murder case.

Jessie makes the call from her office desk at 5:45 a.m., the first time she has ever been there so early. The unfamiliarity of the overnight staff adds to her negatively charged state of mind.

"Chris, I have an email from Gayle Kidd you need to see."

Chris is still at home. "Send it over to me. What is the gist?"

"I don't want to send it. It could have ramifications on the backside. I'll make you a copy of the email and file she sent. It explains a lot. I'm at the office. Please get here quickly."

"Leaving now. See you shortly." Chris gets himself together quickly and drives away from the house, alerting Bobby Rabold to meet him at the paper.

Jessie forwards the file and email to the copying center on the second floor. It is now 6:05 a.m., and nobody is in the building except a cleaning crew on the first floor and the press workers in the basement.

The file is several hundred pages long and will take fifteen minutes to copy, so Jessie heads to the breakroom to make coffee. She adds a filter and water to the coffeemaker and gets the process started. She opens the refrigerator and sniffs the half-and-half. It passes the smell test. When the coffeemaker chirps its completion, she pours some of the hot liquid into an oversized cup decorated in a Saints logo. Blowing on the contents, she moves back to her desk and takes a drink. The lack of sleep has caught up with her, and the steaming coffee jolts her tongue and throat, a warning to slow down and think about what she is doing.

"What the hell?" The words are a shock to her ears, and she spills coffee all over the desk, some of it splashing onto her lap.

Stony Fetter leans over the padded partition, his lips having originated the question.

"Sorry, Jessie. I'm just shocked by your appearance before nine."

She pulls out several Kleenex tissues to sponge the mess now dripping onto the floor. "I have something I need your input on. I couldn't sleep last night. I'll forward it, but I have to show it to Chris Dale first. He'll be by shortly."

"Really? If the law needs to see it, well, you know where I'm located." He walks away.

The sticky liquid makes a mess of the Kleenex despite emptying half the box to clean it up. Jessie has zero patience at this point. She throws the wet tissues into the trashcan and walks to the elevator. Several pushes on the button show no cooperation. The elevator appears glued to the first floor. Jessie enters the stairwell and clears the first landing area when she hears someone moving above her. Footsteps bounce loudly off the the narrow walls and are heading rapidly her way.

Finding panic in plain sight, Jessie speeds downward, bypassing the second floor and clearing the first floor door, standing face-to-face with a janitor polishing the tile. Their eyes meet, and the man stops the machine, taking a couple steps in her direction.

"Are you, okay?" he asks, reading the obvious stress on her face.

The stairwell door opens behind her, and she jumps forward.

The press manager looks surprised at seeing her. "Hey Jessie, what's going on?"

"I'm fine," is all she can manage to spit out.

She returns to the stairwell, finds the pile of printed paper she needs on the second floor, and retreats to her desk. Trying to calm her nerves, she refills the empty coffee mug.

Jessie looks at the inch-thick printout of *Hell Raising* resting on her desk and feels disturbed by her behavior. Having the document only a few hours, she is frightened by footsteps in the stairwell of the building where she has worked for sixteen years. Is this her Monkey's Paw, a short story by Edgar Allen Poe that gave the owner of the monkey's paw wishes that come true. But all of the wishes ended in terrible tragedy for the owner, and Jessie has the feeling that all of the fame and notoriety coming with Hell Raising will exact a terrible price on the backside.

She can hear Chris Dale's deep voice talking to Bobby Rabold as they approach her desk. Jessie is glad to hear it. Chris has always been her rock, and right now that is exactly what she needs.

She stands and smiles. Grabbing the printout, she walks with them to the boardroom and sets it on the table.

"You expect me to read that?" Chris asks coldly, in his usual banter of joking.

"In that pile Gayle Kidd lays out the murder sequence starting with Joe Bailly. She points the finger at her twin sister, Maria, for the manipulation and crimes."

Rabold takes the stack of papers and starts thumbing and reading for several minutes. "It appears she has the inside track behind several events, but blaming her sister won't hold up in court. Did Kidd give any hints on where she might be?"

"No, but I believe her. I've met Maria. She's a certified, dangerous bitch."

"Is Maria Kidd here or Utah?" Chris asks.

"Maria threatened to kill me in Utah two weeks ago. She could be anywhere right now."

"We'll take this and pick it apart. At the very least, it should tighten down the investigations on several fronts." Chris stands, and Rabold follows suit.

"One last question. The *Hell Raising* story answers many questions on UFO integration with the human race. I want to expose it to the world. Is there a legal problem or conflict with what you are doing?"

"Bobby, what say you?"

"Long as no details are revealed concerning the ongoing criminal investigations. The document was sent to you. Do as you please."

"I'll call you later today," Chris says, hugging her, and the two detectives leave.

Jessie feels relieved, but she also realizes that the decision to walk this new road, loaded with landmines as it is, is solely hers. She forwards the email to Fetter then walks to his office, fully aware that he might have a stroke from an overload of joy when he reads it.

◆

Jessie calls Chris late afternoon on her way home. "Did you read any of the manuscript?

"Honestly, no. Bobby is knee deep in it and making notes on every page."

"Chris…" she hesitates.

"What's wrong?"

"Nothing … just one of my female moments." She cannot seem to pull the trigger and expose her thoughts.

"I am capable of listening, although I know it's fairly rare."

"Stony is giving me a fully paid leave of absence to write this book."

"Wonderful news! Why aren't we celebrating?"

"That time is coming … a little premature right now. To be honest, I'm frightened about doing the book."

"Want me to come over tonight and tuck you in?"

"That's not the answer to everything."

"Sorry, having one of my man moments."

"Saw what you did there, but this is a real internal conflict."

"Jessie, writing is what you do. Being a cop is what I do. All ego aside, we're damn good at both. Go win a Pulitzer. It's in your DNA."

"Thanks. Gotta' go." She ends the call.

Jessie stirs the pasta on the stove and takes the boiling liquid to the sink to drain the water. She mixes in the sauce and takes baked bread from the oven. A glass of wine and grated parmesan top off the meal.

Unlike the previous night, the day had flown by in the office fueled by Fetter's offer, which could lead to the crowning moment in her career. Chris did make sense; writing is in her DNA, and ignoring the story is not really an option.

Dishes washed, Jessie heads to bed early, feeling better about her direction.

◆

At 2:20 a.m., Jessie has been in a deep sleep. But now she rises slightly off the pillow, thinking someone is standing in the doorway of the bedroom. When tired, Jessie has visualized people in the room over the years, and she fights against the mirages of her imagination. It only disrupts the sleep, and in defiance, she turns the pillow sideways, blocking the doorway man. Thirty seconds later, Jessie feels strong hands around the back of her neck, and she tries to kick the attacker. The man, wearing a ski mask, by sheer strength lifts her body around facing him.

"Be still," the mask man demands, placing his full weight on her frame and immobilizing her movement.

She does as directed.

"I only want information you can provide. Do you understand?" The mask man speaks in a low tone.

Jessie shakes her head up and down.

The man releases her body and sits on the side of the bed, creating a far less intimidating figure. "Who is responsible for killing Joe Bailey and coming after Louis Fleck?"

"Why are you asking me this?"

"You have written numerous articles on Bailly's grandson. You are the paper's crime reporter. You know. Tell me." The man's voice is losing its softness, and Jessie understands the seriousness of the matter could compound rapidly.

"Gayle Kidd told me her twin sister, Maria, is responsible. But other than Gayle's word I have little proof."

"Where is Gayle Kidd?"

"She disappeared after the death of her boyfriend, Trey Stephens."

"Where is Maria Kidd?" The man cocks his head at an angle, and something about him frightens Jessie well beyond the circumstances she is experiencing. Everything in her body speaks to the subject. This is a dangerous individual.

"Maria is all over the place. I'm not sure. She did reside at Water's Edge in Oden, Utah, but you can't get to her."

"Why?"

"It's a mental institution with strict access protocol. I tried to get in with no luck."

"Luck won't have anything to do with it. Sorry to break in. It was the only way. Call the cops after I leave if you want to, but it won't serve any purpose." The mask man moves quickly out of the bedroom and disappears into the night.

Jessie fails to make it to the toilet before she urinates on herself, her heart now pounding uncontrollably. She sits on the commode going over what just happened. Finally calming, she pulls a suitcase from the closet and packs causal clothes for a long-term stay. The man was right about one thing. Calling the cops would be futile.

◆

Her laptop and a portable copying machine placed in the back seat of the car, she also carries five-hundred dollars in cash, withdrawn from an ATM before heading toward Arkansas and her father's cabin on the White River.

Jessie has plenty of time driving to analyze her actions, including surrendering information about Maria Kidd to the masked man. Wrestling with the ethics of giving such information to someone of bad intent, she takes comfort knowing the woman is evil. Whatever comes her way will be deserved and earned. One real advantage from Jessie's action, Maria Kidd probably will not be knocking on her door in the future.

◆

Israel Hamric had removed the ski mask after leaving Jessie Mc-Gaha's home and running the five blocks back to his rental car. Mentally prepared to do anything to kill the source of his attempted murder, driving to Utah is a small price to pay. The trip places him closer to the West Coast and, eventually, to the bungalow.

Jessie and Israel drive 900 miles between them, going in separate directions over the next several hours, one running away from danger and one running toward it.

Forty One

DEAD LIFT

Nancy Rapport is Madam Faith Hendrix's sister, and she is saddened by her only sibling's death. Nancy has the emotional task of going through Faith's home, removing her personal belongings, and placing the house on the market. Madam Hendrix was a financial success in life, owning the building that housed the frogs and baby gators, all floating around in a secret liquid recipe she took to her grave.

One of the few items Nancy wants to keep is an antique rolltop wooden desk her sister loved. Going through the desk brings a smile to Nancy's face. She remembers how the two bought it at an auction in Hot Springs, Arkansas, and brought it back via U-Haul trailer some twenty years earlier. The trip is a fond memory she cherishes.

She finds, in a small pocket tucked in the back of a larger drawer, a safe-deposit key at a local branch of Bank of America. She goes to the bank with Faith's death certificate and accesses the box. In it she finds cash, jewelry, and an envelope marked "Upon My Death Open." When she reads the note, she immediately heads for her car and drives to the NOPD.

◆

Chris sits in the break room with Bobby Rabold, drinking coffee and talking Saints football when Rolo Silva approaches.

"The sister of Madam Hendrix has brought something you'll find interesting."

"Well, let's go have a talk with ... who?"

"Nancy Rapport."

Chris, Rabold and Silva find her sitting in front of Chris's desk waiting on them as they approach.

"Ms. Rapport, I'm Detective Dale and this is Detective Rabold. We're investigating the death of your sister. I'm told you have something of interest in the case."

She lays an envelope on the desk. "Going through my sister's belongings, I found a safe-deposit key leading me to this envelope. She sold a Hell Raising to Lilly Mathis several months ago.

Seems Lilly's niece was murdered in eighty-eight by the Stephens family, and she wanted revenge. According to this document, my sister was convinced that Lilly wanted her dead, too."

"That does add investigative value to the case," Rabold responds.

"My sister felt strong enough about the situation she had the document notarized by her attorney. I called him on the way over, and he's willing to testify on behalf of her wish to expose the crime. I'm sure you will do your best to bring this Lilly woman to justice." She stands and shakes everyone's hand.

"We'll keep you apprised of the case as it advances," Chris tells her.

"Thanks. One last thing, Detective. Faith was not your normal woman trying to make a living. Most people looked down on what she did. But she was an honest and caring person. She helped more than a dozen families resettle in Texas after Katrina, and that was just a small part of her giving history. Bring my sister justice. That would be fitting."

She leaves and Chris turns to Rabold, who is already reading the document.

"What do you think?"

"Documents like this are admissible in court. The problem is, the instrument of death is a so-called Hell Raising, so I'm not sure if the prosecutor will touch it."

"The one thing it does give you is motive and the person responsible. If you can retrofit other facts around it, you might have something to prosecute with," Silva comments.

"Write it up, Bobby," Chris says. "Work your magic words and we'll go to the big man's office."

◆

The next afternoon, the two detectives are sitting in the prosecutor's reception area, waiting on Mike Broadaway to finish a briefing with a city commissioner.

"If this goes sour, I'm not going to let Lilly Mathis walk away unscathed," Chris says matter-of-factly.

"It's obvious this whole series of murders originated with this woman," Rabold responds. "But I'm not feeling good about it. What do you have in mind, if it doesn't work out legally?"

"A few phone calls and a little footwork will make her life miserable, and I'm just the man to do it." Chris smiles.

The commissioner walks out of Broadaway's office. They walk

in, and he is leaning over a thick stack of paperwork making notes and frowning.

"Batman and Robin in person," Broadaway says, not looking up from the paperwork. "As you can tell, my work schedule is intense, and I'm watching my two sons grow into men at long distance. I spent more than an hour last night ignoring them, yet again, to read this case history. Detective Rabold, you do have the gift of writing bullshit into something legible and entertaining. But from a legal standpoint, I would probably be disbarred by a judge if I brought charges against this woman for buying a 'Hell Raising', whatever that is. You know the direction of the door."

Chris realizes where they stand, so he and Rabold do as directed and leave the office.

Riding down the elevator, Rabold looks at Chris. "What can I do to help put the squeeze on Lilly Mathis?"

"Let me call Mrs. Stephens. I don't believe Trey killed his grandfather, and she should hear it from me. We'll need her help to deal with Lilly, and with this document I'm sure we'll get a yes."

They drive back to the station.

◆

Lilly takes a grilled-cheese sandwich out on the back deck and watches two robins fly back and forth across the yard, building a nest in an evergreen tree. It is that time of year, Lilly thinks. There will be new, young critters in the yard for her to feed.

Life has finally turned in all the right directions for her. Trey and old man Stephens are gone, never to boss her around again. Mrs. Stephens is in Florida, shocked to the core over the losses and probably away for months. She will have the run of the house for an extended period, and when it is finally sold, Mrs. Stephens will hire her to work at the other house. Lilly is thinking Trey probably has her in the will, and no telling what size check she will be able to cash.

Chris and Rabold ring the doorbell out front, to no answer.

"Think she's skipped town?" Rabold asks after the third ringing.

"No, she's still here," Chris answers. "Would you leave this house thinking you got away with it?"

"You're right. She's probably out shopping."

"Let's go around back. If she's not there we'll come back in the morning."

Lilly stands when the two men walk around the corner of the

house. More questions for her, she is sure, but Lilly is never at a loss for words.

"Detectives, how can I help you today?" she asks, donning her depressed, everyone-is-dying-around-me look.

"Lilly Mathis, you can start by packing your bags," Rabold asserts. "You have one hour to exit the premises."

"What the hell are you talking about? I have lived here for years."

"Not anymore We have an eviction notice signed by Mrs. Stephens and the court." Chris hands her the paperwork, which she reads then extracts her cell phone from a pocket. "Mrs. Stephens wouldn't do that to me." She calls her remaining employer but reaches only her voicemail.

"Mrs. Stephens now understands you ordered the Hell Raising that led to the death of her husband and grandson. I don't think answering your call would be high on her list."

"The State's Attorney's office is contemplating charging you with capital murder, so losing your cushy lifestyle is the least of your problems." Rabold hands her a copy of the sworn document, signed by Madam Hendrix.

Lilly is stunned but manages to pack two bags in front of the detectives then leaves the house without without a key.

◆

The drive across town is filled with boiling anger. No one has a clue what she has endured since her beloved niece was murdered by old man Stephens. In Lilly's mind, the Stephens family owes her far more than the money all of them worshipped.

Pulling herself together mentally, Lilly pulls into the driveway of a middle-class home in West New Orleans and parks next to a new Lincoln Continental and a ten-year-old Chevy pickup. One of her nephews lives at the house, and she is sure the Lincoln does not belong to him. Knocking on the door, Lilly cannot take her eyes off the car, thinking maybe her nephew might be dealing drugs if he owns it.

Lamar answers the door. "Aunt Lilly, what brings you to the poor side of town?"

"My boss jumped off a building. Ain't got a job anymore." She walks through the doorway and sees her second nephew, Dallas, rolling a joint.

"That shit will rot your brains," she sputters. Lilly cannot help herself when it comes to lecturing.

"Aunt Lilly, I'm 46 years old, and you are not my momma."

Dallas responds.

"If your momma was alive and saw you smoking pot, she would put a lump on your head."

Dallas looks at an incoming text on his cell and moves to the door. "Gotta' go. Great to see you, Aunt Lilly," He trades palm slaps with his brother. "I'll call you later."

"Don't be smoking that shit and driving," Lilly says, giving departing advice.

Dallas shrugs his shoulders in Lamar's direction, as if to say "she is all yours."

"Where did that boy get a pimp's car. Is he selling dope?" Lilly asks, seeing Dallas drive off in the Lincoln.

"He doesn't sell dope, Aunt Lilly. He's a fence," Lamar responds, sitting on the couch.

"A fencepost maybe. What's a fence?"

"Dallas pays people for things they don't want, and sells it for more money in his pipeline."

"What kind of things does he pay for?" she asks, suddenly interested.

"TVs, computers, silverware, antiques ... things like that. You need a place to stay for a while, getting back on your feet?"

"That would be gracious of you ... only for a few days 'til my mind is clear and thinking right. All this has hit me hard. Been workin' for the Stephens family for thirty-one years. Loved those people ... so sad."

◆

Lamar returns home at 6:30 after being out of the house and finds his aunt in the kitchen cooking a large dinner. She had driven to the store during his absence and bought groceries after seeing he had little more than beer in the refrigerator. The nephews have always respected Lilly despite her overbearing personality, which is the Southern way.

"Aunt Lilly, what are you cooking?" Lamar scans the several pots on the stove, drifting steam and adding to their mystery.

"My famous pot roast. You're lucky I'm here. You need some meat on those bones of yours."

Lamar heads to the living room and turns on the TV to a baseball game. "Some things never change," Lilly says, to no one.

While they are eating, Lilly asks a question of Lamar. "This fencepost thing, how much could you get for a seventy-five-inch TV?"

"If in it's good shape, maybe five-hundred."

"Silverware?"

"Good sterling silver? Forty dollars a pound. What are you thinking?"

"The Stephens family owes me a lot of money, and right now old man Stephens' house has no one staying there."

"You're going to steal from the Stephens' family?"

"Just an advance on what they owe me."

"How do we get past the alarm system?" Lamar asks, guessing what kind of valuables are in the home.

"I know where a spare key is hidden and have the alarm code."

Lamar smiles. "Let's do it."

◆

Lamar's pickup eases around the corner from the Stephens mansion and drives by the front gate.

"That gate has been pushed in," he says to Lilly. "You sure nobody is home?"

"It's a crime scene. Nobody is home. Turn around and go through the gate."

He turns the truck around and drives over the collapsed gate and up the long driveway, parking next to Gayle Kidd's car.

Lilly is surprised by the sight of the car, but the house is dark, and the crime-scene tape is still visible.

"Are you sure this is okay?" Lamar asks, somewhat intimidated.

"Get the bags, put your gloves on, and follow me." Lilly takes a flashlight and approaches the front door. It is open, confirming Lilly's assumption that the incompetent detectives did not have enough sense to lock it when leaving.

The two follow the flashlight beam to the kitchen and fill a bag with silverware.

"There's two seventy-five inch TVs in the den. Pull them off the wall. I'm going upstairs."

Lilly is in her element, giving directions and taking from the family that owes her so much.

Lamar turns a light on in the den and begins to dismantle the mountings on one of the big-screen televisions. Lilly disappears up the staircase. After removing the first television, he carries it out and places it in the bed of the truck then returns for the second one.

Lilly heads straight to the wall safe in the master bedroom and taps the right numbers into the keypad. She had known where Mrs. Stephens kept the combination in the kitchen pantry and had memorized it. Three diamond necklaces and a set of earrings go into her pocket. Lilly is excited by the find.

As Lamar removes the second TV from the den wall, he turns to see the giant man Trey had desperately tried to outrun. He stands ten feet away, machete in hand.

Lilly continues on to the dressing room and takes several more pieces of jewelry, mostly costume. She wants to hurt Mrs. Stephens, understanding the sentimental value attached. Pampered bitch is all Lilly can think heading to the bedroom door.

Lamar screams from the den, and Lilly stops cold in her shoes. Something has gone wrong, and her imagination and lack of faith in her nephew make her think he received a shock removing the TV. Hopefully he has not killed himself is the last coherent thought running through Lilly's mind as she steps into the hallway. At the top of the stairs is the machete-wielding giant waiting on her. She has nowhere to run.

Forty Two

BAD MAN/BAD WOMAN

Israel Hamric unwraps a piece of gum, slides it in his mouth, and places the wrapper in the top of an empty Coke bottle. The paper falls to the bottom, and he twists the top back on. The foot traffic in front of the Water's Edge Asylum gains momentum around the noon hour, with visitors and staff members alike coming and going. Hamric had arrived in Ogden the previous day and spent a few hours watching the facility's activity.

From his hotel room, Hamric had scanned the Water's Edge website and took a virtual tour of the complex. It is impressive and has a tight security system in place. It will be a challenge to his creative ways.

A sport coat adds to his profile of authority, walking into the door and approaching the receptionist busy on the phone.

When she hangs up, she looks his way.

"May I help you?"

He flashes a sheriff's badge, actually from the State of New York, and quickly replaces it in his coat pocket.

"We've received a rodent complaint from several patrons' families in the last thirty days. The first step in resolving the issue is contacting your pest-control company to see how they will handle the issue. I need their contact information." Hamric presents a stern face.

"That's horrible! Hold one second." The receptionist accesses the computer and writes on the back of a Water's Edge business card the pest company contact information. She hands it to him.

"Obviously this is a delicate matter, please keep this information between you and me. We'll contact Jackson Pest Control to see what their process is to eliminate the problem. Are you working tomorrow?"

"Yes, nine to five ... why?"

"I'm sure they will have someone here in the morning, as a fast response."

"That makes sense." The receptionist receives a call, and Hamric leaves.

◆

The Jackson Pest Control Company is a family-run business located in a warehouse district a few miles from Water's Edge. It is late afternoon, and Hamric witnesses four pest-control trucks pull into a warehouse and get locked inside.

He returns at 6:00 a.m. and waits for the warehouse to open. Drivers start arriving at 6:30, loading the trucks and heading out on their rounds. The second truck leaving has a driver with a medium build, and he follows it onto the highway. He hijacks the truck after it pulls behind an office building.

Soon, the Jackson Pest Control Company truck is parked in front of Water's Edge. Wearing a surgical mask, Hamric removes a backpack tank of chemicals from the rear and straps it on his shoulders. Approaching the door in full gear, the receptionist waves him through, and he walks to a security desk manned by an orderly.

"You have a bug issue in Maria Kidd's room. I need help with the access."

The orderly calls the janitor on the in-house intercom system. "Pete will take you to the room," he tells Hamric.

As he sweats under the overalls, mask, and equipment strapped to his back, he wipes his hand on the cloth above his belt, trying to keep the shooting fingers dry. It takes Pete six minutes to appear, and even the orderly is losing his patience.

"Pete, take this man to Maria Kidd's room to spray."

◆

The walk is through several hallways, and Hamric is memorizing a fast exit. Ten feet from Maria's door, Pete turns to him.

"That woman is crazy. I ain't getting close to the door." Pete hands him the key and moves back a few feet.

"Thanks. I can handle it from here."

Through wire mesh and a cracked glass door window that has tape holding it together, he peers into the room and sees Maria in a chair reading a book. He unlocks the door and tosses the key back to Pete.

He enters, holding his hands high. "Excuse me. I need to spray for bugs."

Maria looks not at Hamric but through the outside window at something in the distance. "Get the hell out," she demands.

"It won't take but a minute ... just doing my job." He strides a few steps into the room.

The hardbound book Maria has in her hand suddenly whizzes

by Hamric's head and thumps into the wall behind him.

"Damn, lady! You want to sleep with bugs, go right ahead." He seems to turn toward the door but suddenly releases the backpack and pulls out his .40-caliber pistol with a suppressor. Wheeling around, he raises the weapon. In the same instant, Maria jumps straight off the floor and crashes into the ceiling tile. The first bullet is low, pounding into the bed backboard, and the second shot hits her in the calf.

Hamric fires two more shots into the ceiling tile trying to follow Maria's fast movement in the ductwork. He is not sure if he has connected, so he fires eight more shots at random. The tile is no longer moving, but he has no clue where she is.

Placing a new clip in the pistol, Hamric walks under the hole Maria disappeared into a few seconds before. Standing on the bed, he looks into the dark space. It reveals nothing. Backing up to the door, he takes one last look into the room. Then he opens the door and exits. Pete is no longer in the hallway, and Hamric does not know if he heard the shots or just decided to retreat out of fear. Regardless, it is time to leave for the coast and his beloved bungalow.

Forty Three

SKY BLUE PLUNGE

Gayle Kidd awakens in a metallic tube conforming tightly to her body. A glass window wraps across the top half of her shoulders to the forehead, allowing a certain amount of vision if she moves her head side-to-side. Gayle hates the confinement and, even worse, anticipating the intense pain she will have to endure in short order. She is lying in a large test tube waiting for a foil draped freak to arrive in this sterile environment, injecting chemicals into her brain and recording the reaction. Her body will then be suspended upside down, a microchip inserted in the base of her neck.

The glass window slides out of sight, allowing Gayle to hear the magnetic-propulsion engine moving the craft across the sky. The engine never changes its vibration and rhythm, even when the craft is accelerated ten times faster than its cruising speed.

A series of clicks and pops alerts Gayle that the freak alien of science from a far-away world is coming. It will not be punishment for her insurgency, or thoughts of love, or leaving their code behind. No. The aliens have zero emotional attachment to anything, including themselves. They are merely re-indoctrinating Gayle to live under their control. The process will chemically and electronically alter her thinking into a more manageable pattern.

After the glass is opened, Gayle can move her shoulders and arms more freely, and she is thankful. It gives her trembling hands and fingers more working space to complete her own self-designed experiment.

Areas of her body have gone to sleep, and Gayle has lost some mobility. Moving her toes and feet give better circulation by sliding them slightly up and down at the same time. She coordinates other extremities to rid the numbness and mitigate any mistakes when she needs to perform.

◆

The security guard at Skinwalker Ranch watches two Land Rovers approach, clouds of dust boiling up behind the vehicles. A guard raises his hand, shouldering an AR-15 to halt their movement short of the gate.

A tall man opens the passenger door and walks to the metal-framed barrier. He speaks with a heavy British accent.

"Wendell Harrison. We're with National Geographic." He hands a business card to the guard.

"Give me one minute." The guard takes a few steps in the opposite direction and calls the control center. The guard nods to the second security officer, and he opens the gate, allowing the Land Rovers access to the road leading to camp.

Trent Delaney and Jason Mansion quickly leave the control center and wait for the incoming vehicles. They exchange a high-five as the two SUVs park under a scrub oak tree. Six individuals exit, all shaking hands with the control-center staffers. The visit has been expected, but the staff has not known exactly what day it might be.

The Nat-Geo group is visiting to video and photograph the unusual events occurring on a regular basis to help promote the ranch's program launch on the magazine's cable channel. A third ranch executive, Dr. Robert Higgenbottom, joins the group, abandoning the radiation tests he has been conducting in the numerous caves found on the property.

The ranch staff takes the Nat-Geo crew into the control center, and they present the many videos of UFOs appearing in the skies above. Extending the welcome, the staff explains their experiments involving magnetic and microwave anomalies. Two hours later, both teams ride to the launching pad. The intent is enticing UFOs to appear in the sky by firing rockets one mile into the afternoon haze.

This is a big moment for the Skinwalker Ranch. National Geographic is well-respected across the science field, and television audiences around the world will tune in to the show if their team endorses what they see. The staff also knows it will be a crapshoot to invite the team to see their experiments. If something dramatic does not happen, they will lose a ton of PR worth countless dollars.

Two rockets are launched, each reaching six-thousand feet before deploying parachutes and falling back to earth. Shortly after the second rocket blasts off, a UFO appears at ten-thousand feet and hovers over the valley below.

Those on the ground point their fingers skyward, some having expected the UFO appearance and some surprised at the phenomenon. Cameras are shouldered and photos clicked off at a rapid rate.

Harrison pulls his camera down. "Are you videoing this

beautiful craft for us to take back?"

Dr. Higgenbottom moves closer to him. "Absolutely, the equipment is HD, and the clarity is great, even when shooting the UFO at ten-thousand feet."

"We'll have plenty to work with for the advance-marketing ads," Harrison confirms. "It will generate a large audience for your first program and gather speed after that." Higgenbottom listens, feeling high as the UFO flying above.

◆

Gayle sees a robotic arm swing in motion with her peripheral vision. It is time to act before a five-inch needle penetrates her throat, followed by two other needles searching her nasal cavity. Two aliens, their voices producing clicks and pops, grow louder moving next to the tube. Gayle knows too well the injections will start after the final body lockdown, making any movement on her part impossible.

Her left hand slides her jacket to the side, and her right hand wrestles Trey's grenade from a pocket. She pulls the pin.

The pops and clicks suddenly accelerate. Gayle has no doubt the excited banter is about her revolt and a total lack of respect for their superior intelligence. One of the aliens grabs the grenade, and Gayle holds on with all her strength, hoping Trey actually knew it was live. The struggle between alien and human lasts for several seconds.

◆

Wendell Harrison would never admit it, but he missed the UFO's explosion while reviewing the images he had already taken on his camera's screen. The unified group gasp could be heard fifty feet away as the craft disintegrated, each witness in total disbelief of the history caught on six cameras and two video systems. After the gasp, the launching-pad crowd can barely breathe, much less speak, for the next few minutes. A difficult feat for a group of experienced PR and TV executives, people used to making their living by visually and verbally expressing their views to millions.

Forty Four

SUN OF A GUN

Jessie sits on the back porch of the cabin, listening to the White River roll over and around the endless boulders strewn bank to bank. Her father is downriver, fishing, and has assumed a new role of teacher by becoming a working guide. Word of mouth and cheap Facebook ads created and posted by Jessie have Michael McGaha booked over the next six weeks. Jessie has enjoyed helping her dad build his business, and she cannot remember seeing him more happy. Making money at something he is so passionate about has endowed him with smiles and renewed energy.

The back porch is not just a tool of tranquility, Jessie has rearranged the furniture into an office layout to facilitate her book-writing. Her father has installed a new electrical outlet to keep the tools of her trade charged and connected online.

The cell rings a familiar tone, and she sees Chris Dale's number. Chris had called five weeks earlier, but she ignored him. Instead, she texted him a response: "Busy on the book. Will talk later." It was not personal. The book has indeed been demanding and Stony Fetter wanted and deserved her total focus.

Now she feels comfortable about her progress and takes the call. "Chris, is New Orleans still in one piece?"

"No bullet holes in my clothing. I have that going for me. How's my favorite reporter?"

"Making progress. Maybe another month or so before turning it over to the publisher. To be honest, I'm not missing anything about New Orleans right now. I don't go to sleep wondering who or what is crawling through my window."

"Now I'm really hurt. You don't miss me?"

"You are the exception. That's not a shock, I'm sure."

"Would you like some company? I have a few days off next week."

"All I can say is maybe. Give me a couple more days to judge my progress. I'll let you know then." She is not opposed to seeing him, but it has to be on her terms.

"Fair enough. How's Mr. McGaha doing with you around the last couple months?"

"He's been great. He's doing a lot of guiding on the river and leaving me alone all day. We share stories and beer at night."

"You have my number. Lemme know what time I should arrive."

"I'll call you. Be safe."

The doe and her fawn walk through the back yard looking for bean sprouts. Jessie has seen the deer numerous times now, but she remains in awe of nature being so close. Michael has picked all the beans and replanted tomatoes, leaving the doe without an easy meal. To make sure the mother deer has plenty, he bought thirty pounds of grain, and Jessie walks out onto the lawn frequently with both hands full of corn.

The fawn has been weaned off its mother's milk and runs to Jessie for the handout. Momma soon follows, and she can pet the deer as the two eat from her hand. It has become a daily routine that makes her heart beat faster, anticipating the approaching animals. She feeds them, and soon both have disappeared into the woods. She returns to the desk and jumps back into the work.

Story-writing has always come easy for her. She visualizes the event like a video in her head and writes the scene. Merging Gayle Kidd's writing with Jessie's mental video has interrupted that process at times, but three months into the writing it has become seamless.

Gayle's legacy of *Hell Raising* has allowed Jessie an intimate view into Gayle's intelligence and writing gifts. It also has given her an insight into her emotional and physical love for Trey Stephens. It was an intense love and, deep down, Jessie admires it. At the same time, she feels some jealousy about two people who could create a strong union in such a limited span of life.

◆

Michael McGaha has been a strong asset for his daughter during this turbulent time. The cabin has felt safe in its remote location, and Michael with his twelve-gauge shotgun one room away has made the nights far more sleep-inducing than her own home. Safety notwithstanding, Michael reads the book chapters as Jessie produces them and makes suggestions to sharpen the story fiber and strengthen the dialogue. The McGaha team has been clicking away on all cylinders.

Against this background, Jessie wrestles with seeing Chris. There is a flow to her writing she does not want to interrupt. But she misses his over-the-top personality and knows her father would love him. Plus, she would be lying to herself if the thought of sex has not raised its hormone-driven head. After twelve weeks in the cabin, and the only petting involved has been with the deer.

◆

A few days later, Jessie calls Chris and is treated to, "Take the next train to Clarksville, and I'll meet you at the station…" an old Monkees tune. Chris is singing it when he answers.

"Damn, you actually sang that pretty well," she coos, impressed by his voice, which she has never heard before.

"So many talents and so under-appreciated," he answers. "How's the book coming?"

"Trying to meet the publisher's deadline in two weeks. They want a September launch for the Christmas selling season."

"I want to come and see you, but if you need two weeks to finish, maybe it's better if we wait until you get back—unless you're going to extend your stay."

"You're right. I'm so focused now it probably wouldn't be much fun. The target to launch the book is September eighth, and Stony is throwing a big PR party for the media. Please set that date aside." She is having second thoughts, wanting him to come next week but keeping it to herself for no other reason than pride.

"I would never miss the launch date. I'm gonna take pictures and tell everyone I used to know you before Hollywood called."

"Go back to singing. I liked you better that way."

"I'll do Elvis next time," he says, jumping into the Elvis classic, "Kentucky Rain."

"Should never have encouraged you in the first place," she laments. "Goodbye."

""Love you. See much success coming your way." The call ends.

She stares at the cell for a few seconds and tries to digest the "love you," which Chris has mentioned several times recently. He is no Mr. Sentimental; however, it has become somewhat a habit. After digesting the exchange for a few minutes, Jessie decides to place a positive spin on his reaction and feel good about the intent.

◆

The next two weeks move past the cabin like the White River below, and Jessie meets the publishing deadline. Like all professional writers, she has gone over the manuscript dozens of times. With each new read, she finds yet another word or sentence to change, adding just a little more value to the product, in the process making her feel that much better about it. At last, as they say in the South, the hay is in the barn. Jessie signs off on the final proof and waits impatiently for the press run.

Every day she walks to the mailbox under the guise of retrieving Michael's mail while he fishes. On August 19th, a nondescript cardboard shipping box lies beside the wood post supporting the mailbox, too large to fit inside.

Jessie holds the carton close and walks the three-hundred feet uphill to the cabin, almost afraid to open it. Laying it on the kitchen table, along with a few assorted bills for Michael. She goes to the refrigerator and pulls out a bottle of beer. The cap sails short of the trashcan, and she takes a rather large gulp. She sits next to the book box and stares. Finishing the beer in record time, she uses a knife to slice the top flaps off the box carefully and unwraps the packing material.

The topmost of the three books inside is wrapped with a dust jacket reading:

JESSIE McGAHA

The Truth About UFOs

Her tears roll quickly in the remote hilltop cabin, as she contemplates all the pain and death behind the making of this story. Soon the world will discover all the suffering inflicted on the human race and the why's behind the alien realities. It is a joyous and scary moment rolled into one. Michael walks into the kitchen and sees the books now stacked on the table. He hugs his daughter, his pride obvious.

Just then, her cell rings.

"Did you get it, yet?" Stony Fetter asks, excitedly.

"Yes, I literally just opened the box. It's beautiful!"

'Tell your dad he has to dust off a sport coat for the book-signing on the eighth."

"He'll be there. The fish won't bite that day, anyway," she jokes. "Thanks, Stony for believing in me. This couldn't have happened without your generosity and confidence."

"I will take any amount of credit you give me. I'm greedy that way. Get back to New Orleans. We have a party to plan. Congratulations, Jessie. You are one talented woman!"

♦

Book-signing day jumps onto Jessie's lap in what has seemed like a couple of hours. The excerpts from the book, printed on consecutive Sundays, have been profiled by all the media players, and Jessie has TV appearance invitations constantly flowing in. The book signing has so many invitations and media credential requests that Fetter has rented an auditorium a few blocks from the paper.

Jessie walks into the auditorium, and applause breaks out. She makes her way to a large table stacked with several hundred books, and an assembly line of newspaper staff helps manage the event. A news conference will be held at the end of the signing, and cameras are being assembled as she takes a seat at the table.

Michael McGaha, Eva Czapleski, and Emrik are standing behind the media placement, along with Chris Dale, Bobby Rabold, and Victor Mirontshuck. Jessie looks at the large crowd and is overwhelmed by the intense scrutiny her book has generated. Fetter stands next to the table and talks over a microphone, giving a series of facts about the book and how it came to be published.

Jessie focuses on the familiar faces in the crowd, and her eyes meet Chris's large smile, with her father standing beside him. Emrik breaks away from Eva's side and moves toward the book-laden table. Jessie thinks nothing about Emrik's energy and will seat him next to her. Chris instinctively starts after Emrik, and Jessie stands to make clear that Emrik is welcome.

Several steps into Emrik's advance, he pulls the .40-caliber pistol from his jacket and starts firing the weapon, trying to kill Jessie. The first shot grazes her shoulder, and the second flies over her ducking body. Chris moves quickly and tackles Emrik before he fires a third time. The pistol slides across the floor under the table.

Jessie is on the floor watching the struggle happening only a few feet away and eyes the pistol lying next to her. Gayle Kidd's prophesy of retribution rings in her ears, long after the sounds of the .40-cal shots stop echoing off the auditorium walls.

Forty Five

A GIFT TO MANKIND

Dr. Aiguo Wang is head of the Infectious Disease Council located in Wuhan, the only super-level-four laboratory in China. He is also a loyal subject of the Chinese Communist Party. Educated in the United States at UCLA, he has risen to the top of his profession at age forty-six through hard work and connections within the government. The loyalty and favoritism dates back to his grandfather, who had originated the largest newspaper-publishing group in the country. All of Dr. Wang's family are deeply dedicated to the ruling-class party, and they enjoy the financial rewards that go along with that commitment.

On October 4, 2019, Dr. Wang is a guest speaker at the World Health Organization's annual conference in Hong Kong. He receives international accolades for his speech identifying the spread of disease from contaminated bats to humans. Three years into the research, Dr. Wang has identified the bat virus isolated in the species and reveals the genetic mutation that infects people through touch or airborne inhaling.

When the WHO convention anoints a doctor for forward-thinking research, it creates a rock-star-like following in China. Dr. Wang is living it to the fullest. Even though he is married with four children, he goes to the Hong Kong financial district where the nightclub activities abound. Wang and many of his colleagues enjoy free drinks and free women every evening of the conference.

On October 5th, at 10:30 p.m., Dr. Wang is sitting in a VIP area of the Blazing Sky Bar. The nightclub has a laser light display changing colors and angles according to the musical notes played by one of the most sophisticated and loudest speaker systems in the world. Strippers and other working ladies are clinging to any doctor found as the evening wears on, hoping to impress the targets with their willingness to do anything asked of them. Finding a doctor is not a problem; the conference attendees wear their name badges to the club.

Maria Kidd has come to the Blazing Sky Bar looking for doctors also. She does not know Dr. Wang personally, but that is of little matter. He is about to become the biggest patsy on Earth. Maria is dressed for the part. Her short skirt and stiletto heels gain her easy access to the club. She spots Wang in the VIP section. Men approach Maria, and she accepts the free drinks and dancing on the wooden floor, but she also keeps an eye on Wang and his movements.

Maria retains a slight limp, an injury from the bullet fired by Israel Hamric into her calf. But highly advanced medical science has all but healed the wound that would have normal humans walking on crutches or confined to wheelchairs. That same medical science has developed a complicated and deadly viral disease about to be introduced to mankind through Dr. Wang.

The alien gods are unhappy about their autonomy being challenged, and the best way to distract from their existence is to rain down disruption on the political, economic, and everyday human worlds by infecting the entire globe. And the first step into this chaos is walking onto the dance floor.

Following her assignment, Maria retrieves a hypodermic syringe loaded with the new virus from her purse and dances her way toward Wang. The needle is only three-eighths of an inch long and takes the slightest skin penetration to inject the disease.

Wang is totally engrossed in his partner, and Maria's approach is masked by hundreds of people on the floor dancing shoulder-to-shoulder. The doctor feels a slight discomfort in his buttock and rubs the area of penetration. But he quickly returns his gaze to the tall woman moving her hands up and down his torso.

The job complete, Maria seeks out another overbearing man who would not leave her alone earlier in the evening. He had the gall to place his hand on her hip during a dance, infuriating her.

Maria Kidd is not someone to piss off. She notes the man dancing with another woman and works her way to his backside. A swing by Maria pricks him in the hip with the same infected needle, and she soon leaves. A pandemic, causing millions of deaths and financial ruin for billions, has begun.

Three days later, Dr. Wang is back to the research center. He is greeted by an adoring staff, congratulating him on the recognition he has brought to himself and the Wuhan facility all are proud to represent. None of these highly trained and educated individuals has a clue how much negative recognition and scorn their facility is about to endure, now and forever. Dr. Wang, his family, and most of the research center staff will be dead in the next thirty days. The Wuhan virus known as COVID-19 will spread around the world at a breathtaking rate, infecting hundreds of millions.

Made in the USA
Coppell, TX
05 August 2021